Benjamin Franklin

&

The Vanishing Messenger

a novel set in Philadelphia in the summer of
1787 as the Constitution of the United States
is being written

by

John Harmon McElroy

www.gallopinggiraffepress.com

Benjamin Franklin

&

The Vanishing Messenger

Galloping Giraffe Press is dedicated to publishing works of fiction and non-fiction which affirm the value of America's culture and history. Its motto, Grateful To Be An American, expresses this disposition. For further information on this press and its publications see GallopingGiraffePress.com.

In memory of
Curt Andre Charles Pedersen
born Aarhus, Denmark 1925
died Rolla, Missouri, USA 2022
a Christian Gentleman and Grateful American
and in memory of
our much beloved, brave, intelligent,
handsome, affectionate terrier
Milou (2006-2023)

Table of Contents

Historical Prologue

Benjamin Franklin (1706-1790) had an extraordinarily versatile genius. A master printer. Successful shopkeeper. Internationally renowned humorist. Justice of the Peace. Newspaper publisher. Longtime member of Pennsylvania's legislature. Amateur musician and songwriter. Longtime Lobbyist in the British Parliament for American colonial interests. Author of America's first proposal for general government (the Albany Plan). Governor of the State of Pennsylvania. U.S. Postmaster General. U.S. ambassador to France. Inventor extraordinaire (Mozart and Beethoven both composed music for his "glass harmonica"). A leading member of the committee that wrote the Declaration of Independence; a leading framer of the U.S. Constitution. The first person to plot the course of the Gulf Stream, using data he gathered during the last six of his eight crossings of the North Atlantic. One of the most important early research scientists to investigate the mysteries of electricity. A colonel of militia on the Pennsylvania frontier.

Franklin's exceptional, self-taught writing skills (he had just two years of formal schooling) combined with his innate sense of humor and keen perception of middle-class interests made him the author of a witty, lucrative almanac read by more Americans than any other printed work but the Bible in the twenty-five years he annually wrote and published *Poor Richard's Almanac*.

Franklin's most remarkable activities were perhaps as a civic entrepreneur. He had an unsurpassed ability to envision public improvements, promote acceptance of them, and raise money to fund them. His activities resulted in Philadelphia having America's first volunteer fire company, street lighting, garbage collection, nightly patrols to protect private property, institute to promote science, college not established to educate ministers, circulating library, public hospital, and fire insurance company. To facilitate his fundraising for civic improvements, he invented the concept of matching funds; to give Americans working 72 hours a week some time for daylight leisure during the longer days of summer, he promoted the concept of Daylight Savings Time.

Accumulating unlimited personal wealth was not on Franklin's agenda, as can be seen in the fact that he never patented his invention of the lightning rod, bifocal reading glasses, the Franklin Stove, swim fins, a flexible medical catheter, or any of his other ingenious inventions. His overarching goals seem to have been to make life easier, safer, and healthier for everyone, including himself. Franklin referred to this outlook as "enlightened self-interest." In the 1740s when he began his experimental research on electricity and was asked what good that would do, Franklin quipped, "What good is a newborn baby?"

The Royal Society of London, Britain's foremost scientific society, published his research findings on the nature of electricity in illustrated volumes and awarded Franklin the Copley Medal, the Society's highest honor. He was the first non-Briton to receive the Medal. And after St. Andrews and Oxford, the oldest universities of Scotland and England, bestowed honorary doctorate degrees on him for his work on electricity during the 1760s, "B. Franklin, Printer" became known throughout Europe and America as Doctor Franklin.

Benjamin Franklin & The Vanishing Messenger takes place in Philadelphia in the summer of 1787 when America's largest city, and the second-largest English-speaking city in the world, hosted the Convention that would write the Constitution of the United States. It shows this American polymath creating the security system that was needed for writing the Constitution, and directing the repair of a breech in the system that had the potential to destroy the Convention to produce the new constitution for a rapidly growing nation.

This novel completes the trilogy of historical fictions imagining Franklin in the role of a detective, aided by his devoted legman James Jamison, who is imagined as the grandson of one of the founding members of the self-improvement club Franklin created as a young man shortly after his arrival in Philadelphia and called the Junto. The preceding Franklin detective novels are *Benjamin Franklin & The Quaker Murders* and *Benjamin Franklin & The Innocent Duelist*. All three of these novels may be ordered through your local bookseller or on Amazon.com. For more information on the Galloping Giraffe Press and its publications, see www.gallopinggiraffepress.com

JHM

Historical Prelude: Shays' Rebellion
Chapter I

THE SUN GLITTERED that afternoon off the fresh top layer of accumulated knee-deep snow through which the column of armed farmers slogged, eight ranks wide and fifty files long. Their goal was to capture the cluster of two-story buildings in the near distance. The two cannonballs that had just ripped the bitter-cold winter air above their heads had not diminished their determination to seize these buildings. Most of these "Regulators," as they called themselves, were veterans of the war for independence from Britain, only four years in the past, and the sound of cannon fire did not intimidate them unduly. Instead of uniforms, they wore sprigs of evergreen pinned to their hats to identify themselves to one another.

The Regulators wanted the thousands of stands of muskets, the ample stores of gunpowder and shot, and the cannon kept in the federal arsenal in the countryside outside of Springfield, Massachusetts. Once these military stores were in their hands, they would be better armed than their State's militia, and the Massachusetts lawmakers would have to answer the many petitions they'd been sending to Boston for months, asking for some sort of negotiated relief from the excessive taxes newly enacted State laws said they had to pay or lose their farms.

When the grim-faced farmers broke out of the deep snow onto the cleared road a hundred yards from the arsenal, their commander, Captain White, told his drummer boy to rap out the order "Quick Step," and the 400 farmers broke into a sort of shuffling trot. Seeing this acceleration, William Shepard, the Massachusetts militia general assigned to defend the federal arsenal, ordered his gunners to fire another warning shot over the heads of the farmers.

But that warning had no more effect than the two previous ones. So Shepard ordered that the cannons which were already *lo*aded with grapeshot be fired into the advancing column of men, and a scythe of iron balls the size of a newborn baby's fist hit the densely-packed farmers, killing some outright and leaving many more prostrate and bleeding on the snowy roadway.

Daniel Shays, the overall commander of the assault, was untouched by the storm of grapeshot, because he was leading the Regulators' cavalry behind Captain White's infantry which was breaking a track through the deep snow for the horses and had absorbed the volley. Shays was a Massachusetts tiller of the soil who'd volunteered as a private in the Continental Army in 1775 at the outset of the war with Britain and had served for the next six years, until the major fighting ended at Yorktown in 1781. During that time, he had risen from private to the rank of captain because of his valor and leadership on the battlefield.

Captain Shays' plan for the assault on the arsenal had been simple. After the infantry column and the cavalry were both on the part of the road to the arsenal that had been cleared of snow, he would lead his mounted troops around Captain White's foot soldiers and overwhelm the arsenal's defenders in one swift charge. The plan might have succeeded even after the infantry had been leveled by the grapeshot, except the roar of nearby cannons firing in unison had panicked the farmers' horses.

Seeing all but a few of their cavalry in disarray and most of their infantry prostrated, either bleeding or dead, the mounted troops who'd managed to retain control of their mounts, including Daniel Shays, retreated on the track that had been trampled down for them through the deep snow. And most of the infantry who could still walk followed. The assault on the federal arsenal at Springfield had been defeated. General Shepard and his men, who considered themselves the representatives of law and order in Massachusetts that day, triumphed because of their withering, well-timed blasts of grapeshot, the terror among the Regulators' cavalry, and the fact that a second body of Regulator infantry—as large as the one that made the assault—never got the message to join in the attack on the arsenal which they were supposed to receive.

But was the righteousness Shepard and his men felt justified? Didn't the rebellion of farmers threatened with losing their farms stem from their belief in the Natural Law of right and wrong the Declaration of Independence invoked in justifying America's revolt against the king's authority? Wasn't their conflict with the State of Massachusetts reminiscent of America's conflict with Britain over taxation?

When word of the attack on the federal arsenal in Massachusetts reached George Washington in Virginia, he wrote letters to friends of his there and in other States in which he said:

> Regarding what I have heard of the events in Massachusetts, if anyone had told me three years ago that such a formidable rebellion against the laws & constitutions of our own making would ever occur I should have thought him a bedlamite—a fit subject for a mad house.
>
> A cloud of evils threatens not only Massachusetts but by spreading its baneful influence the tranquility of the Union.
>
> Surely Shays must be either the dupe of some characters who are yet behind the curtain, or has been deceived by his followers. Our Affairs, generally, seem really to be

approaching to some awful crisis. God only knows what the result will be. There are combustibles in every State.

Among men of reflection, few will be found, I believe, who are not beginning to think that our system of government is better in theory than practice—and that, notwithstanding the boasted virtue of America, it is more than probable we shall exhibit the last melancholy proof that Mankind are not competent to their own government without the means of coercion in the Sovereign. Yet, I would try what the wisdom of the proposed Convention in Philadelphia will suggest; and what can be effected by its Councils.

Before organized rebels forced county courts in western and central Massachusetts to close to prevent further farm foreclosures for debt—the rebellion that climaxed on January 25th, 1787, in the assault on the Springfield arsenal— Washington hadn't been sure whether he would accept leadership of the Virginia delegation to the Constitutional Convention scheduled to meet in Philadelphia on May 14th of that year, as Virginia's governor wanted him to do. The insurrection in Massachusetts, however, convinced him he had to attend the Convention and do all he could to correct the impending threat of anarchy looming over America.

For if Americans were incapable of peaceably and justly governing themselves, what had the war with Britain to establish the principles expressed in the Declaration of Independence accomplished?

Washington Arrives
Chapter II

WHEN GEORGE WASHINGTON left Mount Vernon, Virginia, before dawn on May 9th, 1787, several days of gales and heavy rain impeded his progress to Philadelphia. Sometimes the rain came down in such torrents that the roads became an inch or more of slithery mud, and at times the wind pummeled the carriage so hard it took every bit of skill Washington's expert Negro coachman Paris had, to keep it from sliding into a ditch.

But now, at midday on May 13th, the fifth and last day of the journey, the air and sky were clear and calm as Washington crossed into Pennsylvania from Delaware. When he and his traveling companion, one of his twelve nephews, rolled up to the inn outside Chester owned and run by a Mrs. Withy, they were welcomed by half a dozen former Continental Army officers. These three generals, a pair of colonels, and a major spoke for a larger group of former officers of lesser rank from this part of Pennsylvania who wanted to take advantage of Washington's trip to Philadelphia to honor their former Commander-in-Chief by feasting with him on seafood brought in fresh that morning from Delaware Bay. Informants of theirs on the road south of Chester had kept these six planners and coordinators of the feast apprized of Washington's northward progress, and the previous evening they had sent word by courier that the General would be arriving at noon in Chester, which had proven to be a reliable prediction.

Because of all the toasts that the feast in honor of Washington involved, it took a good while to consume the huge platters of succulent shellfish and savory fish. There were, of course, many toasts of praise for, and blessings on, the stately six-foot Virginia planter. But there were also quite a few on related matters. Toasts to freedom as God's gift to mankind. To the glorious future of America. To the flag of the United States, that its stars and stripes should fly forever over a land of the free. To the Union and its indivisibility. To the independence of the United States of America from all foreign powers. To the Convention Washington was going to attend, that it might make the Union stronger and more just than it was at present.

Once the feasting and toasting finally ended, this company of former army officers was considerably more pleased with itself and the world in general than it had been three hours earlier. Nonetheless, the former comrades in arms still didn't feel like calling it a day and going home. As they loitered in the inn's spacious dining room talking amongst themselves, while their leaders said their farewells to Washington, one of the captains among them had an idea. Maybe they ought to accompany Washington on the final part of his journey to Philadelphia. The proposal met with instant and complete approval, and was immediately acted on. By the time George Washington emerged from the inn, they had gotten their horses, saddled them, and were waiting to set off with him for the city.

At Gray's Ferry across the Schuylkill River, which in 1787 marked the beginning of the sparsely inhabited westernmost precincts of Philadelphia, the impromptu cavalcade from Chester encountered Philadelphia's City Cavalry Troop in their resplendent black-and-white uniforms with silver buttons, round flat-crowned black hats bound in silver, and magnificent black-leather boots which flared out halfway between the knee and the hip. The City Cavalry Troop had been planning and rehearsing for weeks a formal ceremonial escort of Washington into the city, and as soon as the General's carriage and four matching horses were on the Philadelphia side of the Schuylkill River, the sound of the entire Troop unsheathing their swords on command in unison greeted his ears, followed by three loud huzzahs. Then, on further command, the City Cavalry placed their drawn swords vertically against their right shoulders and wheeled into a jingling column five-horses-wide to lead Washington's carriage into America's largest city.

As the coach and its four matching white horses in shiny black harnesses, which Washington's groom had risen before sunup to clean and polish for the entrance into Philadelphia, rolled sedately toward the city's center, accompanied before and after by men on horseback, word of its approach reached some of the churches in the city. And they began a joyous pealing of their bells, which before long was joined in by all the churches in the city with bells. The ringing bells signaled the battery of artillery parked beneath the shade trees in the promenade behind the Pennsylvania State House to begin firing salutes. These clangorous acclamations of bells and the volleys of cannon fire sent thousands upon thousands of Philadelphia's citizens hurrying to line both the north and south sides of Market Street, the city's principal thoroughfare, which the papers had announced would be the route down which the City Cavalry would escort the General.

Washington's Negro valet Billy Lee, who had served him all through the eight years of the war and for years before and since, occupied the carriage seat beside Paris the driver. Giles the groom sat in his accustomed place at the rear of the coach. All three servants wore the red-and-white livery of Mount Vernon.

An atmosphere of overwhelming jubilation prevailed. Everyone who could, congregated in Market Street. Amongst the exuberant crowds lining the sidewalks, someone would be moved to make an exclamation, and the people around him or her would echo it. "God Bless General Washington!" "God Bless the United States!" "Long Live Washington!" "America! America Forever!" "Franklin and Washington!" "Praise Be Our Independence From Europe!" "Thanks Be to God for His Blessings Upon Us!" Handheld flags in many sizes affixed to staffs of many sorts were being enthusiastically waved. And there were many wordless cheers and shrill whistles.

Clusters of pretty girls on both sides of the street blew kisses and waved their dainty handkerchiefs at the passing coach-and-four. Small boys dashed back and forth along the edges of the street in front of the crowds. Little dogs lowered their front ends, wagged their elevated tails, and barked loudly and excitedly in imitation of the human celebration. Children holding tight to their mamas' hands peered wide-eyed at their surroundings with inquiring looks on their little faces. Fathers held their offspring on their shoulders, above the heads of the crowds, to see the procession. The frail as well as the hale. Those recently arrived in America, no less than Americans born of generations born in America. The city's quality as well as its humbler folk. People of all conditions and ages. All were drawn to Market Street by the glad-sounding bells and martial thuds of the cannon. Everyone wanted to be part of the expressions of affection and respect for the dignified former commander of the American army, whose faith in America and determination to see it triumphant had inspired the men he led to believe they could win their independence from British rule.

At last the procession, with the long tail of sidewalk onlookers who had fallen in behind it after it passed them, arrived at its destination, the celebrated boardinghouse of Mrs. Mary House at Market and Fifth. General Washington had written to Mrs. House from Mount Vernon weeks before, asking if he might have rooms with her for the duration of the Constitutional Convention, and had received her affirmative reply. But, as it turned out, Washington was not destined to stay at her boardinghouse.

Upon arriving at Mrs. House's establishment, the City Cavalry dismounted without command, by pre-design, and the Troop's thirteen oldest members handing the reins of their horses to the Troop's younger members, formed two lines facing each other, and created an arch with their swords from the door of Washington's carriage to the front door of the most elegant of Philadelphia's more than one hundred boardinghouses. The preferred lodging of Virginia gentlemen visiting Philadelphia because Mrs. House's daughter had married into the Virginia gentry. The place where James Madison was now a guest.

Mrs. House was standing by the door to welcome Washington. And, as he walked toward her under the arch of sabers created by the City Cavalry, he saw standing next to her his old friends from the war years Mr. and Mrs. Robert Morris. And they, as soon as greetings had been exchanged, started explaining to him how much better off he, his equipage, and his servants would be staying with them rather than Mrs. House for the duration of the Convention. They told him how much pleasure it would give them to have him as their guest to dine and entertain. They said their mansion had a full-size ballroom where the dances he was so fond of could be held, and that they might occasionally convert it into a theater where plays—his other favorite social pastime—could be staged. And, they said, they lived only a block from Mrs. House's so there would be no sacrifice of central location if he stayed with them instead of with her.

The Morrises implored him to accept their hospitality as longtime friends of the General and his wife Martha. Robert

Morris pointed out that since he and Washington were both delegates to the Constitutional Convention, they could walk together every morning to its ten o'clock openings and return home together at four after each day's adjournment for dinner. Mary Morris said they employed an excellent Southern cook, who could prepare Washington's favorite dishes. And, Mrs. Morris added, it would comfort Mrs. Washington—since she had been unable to come with him to Philadelphia—to know that his health needs were being taken care of by old friends, as they'd heard that his health had been none too steady of late.

Furthermore, were the General to stay with them, he would have society when that suited him and privacy whenever he wanted it, because the suite of rooms they had prepared for him had a private, lockable entrance. By using his house key, he would not even have to let it be known to them that he was in their house. Finally this deluge of friendly pleas, arguments, and representations had its intended effect, eroding enough of Washington's reluctance to alter his understanding with Mrs. House so that he accepted the invitation of Robert and Mary Morris to stay with them during the Constitutional Convention.

Robert Morris, born near Liverpool, England, had emigrated to America at age thirteen, and was now considered by many Americans to be the richest man in the United States. During the war, as Superintendent of Finance, he had come up with so many imaginative, daring, and successful ways of getting the money the Continental Congress needed that he was popularly referred to as the "Hannibal of Finance." The fire-gutted grand mansion on Market Street that he and his wife, the daughter of a distinguished Maryland family, had bought, and refurbished at tremendous expense, was now spoken of by some people in Philadelphia as the city's most opulent, well-appointed residence.

When Washington, with profuse apologies, announced to Mrs. House his decision to lodge with his old friends Robert and Mary Morris instead of with her, she said she understood. Though not pleased with his decision, she accepted it with more grace than she otherwise might have, had she not known that four other conventions were in town besides the Constitutional Convention General Washington had come to attend. A convention of the Society of the Cincinnati, as commissioned officers of the Continental Army styled their fraternal association. A conclave of abolitionists. And two religious conventions, one Presbyterian and one Baptist. With so many gentlemen from out of town in the city, lodgings of excellent quality in a handsome, conveniently located house serving excellent meals and having smart, genteel service and the freshest linens would not remain vacant long.

No sooner had Washington gotten settled into his rooms with the Morrises and arranged accommodations for his nephew, who would be returning to Virginia in a day or two, and for his three slaves from Mount Vernon, than he began to make preparations to visit the President of Pennsylvania's Executive Council, as Pennsylvania's governor was called. He reminded the Morrises that Benjamin Franklin, as the chief executive officer of Pennsylvania, was the host of the Constitutional Convention, and that he really should pay his respects to Franklin as soon as possible.

While George Washington was indeed a strict observer of social protocols, and had been all his life, that was not the main reason he wanted to see Dr. Franklin as soon as he could after arriving in Philadelphia. He wanted to know what analysis the eighty-one-year-old Franklin—one of the world's most renowned scientists, whose research on electricity was often compared in importance to that of Newton's research on gravity, and America's most seasoned statesman—had made of the government crisis that had moved the Confederation

Congress to call a constitutional convention of the States to address it.

Washington and Franklin had spent time together on three previous occasions. First at Lancaster, Pennsylvania, in 1755, the second year of the French and Indian War, when Franklin as agent for the Pennsylvania Assembly had arranged for the wagons and teamsters to transport the English General Edward Braddock's supplies and military equipment into the wilderness of western Pennsylvania. And Washington had commanded the Virginia and Pennsylvania militia companies that accompanied Braddock on his disastrous expedition against the French and their Indian allies.

The second and third times were in 1775, during the initial year of the war with Britain, when Washington and Franklin were both elected members to the Second Continental Congress and spent several weeks together in Philadelphia, where the Congress was meeting, before it sent Washington to take command of the Continental Army, and he left for the principal scene of military action, the siege of Boston. During the fall of that same year, Congress sent Franklin to his native city of Boston to report on the progress of the siege, and Washington and Franklin lived together for ten days in the house the General was using as his Boston headquarters.

That was before Congress had appointed Franklin to be America's ambassador to France, where he spent the remainder of the war arranging with the French government the immense loans of money, large shipments of military supplies, and the use of French troops and warships which America had to have if it was to be successful in its war with imperial Britain, a complicated mission in which Franklin had been supremely successful. After major combat in America ceased in 1781, Franklin had stayed on in France to lead American negotiations in Paris for the treaty of peace with Britain and had not returned to America until 1785.

As the two chief representatives during the war of their country's vital interests—its alliances in Europe and its military operations in America—Franklin and Washington had often communicated by letter. But Sunday evening the 13th of May in Philadelphia was the first time in twelve years they'd had an opportunity to speak in private; and Washington was eager to take advantage of that opportunity.

Robert Morris, in answering his house guest's question on how to find Dr. Franklin's residence, told Washington to go east on Market toward the Delaware River and, on the south side of the street just past Fourth, he would see a brick-vaulted carriageway with its gates wide open. This was the entrance to Franklin Court, the enclosed space, or "Court," formed by the continuous rows of buildings on Market, Third, Chestnut, and Fourth where Franklin had constructed years before a three-story mansion-house of his own design for his residence. He had recently enlarged it by one-third, including a spectacular new library occupying the entire second floor of the addition.

Morris told Washington he should feel perfectly free to walk in the open carriage gates because not two days earlier Dr. Franklin himself had told him that he intended to make himself available to any delegate to the Constitutional Convention who might want to come by, unannounced, for a conversation.

Washington asked whether it would perhaps be best to send his valet to Dr. Franklin with a note informing him of his desire to come to Franklin Court, and Morris replied that he should follow his inclination; and George Washington sent the note.

Dr. Franklin, after receiving Washington's note, told the valet to inform his master to come to see him whenever he pleased, the sooner the better, and sent his majordomo, Francis Mahoney, out to Market Street to bring him up to the new library, where the elderly American genius was now spending most of his time.

Washington waited until Billy Lee had returned with Franklin's response to his note before setting out on foot to talk with Dr. Franklin.

Franklin & Washington Talk
Chapter III

WASHINGTON HAD NO difficulty finding the carriageway tunnel into Franklin Court on the south side of Market Street near Fourth. Nor did Mr. Mahoney have any difficulty identifying the tall man with a pronounced military bearing striding toward him down Market Street in the light of the whale oil lamps that illuminated it.

Mr. Mahoney took George Washington up to the new library that occupied the entire second floor of Franklin's recent addition to his home; then retired in obedience to Franklin's instructions.

The General was amazed by the thousands of books in stiff white, grey, and tan paper covers intermingled with books in covers of brown, tan, green, red and blue leather, many with gold lettering. The framed honorary degrees on the walls from universities and colleges in America and Europe were also impressive, including doctorate degrees from the two oldest universities in the British Isles, St. Andrews and Oxford. Framed certificates of membership in the learned societies of America and Europe also adorned the library, including one from England's most prestigious institution of learning, the Royal Society of London.

Another impressive sight that was immediately evident was an intensely burning lamp suspended from a pulley above Franklin's chestnut-wood worktable, a gift from its Swiss inventor, which lit every cranny of the lofty, ornately plastered library.

But the most awesome sight in Franklin's library was the portrait of Louis the Sixteenth, King of France, in a frame studded with more than four hundred diamonds. The young monarch had given this royal gift to the first U.S. ambassador to France at the end of his nine-year stay in France, in recognition of his extraordinary popularity among the French. The portrait hung beside Franklin's worktable in his new library with nothing else near it.

"How good to see you again, General! Welcome to Franklin Court!" Franklin called out as Washington entered his library and he struggled to his feet with the aid of the gold-headed cane that a French noblewoman had given him when he left France.

As the two American leaders beamed at each other and clasped hands across the table in their mutual satisfaction at seeing one another again, the 55-year-old general took the 81-year-old scientist's right hand in both of his and said with more feeling than he usually displayed, "Your Excellency, it is good to be in your company once more after so many eventful years!"

Dr. Franklin invited his guest to please take one of the pair of blue-upholstered armchairs in front of his chestnut-wood worktable; and as soon as he saw Washington comfortably seated, he resumed his own chair on the other side of the table.

"The last time we spoke, Dr. Franklin, was, I believe, in the house where I lived in 1775 during the siege of Boston," Washington observed.

"As I recollect, it was the middle of October," Franklin replied. "I'd been sent to the city of my birth, and first seventeen years of my life, with two other members of the Second Continental Congress, to write a report for Congress on the progress of your siege and the prospects of its success. But, if memory serves me, our conversations during the week and a half we spent together were mostly concerned with what regulations would best suit an American army to discipline it, a subject on which you seemed to value having my opinion."

"I have never forgotten, Dr. Franklin, a jest you told on that occasion," Washington said. "I've remembered it, I think, because of your way of telling it and the confirming proofs I had of its truth during my years as commander of the army. The story was of a discussion you said you had had with Dr. Benjamin Rush and Mr. Jefferson concerning what was the oldest profession. Was it medicine, architecture, or politics? Dr. Rush, of course, contended it was medicine because God removed a rib from Adam to create Eve. Jefferson thought architecture was the oldest profession because God had given structure to chaos. But you thought politics should be considered the oldest profession since politicians created the chaos."

Franklin reacted to this remembrance of his witticism many years past with one of his distinctive, chortling laughs.

Washington changed the focus of their talk by remarking that although Mr. Morris had described to him the magnificence of Dr. Franklin's new library, no one could appreciate its splendor without seeing it. "I congratulate you, Dr. Franklin, on your combining beauty with utility, manifested in this room's architecture and decoration."

Franklin smiled in acknowledgement of this compliment and, nodding, changed the focus of conversation yet again by remarking, "We had reports here in Philadelphia this past week of how wretched the weather to the south has been. I hope it did not discommode your coming to the Convention overmuch."

"Withal, the weather was wretched," Washington replied. "What should have taken four days to go the 150 miles from Mount Vernon to Philadelphia took five. But the weather today, the last day of the journey, was exceptionally fine; and the reception the inhabitants of this city gave me more than compensated for the previous inconvenience."

"Sitting here in my library, I heard the ringing of the city's bells and the cannon salutes in your honor," Franklin said. "And Mr. Mahoney, the man who escorted you into Franklin Court from the street, gave me all the particulars of your welcome in Market Street, in which he participated."

"I must tell you, Dr. Franklin, I was uncertain up until just before I started off from home whether I would be able to attend the Constitutional Convention," Washington remarked. "A few days before I commenced my journey my right shoulder was afflicted by as barbarous a case of rheumatism as I have ever experienced. Had it continued beyond the 9th of May, I confess I couldn't have undertaken days of jostling travel in a carriage and would have had to stay home with my right arm in a sling."

"I, too, Sir, as it happens, was until recently also experiencing incapacitating pain, on account of the stones in my kidneys and bladder," Franklin said. "Then, as sometimes happens, week before last the severity of the pain left me, and I became fit for service. May I remain so for the duration of the Convention, which, given the complications we must overcome, could last the better part of the summer.

"I tell you, as a plain matter of fact, my dear Sir, without fear you will misconstrue what I am about to say for vanity, that you and I are the Americans our countrymen most trust. You perhaps may recall my saying something to that effect in the letter I wrote to you a few weeks back, pointing out the necessity of your attending the Convention. What I said in that letter is so. Our presence together at this Convention gives it a credibility in the eyes of the people of the States that it otherwise would not have. One of us, I think, has to preside over this assembly for its result to have credibility with the people. And I, my dear Sir, am too advanced in years to take on the task. Besides, I do not have the temperament to be continually making the rulings that must be made from the president's chair on procedural matters, to keep the Convention in good trim and moving along.

"Therefore, as soon as a quorum of State delegations is present and the Convention can proceed to business, I intend to nominate you for the presidency of the Convention. Your merits certainly entitle you to the office, as proven by your long-suffering and, in the end, successful command of America's military power during the war. Despite repeated setbacks and the chronic shortages of supplies that impeded your efforts, you persisted. Even when cabals of lesser men tried to undermine your authority, you remained undaunted, and never lost faith in the eventual triumph of American arms in the cause of independence. Your steadiness in adversity has won you the enduring trust and affection of your countrymen. You believed we could win, and we did."

Washington said nothing to this speech of high praise from a veteran statesman for his character and conduct in a time of prolonged trial; and there was a lull in the conversation as Franklin's visitor sat silent, with a pensive expression on his visage.

Franklin continued, "As President of the Convention, you will have my constant support, General, both from the floor of the Convention and behind the scenes. I've already spoken several times with Mr. Madison and other delegates who have arrived early for the Convention, and I've let it be known my doors are always open to speak with anyone who wants to come by Franklin Court to converse with me and get my thoughts, and give me the benefit of theirs.

"Perhaps you may know, General, that soon after the Confederation Congress issued its call for a Convention of delegates from every State to reexamine and rethink the Articles of Confederation, I proposed that a Society for Political Inquiries be organized in as many states as possible to get more of our leading citizens discussing the deficiencies of the government we presently have, and thus influencing the selection of delegates to the Convention. I'm pleased to say all eight of the Pennsylvania delegation are members of this Society and have been meeting weekly for several months at Franklin Court, most recently four days ago, to put our thoughts in order.

"At my instigation chapters of the Society for Political Inquiries have been started in other States, as well as in Pennsylvania, and the effect has, on the whole, been salutary, I believe."

Shifting to an even broader topic, Franklin said, "Permit me to say, General Washington, that this Convention will either do great good or great harm. If we can find a way to increase the powers of the national government without decreasing the appropriate powers of the States, the benefits which will accrue to us and to our posterity will be immense and will endure far into the future, I assure you. We shall also have proven to the world that republicanism is a practical form of government, and will have provided a model for it which other nations may want to imitate. If we fail in our endeavor, the harm that will result will be just as tremendous and long lasting. For then we shall have shown that we Americans, despite the virtues we pride ourselves on having, especially our love of liberty—which we derive from our immigrant ancestry and our extraordinary natural resources, particularly our seemingly limitless unsettled land—lack the wisdom to create a government worthy of our potential.

"But I don't think we shall fail. Too many honest men of good will and practical experience are coming to Philadelphia to frame a new general government. Men of this sort, I believe, will not tolerate failure."

George Washington broke his pensive silence by thanking Franklin for his intention to nominate him for election to the Convention's presidency. "Your nomination will do me great honor. But should I be elected President of this assembly, as you think I will be, it may have untoward consequences for me personally. At the end of the war, it was with a sense of relief that I resumed my life of bringing forth good things from the earth. The life of a planter. Now, my yearning to continue that life at Mount Vernon is in conflict with my sense of duty to our country. I see the tremendous opportunities we gained in our victory over Britain slipping from our grasp because our present government is based on the chimera of State sovereignty. Unlike myself, more Virginians than you might suppose believe in the superiority of State sovereignty to national sovereignty, and consider themselves Virginians first and Americans second, if at all.

"I've just been contemplating my dear wife's refusal to accompany me here to Philadelphia, Dr. Franklin. She is of the opinion that this Convention will draw me once more into national service, and that another extended absence from Mount Vernon would blast our hoped-for domestic felicity. She has told our relatives and friends she couldn't come to Philadelphia with me because her grandchildren could not spare her. But Martha's real reason for not coming was not that. It was her disapprobation of my entanglement again in national affairs."

"But, my dear Sir, with all due respect for Mrs. Washington's sensibilities, if you will pardon the frankness of an old man, are you not already in the nation's service?" Franklin asked. "Did not your reception in this city this afternoon prove that? The people of the States in both high and low places, in both the North and the South, claim you as one of their own. They feel they can trust you. Whatever apprehensions your dear wife may have, your virtues have already stamped you as a public man in the eyes of your fellow Americans. I believe once you've been nominated to preside over this Convention, your election is assured and will be unanimous because of the confidence you have inspired and continue to inspire in your countrymen."

Just then Mr. Mahoney came through the library's door bearing a large silver tray on which reposed a small wooden cradle holding a little keg with a spigot, a bottle of French spring water, a tankard, a cut-glass goblet, and a plate of crackers accompanied by thin-sliced ham and cheese, and two napkins of soft linen, which he set down on Dr. Franklin's worktable.

"If you would be so kind, Francis, please serve our guest a tankard of this porter," Franklin requested. "A London brewer sent it to me, General, saying that it was from an exceptionally good batch of porter, the best he'd brewed in many a year. I've been saving it for you. Give me a glass of French spring water, Francis. That's the only treat my enemy the gout allows me these days, General Washington."

Mr. Mahoney, after deftly carrying out these orders, departed, leaving his master and his visitor to the pleasure of their refreshments and each other's company.

"This porter is indeed excellent, Dr. Franklin," Washington remarked. "Thank you for reserving it for me. How did you know I was fond of this sort of beer?"

Franklin replied, "I remembered from our time together twelve years ago in Boston that you were particularly fond of porter. So when Mr. Claymore kindly sent me from London this small keg of that sort of beer, and endorsed it so highly, I naturally thought of you and put it aside for your arrival."

"This ham is from Virginia, if I am not mistaken."

"It is indeed, General. One of your native State's distinctions—besides producing eminent leaders—is producing America's best ham."

After the two men had taken their fill of refreshments, which Washington declared suited his needs exactly, Franklin asked Washington if he might have his views on what they had been discussing before the refreshments were brought.

"My thoughts coincide with yours, Dr. Franklin. The Union is in peril. We must avoid partial solutions, I think, and seek a change in our general government suited to the growth of a large republic in which the States treat each other as equals without demanding sovereignty.

"We're at a crossroads, Your Excellency. In one direction lies the stronger, more equitable government America needs, which will assure domestic tranquility in every State, justice among the States, and the general welfare of the States. If we continue governing ourselves according to the requirements of the Articles of Confederation, I believe we will find ourselves, in another few years, in a state of anarchy where Americans are killing Americans, as happened last January in Massachusetts.

"The next uprising, however, may involve more than one State. The violence that occurred at the federal arsenal in Massachusetts presages what may occur on a more extensive scale the next time, unless we establish a genuine Union of the States in accordance with the natural laws of right and wrong our Creator has ordained, and which we proclaimed when we declared our independence from Britain.

"What made the armed uprising of farmers in Massachusetts so deeply disturbing to me, Dr. Franklin, was not only that it happened in one of the oldest, most republican, and largest States, but that the men prosecuting it were yeomen of the sort who were the backbone of our struggle against British tyranny. We could never have won that struggle without the unyielding commitment to our cause by the farmers of the land, who comprise the greatest portion of our population. They refused to give in to the King's troops even when Congress could not pay them or provide them their lawful rations and other fundamental necessities such as boots and gunpowder, sometimes for months on end. I speak of what I saw and know to be true.

"The Massachusetts men who resorted to force to save their farms were protesting what they perceived to be violations of God's natural law, and were the same sort of Americans who left bloody footprints in the snow at Valley Forge and on the road that Christmas morning when we marched on Trenton to do battle with the Hessians. My tribulations as commander of the American army were nothing compared to the suffering of the men I led. Their dedication to the American cause of independence, and their faith in it, remained firm no matter what tribulations befell them."

There was a slight pause in Washington's comments before he went on. "I happen to know something of this Daniel Shays who, though he did not instigate the insurrection in Massachusetts, reluctantly became its leader, as I am told by my informants in that State. What I know of his character came to me, years ago, by way of testimony from no less a witness than General Lafayette. He was so impressed by Shays' conduct under fire at Yorktown that he had a handsome dress sword engraved with Shays' name and the date and place of his heroism and presented it to him. This Massachusetts farmer, mind you, left his farm and family at the beginning of the war and served in the Continental Army for six years, from Bunker Hill to Yorktown; and, without any patronage, because of his good conduct was commissioned a captain. If since the end of the war such men have become desperate enough to take up arms against their State government and the government of the United States, then something is terribly wrong with the way we're governing ourselves, Dr. Franklin, and it must be put right without delay."

Immediately Franklin responded, "In my opinion, General, the Articles of Confederation must be replaced rather than tinkered with by amendment. Mr. Madison's judgment on that question is sound in my estimation. He is also right, I think, in saying the new constitution must be ratified in conventions elected in each State by the people thereof for that explicit purpose, not as the Articles of Confederation were ratified by the State legislatures. The last time Mr. Madison came by Franklin Court to talk with me, he said he's heard you compare the Articles to a bird without feathers fit only to hop about on the ground, a prey to its enemies. The Articles were hurriedly written during wartime without sufficient debate.

"The Declaration of Independence, in contrast, benefited from many public debates and coffeehouse discussions, countless sermons, innumerable pamphlets, and not a few books on our political relations with England. The Articles had no thorough consideration of the sort of government America should have. The British army in our midst, waging war upon us, provided the only real unity the States had under the Articles of Confederation. The instant the signing of the peace treaty with Britain ended the war, that source of unity disappeared.

"The theory of government which the Articles of Confederation embody, General Washington, is the unrestrained sovereignty of each State, an impractical theory rife with incipient anarchy. The Articles have never provided a basis for just relations among the States. Nor have they provided a basis for reliable funding for general government."

Franklin paused for a moment before saying, "Americans require written constitutions, General, because from the first permanent English settlement on the North American mainland in 1607 down to our renouncing of British authority over us in 1776, as each colony was founded the Crown issued to it a written charter that included instructions for its governance. That is why when the Declaration of Independence terminated British rule over the thirteen English-speaking colonies on the mainland of North America in 1776, each former colony immediately wrote its own constitution for self-government.

"What has been lacking in our tradition of government is a written prescription for relations among the colonies which are now States. The king was our sovereign before the war, and each colony looked to him as such. When his authority was banned by our Declaration of Independence, the people of each former colony became their own sovereign authority. But there was no custom for establishing a Union of American States. Our problem is to institute a written constitution stipulating the sovereignty of the Union of American States.

"The Articles provide no practical basis for general government. The States have not had their need for mutual defense, justice, and law satisfied under the Articles of Confederation because the Articles mistakenly assume the States should be independently sovereign. All semblance of a mutual obligation among the States to satisfy their common needs is being destroyed under the Articles of Confederation by a tyranny every bit as oppressive and intolerable as that of a king who acts only in his own interest. Namely, the unbridled interests of each State. Since 1781 when the Articles were ratified, it's been as though thirteen self-centered monarchs, not just one unruly tyrant—the thirteen State legislatures—ruled America.

"General Washington, we lack an effective Union. Until we have that sort of Union, we are merely an alleged nation composed of thirteen separate governments. We are not acting in unison but, rather, in discord, and occasionally in outright hostility toward each other. The thirteen States are losing their sense of the need for a common defense, a common regulation of commerce, and a common supply of sound money instead of each State supplying its own currency.

"There's likewise a need for a uniform process of admitting new States into the Union on an equal footing with the existing States. Each State in the present Union—if what we now have can actually be called a Union—regards itself as more or less an entity unto itself. As Mr. Madison has often said, the Articles of Confederation regard the States as being only in league with each other, not as the integral parts of a single nation. This must end."

"Indeed, it must, Dr. Franklin," Washington agreed. "What you have just stated is the plain truth of America's present condition. The States cannot go on regarding their so-called sovereignty as constituting something superior to the sovereignty of the United States. To continue to do so will make it impossible for any State to maintain its independence from foreign powers. We won our independence from Britain because of the unity with which the States acted. The States are not thirteen independent entities. Virginia cannot by itself be sovereign. Nor can any State. The States can only have sovereignty in union with one another. Nothing could be clearer to me than that.

"Independent State sovereignty is a chimera when it is regarded as an attainable and desirable prerogative of the States, Dr. Franklin. The independence and prosperity of every State depend on its effective unity with all the other States. That alone can assure each State protection from foreign as well as domestic enemies."

Franklin replied, "I agree, General, that that is the case. And I would further observe that framing the new general government to replace the inherently flawed Articles of Confederation requires that the reformation take place in secret. Otherwise, it cannot be achieved.

"The delegates to this assembly, many of them notable men with valuable experience in government, ought to be able to frame the new constitution that is needed. But they must be free to express their views on any subject with no apprehension that an intemperate remark of theirs made in the heat of debate could be reported to the people of their home State, as might easily happen if the proceedings of the Convention appeared in the press and thus subject day by day to public scrutiny. Without keeping our proceedings hidden from such scrutiny, that sort of apprehension will dominate the Convention's debates and make it impossible for the delegates to arrive at the informed and authentic agreements that are needed to frame an enduring constitution. We have not come to this Convention to contend with our fellow delegates, but to confer with one another in an atmosphere of respectful frankness and adjust our differing views, and thus arrive at a workable general government.

"To achieve agreements that will endure—that is, agreements that will be useful not only to ourselves but to posterity—each delegate to this Convention must be able to express his thoughts on any subject fully and freely, without fear of public opinion. I daresay, General Washington, no one who sincerely engages in the business of this Convention will leave Philadelphia with every idea he had when he arrived here still intact. Each of us will have to listen to the arguments our fellow delegates make in debate with a willingness to be persuaded by them.

"A coherent new constitution for general government

cannot have three million authors, or even three thousand, or three hundred. That is certain. Therefore the people of the States cannot see the constitution as it is being written. Only if the Convention's debates are conducted in private, without public knowledge of them, can the needed reform be achieved. Secret debates alone will prevent the intrusion of the rest of the country on the thinking of the State delegations at the Convention as the framing of the new government proceeds. The public must not see the new constitution in bits and dribbles while it is being written, as would happen if the day-to-day proceedings of the Convention were made known to persons in the press who are not a party to it, or made known through letters written by the State delegates to friends, family, and political allies at home.

"Compromises will be required to reach the necessary agreements on the provisions for the new government, General. When making a broad table, something has to be taken from each board to make the needed tight joints. The same is true of the task before us. Delegates to the Convention must be willing to concede something for the sake of framing a broad government to serve all the States and our posterity. As we enter into the work of making a national government, we must reject the attitude of the Anglicans who say they're never wrong in the form of their worship, and the Roman Catholics who say the doctrines of their faith are infallible. Such attitudes ill become us and would make it impossible for us to form a new government. They resemble the attitude of the woman who, though comely, never received a proposal of marriage, and when asked why she was forever contradicting other people, said, 'I don't know how it happens, but I meet with nobody except myself who is always in the right.'"

"What exactly do you have in mind, Dr. Franklin?" Washington inquired.

"The East Room of the Pennsylvania State House, where the Convention will hold its meetings, must be secured against newspapermen, idle eavesdroppers, gossipers, domestic enemies, and foreign agents. As Pennsylvania's chief executive and therefore host of the Convention, I have taken steps toward that end. I've asked a sergeant in the Pennsylvania militia whom I've known for many years, and trust, to recommend a list of twenty or twenty-five reliable militiamen to act as a Convention Guard. I will appoint fourteen of these to the Guard after interviewing all of the nominees, and will make Sergeant Corbin the commander of the Guard.

"Corbin and I agree that three posts should be manned when the Convention is in session. Inside the State House at the door going into the East Room, where he will have his administrative table. Outside the State House under the East Room's three large windows facing Chestnut Street, and under the three large windows facing the shaded walks behind the State House, known as the Promenade. Each post will have four men—a corporal in charge of it and three privates—all of them armed with musket and bayonet— to keep it free of persons who are not members of the Convention. As an added precaution, I have had the six windows of the East Room nailed shut for the duration of the Convention.

"Besides the dozen armed Guards, two extra militiamen will be assigned to sit with Sergeant Corbin, to be on hand to substitute for any guardsman who may not show up for duty on a given day because of an indisposition. These extras will be younger men in the prime of health, to make it more likely they will be on hand every day. They will also run errands for Alexander Corbin and sweep out the East Room and the small library attached to it after every session of the Convention. Any pieces of paper with writing on them that they find on the floor, or on the delegation tables, they will give to the

Convention's Secretary, who will inspect them carefully before burning them in one of the East Room's two fireplaces.

"Most important to securing the proceedings of the Convention from outsiders is to have each delegate sign a Rule of Secrecy that has been moved, debated, and passed by the Convention. The Rule will pledge each delegate never to speak to anyone not a party to the Convention concerning its proceedings, and never to put in writing or print anything said in the East Room or in the Convention's committee meetings without permission from the Convention's President, who will retain possession of the signed pledges.

"The people of the States must not be part of the processes of writing the Constitution. That would be far, far too many cooks. If the people were to be informed of what the Convention is considering, it would expand the scope of disagreement to such an extent that arriving at agreements would be greatly impaired."

"Dr. Franklin, I concur with your argument for secrecy if the Convention is to achieve its goal of framing a new constitution for the people of the States to ratify," General Washington said. "And if I am elected to preside over the Convention, I would like to see a Rule of Reconsideration adopted. This Rule would allow any decision made in the Convention to be reconsidered within forty-eight hours if only one delegate made such a request, and to allow reconsideration of it after more than forty-eight hours if two delegates requested its reconsideration. That way, no member of the Convention can ever claim his ideas and concerns and the interests of his State were not given the fullest consideration by the Convention.

"I likewise think the parliamentary procedure by which an assembly declares itself to be in a Committee of the Whole House should be liberally used at the outset of the Convention, when many, perhaps most, of the delegates to the Convention will be trying to understand the issues they must resolve, and what their views are on those matters.

"As you know, Dr. Franklin, nothing decided when an assembly is in a Committee of the Whole House is final. Every decision made in that mode of assembly must be voted on again when the assembly reverts to its normal condition of assembly. Being in a Committee of the Whole House allows an assembly to acquire a sense of its members' thinking on a particular subject without making a final decision on it."

Washington continued, "Another thing. One of the chief deficiencies of the Articles of Confederation which must be remedied is denying Congress the power to raise money by taxation to meet the expenses of government. Under the Articles, Congress can only request the States to contribute the money needed to run the government. The amount each State is asked to contribute varies according to its estimated population and wealth. Some States pay the asked-for assessment; others do not. Some pay it sometimes, or only partly. States like Virginia which always pay the full amount requested naturally resent the behavior of a State like Rhode Island, which has acquired the byname 'Rogue Island' because it never pays its assessment. A State that pays only part of the requested contribution, or pays it only occasionally, likewise rouses the ire of States which always pay the full amount of their assessment.

"Worse still, Dr. Franklin, the laws enacted by the Confederation Congress are not uniformly obeyed throughout the Union because the Articles of Confederation do not provide for an executive department of government to see to the execution of the laws Congress enacts. Such a department is needed. The national government also needs a department consisting of judges having the duty to defend and uphold the constitution, because disputes over its provisions are bound to arise, no matter how carefully they, and the laws passed under the authority of the constitution, are worded. There has to be a judicial branch of the general government to settle such disputes by having a judge or judges hear the evidence on both sides of a dispute and say what the constitution, or a law enacted under its authority, allows and does not allow in a particular case.

"You must, I suppose, Dr. Franklin, be aware, as the principal negotiator of the treaty ending our war with Britain, that British soldiers still occupy six formerly British forts now on American soil, four in northern New York and two in the Great Lakes region, even though four years ago the Crown agreed, in signing the treaty of peace with us, to evacuate them with all reasonable speed. This is an example of how weak our government is at present, and how little respect it has in Europe."

"Indeed, General Washington, I am aware of these violations of the Treaty's seventh clause," Franklin responded. "I'm also aware that British agents are here in Philadelphia and in New York gathering information for their government to use to divide us and bring about the collapse of the United States. Correspondents of mine in London tell me the papers there predict every day the imminent collapse of the United States of America, and that it is also common for the governments of European countries to say that the Confederation Congress under the Articles of Confederation does not deserve to be called the government of the United States because its relation to the States is more like that of a petitioner or advisor. The British spies among us are working diligently to make good the predicted demise of our country. They especially want to learn as much as they can of our upcoming Convention to strengthen our Union of States.

"Besides foreign agents trying deliberately to harm the Union, some State leaders, such as the governor of New York,

George Clinton, oppose strengthening the general government because that would diminish their local political power. These Americans seem to regard the weakness of the general government as freedom for their State. This attitude makes as much sense as the man who burned down his house to roast his breakfast eggs.

"But the stronger government that you and I, Mr. Madison, Colonel Hamilton, Robert Morris, Gouverneur Morris, James Wilson, Roger Sherman and other delegates to this Convention want must not be made so strong that it could endanger the liberty and rights that God has bestowed on Americans, or eliminate the legitimate and needful powers of the several States. The new constitution ought to be so constructed that its powers are plainly specified, clearly limited, and checked in as many ways as possible. Care must especially be taken, I think, to keep the new government from gradually usurping powers it has not been granted. If steps are not taken to prevent gradual usurpation, General Washington, a tyranny may develop over time, much worse than the present unbridled power of the States, because it would have the appearance of being constitutional.

"You will remember, Sir, that the Declaration of Independence limits the legitimate purpose of government to protecting the rights to life, liberty, the pursuit of happiness, and government by consent of the governed that God has bestowed on us. In writing the new constitution, we must keep that definition of government specified in the Declaration before us at all times.

"The essence of liberty in America, General Washington, has always been, and remains, self-determination. Wanting to lead lives they determined for themselves, under God's natural law, brought your ancestors and mine across the Atlantic to civilize the primitive shores of North America. Unless we recognize in the new constitution that meaning of freedom, America's unprecedented potential for greatness cannot be realized."

The tall sash windows of the library where Franklin and Washington sat talking had been raised before the General's visit to admit fresh air, and a slight breeze now rippled the topmost sheets of the stacked papers on Franklin's worktable, each held down by the weight of a fossilized molar of a prehistoric mastodon excavated in Virginia by Thomas Jefferson many years before, and sent to Philadelphia for America's foremost scientist to inspect.

Washington yawned and covered the yawn with the back of a hand, as he excused himself for doing it.

"It seems, General," his elderly host mildly observed, "that the fatigues of your journey to Philadelphia are beginning to tell on you. Perhaps it's time we adjourned our conversation. Therefore, until the morrow, when the Federal Convention is scheduled to begin, I bid you a pleasant night's rest."

As George Washington rose from his chair he reached across Franklin's chestnut-wood worktable and once again grasped the right hand of his host in both of his hands, saying, "Your Excellency, it has been of inestimable benefit to me to converse with you."

Mr. Mahoney was waiting for the General on the landing outside the library door, holding a lighted lantern to escort him downstairs and out to the street.

Finally, A Quorum

Chapter IV

IN CALLING A CONVENTION of the States in Philadelphia, the Confederation Congress sitting in New York had referred to the need for such a gathering to correct "the defects" of the Articles of Confederation and to produce what it termed "a firm national government." The date and time designated for the State delegations to convene was Monday, May 14th at ten o'clock, the morning after Franklin and Washington had their private tête-à-tête in Benjamin Franklin's new library. The place for the Convention was the East Room of the Pennsylvania State House.

But the Constitutional Convention did not begin on the appointed day because on the 14th of May a quorum of States to conduct the business of the Convention was lacking. Rhode Island was the only State that had refused to answer the Confederation Congress's call to "render the federal constitution adequate to the exigencies of Government & the preservation of the Union," which were two other ways the Confederation Congress had phrased the purposes of the Convention. And the delegations from New Hampshire, Massachusetts, Connecticut, New York, New Jersey, Delaware, Maryland, North and South Carolina, and Georgia had yet to arrive. But the two most populous States in the Union, Virginia and Pennsylvania, had majorities of their delegations present that day at 10 o'clock in the morning in the East Room of the State House in Philadelphia, ready to vote in Convention. Foremost among the delegates from Virginia and Pennsylvania were George Washington, who had led America to victory in it's war for independence from Britain, and Benjamin Franklin, whose consummate diplomacy in Paris had made possible America's military alliance with the kingdom of France which had been essential to that victory.

Franklin had been brought to the East Room in the sedan chair a French nobleman had given him so he would not have to suffer the agitation of the stones in his kidneys and bladder that made walking and riding in carriages excruciating experiences. His chair bearers were four brawny inmates from the Walnut Street Jail who'd been imprisoned for debt. It was Franklin's way of giving them the employment they needed to pay their debts and obtain release from prison because they had no friends or family with the means to discharge their debts, which the law required to be paid or the debtor would stay in jail.

Other delegates living in Philadelphia who were present were James Wilson, a lawyer educated at St. Andrews University in his native Scotland. Thomas Fitzsimmons, a merchant who had immigrated to America from Ireland. The entrepreneur George Clymer. The lawyer Jared Ingersoll. The financier Robert Morris, a native of England. General Thomas Mifflin. And Gouverneur Morris, a business partner of Robert Morris, but no kin of his, the only man missing from Pennsylvania's eight-man delegation. He had been called out of town on urgent family business and was not expected back for several days.

Four of the seven Virginia delegates besides Washington were present. The professor of jurisprudence at Virginia's William and Mary College and Chancellor of Virginia, George Wythe. John Blair, a judge on Virginia's highest court who had been educated in the law at London's Middle Temple. James McClung, the Edinburgh-trained physician who had replaced

Patrick Henry when that worthy refused his election to the Virginia delegation. And James Madison, a member of the Confederation Congress and close friend of Thomas Jefferson.

Jefferson of Virginia and John Adams of Massachusetts were in Europe, serving as America's ambassadors to France and Britain. Two other Virginia delegates were still absent from Philadelphia—the State's aristocratic young governor, Edmund Randolph, and George Mason, another eminent member of the Virginia aristocracy. Like his neighbor and good friend George Washington, Mason was a planter who also had the distinction of authoring Virginia's Declaration of Rights, from which Jefferson had borrowed ideas and language in 1776 in writing America's Declaration of Independence.

Thus, although most of the delegates from the two most populous States were present, the Convention was five States short of the required quorum of seven States out of the twelve which had pledged to attend the Constitutional Convention.

Yet even though the required quorum was not on hand, the Virginia and Pennsylvania delegates lingered in the East Room getting acquainted, or, in several cases, reacquainted. The hope that another delegate or two might turn up was a further incentive for remaining in the 1,600-square-foot room with its twenty-foot-high ceiling.

Of the dozen delegates present, eleven were standing here and there in the East Room talking to each other. The twelfth delegate, Benjamin Franklin, was sitting at the Pennsylvania delegation table on a cushion he'd brought in from his sedan chair to make sitting on the room's hard wooden armchairs less painful to his kidney and bladder stones. The other delegates present were coming up to him, singly and in pairs, to pay their respects and chat.

Various theories were being advanced as to why more delegates had not shown up on the appointed day. The most common speculation was that the recent heavy rains had mired the roads north and south of Philadelphia, which always slowed travel. Other explanations were that some of the tardy delegates, as busy men of affairs, had probably had to finish imperative business before leaving for Philadelphia. Other delegates speculated the long distances some delegates had to come were causing unexpected problems.

After they had conversed for the better part of an hour, Robert Morris proposed that they repair to the City Tavern to continue their conversations over refreshments, which he would pay for.

Benjamin Franklin immediately summoned Sergeant Corbin and asked him to send a messenger to tell the City Tavern to prepare a suitable private room for their use. He also told the Sergeant to dismiss the Convention Guards stationed at their three posts, and to tell them to report for duty at 10 the next morning in case a quorum of States was present then.

At the City Tavern, it came to light that the Virginians had "a plan," as they called it, a list of proposals for the new constitution around which the Convention could organize its debates on what the new constitution should contain. The Virginians proudly reported they'd been working on their plan for weeks under the studious guidance of Mr. Madison and the wise counsel of Chancellor Wythe. They also informed their fellow delegates from Pennsylvania that James Madison—who had opted to return to Mrs. House's lodgings to work on the Virginia Plan, instead of accepting Mr. Morris's generous invitation—had written to Jefferson in Paris more than a year before, requesting him to buy books for him on the history of government, particularly books on ancient and modern confederations. In due course, a trunk full of such tomes had arrived in New York where Madison was a member of the Confederation Congress representing Virginia. He had been studying the books and taking notes on their contents ever since.

It was quite evident from their conversation that the delegates from Virginia and Pennsylvania thought the Articles of Confederation had to be replaced rather than amended. The Virginians had become convinced that a new kind of general government for the United States was needed, one which would put the States into a different relation with one another than they had under the Articles of Confederation. Influenced by their discussions in Benjamin Franklin's Society for Political Inquiries, the eight men in the Pennsylvanian delegation had come to the same conclusion. But they were less explicit and coordinated in their views than the Virginians as to what was needed in the new constitution. The Pennsylvania delegates had no "plan." Thus leadership of the Convention passed to the Virginians, who had a sort of natural claim to it in any case, coming as they did from the largest State in the Union, the first permanently settled English-speaking colony in the New World, and the first to have an elected legislature, the Virginia House of Burgesses.

Once more, on Tuesday, May 15th, not enough State delegations had a majority of their members present, which would have permitted the Convention to begin. Nor were enough present the next day, or the next, or the day after that. Not until the 25th of May, a Friday, eleven days past the scheduled beginning of the Convention, was the required quorum of seven voting States present in the East Room of the Pennsylvania State House. On that day, majorities of the delegations from New York, Pennsylvania, New Jersey, Delaware, Virginia, North Carolina, and South Carolina were on hand. Now, at last, the Convention could proceed and the history of the United States of America could start moving toward its destiny of being one nation made up of many States, of creating an unprecedented national flag that Americans would refer to as "Old Glory." But, it was a close call. For in the early part of July, 1787, it seemed that a stronger American government would not become a reality.

On May 25th voting delegations from Georgia and New Hampshire, the most distant States, were still not present in Philadelphia. Nor were majorities of the delegations from any of the "Eastern States," as New England was called because its four States were all east of the rest of the States. Nor was a majority of Maryland's delegation present, even though it bordered on Pennsylvania.

The Virginians had put this eleven-day delay to good use by meeting every day, except Sunday, May 20th, at Mrs. House's boardinghouse, to develop their plan.

The first order of business on May 25th was, of course, the election of a presiding officer for the Convention. Dr. Franklin, as had become generally known among the Convention's members who were present, intended to nominate George Washington to that influential position. But he was unable to do so because an all-day torrential rain prevented him from attending the first day of the Convention since his sedan chair would not have withstood the deluge. Therefore, via his majordomo Francis Mahoney, he sent a letter through the downpour to Robert Morris, asking Morris to nominate Washington and to get the head of the South Carolina delegation, John Rutledge, the much-respected wartime governor of that State, to second the nomination. That way, even though no voting delegation from any of the Eastern States was present, the General would still receive endorsements from both the Mid-Atlantic and the South, the other two major regions of the United States in 1787.

No speeches accompanied Morris's nomination of Washington or Rutledge's seconding of it. None were needed. Robert Morris said simply that he nominated Washington on behalf of the Pennsylvania delegation, which everyone understood meant on behalf of Benjamin Franklin; John Rutledge said only that he trusted the vote for Washington would be unanimous. No other name being put in nomination, Morris asked that the nominations be closed, and that the voting for Convention President proceed by written ballot, which was done, each State casting one ballot. As expected, all seven State delegations present voted as Franklin had predicted.

After announcing the unanimous result, Robert Morris and John Rutledge escorted Washington to the high-backed chair at the desk on the slightly raised platform at the front of the room, the desk which had been used eleven years before to write and sign the Declaration of Independence, which was to be used again for writing and signing a new constitution for the United States. The General wore the same uniform he had worn in 1775 when the States of the United States had unanimously chosen him to command their army.

James Madison, by previous arrangement, also rose from the Virginia delegation table and followed the other three men to the front of the East Room, where he sat down at a small desk that had been placed for him in front of the raised presidential platform, facing the tables covered in green baize. The desk had been equipped with paper, ink, and quills for him to record the debates and all the other proceedings of the Convention, a demanding task which he had asked to be allowed to perform.

Washington, in his first act as President of the Convention, made a little speech from the President's Chair, as he had done in 1775 after being appointed unanimously by the States in the Second Continental Congress to command America's armed forces in the war for independence. He thanked the Convention for the honor the gentlemen had bestowed on him, and said he would do his utmost to justify their trust.

The Convention's next order of business was to elect a Secretary to call the roll of the States when votes were taken and to record the official yeas and nays of the State delegations. Votes would, by custom, start in the north and go south, New Hampshire being the first to vote, Georgia the last. If a State delegation was evenly divided in its yeas and nays on a motion, its single vote as a State would not count one way or the other but be recorded as "divided." The modest stipend attached to the position of secretary was not what made it attractive, but rather the possibility that it might lead to a substantial government job when the new government was implemented.

Two men were nominated. Twenty-seven-year-old Temple Franklin who had accompanied his illustrious grandfather as his secretary on his nine-year mission to France was nominated by James Wilson of Pennsylvania, a longtime confidant of Dr. Franklin. Alexander Hamilton nominated Major William Jackson, an English-born South Carolinian who during the war had served on General Washington's staff and briefly as Assistant Secretary of War for the Second Continental Congress.

Of the seven State votes cast, Major Jackson got five and Temple Franklin two. The widely known fact that Temple Franklin had fathered children in Europe out of wedlock and not supported them influenced this result, as did the notorious behavior of his father, William Franklin, Dr. Franklin's only son, who, as royal governor of New Jersey was the only American-born royal governor to remain loyal to the Crown. William Franklin had also raised a troop of cavalry among loyalist Americans and led them in battle to kill his fellow Americans. This conduct had permanently estranged Dr. Franklin from his only son, who after the war fled the United States to live in England on his pension as a former royal governor in the British empire.

Following the election of the Convention Secretary, the rest of the first session of the Constitutional Convention was devoted to listening to the Secretary read the instructions each State delegation had received from its legislature, none of which caused any dismay except Delaware's, which forbad its delegation from ever voting to change the provision in the Articles of Confederation that gave each State a single vote in Congress. This limitation caused some consternation because the One-State-One-Vote Rule had been considered one of the major defects of the Articles leading the Confederation Congress to call a Constitutional Convention.

Before adjournment on the 25th of May, a three-man committee was chosen to draft a set of Standing Rules and Orders to regulate the Convention's procedures, with George Wythe of Virginia as chairman and Charles Pinckney of South Carolina and Alexander Hamilton of New York as members. They were to present their recommendations to the Convention on Monday, May 28th.

All in all, the delegates who participated in the opening day of the Convention on Friday, May 25th, were pleased with the start they had made to their task of formulating a constitution adequate to "the preservation of the Union," which the Confederation Congress had stipulated as the concluding instruction to the Convention delegates.

Washington went to Franklin Court immediately after the opening session of the Convention adjourned, to report to Dr. Franklin the results of the first day, which the heavy rain had kept him from attending. America's greatest scientist and most experienced statesman agreed that the Convention had gotten off to an auspicious start, even though his grandson Temple had not been elected Secretary of the Convention.

"May I say in congratulating you on your unanimous election to the presidency of the Convention, General, that it is my conviction that we will do ourselves and our posterity the most good if we create the best practical constitution, not the best conceivable one. As my friend of many years John Dickinson, now a resident of Delaware and a delegate to this Convention from that State, has said to me on more than one occasion, 'Experience must be our guide. Reason may mislead us.'"

The Convention's session on Monday, May 28th, and part of the next day as well, was devoted to the Standing Rules and Orders recommended by the committee charged with writing them. The house rejected only one of the recommendations, the proposal that a record be made of how each delegate individually voted if just one delegate to the Convention asked that such a record be made. A majority of the State delegations agreed with George Mason of Virginia, who said that if this rule were adopted it would serve no useful purpose and would tend to discourage delegates from changing their minds once their personal vote on a specific matter had been recorded in the Convention's Journal. And delegates would have to change their minds on occasion if agreements were to be reached on provisions for the new constitution.

The Rule of Reconsideration that Washington wanted to see adopted was approved as a Standing Order, as was the Rule of Secrecy that Franklin deemed necessary to the Convention's success. But the secrecy rule underwent a significant modification. Instead of having every delegate sign a printed pledge to obey the rule, it was decided it would be more efficacious if General Washington as President of the Convention administered to every delegate in private an oath pledging him to obey the Rule of Secrecy.

Following approval of the Standing Rules and Orders, Washington recognized Virginia's governor Edmund Randolph who was to present the Virginia Plan to the Convention. By way of introduction Randolph summarized the defects of the Articles of Confederation before he introduced the fifteen "resolutions," or propositions, of the Virginia Plan.

He said the propositions of the Virginia Plan were intended to correct the doctrine that full sovereignty of the States, the principle on which the Articles of Confederation had been based, was the foremost principle of American government. The Virginia Plan replaced that principle with the doctrine that the nation's sovereignty had precedence over State sovereignty. For without national sovereignty, Randolph said, the liberty, happiness, and security of the people in the several States would be in jeopardy. If anything was certain, it was that the wellbeing of every State was bound up in the general welfare of the Union. No State could be safe, happy, and free when the sovereignty of each of them took precedence over the nation's sovereignty, which is to say the Union's. Under the Articles of Confederation, no law of general importance could be passed if even one State objected to it.

Randolph then read in a clear, steady voice the propositions of the Virginia Plan. Its radical departure from the Articles of Confederation was immediately apparent in the Plan's proposal that the States be represented in Congress in proportion to the number of their respective inhabitants rather than by every State having a single vote in Congress as the Articles mandated. Other propositions in which the Virginia Plan departed from the existing constitution were in proposing that executive and judicial branches be added to the Confederation's legislative branch, and that Congress have two houses instead of one, the first to be elected by the people of each State, and the second house by the first. Moreover, the new Congress was to have the power to levy taxes and compel their payment.

The Convention adjourned after Mr. Randolph completed his reading of the propositions of the Virginia Plan so the State delegations could study it and prepare to debate it.

Upon reconvening the following day, May 30th, the Convention voted to go into a Committee of the Whole House to debate the Virginia Plan. Nathaniel Gorham, who had just arrived in Philadelphia as a delegate from Massachusetts and had recently served as President of the Confederation Congress, was made chairman of the Committee of the Whole House, and George Washington resumed his seat at the Virginia delegation table.

In voting to become a Committee of the Whole House, the Convention opened the way for all manner of proposals to be discussed if they were put in the form of a motion and got a second, because nothing said or done in this mode of assembly was binding on the Convention. And the Rule of Secrecy prevented whatever was said in the Committee of the Whole House from becoming known to the people of the States.

Therefore ideas started to be put forward that had long been pent up. One delegate, for instance, proposed that when new States were formed from the extensive lands west of the Appalachian Mountains, and they applied for admission to the Union—as surely would start happening before too long—under the new constitution they would be subordinate to what he called "the Atlantic States," the original thirteen States of the Union, all of which had a port on the Atlantic. He declared that if such steps were not taken and the new

States were considered equal to the Atlantic States, they would soon outnumber and dominate the original thirteen States in Congress, to the detriment of the Atlantic States.

Another delegate proposed abolishing the existing States altogether and forming new States which would be equal in area and population.

While the Convention was in a Committee of the Whole House more than one delegate excoriated "cheap paper money" as a form of theft, in that it diminished the value of private property and of debts.

For the most part, however, the outline for reform presented in the Virginia Plan kept discourse and debate on a generally sensible track, and it soon became apparent while the Convention was in a Committee of the Whole House that most of the State delegations, if not every one of them, agreed that a rewriting of the Articles of Confederation was needed, not mere amendments to that constitution for general government. It also became evident that most of the State delegations were willing to consider replacing the Articles of Confederation. In fact, a motion to do that and institute a national government having a supreme legislative, supreme executive, and supreme judiciary was passed by a vote of six States to one on May 30th, the fourth day of the Convention, and the first day of being in a Committee of the Whole House.

The irony of the Convention's decisions, whether in a Committee of the Whole House or in the normal mode of assembly, was that they were made according to the One- State-One-Vote Rule which most delegates appeared to consider one of the worst features of the Articles of Confederation and which they wanted to eliminate.

The Rule had been established in America when representatives of the colonies had begun to meet in an assembly they called the "Continental Congress" to discuss leaving the British empire and becoming independent. The "Second Continental Congress," which issued the Declaration of Independence, had used the One-State-One-Vote Rule to do that and to govern the United States during the war for independence. The Confederation Congress was still using it. The Rule had become so entrenched that the leaders of the Convention, despite their unhappiness with it, feared that if they did not use it during the Convention while conceiving a new form of Union, the ratification of the proposed constitution might fail if the people learned that a novel method of voting had been used in writing it. For eventually not only would the proposed constitution have to be submitted to the people of the States for their approval or rejection, but the means by which it had been written would have to be made known as well. And if the perfect equality of the States had not been upheld by the Constitutional Convention by using the One-State-One-Vote Rule, and the States with more people in them had been given greater weight in framing the new constitution, the people of the smaller States might not ratify the proposed new constitution.

Government by consent of the governed was a much older rule in America than the One-State-One-Vote concept. It dated from the earliest settlements in the wilderness of North America, which had all been made by persons who had consented to live there. Government by consent of the governed was explicitly enshrined in America's Declaration of Independence as one of the four "self-evident" rights of mankind ordained by God, along with "Life, Liberty, and the Pursuit of Happiness." These God-given rights were all inherent to the act of immigration.

On the 2nd of June, 1787, a Saturday—for after just a week in session the realization of the immensity of their task moved the Convention's delegates to meet on Saturdays as well as Monday through Friday—Benjamin Franklin made a long speech. That is, he wrote a long speech, which his friend James Wilson read for him because standing on his feet for more than a few minutes caused Franklin unbearable pain from the stones in his kidneys and bladder. The subject of Dr. Franklin's speech was whether the president of the new government should receive a salary.

Franklin, who was by far the oldest delegate to the Convention, informed his fellow delegates that his seventeen years in London lobbying for American colonial interests in the British Parliament had taught him that the desire to exercise power is one of the primary passions of human nature. "When that passion is combined with man's passion for wealth," Franklin said, "the result is detrimental to good government. The combination of power and money in a government office will make men move heaven and earth to obtain it. Therefore, the most powerful office in the new government we are devising, the presidency, should carry no stipend. Only the expenses entailed in carrying out the duties of the office should be compensated.

"Lest this view be thought 'Utopian,' may I remind the Convention that the powerful office of Sheriff in the counties of England is not compensated, yet never lacks for candidates of the highest character and ability who seek the honor of serving in it. The same thing is true in France in respect to the Counselors in the Judiciary Parliament. In America, in the Quaker religion, which prohibits its practitioners from resorting to law to settle disputes, judicial tasks are well executed by the elders of that religion for no compensation. Also in America, during the war with Britain, we have the example of the commander-in-chief of the Continental Army serving without pay for eight dangerous, anxious years, with the certainty of execution if Britain won the war and captured him. This sort of disinterested service, carried out for the honor of it, ought to be encouraged by making the U.S. presidency an office of honor only, without remuneration. Therefore, I move that the new republic's presidency, whether vested in one person or—as I, Mr. Randolph, and others would prefer—in three persons, carry no compensation other than repayment of the costs incurred in carrying it out."

Alexander Hamilton stood and said, "I second Dr. Franklin's motion. I do so in order to bring so respectable a proposal before the Committee and because it is based on experience."

But the house neither debated nor voted on this seconded motion; instead, it was tabled for further study.

Several members of the Convention then pointed out something else regarding the new office of President that would have to be considered. A provision for the President's removal from office. Such a provision had to be included in the new constitution in case the President's conduct in office proved venal or otherwise unacceptable. For, as James Madison had observed, if men were angels, no government would be needed; but since men are not angels, and the new government for the United States was to be administered by men, the failings of human nature would have to be taken into account in instituting it. Human beings were susceptible to corruption. Therefore provision had to be made for the impeachment and trial of a President whose behavior appeared corrupt, and for his removal from office if the charge was proven on evidence in a trial. Not only were officeholders liable to corruption, but voters were likewise fallible in their judgments, which was another compelling reason for a constitutional provision for impeachment and removal from office on evidence.

It was suggested that the power to overturn the result of an election, which is what a removal from office amounted to, should be exercised by Congress, but only if a majority of the State governors requested the impeachment and trial of a sitting president.

Though the need to provide for removing a president from office was acknowledged, this matter, too, like Franklin's motion on presidential compensation, was tabled.

As sweltering week followed sweltering week during the first month of the Convention, it became clear that one question above all others had to be resolved or the attempt to write a new constitution would fail. That question was, "Are the States to continue to be represented in the new Congress in the way they were represented in the Confederation Congress?" The Convention's success depended on reaching agreement on that question. Indeed, it became evident early in the Convention that the continuance of the Union, which is to say the continuance of the United States, might well depend on this issue more than any other.

Virginia and Pennsylvania were adamant in expressing their determination not to tolerate any further having their large populations represented in Congress by one vote, the same as the least populous States, a practice which gave Delaware the same weight in Congress as Virginia in making laws for the nation, even though Virginia had more than ten times the number of people Delaware had.

The small States were just as firm in insisting that they had to retain their present equal representation in Congress, which gave them the same voice as the big States in making federal laws. They would leave the Convention and go home rather than surrender their equal sovereignty in Congress, they said.

The big States said the One-State-One-Vote Rule, if continued, would hamper America's expansion into the trans-Appalachian wilderness, because as Americans settled that immense territory and applied for statehood in the Union of States, they would want the size of their growing populations to be taken into account in their representation in Congress.

This question of how the States were to be represented in Congress was more important than how the President was to be elected, or whether he was to be compensated, or how powerful his office ought to be, or how long his term in office would be; indeed, it was more fundamental than all the questions associated with establishing a national judiciary and the disturbing question of slavery. Because on the answer to that question depended how national laws would be made which all the people in all the States had to obey. And in a society of free men that would determine whether persons would have their God- given rights protected. Should each State continue to have a single vote in Congress, or be represented according to its population? And if population was to be the criterion, were slaves to be counted in calculating a State's population, or only free men?

It was as the conflict over State representation in Congress was coming into sharp focus that the Secrecy Rule the Convention had adopted was breeched.

A delegate from Massachusetts wrote a letter without permission from Washington as Convention President summarizing controversial matters that had been discussed in the Convention, such as the One-State-One-Vote Rule, in violation of the Secrecy Rule. He sent the letter by paid messenger to a delegate from Virginia, and both the messenger and the letter he carried had vanished.

If the contents of this letter were to become known outside the Convention, it would cause widespread consternation and protest in the land. If that happened, the result for the Convention would be catastrophic. It could even result in a hue and cry for the Confederation Congress to close down the Constitutional Convention in Philadelphia.

James Jamison's Commission
Chapter V

"DR. FRANKLIN, MR. MADISON, Captain Jamison," George Washington said in turn to the other men seated with him around one end of the massive mahogany table in Benjamin Franklin's new library, "it's past four o'clock, the time we set for our committee to meet, and Colonel Hamilton has not appeared. Either some unexpected, unavoidable business has intruded on his time, or he's been seized by a sudden malady, or he's suffered an incapacitating accident. In any case, we must begin our conference. Otherwise we'll be wasting our time waiting for him."

The former commander of the Continental Army had a long-standing reputation for punctuality and insisting on it from others, even his former chief of staff Alexander Hamilton, whom he loved like a son. Being late for an appointment was in Washington's view to show inexcusable disrespect for the person you were to meet at a certain time.

"We are here in the quiet splendor of this magnificent library, at Dr. Franklin's invitation, to mount an investigation into a threat to the Constitutional Convention. The disappearance of a letter written by Mr. Gerry of Massachusetts to Mr. Mason of Virginia, containing Gerry's opinions on secret proceedings of the Convention. If these opinions come to the attention of persons outside the Convention who oppose America having a stronger general government, they could be used to bring the Convention into such disrepute as to destroy it. And if this Convention were to be robbed of its legitimacy because of this letter's contents, the final chance we have of peaceably settling our differences on how to govern ourselves would be lost, and the United States of America might come to an end before it has barely begun.

"Captain Jamison, we want you, under Dr. Franklin's direction, to locate and retrieve this missing, illicitly written letter which poses a dire threat to the Convention. I've asked Mr. Madison and Colonel Hamilton to provide you the information you'll need in order to understand why the letter's disappearance is of such great concern and import, and to make effective inquiries. Since Colonel Hamilton is not here, Mr. Madison will provide all this information. Mr. Madison."

As a six-foot-tall, superb horseman and ballroom dancer, George Washington was physically everything James Madison was not. At age thirty-six Madison's almost boy-like stature of five feet four inches, and weight of one hundred pounds were belied by his receding, thinning hair (which he combed over his forehead to hide his balding) and his heavy beard (which, if he were going out in the evening, required a second shaving in the afternoon to maintain a clean-shaven, gentlemanly appearance). High cheekbones, cavernous eye sockets, a small mouth, pursed lips, and delicate chin and jaw lines were the principal features of Madison's alert face. His voice was a rich tenor; and, when he spoke in the Convention—which was often because he was one of its two primary organizers, the other being Hamilton—the delegates to the Convention took heed of what he had to say because whatever "Jemmy" Madison said, whether you agreed with it or not, was always well-informed and well stated.

James Madison was a scholar, a son of the Scottish Enlightenment as surely as if he had been born on the banks of the Firth of Forth and educated at the University of Edinburgh. As a lad he had boarded five years at a school in his native Virginia taught by a Scotsman with a degree from the University of Edinburgh, and he was then tutored at home for an additional three years by a graduate of the college at Princeton, New Jersey, which was presided over by John Witherspoon, an immigrant from Scotland with a doctorate from the University of Edinburgh. Madison had taken his bachelor's degree under Witherspoon, graduating in the class of 1771, and remained at Princeton for another year of private tutoring with Witherspoon.

Madison began explaining the situation in the Convention to Jamison by saying, "Dr. Franklin has recommended you, Captain, as a man who honors his word and can be relied on to keep secrets entrusted to him. My inquiries among my friends here in Philadelphia confirm Dr. Franklin's regard for your character and ability to get to the bottom of mysteries. It seems that in recent years you've gained quite a reputation here in Philadelphia for resolving mysteries. I have, therefore, no hesitation in divulging the Convention's affairs to you, Sir, for I know you will keep them a secret in finding the missing letter.

"As the General has said, a threat to the Convention is building, like the ominous clouds preceding a summer thunderstorm. Before going into the particulars of the situation, you should be made aware of why the Convention has adopted a strict Rule of Secrecy, which is what makes the disappearance of Mr. Gerry's letter so worrisome. Unless the missing letter is retrieved before it can fall into the hands of persons who oppose creating a national government for the United States, the continuance of the Convention is, as General Washington has said, in jeopardy, and so is that of the Union and therefore our country.

"Early in the Convention, at its third session, the delegates debated and passed a motion to conduct their proceedings in secret by not allowing themselves to mention any of their proceedings to anyone outside the Convention, or to put in writing or print anything said or done in the Convention without permission from its President, General Washington. For if persons outside the Convention were to receive news of its proceedings in 'bits and dribbles,' as Dr. Franklin is fond of expressing the matter, while the new constitution is being written, our efforts to replace the Articles of Confederation with a practical, national government would fail.

"First of all, because if people knew of some of the radical ideas gentlemen are bringing up for debate in the Convention, a hue and cry would arise in various quarters of the country to suppress such views, and the outcry might even include a demand that the Confederation Congress rescind its call for a convention to reform the Articles of Confederation.

"It is my belief, Captain Jamison, that only the persons chosen by the States and sent here to separate political wheat from political chaff ought to be privy to the process of writing the new constitution. Nothing worthy of being called a constitution, nothing worthy of being honored as a constitution, nothing worthy of being obeyed as a constitution, can be framed by thousands of persons. If the delegates to this Convention had to give heed to every theory of government their friends, family, and associates back home urged on them, and had to keep them informed of what was going on here in Philadelphia, they would be overwhelmed by contrary opinions, and unable to coordinate their own thinking as an assembly.

"Writing a constitution is a matter of selecting the provisions to go in it and making sure none of them contradict one another. To do this, the framers of the constitution must consult each other fully, honestly, and constantly, until the work is finished and a coherent constitution has been framed. A multitude of men simply cannot do that. Nor can a multitude of men forge the practical principles on which a constitution must be based in order to have authority over time. If the delegates to a Convention like the one now in train here in Philadelphia were constantly consulting with persons outside their assembly, and the newspapers of the land were able to publish what was being discussed in the Convention, the proliferation of contending ideas that would result would certainly impede the framing of the new constitution.

"The writing of the constitution now in view must be done in private. Only when it is completed can it be shown to the people who are to live under it so they can give it their approval. must be It must be approved, or disapproved of, as a whole, as written. The people of the States cannot be allowed to amend it, because that would mean the people of the next State to consider its ratification would be looking at a different constitution. The people of the States must all be shown the same constitution. There is no other way to conduct the ratification process.

"The authors of a constitution have to be left in peace to write it. The Rule of Secrecy which our Convention has adopted protects us from undue outside influence as we perform our work. If we are approached to report on our work, we have only to say that we are bound to secrecy.

"To permit persons not a party to our Convention to sit in judgment on the constitution as it is being written would be to subject the Constitutional Convention to a continual barrage of criticism from persons who can have no awareness of the principles being developed in framing it.

"Framing and ratifying a constitution are distinct processes. They are performed by different groups that represent different enterprises. The framing group is small and intimate; the ratifying group, large and not necessarily known to each other. The ratification of a constitution can only take place after the writing of the constitution is complete.

"I cannot impress on you too strongly or too often, Captain Jamison, that if the Articles of Confederation, the present constitution of the United States, are not replaced in the next few years—four at the utmost, I would say—all the sacrifices of life, property, wellbeing, and personal connexions that the war for independence from Britain required of us will have been in vain. I trust I am being clear on what is at stake in this Convention."

"Perfectly clear, Mister Madison," Captain James Jamison replied. The agent being approached on Dr. Franklin's recommendation was a brown-haired, muscular veteran of the War for Independence in his thirties, whose most striking physical feature was his maimed left hand encased in a specially made black kid glove. The mutilation had been conferred by a British cannonball at the Battle of Monmouth, N.J. which resulted in his being mustered out of the Continental Army with his highest field rank of Captain. "I have only one question," the Captain continued. "I'm curious as to why Mister Gerry made known to you and the other leaders of the Convention the contents of his letter. Was it because he felt guilty for having violated the Convention's Rule of Secrecy?"

"Not exactly," George Washington interjected. "If you will permit me, Mr. Madison, I will answer this question."

"Please do, General."

"Mister Gerry has yet to speak of his letter to me or to Dr. Franklin, or to anyone engaged in the work of the Convention except Mr. Mason. The only people who know of his letter's existence are the persons on this ad hoc committee, along with Mr. Gerry, the messenger he hired, George Mason, and now yourself, Captain. And, of course, whoever may now be in possession of the letter. The other members of the Convention are unaware that their Rule of Secrecy has been violated. And, if the Author of every good, Who has thus far blessed our every endeavor to make our country independent, grants you a swift success in retrieving Mr. Gerry's missing letter, no one else will ever know it existed."

"How, if I may ask Your Excellency, did you learn of the letter's existence if its author did not provide that information?"

"Through George Mason, my neighbor in Virginia and a good friend these many years. Mister Gerry told him, and he informed me that Gerry did not attend the Convention last Friday so he might write his letter to George expressing his most candid thoughts concerning crucial matters being debated in the Convention. He said that he turned his letter over to his paid messenger for delivery to George late that afternoon. At the end of Saturday's session of the Convention, when Gerry asked my friend for his opinion of what he had said in his letter, and Mr. Mason expressed ignorance of what he was referring to, the two of them discovered what had happened.

"George immediately came to my lodgings to inform me of the situation, and said that Gerry declined his invitation to come with him. After Mr. Mason's visit, I came to tell Dr. Franklin what had happened. We discussed forming this committee with Mr. Madison and Colonel Hamilton. It met yesterday evening. At that meeting, on Dr. Franklin's advice, it was decided to speak with you today and ask you to look into the matter as quickly as possible."

"Thank you for satisfying my curiosity, General."

"You're welcome. Please continue, Mr. Madison."

"Do you have any further questions, Captain Jamison, on which you would like information?" Madison inquired.

"Not at the moment, Sir."

"Then, having made clear why secrecy is essential to our Convention's proceedings and purpose, I will now proceed to tell you of the present state of affairs in the Convention, which makes finding the missing letter so urgent—the information Colonel Hamilton was to have imparted."

After intertwining his fingers, rotating his hands palms outward, relaxing his fingers and hands, and then unlocking his fingers, Madison said, "What you should know, Captain, is that the disappearance of Mr. Gerry's messenger, who was in possession of his letter, would have been an untoward occurrence at any time, but it has happened at a particularly precarious moment in the Convention. Since we began meeting, a little less than a month ago, many delegates to the Convention, perhaps as many as a third or more, have spoken with various degrees of seriousness of going home if matters dear to their hearts are not arranged to their satisfaction. The strong spirit of goodwill and cooperation in which we began our work is starting to show signs of deterioration.

"From what we know of Elbridge Gerry's letter, this much is certain. The reactions of some people in the United States to various opinions he expresses in it would greatly harm the Convention's reputation as a body of disinterested patriots; and a good many of the delegates who've spoken of going home would actually quit Philadelphia. Of course, were that to happen, the Convention would collapse; and there would not be enough time to organize another one before the Articles of Confederation destroyed the Union. I say this, Captain, as someone who has been for the past several years, and still is, a member of the Confederation Congress, as well as one of the principal organizers of this Convention.

"Believe me, Captain, the Union cannot survive more than another few years under the Articles of Confederation. Some form of national constitution simply must replace the Articles in the next few years if the United States is to continue to exist. A new constitution is also necessary for America to expand and grow in a manner commensurate with our great potential, which an overwhelming portion of Americans want it to do, but which the Articles of Confederation does not provide for.

"Prolonging the authority of the Articles of Confederation would make certain the destruction of the Union. Were the revelations in Gerry's letter to come into the hands of British agents, they would be of enormous use to them in implementing the Crown's policy of regaining as many of her alienated colonies on the American mainland as possible."

Just then voices were heard on the staircase landing outside the library where Benjamin Franklin had stationed his personal servant to prevent any interruption of the ad hoc committee's meeting. Mr. Mahoney opened the library door to announce, "Colonel Hamilton."

"Gentlemen, you must forgive me!" Alexander Hamilton exclaimed as he swept past Mr. Mahoney, who was holding the door for him. "Upon my word, in coming here I stopped to get something from my room at the Indian Queen and as I left the hotel I was accosted by a Mr. Wallingham, a client of mine in New York, and his brother, who have come down to Philadelphia in a specially-hired express coach seeking my assistance in a legal matter which, according to them, will brook no delay and must be attended to immediately or their family will face imminent ruin. The pleas of the Wallinghams were so importunate, I have only just now gotten free of them by promising to take supper with them this evening to discuss a stratagem to avert the disaster they fear. My most profound apology for my inexcusable tardiness!"

The whirlwind of energy who delivered these remarks was a trim, dapper, well-proportioned man in his early thirties, of average height, shoulders-back military erectness, eyes the color of woodland violets, and wavy reddish-brown hair. His movements were as quick as his speech, as he took the chair beside James Jamison, two places to the right of Benjamin Franklin, who occupied the head of the table. Washington and Madison were seated on its other side.

"A good afternoon to you, Dr. Franklin," Hamilton said cheerily, looking in his direction; then, looking across the table to Washington and Madison, he said, "General. Jemmy."

Dr. Franklin returned Hamilton's cheery greeting in kind. Madison acknowledged it by replying familiarly, "Ham." Washington's response was a forbidding look accompanied by a curt nod of the head, a gesture familiar to Hamilton from his five years as Washington's adjutant during the war.

"And you must be Captain Jamison," the newcomer said, turning to the man he had sat next to, and James, sensing Hamilton's desire to shake hands, extended his right hand. "Good to meet you, Colonel Hamilton," James said.

Washington did his duty as chairman of the committee and summarized for Hamilton what Madison had told James before his arrival.

"If you would be so good, Colonel," Washington concluded, "as to make sure the Captain fully comprehends the situation in the Convention, I'd be obliged."

"Yessir."

Hamilton sat in silence a brief moment, collecting his thoughts, then declared, "I'll not trouble you, Captain Jamison, with my ideas on what ought to be in an enduring constitution beneficial to the United States. I discovered from my fellow delegates' responses to a recent speech I made on that subject, that my thinking differs from the views of all but a handful of my colleagues in the Convention, the greatest part of whom want the power of the general government to be as diffused and weak as possible, whereas I want it to be concentrated and potent.

"Differences of opinion in the Convention on how the States should be represented in Congress are increasingly dividing us, Captain, and no house divided can produce a constitution. A few delegates even seem to prefer the current practice by which each State has a single vote in Congress, and want to continue it. Many more want a new principle, such as population, perhaps, to determine the apportionment of each State's representation in Congress, but are unsure of how exactly that should be done. If the number of a State's inhabitants is to determine the number of its representatives in Congress, how would States with large populations be kept from perpetually lording it over the States with few people? That's what delegates from small States want to know. And they say any arrangement based solely on population would be a tyranny they are unwilling to suffer.

"And another quarrel is building, over whether slaves ought to be counted in calculating population for the purpose of determining a State's representation in Congress. States in which slaves are plentiful naturally say they should be counted, or at least a portion of them. States with few, say slaves are property, and only free men should count in determining congressional representation.

"While these conflicts over how States are to be represented in Congress threaten to bring the Convention to a halt, they are not, in my judgment, the main issue. I think the principal issue before the Convention is whether the United States of America deserve their name.

"Are the States comprising this country genuinely united? In my view, they are not. What exists on these shores under the Articles of Confederation is a league of States, none or few of which regard themselves as inextricable parts of one nation. To win the war, it was necessary for all the States to work together, like horses hitched to the same wagon, and for that wagon to have but one driver or commander-in-chief. Now, that sort of unity and obedience to a supreme authority must be given permanent form in a constitution designed to replace the Articles of Confederation, if for no other reason than to make foreign powers respect our independence and territorial rights.

"Britain is violating every day the territorial integrity of the United States, as designated in 1783 in the Treaty of Paris, by continuing to garrison six forts now inside the boundaries of the United States which the British government, in signing the Treaty *four years ago*, pledged to evacuate with all deliberate speed. If the American government instituted in 1781 under the Articles of Confederation is so weak that foreign troops can garrison forts within the United States with no end in sight to their occupation of these forts, I would say such government must be replaced with another capable of enforcing America's territorial integrity. Wouldn't you—or any American worthy of the name—agree, Captain Jamison?

"Does any dispute over a constitutional issue really matter if we are not, first, perfectly clear among ourselves on whether we are one nation or thirteen?

"It seems to me, Captain, that each State should exercise within its own boundaries only the police and other local powers needed to meet its internal needs. All other powers should be vested in a general government designed to unite the States into one nation, and promote their general welfare as components of that nation. It is the Union of the States that provides every State its safety from foreign aggressors, justice as parts of the same nation, and domestic tranquility.

"You were in the Continental Army, Captain Jamison. An artillery officer like myself, I believe. I ask you, have our efforts in the war gained us the safety, growth, justice, and domestic tranquility we thought we were fighting to obtain? Haven't the four years since the war ended been full of uncertainty? Look at the disturbance in Massachusetts in January!

"Are not the States of the so-called United States actually Divided States?" Hamilton said. "By fostering the delusion that each State is 'sovereign,' the Articles of Confederation prevent a sense of national unity from developing, and we sorely need that unity to become a powerful, prosperous nation that other nations will not trifle with—the nation we should be, the nation the God of Nature intends us to be, the nation it is our destiny to become.

"Our strength lies in the people of every State acknowledging their dependence on the people of the other States. That is the fundamental reality of the United States. The foundation for a sound national currency to promote an expanding national economy. The bulwark protecting us against foreign ambitions. And our shield against disturbances within any State. But such a Union cannot be imposed. The need for it must be understood and embraced by us as free men. Our destiny lies in writing and ratifying a national charter for a workable unity, to replace the inherently flawed Articles of Confederation.

"Even during the war, when regiments of Redcoats and their Hessian mercenaries were marching up and down our land, leaving destruction in their wake, the Confederation Congress under the Articles could not compel enough States to provide a sufficient amount of money to unfailingly provide our soldiers their lawful rations of food and their lawful pay; or unfailingly provide our troops the uniforms, boots, gunpowder, and other sundry necessities that were their due. What much greater triumph than the trouncing we gave the Redcoats at Bunker Hill might we have inflicted had our troops not run out of ammunition during the fight? which forced them to use their muskets as clubs instead of firearms.

"Without Dr. Franklin's ability to persuade the French—on more than one occasion, I might add—to part with immense gifts and loans of money, and even to provide us brigades of French troops and fleets of French warships, as well as large stores of military supplies, our chances of winning the war with imperial Britain would have been zero.

"Mr. Madison and I first became acquainted here in Philadelphia five years ago when we served together in the Confederation Congress, which at that time met in this city, not New York as at present. I had just been elected to represent the people of New York. Mr. Madison had been grappling with the defects of the Articles of Confederation for two years as a representative of Virginia in the Confederation Congress. I well recall, as I'm sure he does also, the two of us being on a committee to address Rhode Island's constant refusal to pay its share of the cost of general government. Rhode Island claimed 'sovereignty' then, as it does now, you see, and said it did not have the means to pay!"

"Tell the Captain, Ham, why we think Mr. Gerry's letter has not appeared in the press," Madison prompted.

"Ah, yes! That is important. Thanks for reminding me, Jemmy. The letter Mr. Gerry wrote three days ago, Captain Jamison, was supposed to have been delivered that day, but wasn't. It vanished three days ago; yet since then none of the city's newspapers have published any of its contents."

Benjamin Franklin spoke up. "The messenger who carried the letter, James, is one of the pair of young men in the Convention Guard who substitute for anyone unable to serve on a given day. I'll tell you everything we know of him when you and I have our talk following this meeting."

"Captain Jamison, Mr. Madison and I think several explanations are possible for the letter's contents not appearing in the press," Alexander Hamilton said. "Perhaps the messenger met with an accident such as drowning while attempting to deliver it, and there's been no discovery yet of his corpse, and thus of the letter he was carrying. Or, perhaps, he met with foul play and was buried without anyone searching his clothing, after his killers took from his finger the large gold ring he's been wearing of late. Or, maybe the person now in possession of the missing letter believes, from having read it, that the Convention will soon fail due to its internal conflicts, and has decided to wait until that happens, and then publish the letter to explain the failure.

"We also believe it possible a foreign agent in the employ of the British government obtained the letter in some way, and has sent it to London to decide how such a prize can best be used. If that is the case, it may be a long time yet before its contents appear in print."

Washington interrupted Hamilton at this point.

"There's a further possibility, I think, Captain. Perhaps Gerry's letter has not appeared in the press because the messenger who was to deliver it is a common thief acting in concert with other low-minded persons, and they are offering the letter to the highest bidder, which is taking time to arrange."

As Washington was making this observation, he withdrew from his coat a twice-folded sheet of heavy paper sealed along its final fold with blue-and-buff-marbled wax. It was addressed in swirling script: "To Capt. James Jamison, Esq." and below that salutation in the same hand appeared the words: "From Geo. Washington, Pres. of the Constitutional Convention, Philadelphia 1787."

"I take it, Captain Jamison, you do not refuse the task of looking for the missing letter?" Washington asked. As he spoke, Washington placed the paper on the table in front of James with an air of formality.

James asserted, "I'm willing, Your Excellency, to try to do whatever you and Doctor Franklin would have me do and to give it my fullest attention, particularly since Mr. Madison and Colonel Hamilton have made me aware of how much depends on finding the letter without delay."

"Then please be so good as to read what I've just set before you as your commission in the matter."

There was an attentive silence around the table as James broke the two wax seals on his "commission" and read it.

KNOW YE by these Presents, that CAPT. JAMES JAMISON, ESQ. of Philadelphia, a former Officer serving honorably in the Continental Army, & a recipient of the Purple Heart Medal, is hereby Appointed To Serve in a Confidential capacity the President of the Constitutional Convention now meeting in this City; & THAT

WHOMSOEVER may be Party to the said Convention, respects it, or wishes it Well, is Admonished, Charged, & Directed to give CAPT. JAMISON whatever Aid & Assistance he may request in carrying out the confidential Service Herein Authorized; & to treat his Requirements with the same Deference, & render them the same Support as though the request came from me.

Given this day, the 24th of June 1787, under seal, in
the City of Philadelphia,
by Geo. Washington.
/S/ President of the CONVENTION

"Is the commission adequate, Captain?"

"Most assuredly, Your Excellency."

"Good. Then it's understood you will attempt to find and retrieve the missing epistle with all speed and diligence."

"I will do my utmost."

"That is all anyone can expect of a man of honor, Captain."

Washington, Madison, and Hamilton rose from their seats at the magnificent library table, as did James. Only Franklin, because of his painful affliction, remained seated as the other members of the committee said their good-byes to each other and to their host, and bade James Jamison Godspeed in his search for the missing letter.

Washington, in shaking Hamilton's hand, withdrew from a capacious pocket of his coat two thin, rectangular packages, one neatly wrapped in pale blue paper and tied with dark-blue ribbon; the other, in handsome forest-green paper tied in light-green ribbon. He handed both to Hamilton.

"The blue one is for your dear wife, my boy, from Mrs. Washington. I believe it's a chapbook of Christian verse. The other is for you. I ordered it from my London bookseller. It arrived here yesterday from Mount Vernon. It's a copy of Demosthenes' *First Philippic* which contains the passage on leadership you so often declaimed at Army headquarters, whose sentiment meets with my entire approbation. I believe it reads something like, 'A leader walks at the head of affairs and produces the event.'"

As Mr. Mahoney escorted Washington, Madison, and Hamilton downstairs and out to Market Street, James Jamison remained behind in the library to speak with Benjamin Franklin, who had directed him in two previous investigations, once to absolve a Quaker stonecutter, a friend of the good Doctor, wrongfully accused of strangling his housekeeper; the second time, to prove the innocence of a young gentleman jailed for premeditated murder under the Pennsylvania statute prohibiting dueling.

Franklin & His Agent Confer
Chapter VI

"WHAT DO YOU THINK of General Washington, the man, James? I suppose you have never spent time in his presence before this afternoon."

"While I was in the Army, he addressed my battalion on several occasions. And at Trenton, Princeton, Germantown, Monmouth, and the campaigns to keep New York and the areas around it free of British occupation, I saw him in action on the field of battle. But this afternoon, as you say, has been my first personal acquaintance with him. I'll be glad to tell my just-born daughter, when she's old enough to understand, and the other children Livy and I hope to have, that I once shook the hand of the great Washington and had the honor of serving him in a confidential matter.

"I'll also be telling our children of the connection their father and mother had with you, Dr. Franklin, and I'll make sure our children know why their Grandmère calls you *'l'Américain extraordinaire,'* and what she means in saying that."

"And what is your opinion of Washington the man?"

"That he deserves the respect and adulation he received in Market Street when he arrived in Philadelphia for the Convention over which he has been elected to preside. General Washington's love for our country and sense of duty toward it are palpable. Those who served in the Continental Army under him, as I did, were inspired by his example to believe we could defeat the British army and their Hessian mercenaries. Livy and I took our baby to Market Street to see Washington's arrival in Philadelphia so she can honestly say when she's older that she saw him. The time I spent with him today here in your library leads me to regard him as a man of uncommon integrity.

"I was struck, however, by his disdain for Colonel Hamilton's explanation of his lateness to our meeting, even though I considered it convincing. Yet he gave the Colonel a token of his affection and esteem, which he had evidently made a considerable effort to obtain."

Franklin smiled in the library's fading, late-afternoon sunlight and said, "Anyone who knows the General knows his dignity is not to be trifled with, James, not even by a man for whom he feels the sort of paternal affection that he feels for Colonel Hamilton, who reciprocates that affection with filial sentiments, as I'm sure you noticed.

"The gift he delivered to Colonel Hamilton for his wife, from Mrs. Washington, the chapbook of religious verses, was likewise revealing. Elizabeth Schuyler and Martha Washington met at the winter encampment of the Continental Army at Morristown, New Jersey. Colonel Hamilton was then on Washington's staff and courting Eliza. The two women—the future Mrs. Hamilton, twenty-two, and the older lady who was twice her age—discovered they shared a strong faith in Christ; and that discovery, I'm told, has grown over the years into a sympathy much like that between a mother and a daughter.

"I myself first met the worthy Eliza in her youth at the splendid home of her father, General Schuyler, in Albany, where I stopped to rest on my way back from my unsuccessful two-month-long attempt as an agent of the Second Continental Congress to persuade the Canadians to join our struggle to throw off British rule. The Canadians, however, had become too accustomed to monarchical rule from Europe. They wanted no part of the self-government republicanism entails.

"When Elizabeth Schuyler and I met she was a trig little beauty of sixteen with a merry disposition and the blackest eyes I've ever seen. I passed many hours of my five-day stay of recuperation at the Schuyler mansion teaching the vivacious future Mrs. Hamilton and her older sister the rules of backgammon, and playing that delightful dice game with them.

"The marriage of the handsome, ambitious Hamilton to the beautiful, wealthy second daughter of General Schuyler has been of great mutual benefit to them. It wed her exalted social position and access to riches to Hamilton's brilliance and aspirations. It created a joint enterprise, as it were, dedicated to accomplishing Hamilton's goals." Franklin went on to ask James what his impressions of Hamilton and Madison had been.

"I was surprised to learn they had served together in the Confederation Congress. Both of them seem to have perceptive abilities surpassing those of most men. They are also wholeheartedly committed, it appears, to replacing the Articles of Confederation with a stronger form of government for the United States. Colonel Hamilton seems to be the more forcible of the two in expressing his ideas and Mr. Madison perhaps the more thoughtful. I've heard it said, Dr. Franklin, that the two of them are the mainsprings of the Convention."

"They are," Franklin replied. "Madison has been more instrumental in bringing about the Constitutional Convention, but only because, unlike Colonel Hamilton, he had the prestige and backing of most of the political leaders in his home State, where many men of quality support strengthening our general government. Hamilton was handicapped in his advocacy of a constitutional convention by the political allies of New York's governor, George Clinton, who is opposed to the Convention and the creation of a national government. Clinton and his followers believe such government will diminish their power within New York."

"My impression, Dr. Franklin, is that Mr. Madison is married to his work. That there is no Mrs. Madison," James observed.

"That is correct. I have heard some of the ladies say he's painfully shy in the presence of the fair sex. And someone who's known Mr. Madison quite a long time has told me that after finishing his college studies at Princeton and going home, he was smitten by a young Virginia lady of good family and believed they had an understanding to be married. But while she was on a visit to relatives in New York, she met a man who courted her, and she accepted his attentions and finally his proposal of marriage. To my knowledge, that was the only serious association of Jemmy Madison with matrimony.

"But I'm indulging my curiosity about your opinions. We have important matters to discuss, and you ought to launch your investigation into the problem of the vanishing messenger as soon as you leave Franklin Court.

"The first thing I have to say to you, James, is that you will be more on your own in this investigation than in our previous collaborations. I'm too absorbed in the affairs of the Convention, which are consuming even my evenings and Sundays. I haven't the time to receive and study daily written reports from you.

"But the terrible consequences the missing letter, if not retrieved, could have for the Convention oblige me to make myself available to you whenever you deem it imperative. As I told you when we first collaborated, I sleep only a few hours a night. So I will be free to consult with you in the wee hours of the night whenever you wish. We can use the hidden mail drop in the west wall of Franklin Court, which you are familiar with, to communicate. Or, if need be, I can send Mr. Mahoney to you with a note.

"As I hope you will recall my telling you, James, the investigation of a mystery, whether of nature or of man, is first of all a matter of adopting a method and then of gathering information. In this case, to find out what has happened to the letter, you must find out all you can of the messenger who carried it. If you can find out what has happened to William Best, the messenger, you will find out what has happened to the letter he was carrying. Letters have no interests or habits. Persons do. You must, therefore, trace Billy Best's movements and find out whatever you can of his character, habits, interests, and acquaintances."

James paid strict attention to the advice the eighty-one-year-old statesman and scientist was giving him.

"Another thing, James. I wouldn't spend much effort, if any, on General Washington's reflection that this young man could be a common criminal and has stolen Mr. Gerry's letter, possibly in league with other criminals, to sell to the highest bidder. I myself do not give that hypothesis any credence. General Washington has never spoken with Billy Best, though he's seen him six days out of every seven, every week since the Convention began as he's gone in and out of the East Room. He has not had the advantage I have had, however, of conversing with the young man in examining him for possible appointment to the Convention Guards. Also, prior to that, I discussed Billy's character with Sergeant Corbin, who knows him well and nominated him as a candidate for the Guard.

"Corbin informed me that he met William Best when he joined the Pennsylvania militia here in Philadelphia. He also informed me the young man had tried to join the Continental Army as a drummer boy just after the Declaration of Independence was signed and promulgated, something that caused patriotic feeling to run high among Americans of all ages, even boys of tender years. But his mother got wind of his intention and quashed it. When he was fifteen, he ran away to enlist. But by then the surrender of Lord Cornwallis and his army at Yorktown meant the war was, in effect, over and a treaty of peace between the United States and Britain would soon be negotiated. Consequently, no further enlistments in the Army were being accepted, and Billy had to go home.

"In July of 1785, two years ago, however, when he turned seventeen, this young man joined the Pennsylvania militia and became personally known to Corbin, who was a recruiting sergeant for the militia. Billy's record as a militiaman has been exemplary, Corbin tells me. Eager to be of use. Prompt and thorough in carrying out orders. A defender of republican ideals. Billy is forever asking Corbin and other veterans of the war about the battles they fought in and the life of a soldier. I find it impossible to believe such a young man would endanger the reforms the Convention is attempting to make by stealing Gerry's letter.

"And, hear this. I had Sergeant Corbin bring the fourteen men of the Convention Guard to Franklin Court to meet with me over refreshments in my new dining room. I spoke to them concerning the security they would be providing the Convention and why it is of such great moment. I was pleased to see the serious looks my remarks produced on the faces of the men I had chosen for this duty, which signified that Sergeant Corbin and I had chosen well in making appointments to the Guard and that they understood what I'd said. The look on William Best's countenance, I remember, was particularly solemn.

"Let us turn now, James, to other aspects of the investigation you'll be making. First, you are to tell no one, not even your dear wife, anything of the threat posed to the Convention by the missing letter. You can tell Livy and your grandmother that you've been appointed, on my recommendation, to perform a confidential task for General Washington. That will give them a sense of the seriousness of what you'll be doing. Show them your commission from the General. But do not go beyond that. No one is to know anything of what was said in this room this afternoon. We don't want even members of the Convention to know the security of the Convention has been breeched. Your job, James, is to close the breech as quickly as possible by retrieving the missing letter if it is findable.

"My own speculation is that this young man has most likely met with some mishap while doing Mr. Gerry's bidding. But, whatever the truth may be, James, every hour which passes without finding the letter increases the risk of it falling into the wrong hands, if that has not already happened. Therefore, start your inquiries by speaking with Mr. Gerry and his wife.

"Here's a list I've prepared for you of persons to interview and where you can find them. Speak with everyone on this list. I have also prepared a sequence of the known events related to Best's disappearance and the principal points the missing letter makes, should you need to identify its contents during your investigation. I suggest you memorize this list, then burn it. Your reputation for having an extraordinary memory was one of my reasons for wanting to recruit you for my investigation into the charge of murder against poor Jacob Maul.

"Corbin has given me the names of the Guards that Billy consorted with most. Only those names are on your list, not every member of the Convention Guard. You should make a special point to speak with the Guard he sat with every day by the door going into the room where the Convention meets. His name is starred."

James asked, "Do you think it possible, Dr. Franklin, that foreign agents could have waylaid this William Best to get the letter he carried?"

"At this point, James, nothing can be excluded from consideration. But we do not know the identities of the foreign agents in Philadelphia working to harm the Union, the preservation of which is essential to America's future. We only know from certain events which have happened in Philadelphia that such persons exist. The Commonwealth of Pennsylvania, of which I am now the President, has hired a trustworthy, experienced man to ferret these spies out, along with their American sympathizers. The person recruited to perform this task is a Colonel Tamas Zanzinger, an immigrant from Hungary who came to America shortly before the French and Indian War, in which he fought as a junior officer—the war that cost your dear father his life. The Second Continental Congress commissioned Zanzinger as a Colonel in the recent war because of his service and experience in that earlier conflict. Zanzinger's name and the address of his business is on the list.

"Colonel Zanzinger is well known to me and I to him, and you can speak to him with the same degree of trust as if you were conversing with me. You can rely on having his help. You ought to inquire particularly what Best said and did the day Gerry gave him the letter to deliver, which was Friday, June 22nd. By the way, this was the second letter Mr. Gerry paid Billy Best to deliver to Mr. Mason. He also hired him to take a letter to Mason on June 19th. It consisted of his extensive analysis of Colonel Hamilton's speech recommending that we create a strong executive authority such as the British government has. Mason received that letter the evening of the day it was given to Best to deliver.

"As I recall Hamilton's speech, it was highly laudatory of certain features of Britain's monarchical government, though Hamilton repeatedly said he was not proposing that America establish a monarchy, which he said was entirely out of the question. He was only in favor of concentrating power in the executive branch of the American government, as the British had done with happy results in their government, he said.

"When you speak with Mr. Gerry, James, ask him if he used Best to send letters to anyone else. If he did, get their names and interview them.

"Mr. Mason has informed General Washington that he upbraided Mr. Gerry for putting into writing things said in the Convention without first obtaining permission from the President of the Convention, thus exposing its proceedings to possible public scrutiny, which is precisely what has happened.

"According to Mr. Mason, Mr. Gerry denies he's violated the Rule of Secrecy adopted by the Convention, which he claims was not intended to prohibit one delegate from expressing his views in writing to another delegate, something that is continually going on in conversations. Gerry claims the secrecy rule pertains only to communications between a delegate and anyone outside the Convention. He seems not to appreciate the point that the proceedings of the convention are not to be put in writing or print. The Rule, Mr. Gerry argues, can only be interpreted as a prohibition against the communication of Convention proceedings to persons outside the Convention.

"Mr. Mason says he told Mr. Gerry the secrecy rule requires no interpretation. Its intention is perfectly clear and specific. No record is to be made of Convention proceedings without authorization from General Washington."

"What is this Mr. Gerry like, Dr. Franklin?" James asked. "Does he oppose the idea of creating a stronger Union of the States?"

"It's hard to tell. Sometimes he seems to be making nationally oriented arguments. At other times his thinking seems to favor the sovereignty of the States as expressed in the Articles of Confederation. He is one of the most frequent speakers in the Convention, and his remarks usually consist of negative comments on the views of other delegates. I suppose the best answer to your question, James, is that Mr. Gerry's thinking lacks consistency. The only thing he appears consistent in is his naysaying. General Washington finds Gerry objectionable, since he supported the Conway Cabal to replace him as commander-in-chief of the Continental Army. It must be said, however, that he was not among the principal leaders of the Cabal.

"And Elbridge Gerry was certainly a patriot from the earliest days of resistance to British rule in Massachusetts. He did his utmost to promote the American cause as a member of both the Committee of Correspondence and the Committee of Safety in his home State. He was recruited to the cause of independence and self-government by no less a patriot than Samuel Adams. John Adams is another associate of Gerry's who swears by his ability and fealty. The Adamses and Gerry attended the Second Continental Congress together, and all three signed the Declaration of Independence. From being a member of the Second Continental Congress myself, and a signer of the Declaration, I remember Elbridge Gerry as a well-dressed little fellow who found favor among the ladies even though he has somewhat of a stutter.

"He is now in his forties and a prosperous merchant in Marblehead, Massachusetts. He married last year for the first time. His wife is a remarkably beautiful New York heiress, much younger than himself, who by all reports has charming manners and is quite knowledgeable despite her youth. It is a first marriage for them both. Mr. Gerry has rented a house in Philadelphia for his new bride and their recently born baby girl."

"And Mr. Mason?" James inquired.

"George Mason is one of the most generally respected members of the Convention. A man of firm principles and author of Virginia's Declaration of Rights, the precursor to the Declaration of Independence. He, too, is a frequent speaker in the Convention.

"I don't like to hurry you, James. But it's getting on to sundown, and you ought to be about your business. In concluding our conference, let me tell you what we know of William Best.

"Physically he's of average height, strong build, and good appearance. His cheeks are ruddy and his eyes the color of a clear blue sky on a fine summer day. He wears his hair, which is blond, tied back with a dark ribbon. His most striking feature, however, and the reason, I suppose, everyone calls him Billy instead of William, or Bill, or Will, is his noticeably innocent-looking countenance, which displays an absence of anything that even remotely resembles guile.

"When I was interviewing him for possible appointment to the Convention Guard I asked him what he did for a living. He said he lived with his mother and her maid, and was his mother's dresser at the Southwark Theater where she is the foremost actress.

"The mother is called Rebecca Wellborn. She's from England, I'm told, and came to this country before the war as a young actress in a group of English players calling themselves The American Company. They performed plays in any location where such entertainments were not prohibited by law and that was likely to provide an audience large enough to satisfy the expenses of a stage production. I had Mr. Mahoney make inquiries about her after I became inclined to appoint her son to the Convention Guard on Sergeant Corbin's strong recommendation and my interview with him. Mr. Mahoney discovered the mother's English origins from speaking with her fellow players, who all have a high opinion of her and her talents as an actress. The persons Mr. Mahoney spoke with at the Southwark Theater are identified on your list of names by the letters 'ST.'

"This, too, may interest you, James. When I asked Billy Best who his father was and what he does for a living, he said he didn't know because he doesn't know who his father is. My question caused a sort of shadow to darken his handsome, innocent visage."

The Gerrys
Chapter VII

JAMES LED HIS WELL-BRED Virginia mare by her reins from her stall in Dr. Franklin's stable, and out through Franklin Court's carriageway tunnel into Market Street, where he swung up into the saddle and rode off to seek the Gerrys' residence. And as he did these things he pondered the advice Dr. Franklin had given him, and what he should ask Elbridge Gerry and his young wife.

He was also thinking that he hoped the conversation with the Gerrys would not take overlong, because he had already been away from home long enough to cause his wife and his grandmother some worry, home being the house his grandfather Samuel Jamison had built before the war in Philadelphia's sparsely populated western suburbs. Since the death of his grandfather, his French-immigrant grandmother, whom he called Grandmère, had owned the house. She shared it with James, his wife Livy and their newborn baby, Anne-Louise, named for both Grandmère and Livy's deceased mother. When he'd left home that afternoon James had not told his wife and grandmother that he would not return home until after nightfall because nothing in his summons to Franklin Court, brought by Dr. Franklin's servant Mr. Mahoney, had mentioned that General Washington, Mr. Madison, and Colonel Hamilton would be at the meeting, which had considerably prolonged things.

He also pondered what he had been told in confidence regarding the Constitutional Convention, and the fact that an opponent of stronger government for the United States could use the contents of the missing letter to destroy the Convention.

With these thoughts going through his mind, James rode west on Market Street, then south on Sixth Street past Chestnut and Walnut, to Spruce Street, where he soon found the residence of the Gerrys, the only frame building on a street of brick houses. James wondered if Elbridge Gerry had rented this property because its wooden construction reminded him of his native Massachusetts.

James tied his sleek sorrel mare to the iron horse post in front of the house and went up its three steps to the door, where he knocked using its brass doorknocker in the shape of a horse's head.

A slender man, not very tall, with a long face, intense eyes, pointed chin, and a prominent nose, answered his knock, and said, "Y-Y-Yes?"

James had his commission ready to show to the servant he had expected to answer his knock, not to Gerry himself.

"Mr. Gerry, my name is Captain James Jamison, formerly of the Continental Army," James began. By way of continuing his introduction of himself, he handed his commission to this delegate to the Constitutional Convention from Marblehead, Massachusetts, and continued matter-of-factly, "It has been my honor to be appointed by General Washington to do a piece of business for him, which requires that I speak with you and your wife." As James said this, Elbridge Gerry unfolded the paper he had been handed and read it with deliberate slowness; he then went over it a second time. After that, he opened the door wider, stepped aside, and admitted Washington's emissary into his house, saying, "Follow me, Sir."

He led his visitor down a long hallway to the rear of the house, all the while retaining the paper James had presented to him.

At the end of the hall, he opened a door into a small parlor where three candelabra with six candles each were burning brightly. A well-featured young woman with an abundance of brown, silky curls, dressed in a beautifully tailored, mauve-colored gown of cotton, was rocking a cradle and crooning to the infant asleep in it. She looked up and ceased her lullaby the moment her husband and his visitor appeared.

"Please read this, dear Ann, and tell me what you think," Gerry said, and handed her the paper he held. His wife took it and, having read it, said, "I suppose this has to do with the young man you paid to deliver your disquisition on the Convention to Mr. Mason," and gave James's commission back to her husband, who returned it to James. Gerry neither sat nor invited James to be seated.

Addressing his wife, he said, "That was my c-c-conclusion, too, my love. Perhaps you w-would b-be so good, Captain Jamison, as to explain why you want to speak with my wife and me."

"I've been commissioned, Mr. Gerry, as your wife and you have supposed, to locate the young man who served as your messenger. As you know, he has disappeared, and, so far as I know, he came here shortly before he vanished, to pick up your letter to Mr. Mason. I'm here to ask you about your two letters to Mr. Mason and to find out whatever you and your wife may have to say regarding Billy Best, and to get any information your servants may have to impart if they saw Best when he came here to get those letters."

"We have no servants except a woman who c-c-comes to cook for us and another who comes to keep the house rid up and in good order. Neither of them saw Billy. Do you want to tell this gentleman anything, Ann?"

"Whatever I have to tell him, El, he's more than welcome to it. We have nothing to conceal, Captain Jamison. Why should we? Neither my husband nor I have done anything wrong."

"I appreciate all the candor I can get, Mrs. Gerry. To lessen my intrusion on your time, Madame—it is getting late—perhaps I might ask you some questions."

To this observation, the pretty young woman remarked with charming insouciance, "Ask away. We can hardly do otherwise than cooperate with you, Captain Jamison, since no less a potentate than General Washington charges, admonishes, and directs whoever reads your commission from him to render you any assistance you may require as though the request came from him. Please be seated."

"Thank you."

Elbridge Gerry remained standing.

"How many times did you speak with William Best?" James asked.

"Once."

"And when was that?"

"The first time he came to the house to get a letter from my husband to deliver to Mr. Mason. The second time he came, I was nursing little Catharine and didn't talk with him."

"Do you remember the date of that encounter?"

"I believe it was Tuesday last, five days ago—the 19th, if I am not mistaken. Is that right, El?"

"Quite r-r-right, my dear."

"And how was it you spoke with the young man when he came to see your husband, and what did you and he say to each other?" James continued.

Elbridge Gerry answered this inquiry. "I was i-i-i-indisposed and asked my wife to answer Billy's knock and tell him I would be right down to give him the letter I wanted him to take to Mr. Mason. I knew it was Billy as soon as I heard his knock. He was very punctual."

"So you didn't have any real conversation with William Best, Mrs. Gerry?"

"No I didn't. I gave him my husband's message and stood with him, the baby in my arms, just inside the door, until Elbridge came down with his letter. I think the young man said it was a hot day, and I agreed. As soon as my husband came, I left them to conclude their business."

"Did he make any particular impression on you, Mrs. Gerry?"

"Oh, indeed, he did. He made quite an impression. I've never met a young man with such a thorough look of innocence on his handsome face. I hope no son of mine will reach his majority as innocent of the world as that young man appeared to be."

The infant in the cradle began to stir and make mewling sounds.

"I'm sorry, Captain Jamison, you'll have to excuse me. Catharine usually wakes up hungry. I should take her up to her room and nurse her." And with that, as Ann Thompson Gerry and James stood, he thanked her for her help. She lifted her baby from her cradle and left the parlor. In passing her husband, she paused, and they lightly kissed.

There was a silence in the room as the two men, left alone, looked at each other inquiringly. Elbridge Gerry was wondering what James might ask and James was wondering what he should ask this man who'd broken one of the Standing Orders of the Convention.

James asked if he might sit, and Mr. Gerry nodded his consent and took a seat himself. "So, tell me, Sir, when you first thought of using William Best to deliver letters to Mr. Mason, and whether your opinion of his character coincides with that your wife expressed," James said.

"I noticed him by the door of the East Room the f-f-first time I attended a meeting of the Convention. And he was there every day sitting next to another young man and Sergeant

Corbin. It would have been hard not to notice him. As Ann has said, B-B-Billy is a handsome fellow, and he is obviously a favorite of Sergeant Corbin's."

"Did he make the same impression on you that he made on your wife? Of being too innocent for his age?" James asked.

"He did appear so, b-b-but I have found a-a-appearances to be deceptive. When I spoke with him in passing, as I did on several occasions before employing him as a messenger, he seemed intelligent and to have some education. When I inquired of Sergeant Corbin concerning his character, I was told he was reliable and punctual. I was satisfied he would make a suitable messenger, and gave him a crown each time he served me."

"Generous pay."

"Y-y-yes. But you can't p-p-put too high a price on honesty."

"No, I suppose not. Do you have any opinion on why he failed to deliver the second letter you gave him to take to Mr. Mason? And, did you use Best to take messages to other persons besides Mr. Mason?"

"N-N-No. Only Mason. Twice. My opinion of Billy's disappearance is that he must have been waylaid somewhere between here and the Indian Queen, where I told him—as I had the first time he delivered a letter for me—he would find Mr. Mason. I cannot bring myself to believe he could be guilty of a d-d-deliberate wrong."

"The last time you saw him, did he seem worried?"

"No. He seemed as usual. I had my 'disquisition,' as Ann calls it, ready for him. So we spoke only a minute or so. I reminded him to give the letter only to Mister Mason and no one else. As soon as I paid him his crown, he left."

"What was in your 'disquisition,' as your wife calls the letter?"

"It was a detailed summary of the different positions of various State delegations on how the States should be represented in the legislature of the constitution we're trying to frame. I gave my opinion regarding each p-p-position, and asked Mason to tell me his views on each."

"Did you give the names of the persons who propounded these views?"

"In some instances, yes. In other cases I identified them as the positions of a State delegation, as shown in the way the delegation had voted on motions."

"And what about the first letter Best took to Mr. Mason for you? What was in that?" James inquired.

"My opinion of Mr. Hamilton's astounding speech to the Convention of June the 18th, in which he expressed his views on monarchical government, such as Britain has."

"You stated your opinion of that address, giving Mr. Hamilton's name?"

"Yes. I expressed my disapproval of his p-p-praise for Britain's form of government. I believe I used the word 'insane' to describe it. Mr. Hamilton is a clever man, none more so. His language is elegant, and his facts have a certain immediacy. But when it comes to speaking sense, give me the g-g-good old Yankee soundness of a man like Roger Sherman of Connecticut, who always speaks plainly and bases his statements on experience and never engages in theories, as H-H-Hamilton does."

James had never heard of this Roger Sherman from Connecticut.

"And why, Mister Gerry, were you so interested in having Mr. Mason's opinion of your ideas?"

"I respect him. He has n-n-never spoken r-r-reproachfully of what I have said in Convention, as others have."

"Do you want to add anything to what you have told me? Anything you regard as consequential?" James concluded.

The Massachusetts delegate did not reply immediately to this question. Then he said, "I suppose I ought to tell you my understanding of the Rule of Secrecy, and how my understanding of it differs from the way others understand it. I do not think it prohibits delegates from writing to each other about what they've both heard in Convention. I cannot imagine it was intended to keep delegates from expressing their views to each other in writing w-w-without Washington's permission. The prohibition imposed by the rule can only, I think, b-b-be understood to pertain to writings between a delegate and a person who is not a p-p-p-party to the Convention. That's all I would add, Captain Jamison. Oh, and this," Gerry said. "I think the ruffians who've assaulted Billy were after the ring he's been wearing of late, an unusually l-l-large ring of fine gold, carved with a remarkable bas-relief of a griffin."

By the time James got home and stabled his horse, the dusk which had been gathering as he left the Gerrys' house had become full dark.

Grandmère and Livy were with Anne-Louise having supper in the candle-lit kitchen when James entered by the backdoor and smelled the lamb stew. A plate for him was on the table.

"We waited as long as we could, James," Grandmère explained as Livy handed the baby to her and got up to take James's plate to the hearth to fill it from the pot of stew. James kissed both of Grandmère's cheeks and the top of Anne-Louise's little head. He thanked Livy after she set his plate of food at his place, and kissed her full on the mouth.

"And how have my ladies and my little one been doing today?" James asked, sitting down at his place next to Livy to begin his supper.

"Oh, we're fine," Livy replied. "Anne-Louise is getting another tooth."

"Good for you, Annie! You'll be eating roast beef before long!"

The baby had her thumb in her mouth and was intently watching her father, as she had been ever since she'd caught sight of him when he'd entered the kitchen and she'd heard his voice.

As James had ridden home under the glittering stars, he had mulled over what he was going to tell his family. He would have to tell Grandmère and Livy something of the work he'd taken on. But as he sat with them at table, eating, he sensed that his need to explain to the two women that he would be away from home during most of the ensuing days might not be as urgent as he had imagined. He began to sense the tremendous difference the baby was making for Grandmère and Livy. James was no longer the exclusive center of their thoughts and concern. In corroboration of this, Livy remarked, "I don't know where the day has gone! I honestly don't. The baby has been fussy all day."

"So you didn't miss me?" James asked.

Livy gave him an inquisitive look. "Of course I missed you, Jamie. You know I never feel quite secure when we're apart. But I had a lot to attend to today."

"Well, I'm glad you have things to occupy you because in the coming days I'll be leaving the house before sunup and will likely be away until dark."

"Who've you been with, James, since you left the house?" Grandmère asked.

"Mainly Dr. Franklin. But also some of the other leaders of the Constitutional Convention, and at the residence of one of the Convention's delegates from one of the Eastern

States." James stopped eating and removed from his coat the commission Washington had given him. He handed it to Grandmère, and when she finished reading it he took it from her and handed it to Livy to read, as Dr. Franklin had instructed him to do.

"So, you're going to be doing something for General Washington and Dr. Franklin," Livy said after she had read the paper, "and you can't tell us what that is? Is that it?"

"That's right. Dr. Franklin will be advising me as I do it."

"And you can't tell us anything except that it's important?"

"I'd like to discuss it with you, Livy—and you, too, Grandmère—but I can't."

"Is it dangerous?" Grandmère asked.

"I don't think so," James replied. Then, after a pause, he added, "I suppose it could be, but I don't think it will be. No one mentioned danger in telling me what I have to do, and I think they would have if danger was to be expected."

There was silence at the table as James continued to eat his savory lamb stew with homemade rye bread thickly spread with homemade butter.

Nothing was said for a long time as all three of them pretended to be completely fascinated by Anne-Louise.

When James had finished eating he said, "This stew is really wonderful, Livy."

"Grandmère made it," Livy replied. "I was too busy with Anne-Louise to cook."

The Masons & The Guards
Chapter VIII

JAMES LEFT HOME before sunup while Livy, the baby, and Grandmère were still fast asleep. The sky was just beginning to turn slightly pale in the east as he rode toward the river, and the heavens were still thickly spangled with stars. But by the time he arrived at the corner of Fourth and Market streets and entered the Indian Queen Hotel, the visibility of the dimmer stars had been erased by the light of the rising sun, leaving only a scattering of the brightest celestial bodies, which would also soon be gone. The robust clamor of morning birdsong greeting the new day was in full chorus.

Only half a dozen other early breakfast patrons were present in the hotel's airy, high-ceilinged dining room, and James had no difficulty identifying the distinguished Virginia planter, with his grown son, whom he sought. The Masons, father and son, were just tucking their napkins in, in preparation for their breakfasts. Because John Mason was seated facing the room's wide entrance, he apprized his father of James's approach to their table.

The agent of George Washington apologized for intruding on their meal and extended his commission to Mason in explanation of his need to speak with Washington's neighbor at such an early hour. After reading the commission, Mason invited James to be his guest and partake of the marvelous German breakfast sausages he had discovered at the Indian Queen Hotel. Since taking rooms there for the Constitutional Convention, he had formed the pleasant habit of making

German sausages part of his first meal of the day. James agreed that Philadelphia, because of its many inhabitants of German descent, offered an array of superlative breakfast meats.

After the waiter had taken their orders, George Mason said, "Before we speak of the matter which has brought you here, Captain Jamison, permit me to tell you that I find it reassuring that Washington has appointed a serious man such as yourself to look into the menace which Mr. Gerry's missing letter poses, and to say also that I think secrecy is essential to the successful conclusion of the Convention's business. My judgment is entirely in accord with Dr. Franklin's sentiments. The people of the States should not see the new constitution until it is completed. Learning of it 'by bits and dribbles,' as Dr. Franklin says, while it is being written, would prevent a proper understanding of what we're doing.

"How the various parts of the new constitution will function can only be seen and understood when all the parts of it have been put together into a coherent whole. Only then should the people of the States get a look at the proposed constitution to pass judgment on whether it pleases them enough to ratify it and live under its authority. It would be a disaster, Captain Jamison, to allow the people of the States to see pieces of the new constitution before all of them have been assembled. Only a completed constitution, as I've said, can be truly judged by the people of the States.

"The eyes of America—indeed one might say of the world to some extent—are upon this Convention, Captain, and the expectations of the people of the States have been roused to an extraordinary level of anticipation. May the Lord God Almighty, the maker of all the laws that govern the Universe, guide our efforts to frame a more practical and just constitution for the Union of American States than the Articles of Confederation. This Convention is the true culmination of our war for independence. And I, for one, Captain Jamison, am prepared to spend the entire summer in Philadelphia if need be to see a proper constitution written.

"The interests of posterity as well as our own require the Convention to act in a manner which transcends merely local interests, and the immediate future. We must bear in mind that experience has shown the democratic principle alone will not protect the rights of everyone, particularly when it comes to property. Now, sir, what assistance may I render you in your admirable efforts to retrieve Gerry's missing letter?" Mason concluded.

James said, "What I most need is information on William Best, for if I can find out what has happened to him and locate him, I stand a fair chance of finding the letter, or at least finding out what has happened to it. I particularly need to discover why William Best failed to deliver the letter to you here at the Indian Queen Hotel. Do you have any information or opinion on that, Mr. Mason?"

"As a matter of fact, I do. Billy made it here to the Indian Queen with the letter Gerry entrusted to him, according to what Henry Glebe, one of the hotel's deskmen, told me when I returned to the hotel that Friday from my excursion with my son into the countryside. Glebe informed Billy when he asked for me at the desk that we had gone out to the Schuylkill Fishing Company in our carriage to partake of its famous Friday fish fry."

"Do you know what time he arrived here?" James asked.

"Glebe said it was around five o'clock, which means Billy must have come straight here from Gerry's house."

"Did the deskman tell you what he said?"

"Yes. He said Billy asked for me, and when he was told where I'd gone, he said he had a letter to deliver to me which he had been instructed to give into my hands only. When he asked when I would be returning, and was told by the deskman that he couldn't say for certain, Billy asked where the Schuylkill Fishing Company was located and Glebe told him it was near the mouth of the Schuylkill River, too far to walk to in less than two hours, and in all likelihood I would return to the hotel before the lapse of two hours. Mr. Glebe recommended that Billy and his dog wait in the hotel lobby."

"He had a dog with him?"

"A handsome white terrier. It seems he and the dog are inseparable. I've seen the little fellow with Billy every day at the entrance to the East Room of the State House."

"What happened then?" James prompted.

"Mr. Glebe told me Billy went and sat on one of the sofas with his dog at his feet. But half an hour or so later, when the deskman looked over at the sofa, it was empty, and he didn't see Billy and his dog again. You should, of course, speak with Mr. Glebe himself, Captain Jamison, and not depend entirely on my hearsay."

At this juncture, the three breakfasts of German sausages and baked eggs were served, and conversation lapsed in favor of consuming them while the dishes were still hot.

As they ate, Mason asked James what he did for a living. When James told him he ran a family-owned furnace for blowing commercial glass along with his brother-in-law, Mason informed him of his large ancestral plantation called Gunston Hall on the Northern Neck of Virginia, where he was a neighbor of George Washington. He added that while his wife was still alive, she and he had often been guests of George and Martha Washington at Mount Vernon and had reciprocally hosted the Washingtons at Gunston Hall.

When James asked Mason's son what he planned to do with his life, John Mason said he hoped to become a broker for America's agricultural products, either in France or in England.

James asked the older Mason for his opinion of Billy Best's character.

"My acquaintance with the young man is far too superficial for me to have an opinion of his character," Mason replied. "I've only spoken with him that once, when he delivered Mr. Gerry's first letter to me, which was an exchange of just a few words. I've seen him every day, of course, sitting by the door going into the Convention, always with his white terrier, and I've sometimes exchanged greetings with him and Sergeant Corbin if our eyes met. But that's the extent of my knowledge of him, which is not enough to have formed a judgment on his character, other than to say he was a presentable and seemingly honest young man."

James said, "Mr. Gerry thinks Billy has been set upon by thugs who wanted to rob him of his gold ring. What's your opinion on that?"

"If that happened—and it could have, I suppose—it's now more than three days since Mr. Gerry gave his letter to Best to deliver to me. That's plenty of time for him to recover from an attack and make his way home."

"Then you think he may be dead?"

"It's possible."

"What do you think of the idea that William Best was in league with an enemy of the United Sates, most likely Britain, or with Americans who want the Constitutional Convention to fail so the government of the United States will remain weak under the Articles of Confederation? And that he's given Mr. Gerry's letter to someone of that way of thinking?"

"Father, may I say something?" John Mason interjected.

"Certainly, my son. If you have something to say, tell us."

"I've never laid eyes on this William Best whose

disappearance you're discussing with Captain Jamison," the young man remarked, "but it seems to me inquiries could be made as to the movements of his dog. In light of what you've said, that he and his dog were inseparable, such inquiries might yield useful information. You remember Russell Humphreys down home who was killed in the carriage accident? Weeks passed before his terrier, who was with him at the time of the accident, would quit the scene of his master's death. Perhaps if this William Best met with foul play and was killed, the scene of his death could be discovered by finding out where the dog has been seen. Or, if he was assaulted and left unconscious, and some charitable character took him in, his whereabouts might be found by tracing the dog's movements."

"What a sensible suggestion, John!" George Mason exclaimed. "Don't you agree, Captain Jamison?"

"I think it's certainly worth considering," James replied.

In leaving the Indian Queen Hotel after his breakfast with the Masons, James stopped at the hotel desk to ask if he might speak with Henry Glebe and found out he would not come on duty until five o'clock.

In front of the hotel, James paused to have a word with the hotel's uniformed Negro doorman and greeter, who made an imposing figure in his scarlet knee-length coat, ruffled white shirt, white gloves, bright blue breeches, large tricornered hat of stiff black felt, and black leather boots that came halfway between his knees and his hips.

When James asked the doorman if he remembered seeing a young man matching Billy's description exiting the hotel four days previously, he said he had no such recollection. But as soon as James mentioned the young man was accompanied by a white terrier, the doorman remembered seeing "a handsome young fella with a fine white terrier."

"Did he ask for directions, do you recall? Say, for the Schuylkill Fishing Company?" James asked.

"Not that I remembahs. Nah, Sah. He didn't. The last time I seen dem two, dey's headin' nawth from heah on Fou'th. They sho'ly made a sight, that good lookin' young man with his big strides an' the fine-lookin' bowser's ears aflappin' up an' down like little wings as he trotted 'longside."

Leading Jenny, James walked over to the Pennsylvania State House, which was just two squares from the Indian Queen Hotel. James had guessed right that even though it was still early, Sergeant Alexander Corbin would be on hand at the East Room—and there he was, even though the clock on the State House tower had just struck eight, and the day's session of the Convention wouldn't start for another two hours. Sergeant Corbin sat at his small administrative table by the door into the State House's assembly room where the Convention was meeting.

A man in his late fifties, Corbin looked quite strong and reliable. He had broad shoulders and large calves, and a general air of competence. To his right, on a two-man wooden bench beside his table, sat a fit, robust-looking man in his thirties with a similarly trustworthy air, also in the uniform of the Pennsylvania militia.

Corbin read James's commission with respectful attention and, handing it back to him, stood up and invited James— addressing him as "Sir"—to go across the street with him to the Half Moon Inn for a coffee and a talk. When James accepted, Corbin told the young man on the bench to mark on the printed roll call the names of the Convention Guards who showed up for duty. He then introduced James to the younger man. "This is Noah Day, Captain. Noah, Captain Jamison. Noah and Billy have worked side by side since the Convention began on the 25th of May, and before that."

The Half Moon dining room was as James remembered it from having taken Livy to eat there shortly after they'd become engaged, only it was much less crowded now than it had been then, because the legislature of the Commonwealth of Pennsylvania, which provided the Inn with most of its custom, was not in session. The Half Moon dated from the days of William Penn, the founder of Pennsylvania and, being directly across from the State House, had a natural attraction for the legislators of the State.

After Corbin and James had been served their coffees in the private room they'd asked for, the militia sergeant, who'd been handpicked by Benjamin Franklin to lead the Convention Guard to protect the Constitutional Convention from the press, curious idlers, and foreign and domestic spies, said, "I take it you've been commissioned by General Washington to look into Billy Best's disappearance, Captain. It's my opinion, because of the behavior of Billy's little dog Kemper, that he's met with foul play. The last time Billy was seen by any of us in the Convention Guard was four days ago, on Friday. The next day, Saturday, in the afternoon, Kemper shows up looking for Billy. He would never have left Billy's side if Billy had been all right. The dog hung around, lying on his bed by the door, the old, folded blanket you may have noticed on the floor by the bench where Billy and Noah sat together. When I locked the East Room that Saturday, after Noah and I rid it up and left the State House, Kemper accompanied me. Under ordinary circumstances, he would never have parted from Billy, nor would Billy have parted from him."

"Which way did the dog go when he left the State House with you?" James asked, taking a sip from his coffee.

"He accompanied me east on Chestnut, toward the river, which is in the direction of where I live, and he and I walked along together. He seemed to want my company. Kemper's one of those dogs you wish could speak so he could tell you what he's thinking. He's a well-behaved little fellow, a regular gentleman. Everyone in the Guard knows him and likes him, just as everyone knows and likes Billy. And Kemper is brave. Billy told me he was with Kemper once when a pack of three big dogs attacked him, and he stood his ground and defended himself. Had he run, the pack would have overtaken him from behind and crippled or killed him."

James observed, "Kemper's an odd name for a dog. Does it mean something?"

"I asked Billy that once. It's Danish for 'fighter.' He said his mother told him what the name meant when she gave him the dog on his ninth birthday. She said a friend of hers from Denmark was given a white terrier with that name when he was nine, and she wanted him to have one, too."

"How far down Chestnut Street did the dog go with you, Sergeant?" James asked.

The Sergeant looked off into the middle distance and thought for a moment. "To Fourth Street. He turned left, there, while I kept going straight on Chestnut."

"Billy's dog left you and went north on Fourth?"

"Yes."

"But didn't Billy live with his mother in Southwark, which is in the other direction?"

"Yes, Southwark is south of Chestnut, quite a ways," Corbin agreed. "Billy's mother's an actress who plays at the Southwark Theater. I've never seen her, but I understand she's quite beautiful and talented."

"After I finish talking with members of your Guard, Sergeant, Billy's mother is the next person on my list of people to speak with. A person I've interviewed saw Billy and Kemper come out of the Indian Queen and go north on Fourth on the afternoon of the day he disappeared. Someone else I've spoken with, who shares your opinion that Billy has met with foul play, thinks he was attacked by brigands who wanted his gold ring. Would you please tell me about the ring?"

Corbin complied, saying, "I've never seen anything like it, Captain Jamison. Like the dog, it was a gift from his mother, which she gave him recently, he told me. It was heavy in your hand when you held it. Billy took it off his finger once and let me hold it and inspect its workmanship, which was quite impressive. It includes an image of a sort of dragon carved on its flat upper side. Billy said he liked the feeling that wearing the ring gave him."

"One more thing, Sergeant Corbin," James continued. "Did the young man seem any different to you the day he disappeared? Perhaps worried about something?"

"He did, in fact, Captain. When Noah was off using the necessary, I asked Billy what was bothering him. At first he denied anything was bothering him, but I kept after him, and finally he said someone had threatened his mother. But he wouldn't tell me any more than that. When I offered to help, saying the Sheriff is a friend of mine, and I might get him to speak to the man who was threatening his mother, he said not to bother. He said he knew what he had to do."

"Thank you for your time, Sergeant," said James. "You've been a big help. When you go back to the State House, please send over to me Noah Day, Thomas Whitehall, and Andrew Farrier."

As Corbin left the Half Moon, James ordered another coffee and was just taking his first sips of it when a clean-cut, rangy man in his late twenties, in the uniform of a corporal in the Pennsylvania militia appeared at his table.

"I'm Corporal Tom Whitehall, Captain Jamison. I understand you want to see me," the man said.

Two other militia men in uniform came up to the table together almost at the same moment as Whitehall. One of them was Noah Day, whom James had already met.

Standing up and shaking hands with the three, James said to the militiaman he didn't know yet, "You must be Adam Farrier." He continued, "Please have a seat, all of you. Would anyone like to take a coffee with me? Or perhaps a cup of tea?"

Only Whitehall, who said he'd have tea, took James up on his invitation as the three militiamen sat around the table.

After telling the waiter to bring Corporal Whitehall a tea, James told the three men he'd summoned, "As you know, I'm Captain James Jamison and, like yourselves, I'm in the service of the Constitutional Convention. General Washington has commissioned me to look into the disappearance of your friend Billy, who was last seen on Friday. I want to get from you any information or notion you may have that would help me find out what's happened to him, and where he is."

Adam Farrier, whose head had the unflattering tendency to suggest the shape of a pear, spoke up. "You'll be wanting to speak with Felicity Asquith, Captain Jamison. She is sweet on Billy and is always mooning around him."

"She's always with her confidantes Ruth Tyke and Dulcy Collier," Noah added.

Corporal Whitehall said, by way of explanation, "Miss Asquith, Captain, was supported in her attraction to Billy by her friends Ruth and Dulcy. The three of them have been something of a nuisance, because the Guard is under orders to keep our posts free of persons who are not part of the Convention. But this trio of fair ones pays no heed to anyone's duty except theirs to each other. They won't take orders from anyone. They're somewhat like anarchists."

"Anarchists for the sake of love!" Adam said laughing.

"I see," James said. "What are the ages of these young ladies?"

"Felicity must be going on eighteen," Adam replied.

"And the other two, Miss Tyke and Miss Collier?"

"Probably a year or two younger," Noah Day answered. "Dulcy's probably sixteen, and acts like she's forty. She's the shortest of the three."

"How would I find Miss Asquith and her friends to speak with them?"

"They've stopped coming around, now that Billy's disappeared. No honey pot, no flies buzzing around," Adam said.

"Who would know where these misses live?" James inquired.

"Peter might know," Noah said, looking at Corporal Whitehall. "I once saw him trying to get into Ruth's good graces."

"That's right," Adam said. "I remember telling him it looked like the Guard was becoming a bureau for romance."

"Who's Peter?"

"Peter Broadhurst," Corporal Whitehall said. "He's another of the militiamen guarding the entrance to the East Room." Then James remembered that the name Broadhurst was on Franklin's list of names.

"Is Billy sweet on this Felicity Asquith?" James asked. Whitehall and Day said they thought there was some interest in her on Billy's part, but Adam Farrier disagreed and said Billy had told him he'd yet to find the young woman he would want his mother to meet and approve of.

The line of inquiry then shifted to whether Billy had seemed preoccupied or worried the day he disappeared. None of these Guardsmen believed he had. Corporal Whitehall made the observation that when Billy failed to appear for duty on Saturday, June 23rd, it was the first time he'd ever done that.

On this note, James ended his conversation with these colleagues of the missing William Best, and asked Corporal Whitehall to send over to the Half Moon the militiamen Peter Broadhurst and Gideon Banks, which would complete his talks with Billy's closest associates in the Convention Guard.

In speaking with Banks and Broadhurst, James learned from Broadhurst where Ruth Tyke lived, and the young man said she would be able to tell him where her two friends lived. He added that Ruth's father was a physician; Dulcy's father was a baker who owned two bakeries; and Felicity's was a lawyer.

Apart from that, neither Broadhurst nor Banks had any information to add to what James had already gathered from speaking with the other Guards.

After retrieving Jenny from the front of the State House and getting into the saddle, James headed for Southwark to speak with the mother of Billy Best, who was an actress in the Southwark Theater.

Meeting Billy's Mother
Chapter IX

MEETING THE ACTRESS Rebecca Wellborn, Billy Best's mother, was for Captain James Jamison a singular experience. She lived in a lovely Georgian mansion in Southwark, which immediately struck James as beyond the means of an actress to purchase and maintain.

A well-dressed mulatto maid answered his knock and escorted him to her mistress.

The main part of the experience of seeing Mrs. Wellborn was the perfect harmony of her features. Her exquisitely shaped mouth, for instance, whose lips had the fine natural color of ripe cherries, harmonized perfectly with the russet of her hair, which fell in easy cascades to her perfect shoulders. Likewise, the fullness, shape, and color of her eyebrows suited the shape and color of her eyes and the luscious whiteness of her skin. Seeing her had somewhat the effect of seeing a summer sunrise at the height of its glory.

When James first beheld her, Mrs. Wellborn was seated in an upholstered armchair in a sunny alcove, reading a book. She looked up as her maid entered the room holding a paper and followed by an unknown gentleman whose left hand was grotesquely mutilated and encased in a tight-fitting black-kid glove. She glanced at the page she'd been reading, to memorize its number before closing the book, and said, "Yes, Celta? What is it?" Her voice had a clarity and a sweetness in keeping with the rest of her beauties, but as soon as she spoke, James knew her loveliness resembled those of a sunrise in another way. They could be seen but not touched. Nothing in her words conveyed that impression. It was a certain tone in her voice.

"Dis gen'lman, Meg, he bring dis pepah," the maid said and handed James's commission to her mistress.

The actress absorbed the words of the commission in a moment's reading, and had she wanted to impress her visitor could have recited every word of what she had read, the infallibility of her quick memory, along with the excellence of her unusual beauty and grace, being among the reasons she excelled as an actress.

"Does your visit concern the disappearance of my son, Captain Jamison?" Rebecca Wellborn asked in returning James's commission from General Washington to her servant, who in turn gave it to James and stepped aside, but did not leave the room.

"It does, Mrs. Wellborn. May I sit?"

"Yes, of course. Celta, please move that chair over here for the captain."

As this was being done, Rebecca Wellborn said, "I went with Celta this morning to the Sheriff to report William missing. Today is the fourth day since we last saw him go off with his dog, Kemper, to the State House to be one of the Convention Guards. Kemper came home yesterday alone. I told the Sheriff, it is not like William to vex me, and Kemper returning home without him is cause for considerable concern. The dog is devoted to William and would never leave him unless forced to part from him. Kemper has his bed in William's bedchamber."

"When the dog came home, Mrs. Wellborn, were there any signs on him indicating that he'd been in a fight?" James asked. "Any blood or wound? Was the dog limping?"

"There was nothing like that. Kemper looked his usual handsome self," Mrs. Wellborn replied.

"Would you mind, Madam, if I spoke with your maid?"

Celta, after having moved the chair up for James to sit in, had remained standing in the room, attentively listening to her mistress's conversation with this gentleman.

"Of course not. Go right ahead. Celta, please answer whatever questions this gentleman puts to you."

"Yes, Meg."

"You've known Billy a long time?" James asked Celta.

"Yessah. I knows 'im all 'is born life. Since da day he take 'is firs' breat'."

"Would you say something was bothering him the day he disappeared, or in the days before that?"

Celta seemed to think a moment before answering James's question with a simple negative.

"There was no indication of anything out of the ordinary being on his mind?" James persisted.

Again, there was the momentary hesitation, followed by a simple "No, Sah."

"Had there been any change in his behavior in recent weeks? Anything you heard him say or saw him do that struck you as peculiar?" James asked.

The pause this time seemed to him a bit longer before the "No, Sah" came.

"And how would you answer those questions, Madam?" James asked turning his head toward Mrs. Wellborn.

"I agree with Celta," Rebecca Wellborn replied. "I've noticed nothing out of the ordinary in anything William did or said, either the day he disappeared or in recent days."

"What did Sheriff Tuttleton say when you reported your son missing?"

"He expressed concern and sympathy, and promised to do what he could to find him. He asked me to describe the clothes William was wearing when I last saw him. I told the Sheriff and gave him a miniature of my son that I had Mister Peale's son Rembrandt paint."

"Did you tell Sheriff Tuttleton about Billy's dog coming home alone?"

"I did."

"What did he say to that?"

"He asked for a description of Kemper, saying it might be useful in making his inquires."

"Has anyone gone around to the pawnbrokers to ask whether the gold ring Billy wore has been offered in pawn?" James inquired. "I understand it was quite an impressive gold ring, featuring a bas-relief of a griffin."

On hearing James ask this question, Rebecca Wellborn gave him a searching look.

"That makes sense, Captain," she said. "I hadn't thought of doing that. Celta, early tomorrow morning, go around to Mr. Yarden and the other pawnbrokers and ask them if they've been offered William's ring in pawn."

"Yes, Meg."

"What is the significance of this ring, Madam, that you wanted your son to have it, and how did you come by such an unusual ring? What meaning does the griffin on it have?"

"How I may have obtained the ring is of no concern to you, Captain. Nor is my reason for wanting my son to have it," Rebecca Wellborn replied. "Neither of these matters pertains to William's disappearance. I'm pleased to know a person like General Washington, the President of the Constitutional Convention for which William works, has taken an interest in his disappearance and has assigned you to look into the matter. But I do hope in future you will confine your inquiries to matters that pertain to your investigation."

After delivering this reprimand, Mrs. Wellborn rose from her chair, and out of respect for her so did her visitor. As she stood, revealing the perfect shape of her figure, the smallness of her waist, and the attractive lengthiness of her legs, she said, "Now you must excuse me, Captain Jamison. Celta and I have to go over to the theater where my company is rehearsing a new play, *The Prince of Parthia*. It is by a deceased American playwright. We're going to perform it at the mansion-house of Mr. and Mrs. Morris for the particular entertainment of General Washington. As every actor in America knows, the General loves dramatic performances. They are among his favorite social pastimes along with dancing. I will appear in the role of Evanthe, the principal female character."

In leaving, James thanked Mrs. Wellborn for speaking with him.

She said nothing to him, only nodded her head.

Mrs. Wellborn's maid Celta escorted James to the front door of her mistress's mansion, and told him the house was just one square from the Southwark Theater. In departing the house, he asked Celta who Billy's most intimate friends were at the theater. The two names she gave him coincided with the names on Dr. Franklin's list of persons to be interviewed.

James took his dinner in Southwark at a small establishment on Fifth Street near Lombard called Der Gaststatte, which he'd passed in going to Mrs. Wellborn's. It had a sign over its entrance of a rampant lion wearing a crown. He'd heard people speak of this small restaurant in Southwark as having the best German food in Philadelphia, but had never had occasion to eat there.

Against one wall of the dining room, which contained ten round tables, each with its gleaming white tablecloth of linen, was a pair of crossed flagstaffs. Attached to one of these was the flag of the United States, with its circle of thirteen white stars on a blue field and thirteen alternating red and white stripes. The other flag's top half was solid red and its bottom half solid white; in the center, where these two halves met, was the same crowned lion that adorned the ordinary's signboard. Each flag had the corners farthest from its staff tacked to the wall to make their designs completely visible.

James had to order his meal through the owner of the establishment, Hermann Kriegmann, because none of the waiters spoke English.

On the advice of Herr Kriegmann, James's dinner consisted of sauerkraut and pork. After he finished eating everything on the huge platter of the dish that was served to him and emptying the big tankard of lager beer that came with the meal, he signaled his host to come to his table so that he could thank him for serving such filling quantities of excellent food and drink. Mr. Kriegmann asked James if he had received the Purple Heart Medal, motioning with his head to James's mutilated left hand; and when James said he had, the owner of the ordinary sat down at his table and ordered one of his waiters to bring two more tankards of beer, saying he could not let James leave without having a drink with him, and that he would pay for his meal.

He then told James the story of the wound he'd received at Trenton, which had earned him his Purple Heart. And James related the story of his nearly fatal wound from a British cannon ball at Monmouth, which had cost him the three middle fingers of his left hand and some of its palm.

After this heartening experience, James set out for the home of Ruth Tyke, one of the three young ladies who had been on friendly terms with Billy Best, who had irritated Corporal Whitehall by hanging around a part of the State House that was supposed to be kept free of persons unconnected to the Convention.

The house was on Walnut Street between Eighth and Ninth, three squares north of the Pennsylvania Hospital where Stephen Tyke, Ruth's father, whose medical degree was from the University of Edinburgh, taught anatomy to prospective physicians.

When James explained to the doctor's wife why he needed to speak with her daughter, and showed her his commission from George Washington, Mrs. Savila Tyke told him Ruth was in the garden at the rear of the house with her friends Felicity Asquith and Dulcy Collier. This was pleasing news to James since these were the other young ladies he wanted to speak with to gather information on Billy Best.

Mrs. Tyke explained that the three girls were testing the confections Dulcy's father, a baker, was thinking of introducing to people of quality in Philadelphia and was sending around to get opinions on their delectability.

"Dulcy came to the house with Felicity about an hour ago," Mrs. Tyke said to James as she escorted him through her house to the door to the backyard. "She was carrying pokes of three confections called Pistachio Pralines, French Macaroons, and Almond Fagots, and had me try them. I found them all delicious, Captain Jamison. So much so that I wrote down their names. Dulcy told me a friend of her father's in London named Frederick Nutt is writing a book on making confections and has sent him the recipes for these three delectable to get his opinion of them." At the back of the house Mrs. Tyke gestured toward the grape arbor and said James would find her daughter and her friends there.

James followed the chatter of young female voices to the arbor. The sudden appearance of an unknown gentleman in the girls' midst, even though they knew Ruth's mother must have admitted him into the garden, silenced their jabber. When James gave the young ladies his name and told them he was looking into the disappearance of Billy Best, the fairest and oldest of the threesome, whom Corporal Whitehall had identified as Felicity Asquith, exclaimed, "Billy's dead!" This declaration was accompanied by a gush of tears and comforting words and tokens of affection from Felicity's friends.

The youngest and shortest of the trio, whose name James recalled was Dulcy Collier, got up from the bench under the arbor where she'd been sitting and went to her friend to cradle her head between her ample breasts, which expression of pity briefly increased Felicity's sobs but soon quieted them.

"My pa, who's a doctor," Ruth Tyke declared, "is always saying 'Where there's life there's hope,' and I believe him. But I think people ought to say 'Where there's hope, there's life.' You mustn't think Billy's dead, Felicity! It will bring him bad luck!"

James, still standing, asked, "What makes you so sure, Miss Asquith, that Billy's dead?"

"He loves me. He would never go away without telling me he was going, and he's been gone four days now. He didn't go away. His witch of a mother, the actress, had one of her love slaves do away with him when she couldn't get him to stop seeing me. She's jealous of me! She's evil! Didn't you think something was bothering Billy last Friday?" Felicity asked her friends.

"You're right," Ruth Tyke said. "He didn't say anything, but you could tell something was on his mind."

"It was that mother of his! He suspected she was up to something. But he was too much of a gentleman to say anything against her. What do you think, Dulcy?" Felicity asked her other friend.

"Something did seem to be bothering him," Dulcy Collier said. "It might've had to do with his mother."

"Something awful has happened to Billy. I feel it," Ruth Tyke said. "But I don't think he's dead. That's Peter's opinion, too, and the opinion of some of the other Convention Guards—Peter told me."

James brought up for discussion the gold ring Billy had started to wear not long before his disappearance, asking these associates of Billy's if he had said anything of this ring to them.

"It was a fine, big ring," Dulcy said.

"You could tell Billy liked wearing it," Felicity said. "But he didn't talk about it, except to say his mother had given it to him. I think she gave it to him to get him to stop seeing me. But it didn't work."

"Did he ever say anything about the meaning of the griffin carved on it?" James asked.

The three young women agreed he had never spoken of that.

Dulcy offered James the plate on which she had placed her father's European confections and pointed out each of them by name, telling James to take whichever one he wanted. James took an Almond Fagot because he was fond of almonds, and Dulcy said this confection had been given that name because the almonds in it were sliced thin for easier chewing and bound together, like a fagot or bundle of sticks, by the sticky ingredient called for in the Almond Fagot recipe. After eating one Fagot, James asked if he could have another, and Dulcy told him to take two, that the Fagots were small.

The talk James had at the Indian Queen with Henry Glebe, the hotel deskman who came on duty at five, who had spoken with Billy Best when he had appeared at the hotel to deliver Elbridge Gerry's letter to George Mason on June 22nd, added no information to what Glebe had given George Mason who had passed it on to James.

Before going home to supper, James went around to the concealed letter drop for Franklin Court off Fourth Street, to leave a note requesting a meeting with Dr. Franklin.

He got home and stabled Jenny in time to sit down to supper with his ladies. Grandmère had made a chicken fricassee which she had prepared with fresh peas from the garden and small garden potatoes, augmented by Livy's fresh-baked bread and home-churned butter.

Having gotten the news of the day at the supper table, which was mostly on Anne-Louise's latest doings, James excused himself, saying he had to write a report to Dr. Franklin on his activities and went upstairs to his room which he now shared with Livy and the baby. His twin sister Jane's former bedchamber had become the baby's nursery.

He began his report:

Dear Dr. Franklin—

As of this Evening, my second full day of making Inquiries, I've spoken with 16 people who knew Billy Best and have formed certain Opinions I would like to discuss with you as soon as you can manage to meet with me.

I've come to the same Conclusion as you, that it is quite unlikely this young man would have Stolen the letter to Mr. Mason, in order to sell it to the Highest Bidder. Your opinion of William Best's character, I have found, is generally shared by my Informants, several of whom, including Sgt. Corbin, think he's met with Foul Play; "footpads" & "brigands" are the Characterizations most often offered of his assailants.

I think some sort of Misadventure may likely have befallen Billy, the nature of which has yet to be determined. The involvement of enemies of the Convention, whether foreign or domestic, in what happened to him, cannot be ruled out, I think. But I somehow am not inclined to that Conclusion.

Tomorrow I will speak with Colonel Zanzinger. I want the Opinion of this tracker of spies of whom you Spoke so highly, on the possibility of foreign agents being a party to Billy's disappearance.

I've asked all my informants if they thought Billy was upset the Day he vanished, & only your Sgt. Corbin & three young female friends of Billy's thought he was. Sgt. Corbin informed me that Billy himself told him, after persistent questioning, that his mother had been "Threatened," but would offer no specifics. He refused Corbin's offer to get Sheriff Tuttleton, who is a friend of the Sergeant, to speak to the man who made the threat. Corbin reported that Billy told him he knew "what he had to do."

An interesting Pattern of facts is forming around the mother, who is a surpassingly Beautiful woman who seems to be in her middle thirties, which means she gave Birth to her nineteen-year-old Son quite early in her life. She lives alone in a spacious house in the Georgian style of Architecture near the Theater where she performs as an actress. The House is Richly furnished & seems to me beyond the means of an actress to buy or maintain. I have not looked into the number of Servants she employs, & saw only the one who took me into the House, a good-looking Mulatto woman who serves as her personal Servant. A house of that size would require no fewer than four, I would say.

Her speech & the fact that she was reading Montaigne's essays in French when I first laid eyes on her gave me the impression she's an educated, intelligent Woman. She also has given me the impression of being a Strong-willed Woman.

Somehow she has an air of having experienced some tremendous Sorrow early in Life. I would also report that though Mrs. Wellborn is Concerned about her son's Disappearance, she does not seem Excessively Worried. For instance, she used the expression "gone away" in reference to his Disappearance.

She & her maidservant, who goes by the name of Celta, have been together at least two decades because the Maid told me she had attended Billy's birth. This maid & her mistress seem to Disagree on whether the young man's disappearance should be a cause of grave Alarm, though the maid Pretended to be of the same Mind as her mistress on the matter.

The maid calls her mistress 'Meg,' which suggests the baptismal name of Billy's mother may have been Margaret. It also suggests some sort of extraordinary connexion between this Maid & her Mistress.

Mrs. Wellborn, by the way, always refers to her son as "William," never as "Billy." You should also be informed that she refused to answer my questions concerning the gold ring she gave her Son, and that he started wearing a few weeks before his disappearance.

Perhaps you can make something of these Facts & Impressions. I have not been able to.

I conclude this Report by informing you that the missing young man has a dog named Kemper which everyone says is his inseparable Companion. The dog sleeps on his own bed in Billy's bedchamber. By all accounts, he's a handsome white terrier, notable for his amiable temper, intelligence, and courage.

Kemper was with Billy the last time he was seen by anyone I've talked to, which was the Indian Queen's doorman. He saw Billy & the dog after they came out of the Indian Queen, and saw them head north together on Fourth Street the day he vanished.

I have had an idea of how this Terrier of Billy Best might be enlisted to Assist me in finding him, if I can get Mrs. Wellborn's maid Celta to go along with the idea. I want to speak with Celta alone on this, & I think I know how that might be arranged.

Yr obliging Servant,
James Jamison
June 25, 1787.

After James rode into the city, he left these written comments in the concealed letter drop in the western wall of Franklin Court. When he did so, he saw that his earlier note to Franklin, requesting a conference, had been removed from the letter drop by Mr. Mahoney to give to his master.

Mr. Yarden, & Celta Alone
Chapter X

"CAPTAIN JAMISON! GOOD to see you again!" Abraham Yarden, Philadelphia's most respectable pawnbroker, said as his indentured manservant brought James into the room at the back of his house where he conducted his business. "What may I do for you, Sir?"

"Perhaps it would be best, Mr. Yarden, if you read this first," James replied, presenting his commission from Washington to the elderly gentleman.

James had again left his house in the sparsely inhabited, far-western suburbs of Philadelphia while his grandmother, Livy, and the baby were all fast asleep and had taken breakfast at an ordinary on the way to Mr. Yarden's house. By the time he'd arrived at Yarden's house, the sun of Tuesday, the 26th of June, had fully risen over the houses on Mulberry Street.

After reading James's commission, Mr. Yarden said, "This only tells me, Captain Jamison, that if I wish to be thought of as a good American, which I do, I must give you whatever aid you require. And what aid *do* you require?"

"A maidservant of a woman of some means, whose son has vanished, will be coming to see you soon, Mr. Yarden—probably within the next hour or so. She is going to all the city's pawnbrokers this morning, having been ordered by her mistress to ask if any of you has been offered a heavy gold ring her son wore."

"Is it a ring with a bas-relief image of a griffin carved on the ring's bezel, and bearing the motto '*Ad finem*' engraved on its inner surface?" Yarden asked. "A ring of the purest gold, crafted in the finest tradition of goldsmithing?"

"I don't know about the motto, Mr. Yarden, but the rest of your description fits the ring I'm interested in tracing," James replied. "When did you see it? Do you have the name of the person who pawned it? May I see the ring?"

"It wasn't something I took in pawn, Captain Jamison. The handsome young man who wore the ring wanted to know its value and what sort of ring it was. He said he thought it had belonged to a very rich man, and I confirmed that it apparently had. When I told him the minimum value of such a ring, he was astonished and said he had not expected it to be so costly.

"When I asked him how he came to be in possession of such a valuable ring, he said his mother had given it to him, but that she had told him nothing of its history or how she'd come by it. He said all she had told him was that she wanted him to have it, and that he deserved to have it.

"He asked me if I thought the ring belonged to a noble family and said he was curious to know that more than anything. I told him I had in my library several books on such matters, arranged by countries, and if he gave me a moment I would look in them to see if they might have answers to his questions. But before I could do that, he asked me what the words on the inside surface of the ring meant. I told him '*Ad finem*' is Latin for 'To the end,' and that it probably was the motto of a noble European family, to convey the idea of fidelity in battle. And I told him his ring was most likely the signet ring of such a family, the sort of ring used to impress the family's emblem in the wax seals of important papers, to authenticate them as belonging to that family.

"He was an innocent-looking young man, extraordinarily handsome, as I've said, and of excellent manners. You couldn't help wanting to help him, just as you would any good-looking, polite boy. I told him if he would excuse me, I would go upstairs to my library to consult my books. He thanked me, and I left him to do what I had promised.

"After looking in the indexes of books on the noble houses of England, Scotland, Wales, Ireland, and France for the Latin motto '*Ad finem*,' I finally found it in a book on the noble families of Scandinavia. It turns out it is the heraldic motto of a Danish earl, the Jarl of Jutland, and, as I had supposed, it expresses the idea of unfailing feudal loyalty in the face of adversity, especially in battle. The title and its motto date from the time the kings of Denmark ruled Norway also. The family name of the Jarls of Jutland is Griffenfeld, hence their heraldic symbol of a griffin, a mythical beast whose upper body is that of an eagle, including the wings and talons, but whose loins and tail are those of a lion. In the seventeenth century this family received from the king of Denmark the additional title of 'Count Griffenfeld.' The present count and earl bears the Christian names Vilhelm Peder Anders, according to the information in my book on the noble families of Scandinavia. I reported all of this to the young man, which greatly pleased him. He thanked me several times before his departure."

Mr. Yarden's information deepened the mystery of the ring for James. How had an actress in Philadelphia allegedly born in England—according to information Dr. Franklin had received from his majordomo—come to possess the signet ring of a noble family in Denmark?

"Might I read the entry on the Griffenfeld family in your book, Mr. Yarden?" James inquired.

"Of course. I'll send for it." Yarden rang a little porcelain bell on his desk, which instantly brought into his office the man wearing the blue smock who had admitted James into Yarden's house.

"Karl, please bring me from the library upstairs the book *Scandinavian Families of Royal and Noble Birth*," Yarden requested, adding, "It's on the middle shelf of the bookcase to the right of the entrance."

While waiting for the book to be brought down, James asked the learned, gentlemanly pawnbroker whether he had encountered other signet rings in Philadelphia in the course of his business.

"Never before have I seen a person in America in possession of such a ring, and only once in Europe, in the city of Antwerp, before I came to America. And the signet ring the young man wanted information on was not being offered in pawn. The young man who had it wanted to keep it.

"My understanding of signets, Captain Jamison, is clear. No class of noblemen lives in the United States, which is one of the reasons Europeans of common lineage want to come here to live, and thus articles such as signet rings are not found here. Moreover, because such rings represent the authority of being a nobleman, they are never found here. May I ask, Captain Jamison, what your interest in this ring is, and how the mother of the young man happened to have the signet ring of a European nobleman to give to her son? I have a certain curiosity concerning this matter."

"The young man who wore the ring and spoke with you has disappeared, Mr. Yarden. That is my interest," James replied. "I have been asked by General Washington to find him because he worked for the Constitutional Convention over which, as everyone knows, the General presides. I need to find out as much as I can about the young man, and particularly about the ring he was wearing when he disappeared, because some persons think his wearing it has something to do with his disappearance. The woman I mentioned who'll be coming soon to ask you if you've been offered the ring in pawn has known the young man since the day he was born, and I want to speak with her privately."

James didn't inform Yarden that he'd previously questioned Celta in the presence of her mistress.

"You'd like to wait in my house until the maid arrives, and she and I conclude the business which brings her to me. After that, you'd like to speak with her alone? Is that it?"

"That's exactly what I'd like you to arrange for me, Sir—an opportunity to talk with this woman without the influence of her mistress's presence."

"You can wait for her in my front parlor, Captain, and I will send her to you after she finishes the business that brings her to me. You may use that room as long as you like. I'll have Karl take her to you. How will I know she is the woman you're wanting to speak to, aside from her asking about this so-interesting signet ring?"

"Oh, there can be no mistake about that. She's a good-looking, well-dressed servant of the complexion spoken of in the Islands as *mulatto*."

"Ah, here is Karl with the book you wanted to see." The servant entered the room bearing a thick, folio-size tome, the cover of which was embossed in gold lettering.

"Karl, please carry this book to the front parlor for Captain Jamison. He will be waiting there for a female client of mine who has yet to arrive."

After studying the entry on the Griffenfeld family in Yarden's book of Scandinavian noblemen, James remembered having heard that "Vilhelm," the first baptismal name of the present Jarl of Jutland and Count Griffenfeld, was a version of the name "William," which Billy Best bore. He wondered if this was mere coincidence or had some significance. William was, of course, a common Christian name. But, after everything

James had learned of the signet ring Billy's mother had given him, he was inclined to believe there probably was a connexion between William Best's first name being the same as the first Christian name of the head of this noble Danish family. If he could get Celta to tell him what she knew of the ring, perhaps he would understand what the connexion was, and be able to piece together a reason for Billy's disappearance.

Another thing he would have to find out from Celta was why Billy's surname was Best. Was Best his mother's unmarried name or the surname of Billy's father? One thing was certain. When Dr. Franklin had spoken with this young man in assessing his family background, when he was considering him for appointment to the Convention Guard, and had asked him what his father did for a living, Billy had found the inquiry upsetting because, he told Dr. Franklin, he didn't know who his father was. How did that fact tie in with Billy coming to Mr. Yarden to find out the history of the ring his mother had given him because, she said, he "deserved" it?

As these thoughts followed one another in James's mind, the door to Mr. Yarden's front parlor opened and Celta was escorted into the room. "Miss Celta to see you, Sir," the servant announced before he left.

Celta was more curious than surprised to find the man who'd visited her mistress's house the day before here in the parlor of the city's most prominent pawnbroker, apparently waiting to speak to her. She was particularly curious because she remembered this Captain Jamison had suggested that her mistress find out if the city's pawnbrokers had been offered Billy's ring in pawn, and Meg had mentioned only one pawnbroker by name, Mr. Yarden, in telling her to visit the city's pawnbrokers. And here Captain Jamison was. At Mr. Yarden's place of business, waiting for her.

James began their conversation by saying, "You know from my visit yesterday to Mrs. Wellborn, Celta, that I'm trying to find her son, the young man you've known since the day he was born and helped Mrs. Wellborn raise. Yesterday I had the impression you might have a different opinion of Billy's disappearance than she has. I've come here to discuss that possibility with you. I believe you love Billy as much as she does.

"The paper signed by General Washington that I showed Mrs. Wellborn yesterday in Southwark asks everyone in Philadelphia to help me find Billy." With this James withdrew his commission from his coat. "I'll read the paper to you if you can't read."

Celta replied, "Yessah, it be true, as you say, dat Billy as precious to me as to Meg. But I can read. Dey be no need tah read Gen'l Washington's pepah tah me. Meg's momer, who die birtin' 'er, she teach me me lettahs, when she big wit' Meg an' I jus' a youngstah, livin' wit' me momer in da big 'ouse o' Mastah William an' Mis'ress Marg'ret.

"She tell me I mus' take care o' her baby an' be 'er companion all 'er life, an' see no 'arm come to 'er, be it a girl baby or a boy baby. But she was tinkin' it goin' to be a gal, an' dat be how it turn out. Mis'ress Marg'ret's firs' chil' be her onlyest one, 'cause she die givin' Meg tah da light o' day."

James replied, "Well, I'm glad you can read, Celta. Please read this." And with that he handed her his commission. James was not just being polite when he said he was glad Celta could read, because he thought that if she had grown up reading, chances were she had developed some independence of thought, which James needed her to have if he was to enlist her help.

After reading James's commission, this slender, well-groomed maidservant said, "I guess I's got tah help yah find Billy, Cap'n Jamison. But I mus'na cross Meg. I been lookin' aftah her an' 'elpin' 'er all 'er life, an' dis be da firs' time we evah have a different idea on sometin' big.

"She tink Billy be safe. But I tink 'e be in danjah. She tink she know who got 'im. I be tinkin' she may be right on dat, but, like you say, Cap'n, Billy got to be found quick-like. He mighty upset when Meg tell 'im she done get a lettah from dat man who be pesterin' 'er fah years, sayin' 'e goin' to do sometin' nasty tah Billy lessen she do what 'e want—and I know she nevah do dat, so long as God give 'er life!"

This statement from Celta confirmed what Sergeant Corbin had told James, that the day Billy vanished he had been upset by a "threat" to his mother and had said that he knew "what he had to do."

"So, Mrs. Wellborn thinks this man who threatened her is holding her son, and she believes he won't harm Billy because that would end any chance of her agreeing to become his mistress."

"Dat be it, Cap'n."

"Do you know the man's name?"

"I seen 'im. Some o' da women at da teeahter who laughs at 'im fah moonin' ovah Meg calls him 'Declan.' He be a good-lookin' fella, maybe fifty. When Meg in a play, he be dere in da box closest tah da stage. He allus sendin' Meg bunches o' yellah roses. Been doin' it fah years. She don' like roses, Meg don', on account o' dem t'orns dey 'as, an' she say dey smell be puttin' 'er in mind o' funerals. She say dey's plenty o' flowers wit'out t'orns, as pretty an' fine smellin' as roses be. A time or two he send 'er small jewelry, bracelets an' such."

"Mrs. Wellborn did not, I suppose, let you read this man's threatening letter?"

"No. Meg only tell me an' Billy 'bout it."

"Do you know where he lives, or his occupation? That and his Irish first name might help me identify him."

"No. I not be knowin' where 'e live or what 'e do."

"You were with your mistress when she went to the Sheriff. It doesn't seem she told the Sheriff about this man. Is this right?"

"No, she no tell 'im."

"Why? That seems strange if she thinks he's taken Billy hostage."

"She be pityin' dis man. She be tinkin' she responsible fah 'is passion fah her. Mos' of all, she be convinced 'e not be harmin' Billy. Dat be where Meg an' me, we 'as diff'rent t'oughts. I be tinkin' dis Declan could 'arm Billy, an' we best be gettin' 'im 'ome if dis man 'ave 'im."

"Tell me, why do you call Rebecca Wellborn 'Meg'?"

"'Er name not Wellborn. Dat a name she make up to go on da stage. 'Er name be Marg'ret Godolphin. I been callin' 'er 'Meg' since she a baby an' I be tol' to look aftah her an' keep 'er from 'urt. 'Er Daddy call 'er 'Meg.' Dat be anoddah way o' sayin' 'Marg'ret.' Dat 'er momer's name. Mastah William, 'e say she remin' 'im o' her momer. I musta pick up callin' her dat from 'im."

"Her father's name was William?"

"Yessah."

James then told Celta that the last anyone had seen Billy and Kemper, they'd been walking north on Fourth Street from the Indian Queen Hotel.

"Whatever happened to Billy last Friday, Celta, two things seem clear. Kemper was with him when it happened, but was not affected by what happened because he returned home safe and sound two days later. Where Kemper spent those two days, no one knows. Second, Billy seems to have gotten tired of waiting in the hotel lobby for the man he had to give a letter to. It seems likely he decided to take care of some personal business, thinking he could do that and get back to the hotel before the man he was waiting for returned. From what you and others have told me, Celta, I think the personal business Billy wanted to take care of was to confront the man who'd threatened his mother.

"If this is right, then Billy must have known where to find the Irishman named Declan he wanted to confront. It may be only a mile or two north of the Indian Queen Hotel, somewhere to the east or west of Fourth Street. Whatever has befallen Billy must have occurred in that area, which is too big to search. What I have in mind, Celta, is to get Kemper to take us, with your help, to where he went with Billy last Friday.

"I need you to get Kemper out of the house without your mistress interfering, and to provide an article of Billy's clothing for Kemper to smell so he will know we're looking for his master. Perhaps a piece of his small clothes that hasn't been laundered. Because the dog knows you as someone who lives in the same house he does, if you present him something that has Billy's scent and tell him to find Billy, a name he knows as well as he knows his own, we might get a good result. Will you help me do this, Celta?"

The maidservant said, in affirmation of this reasoning, "Kempah do like me 'cause I gives 'im 'is vittels." Then she added, "I got a feelin' sometin' bad gonna 'app'n tah Billy iffen we don' rescue 'im soon. Yah plan, Cap'n, soun' good tah me. But Meg mus'na know what we be doin' 'cause she done make up 'er mind Billy be safe an' da man what got 'im not goin' tah 'urt 'im. Once Meg make up 'er mind, she be powerful stubborn."

James then asked the maid, "Could you bring Kemper to the Fourth Street entrance of the Indian Queen Hotel tomorrow morning at ten? And bring an article of Billy's clothing to give Kemper to smell?"

Celta's answer came at once, "I will."

She left the pawnbroker's front parlor as soon as she and James agreed to put his plan into effect. James left after going to Mr. Yarden's office at the rear of the house to thank him for his assistance.

James Presses On

Chapter XI

THE DAY CONTINUED hot and thickly humid as James rode from the pawnbroker's house on Mulberry Street to the City Tavern at Second Street and Walnut, two blocks in from the river, to partake of the rich oxtail soup that was always part of the Tavern's bill of fare for Tuesday dinner. And, as always, no matter what day of the week it might be, at midday both the City Tavern's dining room and its bar were full of merchants, ship captains, lawyers, legislators, politicians, men of affairs, and visitors to America's biggest city, all of them conversing at the same time, creating a lively, pleasant hubbub.

James ate standing at the bar, and though he noticed several men of his acquaintance, he did not join any of them or invite any of them to join him. He preferred to eat alone and contemplate the information he had gathered relating to William Best, to see what sense he could find in it. By the time he got to his dessert—extra ripe, skinned and pitted plums mashed in their own juices, topped with whipped cream and freshly grated nutmeg—he was no closer to finding a pattern in what he'd discovered than he had been when he'd savored his first spoonful of the Tavern's rich, dark oxtail soup.

Only two things seemed evident. Billy's mother had given him a dog with a Danish name that meant "fighter," and the signet ring of a Danish nobleman whose engraved Latin motto "*Ad finem*" meant "fidelity in battle." There was also a possible connection to the Griffenfeld family in that Billy's Christian name coincided with that of the current scion of the family, although it was also the same as that of Rebecca Wellborn's father, William. The fact that Billy had told Dr. Franklin he didn't know who his father was could be related to the Danish signet ring and the dog with a Danish name. But how exactly?

Upon leaving the City Tavern, James rode over to the south side of Market Street, to see if Mr. Mahoney, Dr. Franklin's confidential servant, had left the peephole in the Franklin Court carriage gates open, signaling that a message from Dr. Franklin awaited him in the secret letter drop in the west wall of the mansion-house.

The peephole was open. To retrieve the communication, James tethered Jenny to the first available iron post he came upon. Walking back to Fourth Street, he went down the narrow passageway on the south side of the Indian Queen Hotel to the hidden letter drop at its end. The note for him from Dr. Franklin that he found there was brief, written on a small square of paper, without salutation or signature apart from initials.

> J: Your report on your discoveries since Sunday is intriguing. I want to talk with you. Come by at one o'clock Wed. night. I've told Col. Zanzinger of your intention to see him & he says to come to his home, not his place of business, the Address I gave you for him. His Home address will be in the Directory. BF

On going back for his horse, James stopped at the Indian Queen Hotel to look in the Hotel's copy of the Directory for the home address of Tamas Zanzinger, which turned out to be in Appletree Alley, a street he'd never heard of, and he had to ask the hotel clerk for directions to it.

After untethering Jenny, James walked the mare the short distance to Fourth Street before mounting, and rode north on that major north-south thoroughfare. He passed the University and, shortly after crossing Mulberry Street, turned west onto Appletree Alley, which was one square long, going from Fourth to Fifth streets.

The good appearance of the houses on this narrow, brick-paved street made up for its obscurity and small size. The street had eight houses, five on the south side and three on the north, and every one was substantial, of brick construction with slate roofs, most of them in the mansard style of roof construction. Every house was set well apart from its neighbors and had a flower garden in front and, in some instances, also in the rear. The house of the Hungarian immigrant Tamas Zanzinger, who had established a successful trade with the Caribbean islands, principally St. Croix, was one of three houses on bigger lots on the alley's north side. Colonel Zanzinger's front yard was a mass of white, yellow, red, and purple flowers, including dahlias, zinnias, and lavender, and from the street James saw there was a large grape arbor at the rear of the house, and that a nice grove of mature chestnut trees taller than the house shaded the backyard.

At the far end of the street St. Michael's Lutheran Church was visible, and James wondered if this church was the one the Colonel attended.

Zanzinger had been given the rank of colonel during his service in the war, in recognition of his previous military experience in the French and Indian War. His two sons, Tamas and Nicholas, had been junior officers. The younger one, Nicholas, had died of typhus, one of some 2,500 men, a fourth of the Army, who had perished from illness at Valley Forge during the bitter winter the Army spent in makeshift huts without adequate heat, blankets, food, or medical supplies. Zanzinger's wife had died during the first year of the war, with her sons and husband away from her side.

Following the surrender of General Lord Cornwallis and his army at Yorktown, Britain's attempt to put down the uprising of her thirteen colonies on the American mainland was in effect over, and Colonel Zanzinger had requested and received honorable discharges for himself and his surviving son so they could return to Philadelphia and revive his formerly flourishing trade with the Caribbean. Three years after his return from the war, the Commonwealth of Pennsylvania had requested that he take on the task of ferreting out foreign agents in Philadelphia along with their American sympathizers, and Zanzinger had accepted and turned most of his commercial activities over to his son Tamas.

A slender, pleasant-looking man in his late forties, wearing the clothing of a gentleman, admitted James to Zanzinger's house. He told him in an English spoken exactly like that of James's French-born grandmother that Colonel Zanzinger was expecting him. This man did not give James the impression of being a house servant, but of being employed by Zanzinger in some other capacity.

The gentleman James had come to consult was of ordinary stature and nondescript features except for his eyes, which had a greenish-yellow tinge and were of a remarkable intensity. Even when passively sitting behind his worktable, this naturalized American from Szgard, Hungary, had an appearance of alert command. The long wall of his rectangular workplace, opposite a row of windows looking out onto the house's beautiful backyard, consisted of floor-to-ceiling shelves filled with books and small art-objects. Two opened windows admitted the tree-shaded yard's cooling freshness.

As had become customary for James after giving his name to those he needed to speak with, he presented to Colonel

Zanzinger his paper signed by Washington, which the Colonel read while standing after shaking his visitor's hand; then Zanzinger returned the commission to James and invited him to be seated, indicating the three armchairs in front of his worktable. These chairs, a large sofa, and two additional armchairs in a distant part of the room were all upholstered in the same lively chintz material.

"I have been told by Dr. Franklin, Captain Jamison, that you are carrying out something of the utmost urgency for the Constitutional Convention," Zanzinger said.

"And Dr. Franklin has told me, Colonel, that I may speak with you with the same confidence and frankness as if speaking with him."

"For Dr. Franklin, who got the king of France and God's own lightning to do his bidding, to say that of me is really pleasing. And, having just read your carte blanche from General Washington, I assure you that whatever help I may be able to give you because of my special information on foreign agents and their American supporters in Philadelphia, shall be given. Please be seated, Captain."

After taking a chair, James replied, "Since Dr. Franklin has said I may speak to you with complete candor, Sir, perhaps the best way for us to proceed would be for me to tell you everything I've learned in the matter I've been assigned to investigate for General Washington. That way you will have a clear understanding of what I am engaged in, its importance, and the kind of aid I require."

James then recited to Zanzinger all that he'd learned from his many informants he'd spoken to in the space of a few days. The Hungarian immigrant who'd become one of Philadelphia's most successful trading merchants, and had fought for America's independence with as much zeal as any American-born citizen, paid close heed to everything the man seated in front of him said. The recital, including Zanzinger's occasional questions, lasted the better part of an hour.

When James finished, the Colonel summed up what appeared to him the thing of greatest importance. "Captain Jamison, you seem to think this mystery revolves around the mother because a man obsessed with her charms wants her to be his mistress. I've seen Mrs. Wellborn on stage and agree she has a compelling beauty."

"You're right, Colonel. Considering everything I've discovered, that hypothesis seems to suit the facts. But I also think a different hypothesis is possible. That this extraordinarily attractive woman is being paid by the British to provide information on our attempt to create a stronger general government for ourselves, information she might obtain through her son, who is in trusted daily proximity to the Convention."

A long moment of silence ensued after this exchange between the two veterans of the American Revolution.

"Well, Captain Jamison, may I say that I, too, once had similar suspicions of the beauteous Mrs. Wellborn, having been given reports that during the British occupation of Philadelphia she had social relations with the British army's commander and his staff. And when her acting company withdrew from wartime America and went to Jamaica because theaters in America were all closed for the duration of the war, whereas they remained open in the British colony of Jamaica, she did not go with her fellow players but remained in British-occupied Philadelphia. That seemed suspicious to me and to people whose judgment I trust. Furthermore, one of the persons Mrs. Wellborn consorted with was Major John Andre, who was later hung by Washington when caught *in flagrante delicto* in an act of espionage that would have greatly damaged the American prosecution of the war had it succeeded.

"Andre was, as you perhaps know, Benedict Arnold's liaison with the British military commander in North America when General Arnold, through the influence of his Tory wife, was persuaded to betray his command of West Point, America's key stronghold on the Hudson. If his treason, promoted by Major Andre, had succeeded, and West Point had fallen into British hands, their warships would have gained control of the Hudson and split our five northernmost States from the eight States to the south.

"But apparently Mrs. Wellborn could not be seduced by any of the British officers who wanted to have carnal relations with her. Nor could she be swayed by the money she was offered to become a British spy and betray the interests of her adopted country. She did not refuse, however, because of loyalty to American interests, nor did she thwart attempts to seduce her for reasons of patriotism or morality. Her heart had simply been totally and permanently engaged at a tender age by the first love of her life. Very likely, her son is the fruit of that profound youthful affair.

"Aside from the fact that she performed in the plays, dramas, and recitals the British officers put on in 1778 to alleviate the tedium of occupying Philadelphia—most notably her performance alongside the charming Peggy Shippen, Benedict Arnold's second wife and a notorious Philadelphia Tory, in Major Andre's theatrical extravaganza *Mischianza*— I uncovered no evidence of Rebecca Wellborn giving aid or comfort to our enemy.

"A week ago, however, Captain Jamison, on successive days, I received a pair of anonymous letters, in the same handwriting, accusing Mrs. Wellborn of being a paid British spy who was gathering information that would divide the States and bring about the destruction of our Union."

"Did these accusations have any credibility in your judgment, Colonel?" James inquired.

"No. As far as I'm concerned, Mrs. Wellborn is not a subject for investigation for espionage on behalf of His Britannic Majesty George the Third."

"Who, then, do you think is behind the accusations?"

"It could, I suppose, Captain, be the man that Mrs. Wellborn's son told Sergeant Corbin has threatened his mother, and that these anonymous letters represent the form his threat took before he abducted her son."

"What about Mrs. Wellborn's income, Colonel Zanzinger? As I have told you, when I went to speak with her in regard to her son's disappearance, it seemed to me that her home exceeds in opulence the income that even the most beautiful and most talented actress could earn. To live in and maintain a dwelling the size of hers is simply beyond any actress's income."

"Perhaps she has an inheritance of some kind, Captain Jamison, or is the recipient of gifts of money from admirers, which would account for her high life. I will have Jean-Pierre look into the sources of her income. He's the man who opened my door to you. His last name is Latrobe. He is good at things of this sort. Years ago, he came to Philadelphia from Paris as a chimneysweep because he heard chimney sweeping paid much better in America than in France, and Philadelphia is the city with the most chimneys in America. But a short time after his arrival, he became *un preneur de rats*, as a rat catcher is called in France, because that paid even better than chimney sweeping. But rat catching is a disagreeable occupation, as one might imagine, in which success is measured in the number of rat tails one can present to the person who engages the rat catcher.

"After pursuing that lucrative, but unpleasant, occupation for several years, Jean-Pierre became a jockey because he likes fast horses. Now he works for me because he's perceptive and intelligent in investigating the matters that interest me, and has become too old for the dangerous and demanding business of riding fast horses. He can find out for you Mrs. Wellborn's sources of income, apart from acting."

"I appreciate your help, Colonel Zanzinger. Do you think Mr. Latrobe might also look into the connection Mrs. Wellborn has with things Danish?"

"I can do that for you. I know Danes who have family in St. Croix, which is, as you may know, a possession of the Danish crown in the Caribbean. I do most of my trading with that island and will make inquiries among my Danish friends here in Philadelphia on the matter that interests you. They should know of any connection Mrs. Wellborn might have with 'things Danish,' as you put the matter."

"I would be much obliged for your help, Colonel. Thank you."

Thus ended James's long first visit with Colonel Zanzinger. The several points they had discussed regarding Mrs. Wellborn settled to James's satisfaction the principal question of whether Billy Best's disappearance could have, through his mother, a connection with the activities of foreign agents in Philadelphia. He was also pleased that the visit had resulted in an offer to have an experienced investigator of financial matters look into Mrs. Wellborn's sources of income, and for Colonel Zanzinger himself to look into her Danish connections.

The next stop for James, before returning home for supper with his family and resting before going to Franklin Court in the middle of the night, was the Southwark Theater. There he hoped to speak with Elizabeth Swaddling, a seamstress for The American Company that performed at the Southwark, and with Rowena Henderson, a niece of the Company's founding manager who was an actress in the troupe and also in charge of scenery for its productions. These were the two persons at the Southwark who were closest to Billy Best when he worked there as his mother's dresser, according to James's information from Rebecca Wellborn's maid Celta.

The theater was a two-and-a-half story building, the foundation and first floor of which were of brick, and the upper story and a half were of wood. It also had a wooden cupola to circulate air through the building. The theater was 95 feet long and 50 feet wide, and was one of the earliest theaters built in America. It had been constructed more than two decades before the war and had been located just beyond Philadelphia's southernmost limits to evade the laws on theatrical performances within the city limits, which the Quakers imposed when they had full control of both the Pennsylvania assembly and the city government.

After tying Jenny in front, James went up the building's four curving stone steps to its wide, two-part door, both halves of which were painted a vivid red. Opening the right half of the door, he went in to inquire if the friends of Billy Best he wanted to speak with were available and was told they were both on the premises, engaged in preparations for *The Prince of Parthia*, to be performed at the mansion-house of Mr. and Mrs. Robert Morris for the private entertainment of General Washington, two days hence. Elizabeth Swaddling was sewing costumes and Rowena Henderson was painting sets. Even though such details of the production were still being attended to, the Morrises had already sent out their invitations to the play.

James was told he would find the seamstress in a small room off the back of the stage.

Eliza Swaddling did not put aside the garment she was sewing when James introduced himself to her, but merely looked up at him. Because she was so concentrated on her work, he did not show her the paper signed by Washington directing people to cooperate with him in his inquiries.

The seamstress was in her mid-thirties and had glossy black hair, dark-blue eyes, and a pox-marked complexion. She seemed to James to have a cheerful disposition.

"I'm looking into the disappearance of Billy Best, Mrs. Swaddling," James began. "I understand you and he were particular friends. I'm hoping you can tell me what the state of his mind was when he disappeared five days ago. Would you say something was bothering him the day he vanished? And, if so, what was it?"

"Aye, Billy is the friendly sort," Elizabeth Swaddling replied, "as sweet and handsome a lad as could be, who before he got the job at the political Convention in the State House was often among us here at the Southwark on account of his mother. Everyone likes him. His disappearance is causing fear that he may have met with violence. As to whether anything was disturbing him when he vanished, I couldn't say. I can say he didn't seem to be worried, though he did seem a bit broody, perhaps. He came by to get his mother that day."

"Did you hear him say or see him do anything out of the ordinary in the days before he disappeared?"

"Can't say as I did. No, Sir."

"You know Billy's mother. What's your opinion of her?"

"Miss Rebecca? She's a fine player and a fine lady. None finer."

With that, James thanked Eliza Swaddling for speaking with him and left her to finish her work without further disturbance from him.

Rowena Henderson turned out to be an older woman. James encountered her working with a Philadelphia artist named Thomas Braithwaite. They were painting a large street scene showing a triumphal parade of soldiers marching down an ancient street behind a chariot, and having many spectators on both sides of the street and atop the flat roofs of the houses beside the street. James had Mrs. Henderson read his commission from Washington, and after she read it she invited him to go with her "where we can have a quiet talk," and told her fellow worker she would be back as soon as she could.

As they crossed the large plaza in front of the Southwark Theater to the Tea & Coffee Company, the actress-scene painter said Billy's disappearance had been a troubling occurrence for her, and she was glad to know "a serious person" was looking into the matter.

Once they were settled at a table in the tea and coffee shop and had given their orders, Rowena Henderson asked James how she could help him. He asked her for her opinion of Billy's disappearance.

She responded, "I think Billy would never have left his mother without telling her where he was going and how long it would be before his return. Once, when he was young, it's true he ran away to join the Army as a drummer boy. But that was when he didn't know any better. Since he's become a young man he's been as dutiful and attentive a son as Rebecca could hope to have.

"My belief, Captain Jamison, is that Billy's been kidnapped by a man named Declan O'Cormick, who's been after his mother for years, a man who owns brick kilns and has the kind of friends who—judged by their behavior when they're together with him at the Theater—would help him do that. Whenever she's in a play, McCormick and his two chums show up in his box, which is nearest the stage, to inspect her. He wants to force Rebecca to be his inamorata by threatening to harm Billy. That's the way Rebecca sees it. She's told me that herself, and I think she's right. The man seems frantic to have her.

"But I'm not as sure as Rebecca is that Billy's safe in Declan O'Cormick's hands. I think Billy may already have met with violence and could in fact be dead."

"You know this man O'Cormick, then, Mrs. Henderson?"

"I've never spoken with him, but I've seen him at the Theater, always in the company of the same pair of men. Rebecca told me his name and that he owns brick kilns. Mrs. Wellborn and I are on intimate terms, Captain Jamison. We've known each other since before she came to Philadelphia."

"Oh, tell me about that," James urged. "Where did you know her in England and when did she arrive in Philadelphia?"

"Oh, it wasn't in England that we met," Mrs. Henderson answered.

"Where was it?"

"Meg doesn't like people discussing her past, Captain Jameson. If you don't mind, I'd rather not say anything more on that subject. I've already told you more than I should have. She frowns on people talking about her past."

James responded to this by saying, "I remind you, Madam, of the signature on the paper I showed you, and which you read. Would you like to read it again? General Washington has commissioned me to find Billy and admonishes residents of Philadelphia to provide me whatever information I may request. You reside in Philadelphia, I believe."

Rowena Henderson frowned and looked grave as James said this, and nodded in acknowledgment of the truth of what he said.

"How and when did you meet the woman who calls herself Rebecca Wellborn?" James persisted.

"It was the summer of 1767, on a ship called *The Swift Hope*, out of Kingston, Jamaica. The American Company was returning to Philadelphia from Jamaica by way of Santo Domingo, a port on the south coast of Hispaniola. Meg was sixteen. I was in my thirties."

"Rebecca Wellborn is not of English origin?"

"If by that you mean was she born and bred in England, she is not. But her father is the fourth son of the Earl of Myrcia, from an ancient family in the county of England where I was born. His name is William Harold Edward Godolphin. Her mother was from highborn Anglo-Irish stock who've been in Jamaica for generations. Meg told me her family history during the first day or two of our voyage, before the ship reached Santo Domingo, when it came out that I had been born in the same English county her father came from.

"Meg's birthplace was Elderholm, her father's sugar plantation on Jamaica's north coast, which came to him as her mother's dowry when he married her mother. Meg's mother died giving birth to her, and Meg was given her mother's Christian names, Margaret Amanda. Rebecca Wellborn is a stage name."

"So how did she come to be on a ship out of Kingston, Jamaica, bound for Philadelphia with a company of English players?" James asked. "You say you were a member of this troupe?"

"Yes. The American Company had been performing plays in Jamaica, and we were returning to Philadelphia to try our luck again in America. Meg was running away from her father's second wife and her two daughters. Without giving me particulars, she said her mother by marriage and her two stepsisters were intolerable to her. So she decided to run away to America.

"To pay her passage and that of her maid Celta on *The Swift Hope*, she used a small inheritance from her mother, which had just come to her when she turned sixteen. Celta always seemed to me more like a protective older sister to Meg than a servant, and after a few days on the ship I noticed a physical resemblance between them. Something about the forehead and the shape of the face, although I've never mentioned it.

"Meg told me she had bribed the captain of *The Swift Hope* to keep Celta and her out of sight until the ship cleared Kingston, in case her father sent men searching for her. She was prudent and strong-willed even at the age of sixteen."

"There's more to the story, I suppose."

"The main part of it, Captain. In Santo Domingo, two new passengers came on board *The Swift Hope*. A Danish nobleman only three years older than Meg, with his tutor and traveling companion.

"We learned that Johan's father was an earl in Denmark. He had been visiting relatives in St. Croix which, as you undoubtedly know, Captain, is a Danish possession in the Caribbean, a bit to the east of Hispaniola. He'd taken passage on our ship to visit a cousin in Philadelphia whom he'd never met."

"The young Danish nobleman's family name was Griffenfeld," James announced.

"It was. How did you know?" Rowena Henderson asked, startled.

"And he and your friend Margaret Godolphin fell in love," James replied, ignoring the question.

"Deeply in love. I've never seen anything like it. It was as if you were watching some unstoppable process of nature, like a sheet of water falling off a high cliff or the disc of the sun rising above the horizon. They tried not to touch in the presence of others. But if they did, or even looked at one another, it was like two persons merging into one."

"I suppose from their profound attraction to each other Billy Best was born," James Jamison said.

"I think so. I didn't see Meg for quite a while after The American Company landed in Philadelphia from Jamaica. She left *The Swift Hope* with Celta and the two Danes as soon as the health inspector cleared the ship. The four of them and their baggage piled into the biggest of the coaches that met the ship and away they went to the home of Johan Griffenfeld's cousin.

"I ran into Meg on the street a year or so later. She was with Celta, who was carrying this darling infant boy in her arms. Johan and his tutor were nowhere to be seen, and I didn't ask where they were. Nor did Meg offer an explanation.

"I haven't told you yet that on our way up to Philadelphia from Jamaica we were rehearsing a new play, and that the actress in the main feminine role had been incapacitated by severe seasickness from the start of the voyage. The manager of the Company, who was my uncle, asked Meg to read the part because she'd expressed an interest in our work and was so beautiful, and because Johan encouraged her. Meg showed a natural aptitude for the stage, particularly in memorizing lines and delivering them with éclat.

"So when I told my uncle I had run into Meg on the street and spoken with her, he recalled her. He was in need of a talented actress, especially one of exceptional beauty, and he had me take an offer to her, inviting her to join our company. She accepted, and everyone in The American Company was delighted to have her. Meg's success onstage at the Southwark was immediate and large.

"My uncle's the one who, with her permission, I'm sure—perhaps at her request—gave her an English background. Meg probably wanted to conceal her Jamaican origin."

James commented, "Considering the sort of attention Declan O'Cormick has been paying her, maybe she's been too successful on stage for her own good and the good of her son."

At Franklin Court Again
Chapter XII

THE CITY WATCHMEN were calling, "One o'clock and clear skies!" when James appeared at Franklin Court in the small hours of the night. After being admitted into the mansion-house by Mr. Mahoney, he asked him to please go out to Fourth Street where he had tied Jenny and bring her around to Dr. Franklin's stables to keep her safe from horse stealers, while he went up to the library to see Dr. Franklin.

As he entered the library, James saw the good Doctor, as always, writing at his worktable, and went to him. He told his host of having asked Mr. Mahoney to bring his mare into Franklin's stables and said he hoped it had not been presumptuous of him to make the request.

"Perfectly all right. Only a prudent measure in the middle of the night while horse stealing is on the rise in Philadelphia, especially with an attractive animal like your Virginia mare.

"On a quite different note, James, I invite you to partake of the opened bottle of Ligneville here on my table, in celebration of the extraordinarily swift progress of your investigation. Please serve yourself. Also help yourself to the crackers, cheese, and Virginia ham on the plate. A shipment of this wine, from my friend Madame Helvetius, arrived two days ago. It is from her ancestral vineyards. A long while ago, I wrote to her saying one of my closest associates had become an enthusiastic drinker of her family's wine. She says this is the best vintage she's had in many years."

"You may, James, if you would be so kind, pour me some of the only pleasing liquid my health allows me to drink these days, my bottled French spring water."

After these refreshments had been poured and James with his customary glass of Ligneville in front of him, had taken his customary chair across from Dr. Franklin, his host asked him to please tell him everything he'd learned since writing his first report.

"Well, this morning, in speaking with Abraham Yarden, I found out several things related to the gold ring Billy's mother recently gave him. First of all, it is the signet ring of a prominent family of Danish noblemen named Griffenfeld, hence, the bas-relief of a griffin carved on the ring's flat upper side. The family has for generations been the Jarls, or Earls, of Jutland in Denmark. According to Mr. Yarden's book on the Danish nobility, the Griffenfeld family also holds the title of Count Griffenfeld.

"It may be significant that only a day or so before his disappearance Billy went to see Yarden to inquire about the kind of ring his mother had given him. He received from the pawnbroker the same information I was given this morning, including the meaning of the ring's Latin motto, '*Ad finem*'. Yarden said it means "loyalty in battle, even to death." The Christian name of the present holder of the titles Earl of Jutland and Count Griffenfeld is Vilhelm Peder Anders Griffenfeld."

"You're to be congratulated," Dr. Franklin said, "for discovering that the beautiful English-born mother of Billy Best has had an intimate connection with a family of high Danish nobility, because that is the only way she could have come to possess the signet ring of a Danish Earl. Rings like that are never given to persons not born into the direct line of descent in a noble family. Nor are they for sale."

"That is what Mr. Yarden also says, Dr. Franklin."

"I don't believe I've ever told you, James, that I have a particular fondness for the Danish throne because, of all the European monarchs, only Denmark's king found it fitting to invite me to dine with him when I was beginning to become known in Europe for my research on the mysteries of electricity."

"Another discovery I made this afternoon, Dr. Franklin—this one at the Southwark Theater—is that Mrs. Wellborn is not from England. Her father was born there, but she wasn't. Mr. Mahoney was deliberately misled when you sent him to Southwark to inquire into Billy's family background before appointing him to the Convention Guard. Mr. Mahoney naturally believed what he was told, in reply to his questions—that Mrs. Wellborn was a native of England—and naturally passed that information on to you. I, however, spoke with someone at the Southwark Theater who had Mrs. Wellborn's history from her own lips. My informant was another actress, named Rowena Henderson, who sailed with Mrs. Wellborn on the ship from Jamaica that brought her to Philadelphia. And despite some initial resistance on Mrs. Henderson's part, I finally extracted from her everything she knew of Mrs. Wellborn's background.

"She was born into a wealthy Anglo-Irish family on the island of Jamaica, on her father's sugar plantation. He is the fourth son of an English Earl who went to Jamaica seeking his fortune. He found it by marrying into an established Anglo-Irish family on that island who gave their daughter a sugar plantation as a dowry. Mrs. Wellborn's mother died giving birth to her, and her father, whose name is William Godolphin, remarried and his second wife brought two daughters into the family.

"Mrs. Henderson and another informant also told me Mrs. Wellborn's baptismal name is Margaret Amanda, the same as her mother's, and that by the time she was sixteen, she felt so powerful an antipathy toward her stepmother and her step-sisters that she determined to run away to Philadelphia, using a small inheritance her mother had bestowed on her. She had just turned the age at which the inheritance came to her. On the ship that carried her and her maid from Kingston to Philadelphia was a troupe of English actors, The American Company, to which Mrs. Henderson belonged, which is how she met Rebecca Wellborn, born Margaret Amanda Godolphin."

"Did the woman you spoke to tell you who Billy's father was?" Franklin inquired.

"Her information has cast decisive light, Dr. Franklin, on the question of the identity of Billy's father, though not on his present whereabouts."

"Please tell me what your informant told you."

"Mrs. Henderson said the ship on which she and Margaret Godolphin sailed stopped at the port of Santo Domingo, on the south side of the island of Hispaniola, a few days after they left Jamaica. There, the nineteen-year-old heir of the Griffenfeld family and his tutor came on board as passengers for Philadelphia. When this young man and the sixteen-year-old Anglo-Irish beauty from Jamaica saw each other, they fell instantly and desperately in love. Their mutual attraction, Mrs. Henderson said, was like seeing two persons merging into one."

"And when did this chance encounter between the young man from Denmark and the young woman from Jamaica occur?"

"I believe Mrs. Henderson said it was in 1767, if memory serves me."

"What was the name of the young Danish nobleman?"

"Johan. Johan Griffenfeld. Mrs. Henderson also likened

seeing the attraction between Margaret Godolphin and Johan Griffenfeld to watching gravity bring a piece of water all the way down from a high cliff."

"This happened in 1767, you say..." Dr. Franklin pensively remarked, and after a slight pause he smilingly added, "That would account for why Rebecca Wellborn, or Margaret Amanda Godolphin, gave her nineteen-year-old son William the gold signet ring with the bas-relief of a griffin carved on its flat upper surface when she did. This year, 1787, marks the twentieth anniversary of her meeting Billy's father. This year Billy attains the age his father had when Mrs. Wellborn met him.

"What you've said, James, also explains, I think, why Mrs. Wellborn bestowed the name William on him, which is the name of his two grandfathers. Moreover, her history suggests why she always refers to her son as William and never 'Billy,' as most of us do. Apparently to Mrs. Wellborn the more formal appellation 'William' is appropriate in referring to a young man with the blood of English and Danish earls in his veins.

"What Abraham Yarden told you, James, of the noble Danish family Billy's father came from, information imparted to Billy shortly before his disappearance, of which the young man had had no previous knowledge, particularly not of the Griffenfeld family motto, '*Ad finem*,' may have inspired Billy to defend his mother's honor against the man who was insulting her."

"So you think the young Danish nobleman Johan Griffenfeld gave the young runaway from Jamaica, Margaret Godolphin, his gold signet ring as a pledge of his troth, Dr. Franklin?"

"I am most definitely of that opinion."

"Then why didn't Griffenfeld keep his pledge? Why didn't he marry Meg Godolphin? Why has she lived forlorn these past twenty years, with only the memory of their passionate attachment and the presence of their son to comfort her?"

"The marriages of noblemen are seldom uncomplicated, James. The answer to the question you've just posed remains to be discovered, but the most plausible view of it may be that between when Johan and Margaret conceived their son and the baby's birth, Johan Griffenfeld died. It is, of course, also possible that Griffenfeld's father forbad his son and heir to marry the young woman from Jamaica on pain of disinheritance. I tend, however, to doubt that Johan Griffenfeld would have been deterred from marrying Margaret Godolphin by such a pronouncement from his father, the Earl, given the fact that he gave Miss Godolphin his gold signet ring as a pledge of his word, and the further fact that Margaret's father was the fourth son of an English earl. Moreover, the powerful attraction these two young people of noble descent manifested for each other, which you have discovered, James, suggests they were both unusually strong-willed, which may have been one of the things that attracted them to each other.

"What happened to Johan Griffenfeld to keep him from fulfilling his pledge to Margaret Godolphin, a pledge whose strength is shown by her still possessing his signet ring twenty years later to give to their son, is an unanswered question.

"Your swift investigation into Billy Best's life, James, demonstrates, I think, beyond any reasonable doubt that the Constitutional Convention has little or nothing to fear from Billy or his mother. The discoveries you've made with such speed suggest a personal matter rather than any political consideration has precipitated the disappearance of Billy Best.

"We must, of course, continue to try to recover Mr. Gerry's wayward letter, because not knowing its whereabouts represents a continual source of anxiety for us.

"You mentioned in your written report, James, that you

want to use Billy's dog to trace his movements. Please explain that to me, if you would."

James replied, "Dr. Franklin, I spoke with Mrs. Wellborn's maid Celta this morning at Mr. Yarden's pawnshop. My sense that there was a difference of judgment between her view of Billy's disappearance and that of her mistress was correct. They both believe the young man has been abducted by a man named Declan O'Cormick, who is fascinated by Mrs. Wellborn's beauty and wants her to be his mistress. He sent her a letter threatening to harm her son if she continues to refuse his advances. Celta gave me this man's first name this morning, and Mrs. Henderson provided his surname this afternoon.

"Where Mrs. Wellborn and her maid disagree is on the question of whether Billy is in danger from O'Cormick. Celta thinks, as do I, that O'Cormick poses an immanent danger to Billy. Celta tells me Mrs. Wellborn is of the opinion that O'Cormick will not harm Billy. She opposes doing anything that might make O'Cormick feel threatened and provoke him to take some rash action. Her plan is to follow a policy of patient waiting."

"I've heard of this Irish brick maker, James. He is becoming wealthy by making good quality bricks in large amounts and selling them below the price other brick makers charge for wares of lesser quality.

"So, what is it you want to do with Billy's terrier? I've seen the handsome little fellow with Billy every day, by the door going into the Convention. He seems intelligent and alert."

"I've arranged for Celta to meet me tomorrow morning in front of the Indian Queen Hotel, which was the last place Billy and his dog were seen together. She has agreed to bring a piece of Billy's clothing for Kemper—which is the dog's name— to smell when she gives him the command to find Billy. That way, I'm hoping Kemper will get the idea to take us to where he and Billy went together last Friday. What do you think of this notion of mine, Dr. Franklin?"

"It would not be a waste of time, James. It constitutes an admirable experiment using the superior sense of smell canines possess, along with their loyalty and affection for their masters. I think it's an experiment that can be engaged in with some expectation of success."

Benjamin Franklin then wanted to know what Colonel Zanzinger had told James regarding Mrs. Wellborn.

"He says he himself once had suspicions she might be spying for the British, " James answered, "and he therefore looked into her conduct. But he found no evidence of espionage. It is Colonel Zanzinger's view that it's unlikely Billy's disappearance has any connection to international intrigue. He also informed me he recently received two unsigned letters in the same handwriting accusing Mrs. Wellborn of spying for the British. These letters came shortly before Billy disappeared. But when he looked into the accusations, he found no substantiating evidence for their credibility. He believes Mrs. Wellborn guiltless of wrongdoing. He suspects the sender of these two letters may be the person responsible for Billy's disappearance.

"When I told Colonel Zanzinger of my observation that Mrs. Wellborn is living beyond the income she could earn as an actress, he promised to have a trusted assistant of his, experienced in the investigation of financial transactions, look into the matter. He also told me he would make inquiries among Danish friends of his in Philadelphia, regarding this lady's association with Danish matters. I'm persuaded, by what Zanzinger has said regarding Mrs. Wellborn, and the conviction with which he has said it, that Mrs. Wellborn is not engaged in any plot against American interests."

"I think what you've found out, James, explains how

Mrs. Wellborn came to possess the signet ring of a Danish nobleman, but we still do not know why the young man failed to keep his pledge to marry her, why she has lived forlorn these past twenty years.

"Your inquiries have shown, I think, beyond any reasonable doubt, the standard of proof in trials by juries, that the Constitutional Convention has little or nothing to fear from the disappearance of William Best as the carrier of Mr. Gerry's letter. The young man appears innocent of wanting to betray the Convention, and I will report that surmise, and my reasons for it, to Washington, Hamilton, and Madison, the other members of the ad hoc committee for whom you are acting.

"It appears to me, James, from what you've told me, that Billy's delivery of a letter fraught with volatile political information got tangled up in his recent discovery of his connection to a noble Danish family, through his mother, and his idea of that family's lofty tradition of honor. Having learned from the deskman at the Indian Queen that in order to give Mr. Mason the letter from Mister Gerry's he would have to wait an indeterminate length of time for Mr. Mason's return to the hotel, Billy decided to take care of some personal business involving his mother's honor. His just-discovered kinship with a family of Danish noblemen may have prompted him to consider this necessary. He seems to have thought that what he felt he had to do to defend his mother's honor would not interfere with his delivery of Gerry's letter."

"In suggesting, Dr. Franklin, that neither Billy nor his mother have been involved in political intrigue, you are not implying that we have no obligation to find out what has happened to him, are you?" James asked.

"No indeed. You must continue your investigation, James, with all possible speed. Mr. Gerry's letter still needs to be found so that there can be no doubt of who has it and the information it contains. When that is accomplished, if it can be, then all apprehension that Gerry's letter might fall into the wrong hands will end.

"Let me add to what I've just said, James, that although I approve of your experiment of using Billy's dog to discover where he went after leaving the Indian Queen Hotel, I oppose you performing the experiment supported only by Mrs. Wellborn's maid. No one knows where the dog will take you. You should go armed tomorrow with pistol and ball, and I would advise you to take another man, also armed, with you. If you accept my advice, the other man should, I think, be a member of the Convention Guard; and the logical choice would be the Guardsman who worked most closely with Billy, Noah Day. His feelings have probably been thoroughly aroused by Billy's disappearance, and he is therefore the member of the Guard most motivated to want to find him.

"If you agree with this thinking, I will, with your permission, send Mr. Mahoney to Sergeant Corbin early tomorrow morning, to have Noah Day join you in front of the Indian Queen Hotel at ten, with his musket."

"If you think two men are needed tomorrow, Dr. Franklin," James replied, "I, of course, defer to your judgment. I certainly agree with your choice of Noah Day as the other man."

Before he left, James said he was curious to know if Dr. Franklin had been invited to attend the performance of *The Prince of Parthia* in honor of General Washington, which was scheduled to be performed by The American Company in the ballroom of Mr. and Mrs. Morris' mansion-house.

"Yes, I have received an invitation, but am not inclined to attend," his host replied.

The Kemper Experiment
Chapter XIII

AS JAMES MADE his way home from Franklin Court, the neighborhood watchmen that Benjamin Franklin, as a young shopkeeper, had organized and raised money to fund, were proclaiming, "Three o'clock and starry skies!" as they made their rounds.

Because he had given his mount a good currying before his late night conference with Dr. Franklin, when he reached home and stabled Jenny and removed her gear, he had only to dry her sweat-dampened withers and back with handfuls of hay and bring a bucket of fresh water to her stall.

He managed to get undressed and into bed without waking Livy or disturbing the baby's sleep, and he himself fell into a peaceful sleep immediately upon finishing his prayers.

He slept soundly until eight thirty, the hour at which he had asked Livy, the evening before, to wake him. After shaving, dressing, and eating the breakfast Livy prepared for him, James saddled Jenny and rode into town, arriving in front of the Indian Queen Hotel a little before ten. Noah Day and Celta were already there, waiting for him.

The hotel's gaudily dressed doorman and greeter was making a fuss over Kemper, petting him and talking to him.

James wondered as he tied Jenny to an iron hitching ring in front of the hotel, if the Negro doorman was doing this because the dog was on a leash held by a good-looking woman of mixed Negro and white ancestry.

The harness the twenty-five-pound terrier was in had been improvised by Celta from a length of stout four-strand twine.

One end of the twine had been untwisted and the unraveling of the twine stopped by tying a knot in it; then a pair of the cord's strands had been tied to make two holes for the dog's forelegs; the two other strands were tied across the small dog's chest. Over his back, a separate piece of the same twine joined the two leg holes, and a ten-foot piece of the twine was attached to the harness for a leash, with a peg at the end of the leash as a grip.

Celta noticed James regarding her handiwork, and said, "Widdout knowin' what be at da end o' da road Kempah be takin' us on, Cap'n Jamison, I want tah be able tah control 'im if 'e want tah give someone, or anoddah dog, a fight."

"Very sensible, Celta, and nicely done," James observed. "Did you have any trouble getting Kemper out of the house without your mistress trying to stop you?"

"No, Sah. I jes' tell Meg, I's feelin' squeamsy-like' an' tink I walk up to da Market to get a dose of somet'in' tah settle me stomach. I be takin' Kempah along wit me fah da walk. Meg, she go ovah tah da Teeahter tah get ready fah da play dat goin' to be put on fah Gen'l Washington, so I jus' put da harness on Kempah, an' we leff da house wid no trouble. Kempah an' me, we be gettin' along 'cause we be partial tah each uddah. Dis be da firs' time I 'as charge o' him outa da 'ouse."

James then greeted Noah Day, in his Pennsylvania militiaman's uniform carrying his musket, the kind the Convention Guard used, with a long bayonet fixed to the end of its long barrel.

"Your musket is a conspicuous weapon, Noah. It will let whoever we encounter know at once that we're armed and prepared to use force if necessary. You understand, I suppose, what we're trying to accomplish?"

"We're trying to find Billy," Noah Day responded. "It's been nigh onto a week since he went missing, Captain Jamison. I'm all for findin' out today what's happened to him, one way or the other. Myself, I don't expect there's much chance of findin' him alive an' in good condition."

"Celta, please tell Kemper what we want him to do."

Billy's second mother since his birth, and the small dog's usual provider of his daily ration of food, took from a pocket of her skirt a neck cloth belonging to Billy that hadn't been laundered since he'd worn it. Celta knelt alongside Kemper, who was looking at her attentively with his intelligent black eyes set in his handsome, white-furred face, and holding the neck cloth close to his nose, she said, "Billy! Where Billy be, Kempah? Find Billy! Find 'im!" The little dog's stubby tail began moving side to side, and he made an eager half-turn of his body, accompanied by a gruff sound as though saying something. "Find Billy, Kempah!" Celta ordered again, and stood up. Kemper responded with a single bark and another circling motion; then he took off, pulling Celta forward at a rapid pace north on Fourth Street. It was a good thing Celta had made the harness. Otherwise, she and her companions couldn't have kept up with the eager dog.

At the pace Kemper set, nearby Market Street was quickly crossed, and the university's multistoried building on the west side of Fourth was also quickly passed, and since Kemper did not slacken his pace, he soon pulled Celta and the two men beyond Mulberry Street, where Abraham Yarden conducted his pawn business. After passing Mulberry, the little squad of four passed the entrance to Appletree Alley, the elegant short street Tamas Zanzinger lived on, and then crossed medium-wide Cherry Street and then wider Sassafras Street.

Beyond Sassafras they came to Vine, the east-west avenue separating the central part of the city from Spring Garden, the city's large northern residential district of attractive homes on large lots set among orchards and cultivated fields. They were now well away from the river with its miles of wharves and the working-class area north of the wharves known as the Northern Liberties, where the Jamisons had their glass factory. At Vine, the straight-as-a-string Fourth Street, one of Philadelphia's major north-south avenues, angled off to the northwest.

Where this change in direction occurred, the side of Fourth next to Spring Garden took on an entirely bucolic aspect of uncultivated fields, before crossing Callowhill Street, the maiden name of William Penn's second wife. After Callowhill, which was the city's last east-west avenue, Kemper began panting loudly, though he was not out of breath since there was no lessening of his pace. Rather, the panting seemed to indicate his excitement.

James, Celta, and Noah noticed the change in the dog's breathing, and Celta said, "Kempah be tryin' tah tell us sometin'!"

Beyond Callowhill, the now unpaved Fourth Street crossed, by means of a culvert, the little stream called Pegg's Run and its boggy margins. This took the searchers to a place having scattered houses to the east, in the direction of the river, and nothing but empty fields to the west. Though it was the same street, merely going in a new direction, it now had a new designation, Germantown Road.

A little past Noble Lane, which came into Germantown Road from the east, seven shabby cottages—rural tenement houses—were crowded together in a row on tiny lots on a nameless dirt road that went off to the west in a straight line as far as the eye could see. A few hundred feet beyond this long east-west dirt road, the angle of the road they were on put them behind the seven tenement cottages, and the searchers came upon a large brick kiln and its chimney, with a clay pit and two outbuildings next to it.

Kemper continued fifty feet past these structures, then left the Germantown Road and entered a property having two brick kilns and their chimneys on the same side of the road as the first kiln. These two kilns were set much farther back from the road than the single kiln, and had four outbuildings and a much bigger clay pit associated with them. Kemper moved into this compound at the same ear-flapping pace he'd maintained since leaving the Indian Queen Hotel and pulled Celta straight to the kiln whose chimney was billowing smoke. Kemper stopped beside that kiln and looked up at Celta, still panting.

No one was in sight. Nonetheless, Noah swung his musket off his shoulder, where he had been carrying it by its strap, and held it at the ready, peering around expectantly at these buildings. A substantial house was visible off to the west a hundred yards or so from the kilns, along with their outbuildings, and the clay pits.

At that moment, a fair-haired, strong-looking man of above-average height, wearing a workman's leather apron, came around the corner of the kiln whose chimney was spouting the roiling smoke.

As soon as the man appeared, Kemper began barking furiously and lunging at him to the limit of his leash, so that it strained Celta's strength to control him.

Faced with this loud display of hostility, the man instantly turned and hurried back the way he had come and disappeared. Even after he could no longer be seen, Kemper kept up his loud barking and attempts to close with the retreating man. For so small a dog, the terrier's strength was extraordinary and his bark remarkably deep and fierce.

James took the dog's leash from Celta and said, "Stay here!" to her and Noah. With Kemper pulling hard every step of the way, James and the dog went after the man in the leather apron. But when they went around the corner of the building, no one was in sight, and James returned to his companions, dragging the still barking dog, who wanted to continue the pursuit. James reported to Celta and Noah the man's disappearance.

It seemed Kemper had conducted them to a place where he had been with Billy and that he recognized the man in the leather apron.

James did not know what to do next, and it was clear his companions expected him to decide.

As he pondered the situation with Celta and Noah looking at him expectantly, a second man of the same general appearance as the first, but without the leather apron, came around the same corner of the kiln as the first man had come and approached James, who was the obvious leader of this trio of strangers. The man asked what their business was.

"I'm Captain James Jamison. Are these Declan O'Cormick's kilns and is that his house over there? What's your name?"

"I'm John Rankin. I oversee tings for da man who owns dese kilns and dat 'ouse over dere. Also da kiln afore dese, which we call 'Kiln One' because it was da firs' one Declan operatcd. Dese we call 'Kiln Two' and 'Kiln T'ree'. Mr. O'Cormick has recently bought anodder pair o' side-by-side kilns where Ridge Road leaves Nint' Street, a quarter-mile west o' here and a bit sout'.

"But Declan ain't here now. He's off wit' a friend lookin' for a good supply o' da good-burnin' hard coal dey calls ant'racite, to fire 'is kilns. Why youse wanta speak wit' Declan?"

James did not answer the question but asked one of his own. "Who was the strong-looking, fair-haired, tall man in a leather apron who was just here and ran off as soon as he saw us?"

"That was me brudder, Michael. He's da one tol' me de t'ree o' youse was here wit' yer dog."

"Why did he run off like that without speaking with us?"

"He said da dog an' da man wit' de gun scared him. What's dis all about?"

"Where do you live?"

"You passed me house comin' here if youse come from da city, as I s'pose yeh did. It's da one at de nigh end o' da line o' seven cottages on seven little lots. What do youse want wit' O'Cormick?"

"We want to discuss with him a friend of ours who's gone missing," James answered. "We have reason to think our friend came here last Friday, the 22nd of June, five days ago. When did you say Mr. O'Cormick left on his trip to find an anthracite coal mine to supply his kilns with fuel?"

"Da 23rd."

"And when is he coming back?"

"Da day after Independence Day."

"My search for the missing man is being made under the highest authority," James said, and handed John Rankin his commission signed by George Washington.

After reading the paper and handing it back, Rankin said, "I don' understand. What connection does your friend have wit' Washington an' his Convention?"

"He helps keep the Convention free of intruders. When he came here, he was wearing the uniform of a Pennsylvania militiaman, like this man," James said, nodding at Noah Day, "and had this dog with him."

John Rankin asked, "What proof do you have the man who's missin' come here?"

Listening to this exchange and remembering the words of James's commission, Celta spoke up. "Where in Cap'n Jamison's pehpah do it say he haf tah answer questions by people he talkin' to? It don't!"

"She's right, Mr. Rankin. I'm authorized to make inquiries, not answer them. You say no one in the uniform of a Pennsylvania militiaman accompanied by this dog was on this property on the 22nd of June?"

"That's what I'm sayin', Captain."

"I don't believe you."

"Well, yah kin believe what yah want. I'm tellin' yah I don' know nuttin' o' your friend what's gone missin'."

"If you want to help me and General Washington, Mr. Rankin, bring your brother here. I want to ask him what he knows. If you've nothing to hide, and your master, Declan O'Cormick, is an honest man, you'll bring your brother here." John Rankin was silent a moment; then left to get his brother Michael.

As soon as he had gone, James told Noah and Celta that he would question the Rankin brothers inside the kiln building they were next to, and that the two of them, with Kemper, should search the property's other kiln and four outbuildings. He handed Kemper's leash back to Celta.

In a few minutes, John Rankin returned with the man who had caused Kemper's violent reactions. The sight of Michael Rankin this time, however, made the terrier only utter a steady low growl and show his teeth while staring intently at the man. James asked John Rankin if they might go to his office for their talk, away from the dog, and was told that that would be good. The Rankin brothers, followed by James, went around the corner of the building and through a door on the other side of it. When they had gone, Noah and Celta took Kemper to search the other buildings on the property.

The large kiln inside the other big building occupied almost its entire interior. A wooden walkway around its upper part, reached by wooden stairs at each end of the walkway, allowed the kiln to be tended when it was charged with "green" or clay bricks that had yet to be hardened by heat. When Noah looked in the seven iron doors at the kiln's base, through which it was fired, he and Celta saw there were no stacks or clamps of unfired green bricks in the kiln being hardened. Nor did the building have any separate rooms that needed to be searched.

Two of the outbuildings were being used to store fuel for the kilns. One was full of oak billets, the other with coal. The remaining two outbuildings, which were much smaller, were being used to store spades for digging clay, wheelbarrows for hauling clay and fuel, the metal-reinforced wooden molds for shaping clay into green bricks, and trowels for trimming excess clay from the molds.

While Celta and Noah conducted these searches, James was sitting with the Rankin brothers in John Rankin's small, crude office. In going to the office, James saw two men in leather aprons shoveling coal through the iron doors of the kiln's furnace, fuel which two other men were bringing to them in wheelbarrows from a big pile of coal in one corner of the building.

At John Rankin's invitation, James seated himself at the desk in the cramped office, with Michael Rankin in front of him seated in the only other chair in the room, and John Rankin leaning against the wall behind his brother. James Jamison then asked the brother leaning against the wall, "So, you oversee Mr. O'Cormick's brick-making enterprises from this office?"

"I do."

"And what do you do, Mr. Rankin?" This question he directed at Michael Rankin.

"I help me brudder, goin' 'ere an' dere wit' 'is orders an' seein' 'ow da firin' is goin' if we're makin' good bricks. I also take care o' problems wit' da workers an' sees if dey're doin' as dey're tol'."

"And where do you live?"

"In me brudder's 'ouse, wit' 'im and our 'ousekeeper, Grace Noles."

"I take it you both came to America from Ireland."

"County Derry, Declan's 'ome county. Michael 'ere came over da pond jus' two years back. I come twenty years ago."

"Are any of the other workers Irish?"

"All but two. Most from Derry. Declan pays der passage to America after dey signs der indentures in da ol' country to work for 'im eight years. Room an' board. No wages. Da indenture system is makin' Declan rich, but it's also givin' poor, ignorant Irishmen a chance to make der fortunes after dey works off der contracts."

"Your brother John has answered this question, Mr. Rankin," James said. "Did a handsome young man with blond hair in the uniform of a Pennsylvania militiaman, and accompanied by the dog that barked at you as soon as he saw you just now, come by here last Friday?"

Michael Rankin gave his answer instantly. "No."

"You're sure? You don't have to think about it?"

"I'm sure."

"Were you working here last Friday?"

"I'm workin' 'ere ev'ry day 'cept da Lord's day."

"I thank you, Mr. Rankin, for your time, and you, too, Mr. Rankin." And with that, James got up and left the office, nodding at the two brothers without shaking their hands, and went in search of Noah and Celta. He found them waiting for him where he'd left them.

"Any results?" James asked.

"No sign of Billy," Noah answered.

"How did Kemper behave?"

"No barkin'," Celta replied.

"Let's go over to O'Cormick's house and see what his servants there have to say," James said.

As he and his companions approached Declan O'Cormick's home along the fine-gravel-and-coarse-sand path from the kilns, they saw large beds of red, white, pink, and yellow roses in front of the house and near it on both sides of the path.

The house was of a fine pale-pink brick and had a wide, covered porch furnished with small tables, and Windsor rocking chairs that ran across the whole front of this rather imposing country mansion.

As the quartet went up the wooden steps to the porch, Noah said, "These are grand rose beds. I've never seen yellow roses."

As James rapped the door's brass knocker, Celta said, "I seen 'em afore. Da man what own dis 'ouse, 'e be sendin' me mistress big bunches o' dem."

A short, desiccated woman answered the door and solemnly inspected the man in uniform armed with musket and bayonet, the woman of mixed blood with a small white dog, and the man whose left hand was half gone and encased in a specially made black leather glove.

James asked, to see if this person would give the same answer John Rankin had given to the question of where Declan O'Cormick was,

"May I speak with Mr. O'Cormick, please?"

"He ain't here. He's off on a trip."

"Do you know where he's gone or when he'll come back?"

"Somethin' 'bout lookin' for coal of a pa'ticular kind. He'll be back the day after the Fourth, I 'spect. Least ways, that's what he said when he left. And he generally does what he says. I keep house for him."

"May I show you a paper authorizing me to make inquiries in the name of the Constitutional Convention meeting in Philadelphia? And would you please tell me your name, Mrs...?"

"I ain't no 'Mrs.' I 'uz baptized Lucinda Belacre, an' I 'spect to die Lucinda Belacre. I ain't never took no man's name in marriage, an' I never will 'cause when I was a young un, I decided bein' independent meant more to me than givin' myself permanent to a man and havin' his babies. Now, at my age, I'd be mor'n foolish to 'spect offers o' marriage, even if such nonsense appealed' to me, which it don't. That what yuh want me to read, is it?" Miss Belacre asked, nodding at the paper James held in his right hand.

He said it was, and handed the housekeeper the commission. She read its 120 words slowly and deliberately, one at a time, with her lips moving silently. It took her several minutes to complete her reading.

"Are you the only servant Mr. O'Cormick has here, Miss Belacre?"

"No, there's a cook. Esther Wallsend. Course there's Grace Noles, who's a kind o' servant."

"What do you mean?"

The diminutive housekeeper glanced at Celta before stating, "Well, I'll only be sayin' Grace comes to the house regular an' does special things for Mr. O'Cormick."

James took note of this comment on the woman Michael Rankin had identified as the housekeeper for him and his brother.

"Would you be so good as to call Mrs. Wallsend? I'd like to ask the two of you together some questions."

"What should I tell Esther you want to ask us?"

"I'll tell you when you're together. May we come in?"

Miss Belacre said he and "th' gentleman with th' gun" could come in, but not "the lady with th' dog." She didn't want "dog hair all over my parlor, 'specially not white dog hair." Noah said he'd stay on the porch with Celta.

The furniture in the parlor where James waited indicated prosperity, as did the furniture on the porch.

The housekeeper was a long time returning with the cook.

Esther Wallsend, when she was finally brought by her colleague Miss Belacre and introduced to "Captain Jamison," was not a desiccated, small woman like the housekeeper, but a woman of ample proportions, as befitted a good cook. She, too, was a spinster, James learned.

He questioned these two female servants repeatedly on whether anyone fitting Billy Best's description had come to the house five days before, in the late afternoon or early evening of Friday, June 22nd.

"You remember, Esther, that were the day you made the master that fine pot roast with onions and potatoes before he went on his trip."

"I 'member, Lucy. It were a nice dish even if I did cook it my own self."

"It were. The part of it I ate were right tasty."

"No one come by the house that day, Captain—was there, Lucy?"

"Nossiree! I'd 'a' remembered. 'Cause I'd 'a' answered th' door!"

It was after two o'clock before the searchers and Kemper got back to the Indian Queen Hotel on Fourth Street, their point of departure, and went their separate ways.

James rode over to the City Tavern to have his favorite meals, pork and turnip mash, accompanied by German beer. After he'd satisfied his hunger, he wrote in the hotel's library a summary for Dr. Franklin of the results of the experiment with Billy's dog.

The report said the terrier had gone directly and without hesitation from the Indian Queen Hotel to a property belonging to Declan O'Cormick on the Germantown Road. In describing to Dr. Franklin what had transpired during the experiment, James emphasized what each of Declan O'Cormick's servants said, particularly the information that O'Cormick had left town the day after Billy vanished. The evidence that Kemper appeared to know and was hostile to Michael Rankin was also emphasized, along with his impression that the persons in O'Cormick's employ seemed to be repeating what they'd been told to say, which was that no one of Billy's description had been on his property the day of Billy's disappearance. The report also mentioned in passing the different character Michael Rankin and O'Cormick's housekeeper had given Grace Noles.

James said it was his opinion and that of his two companions in the search that the Sheriff would have to question Declan O'Cormick as soon as he returned from his trip.

The report concluded with a request for another conference as soon as Dr. Franklin had the time for it, to discuss what should be done next in searching for Billy Best because he had now spoken to everyone on the list of names Franklin had given him.

When he went to the concealed letter drop in the west wall of Franklin Court to leave his report, James discovered that Franklin had left his invitation to *The Prince of Parthia* there, endorsed to him. Franklin's note said James ought to attend the performance in his stead to see "Mrs. Wellborn acting in a play" and that he should come to Franklin Court at one o'clock, the morning of the following day, to discuss what was to be done next in searching for William Best.

Franklin's message also notified James that Colonel Zanzinger wanted to see him at his home, so he could give him the information on Mrs. Wellborn that he and his assistant Mr. Latrobe had gathered.

The invitation to attend *The Prince of Parthia* said it would be performed in the ballroom of the mansion-house of Robert and Mary Morris on Market Street at four o'clock in the afternoon of the 28th and would include a buffet supper and a ball after the play.

James had only to think a moment before realizing he should not attend the ball since there was no invitation for Livy. The supper would be welcome, however, so he could immediately go home to get some sleep before coming back into the city to confer with Dr. Franklin at one o'clock in the morning.

More Danish Information
Chapter XIV

APPLETREE ALLEY WHERE Tamas Zanzinger lived was as quiet and sunny as it had been when James had met the Colonel, two days before—a little bit of country serenity in the center of Philadelphia. And James's knock was once again answered by the French immigrant of slight stature. The former Paris chimney sweep and Philadelphia rat catcher and jockey, now a gentlemanly assistant to Pennsylvania's chief investigator into the activities of foreign agents in America's principal city and their American sympathizers, escorted James into the Colonel's library-office looking out onto the backyard with its tall chestnut trees. Only this time Jean-Pierre Latrobe did not leave James with Colonel Zanzinger and go about his business.

"Greetings, Captain Jamison," Tamas Zanzinger said as he shook James's hand. "Jean-Pierre and I have some interesting news for you regarding your acquaintance Mrs. Wellborn. Monsieur Latrobe is the best person to inform you of what he has found out. Then I will tell you what my Danish friends in Philadelphia have told me. Jean-Pierre?"

Latrobe removed a paper from his coat and kept it in his hand for ready reference, but never had to consult it as he presented its information.

"*Oui, mon colonel.* It is my pleasure, Captain Jamison, to tell you that after no great effort I 'ave learned that Madame's income, aside from 'er earnings as an actress, which struck you as insufficient to support the manner in which she lives, can be explained. 'Er additional money 'as two sources. The older of these takes the form of quarterly payments to 'er bank in Philadelphia from a bank in Copen'agen. These transfers started in 1769, in the month of May, and are in Danish currency equivalent, per annum, to an amount a little under 700 pounds English sterling. A more recent source is payments which started three years ago in December. The source of this income is the Bank of England in Kingston on the island of Jamaica, and it is in the amount of 750 pounds annually."

Having informed James of the amounts and dates of Mrs. Wellborn's sources of income besides her income as an actress, he handed the paper he held in his hand to James with the words, "You may want to keep this for your records, *monsieur*. I 'ave made a copy of it for mine."

"Thank you for your information, Mr. Latrobe."

"It is an honor to serve you, *monsieur*." And with a graceful bow to James and a polite nod to his employer, which Colonel Zanzinger returned, Jean-Pierre Latrobe left the room.

"That was a remarkably neat and quick piece of work your man did, Colonel Zanzinger," James observed.

"I told you, Captain Jamison, Jean-Pierre is good at this sort of thing. Now you know how good. While in my employ, he has become trusted by the bankers of our city, who all know the work I do for the Commonwealth and that he is my principal assistant. But, more than that, Jean-Pierre has an inborn ability to get people to tell him what he wants to know, which is what makes him so valuable to me.

"Now, Captain Jamison, for my news. The information I've gained from my Danish friends here in Philadelphia correlates with Jean-Pierre's finding that Madame Wellborn has been in receipt of considerable sums of money from Denmark for many years. My friends know of these monies to her and say they come from the Jarl of Jutland, one of the most respected titles of nobility in Denmark, thus confirming the information you have regarding this beautiful lady's attachment to Johan Christian Griffenfeld, the heir of that noble family, whom my friends say they saw in the company of Madame Wellborn two decades ago, here in Philadelphia—an attachment formed on board the ship which brought them here from the Caribbean.

"This young Danish nobleman was undoubtedly, as your informant who was also a passenger on that ship surmised and told you, the father of Madame Wellborn's son. It appears the head of the Griffenfeld family, the Jarl of Jutland, was persuaded many years ago that his son had fathered a son by this lady when they were both extremely young and has been supplying his grandson and the boy's mother funds for nearly two decades now.

"My Danish acquaintances further inform me that you should speak with Carl Jens Waldemar, the cousin of Johan Christian Griffenfeld here in Philadelphia, and his wife Kirsten, who received the young earl and his inamorata into their home off the ship. They also say you should interview the young nobleman's traveling companion and tutor, Anders Sensenborg, who was with him on the ship. Sensenborg is an instructor in Latin at the University, and was with Griffenfeld on the ship and with him at his cousin's home."

"I shall certainly speak with the Waldemars and Mr. Sensenborg, Colonel Zanzinger," James replied. "Do you happen to know why Sensenborg stayed on in Philadelphia when his noble young master did not?"

"I have no information on that. But I did have Jean-Pierre inspect the records of the Master of the Rolls and the Secretary of the Land Office with respect to Mrs. Wellborn, and his inquiries reveal she bought her house in Southwark in 1772, without a mortgage, which suggests to me that she put aside a good portion of the annual emolument she received from Copenhagen with a view to buying a home for herself and her son."

Neither man said anything for a moment. Then James asked, "What is your understanding of Mrs. Wellborn's more recent annual source of income?"

"Well, I would say it seems that her father in Jamaica, the wealthy plantation owner named William Godolphin, has come to his senses, tracked down his runaway oldest daughter, and has begun sending her an annual stipend in acknowledgment of his duty toward her. The fact that she is accepting this money suggests to me that she acknowledges her connexion to her father—that the natural affections of father and daughter between them have been restored."

As he left Colonel Zanzinger's residence in Appletree Alley, James decided it would be better to try to speak with Johan Griffenfeld's tutor and traveling companion before he spoke with Griffenfeld's cousin Carl Jens Waldermar and his wife. For one thing, it would be better to get reliable facts from one informant regarding events that happened decades ago than to try to get them from two persons who might not remember them in exactly the same way. The single informant's account would serve as a standard by which to assess any discrepancies in the joint recollections of Johan's cousin and his wife.

For another thing, all James had to do to get to the tutor Anders Sensenborg was ride the short distance from Appletree Alley to Fourth Street, and then go south one square to the University buildings.

He was in luck and found Sensenborg in his two-room quarters on the third floor of the University building, working on a translation of a passage in The Aeneid by Publius Vergilius Maro, commonly known as Virgil, in preparation for a Latin tutorial he had to give.

Sensenborg was happy to interrupt that work to accommodate Captain Jamison by sharing with him his memories of his first few weeks in Philadelphia in the company of Johan Christian Griffenfeld. To ensure that he would have the Dane's fullest cooperation, James asked him to read his commission from General Washington authorizing his enquiries.

He then said, "I understand, Mr. Sensenborg, that you observed the love affair between your traveling companion, Johan Griffenfeld, the heir of the Jarl of Jutland, and Margaret Godolphin on the ship *The Swift Hope*."

"If you mean that I saw them fall in love, you are correct. I thought Johan was making a grave mistake in taking such a young woman into his affections so absolutely—although she *was* exceedingly beautiful—given their altogether different upbringings, expectations, and responsibilities. I repeatedly counseled him not to do what he was doing. But he was unable to hear reason or control himself when it came to her. My arguments on how his father would view his behavior fell on deaf ears. The young lady was without precedent in his experience. She did not have to play the siren. He was, as you English say, 'smitten,' like a man struck by lightning. He was as helpless in her presence as a leaf being carried on a mountain stream. He could not resist her. She enthralled him.

"And I must say, too, that it was the same for the young lady. She was smitten with Johan and was carried along on the same irresistible current of their passion for each another. It did not seem either of them wanted to resist what they felt. Moreover, Miss Godolphin did not receive from her traveling companion, her maid, the sort of advice I was giving to Johan."

"Please tell me how you came to be traveling with the Griffenfeld heir," James prompted.

"The Jarl wanted his only son to have knowledge of the world from travel, not just from books. I had been Johan's tutor for five years in Denmark, instructing him in mathematics, English, French, philosophy, music, geography, and Latin, when the Jarl announced his plan to further his son's education by travel. So I, a man of known gravity, some learning, and a reputation for responsibility in the Jarl's eyes, and also being six years older than his son, was hired to accompany him on his travels and continue his education from books as he also learned from experience. We spent half a year in the cities of Germany, Italy, and France, and half a year in London to improve Johan's command of English, which his father wanted him to do. Then we returned to Denmark for a visit of several months before crossing the Atlantic to St. Croix, where Johan had a maternal uncle he'd never met; we then started for Philadelphia to meet a cousin of his whom he did not know. It was when we started for this city that he met Margaret Godolphin. His father never anticipated, any more than I did, the consequences of that encounter.

"The pair were completely enamored of each other. I thought once we arrived in this capital things might get better. But they got worse. Johan's cousin and his wife loved Miss Godolphin and completely approved Johan's attachment to her. They welcomed her into their home as though the couple's marriage banns had been duly announced in church. The counsel I gave Johan had no chance of success with such allies on hand as his cousin and the cousin's wife."

"So why, then, pray tell, did a young man so thoroughly enthralled by his beloved abandon her? How did that happen?"

"His father called him home. We had not been in Philadelphia but a few days when a letter from the Jarl arrived, requiring his son and heir to return with all haste to Denmark, saying his help was urgently needed to help put down an uprising of serfs on the Griffenfeld estates. In obedience to his father's summons to help suppress this threat to the Griffenfeld family, Johan left on the next ship that could take him, which was a fast-sailing German vessel destined for Bremerhaven, leaving Philadelphia in two days. Before he departed, he gave his signet ring to Margaret Godolphin as token of his solemn pledge to return for her as soon as possible to make her his wife. Shortly after his departure, word arrived among the Danes in Philadelphia that the uprising in Denmark was countrywide, not just among the serfs on the Griffenfeld estates."

"Why didn't you go back to Denmark with Johan?" James asked.

"I did not go with him because I feared the Jarl would hold me accountable for his son's waywardness in regard to this chit of a woman, Margaret Godolphin. I knew that, sooner or later, Johan would plead his case for her hand with his mother and father, and I felt sure they would reject his arguments as inadmissible. I therefore left the home of the Waldemars when Johan sailed from Philadelphia, and found employment here at the University as a tutor."

"What happened next?"

"Four months later, I was informed by Johan Christian's cousin, Carl Waldemar, that Johan had died in hand-to-hand combat on his father's principal estate. Margaret had sent Waldemar to me with this unwelcome news because she knew I was Johan's sincere friend. Mr. Waldemar told me Margaret was staying with him and his wife until the birth of her baby and as long after that as she should require.

"I should have had no anxiety, Captain, that the Jarl would hold me accountable for his son's surrender to his passion for Miss Godolphin, because not long after getting the news of Johan's death, I received payment in full from that noble lord for all my services as tutor and traveling companion to his son, along with a gracious letter thanking me for the quality of those services, which I have since used as a letter of recommendation."

"Why did Margaret Godolphin give the name 'Best' to her infant when she baptized him? Could she not have used Griffenfeld, a name of noble Danish lineage?"

"I was told, Captain Jamison, that she thought with Johan dead and unable to give his consent to the use of his name, and since he had not even known when he died that Miss Godolphin was with child, that it would be too suppositious for her to use the name Griffenfeld in baptizing the boy. I heard it required a large bribe from Johan's cousin to get a Lutheran minister here in Philadelphia to baptize the infant in the absence of a certificate from the Lutheran Church that the baby's parents were married or a proper certification of the father's death. I suppose the Lutheran priest who performed the baptism thought the absent father was named 'Best' since that was the name he was told to use."

"Are you still in communication with the cousin and his wife?" James asked.

"Not for many years now. Miss Godolphin, who now calls herself Mrs. Wellborn, brought her boy, Johan's offspring, to show me when he was a year old. Though I've read in the papers from time to time of Mrs. Wellborn's triumphs as an actress, she never visited these humble lodgings of mine a second time. I was associated in her mind with the happiest weeks of her life and was a close friend of her beloved Johan, which is why she wanted me to see their infant, the fruit of that happiness. But, as the great Italian poet Dante says, 'No agony is greater than the recollection of supreme happiness in a time of suffering.' And I believe Mrs. Wellborn still suffers keenly Johan's loss, judged by the last time I saw her. Their love was no transient affair but a life-changing event."

The afternoon was waning when James, having descended from the third-floor rooms of Anders Sensenborg in the University building, gathered up the reins of his thoroughbred Virginia mare and swung into the saddle to go to Spring Garden to find Lilac Lodge, the home of Carl Jens Waldemar and his wife, Kristin Waldemar, the whereabouts of which, he had gotten from the City Directory.

The house was at the end of Sachem Lane. A liveried footman admitted James to the Waldemar mansion and conducted him into the waiting room off the entrance. In lieu of a calling card, James gave the servant his commission from General Washington to show to his master and mistress.

The footman returned the commission to James with the message that he was to follow him, and took James to the Waldemars, who were in the paneled library of Lilac Lodge taking tea with their daughters, eighteen and twenty years old, and a son whose age fell in between those of his sisters. After thanking the couple for receiving him, James said he needed to ask them some questions regarding the actress Rebecca Wellborn and her son, who had vanished while in the service of the Pennsylvania militia guarding the Constitutional Convention. He reiterated that this was a matter which General Washington had commissioned him to investigate, as they had seen in the paper he had shown to them. In reply, the Waldemars insisted that James have tea with them.

Kristin Waldemar gracefully passed James his tea in a small white teacup painted with little blue forget-me-nots while telling him that Rebecca Wellborn was her dearest friend, and that she and her husband knew of Billy's disappearance.

"Margaret sent us a letter by messenger the day Billy went missing," Carl Waldemar announced in support of his wife's statement. "She advised us not to be fearful and to remain calm, adding that she was sure Billy would be returned to her well and sound. Billy was born here in this house, you know."

Mrs. Waldemar added, "We are his godparents."

"Meg has told us, Captain, that Billy is being held by a rich man who for years has been attempting to get her to be his mistress. This is the first time, she says, he's ever tried to coerce her into doing his bidding, but she regards him as ultimately harmless and not to be held accountable for his obsession with her."

Kristin Waldemar added, "I suppose you've made inquiries among the Danes of Philadelphia and already know of our close connection to Margaret and her son Billy because Billy's father, Johan Griffenfeld, was my husband's cousin."

"You are correct, Madam, except I did not learn on my own of your close relation to Mrs. Wellborn. That knowledge came to me from someone I know who has friends among the Danes of Philadelphia. I have also spoken with Anders Sensenborg."

"Ah, dear Anders..." Mrs. Waldemar said.

"From all I've learned, Mrs. Waldemar, I take it that you and your husband entirely approved of the match between Johan Griffenfeld and Margaret Godolphin. What you've just said indicates that your fondness for her extended to the child born of her affair with your husband's cousin."

"No one with any sensibility who saw Johan and Meg together could have disapproved of their love, Captain Jamison," Mrs. Waldermar said wistfully. "Never have I seen two dear people more completely devoted to one another. My husband and I often remarked on their feelings toward each other while they were together with us in our home. When Johan returned to Denmark in obedience to his father's orders, he left Margaret in our care. That was before either her pregnancy or the news of Johan's death in battle were known. Those momentous events, of course, made us feel more protective of Meg than ever. I am near her in age and at the time was carrying our second child, our son."

"From the moment Johan and Meg appeared on our doorstep from the ship, holding hands, Captain Jamison," Carl Waldemar said, "they manifested the strength of their love in their every expression, and my wife and I considered them married in spirit, if not in the eyes of Denmark's State religion, the Lutheran Church."

"One thing continues to puzzle me, Mrs. Waldemar. Why didn't Mrs. Wellborn use either her family name, Godolphin, or the name Griffenfeld in baptizing her son?"

"I can tell you something related to that," Carl Waldermar said. "It was because of the respect she had for the Griffenfeld name and my uncle's rank in Danish society. She did not consider herself entitled to use the name since the love between her and Johan had not been consecrated by marriage in the Lutheran Church, which the Griffenfelds, as a noble Danish family, uphold.

"As to her own family name, Godolphin, at the time of Billy's baptism she was still trying to put behind her the memory of her father's second marriage and did not want to use the Godolphin name on her son's certificate of baptism. She did, however, acknowledge Johan's lineage and hers by giving the baby the name William, which was the Christian name of both of his grandfathers.

"I wrote a long letter to my uncle in Denmark concerning Meg and the completeness of her devotion to Johan and of his to her. I think my representation of her character, the genuineness of their mutual love, their intention to marry as soon as possible, which his order to Johan to return home prevented, and the noble blood of Meg's father, moved my uncle to support Meg and Johan's son financially."

"I can tell you, Captain," Mrs. Waldemar said, "why Meg used the name 'Best' on Billy's baptismal certificate. She told me the day we took him to the church to have him baptized. She said Billy would always be *the best* to her. The embodiment of Johan."

By the time James left Lilac Lodge dusk was thickening in the valley of the Delaware River.

When he got home, Livy handed James a letter she said had been delivered for him an hour earlier by a well-dressed, diminutive gentleman of nice manners.

Weds. 27 June

Capt. Jamison, Your problem of the vanishing messenger has become so intriguing to me that I asked Mr. Latrobe to check the City's records to see if Mr. O'Cormick has other property apart from his home and the five kilns you told me of.

It turns out that indeed he does. Last November, he bought the Commonwealth's Old Powder House, the sole building on the square defined by Vine, Sassafras, Sixth, & Seventh streets, nothing else but a Graveyard being Located There. The Papers on the purchase say it was bought by O'Cormick to build a Brick kiln inside the disused Building, & efforts to accomplish that were begun soon after the Sale was recorded.

But the work has been abruptly halted, Mr. Latrobe found out this Afternoon from the Neighbors, who were quite surprised by the Work Stoppage, on June 23. I seem to recall you saying Mrs. Wellborn's son went missing on June 22.

What better place to Confine a man against his Will, I ask you, than an empty, solidly constructed Building situated where only the Dead could hear his cries for help?

Perhaps it would be advisable to put the Old Powder House under surveillance to see if someone is being held there.

Col. Z.

The Old Powder House
Chapter XV

JAMES SPENT A PLEASANT evening with his two ladies, starting with a feast of oysters that had been dredged up from Delaware Bay early that morning and purchased by Livy shortly after their arrival at one of the Market Houses. The meal also featured Livy's fresh-baked rye bread and freshly-churned salted butter. James, Grandmère, Livy, and the baby had supper in the dining room, where it was noticeably cooler than in the kitchen because at this season of the year there had been no fire in the dining-room fireplace for months, whereas the usual fires for cooking had been built every day in the kitchen to prepare meals.

After the dishes had been taken to the kitchen, washed, dried, and put away, the family repaired to the parlor, which was even cooler than the dining room because before supper James had raised the windows in the parlor facing the street and put cheesecloth window screens in them, which let the rain-cooled evening air into the house while keeping bugs out.

In the parlor, by the light of eight candles, James, who was generally considered to have an exemplary reading voice, read from the collection of Philip Freneau's poetry published the previous year in Philadelphia. Grandmère was fond of this Philadelphia poet because he shared her French Huguenot ancestry and because a friend of hers had presented her with Freneau's first major poem, *The Rising Glory of America*, written with his Princeton classmate Hugh Henry Brackenridge, three years before the war began. Grandmère had read this poem on the future glory of her adopted country many times because it pleased her so much.

The next morning, well before breakfast, James was in the saddle headed for Sassafras and Vine streets between Sixth and Seventh to have a look at the Old Powder House.

The building proved to be a large one-and-a-half-story brick octagon whose eight walls were each twenty-five feet wide. To admit light, seven of its eight sides had two slits eight inches wide and twenty feet high filled with thick glass blocks. James recalled his grandfather Jamison telling him, when he was a boy, of making those glass blocks in his manufactory. The side of the octagonal building paralleling Seventh Street had no slits for light but rather a huge iron door which, when both halves of it were wide open, allowed horse-drawn wagons to enter the building. There was also a postern in the right half of the huge iron door to allow pedestrian traffic into the building. The Old Powder House occupied one-third of the square adjacent to Seventh Street close to Vine Street, and some three hundred yards east of Declan O'Cormick's recently acquired kilns at Ninth and Vine. The graveyard, which he of course had not purchased, occupied the two-thirds of the square adjacent to Sixth Street.

Having located the silent former powderhouse, ridden around it twice and explored the nearest streets to it, James rode back to the center of town to the Half Moon Inn across from the Pennsylvania State House, to have breakfast and discuss with Sergeant Alexander Corbin putting the Old Powder House under surveillance.

He requested a private room for his meal and, as soon as he had ordered his breakfast, he asked for pencil and paper and wrote Corbin a note inviting him to join him at the Half Moon as soon as he could, and to bring Noah Day with him.

James had finished his breakfast of fritters and molasses and German sausages, and was drinking a second cup of good strong coffee when Corbin and Day appeared at his table.

"Good morning, Captain Jamison. You wanted to see Noah and me?"

"I would like to discuss an event regarding Billy Best's disappearance. You were with me, Noah, when Billy's dog Kemper took us to the place he and Billy were probably last together, a property owned by Mr. Declan O'Cormick. Late yesterday, I came by information that this man also owns a property ideally suited for holding a man prisoner. The opinion of most of us at the beginning, you will recall, was that ruffians, who wanted to rob Billy of the gold ring his mother had given him, had likely waylaid him and perhaps killed him to get it. But suppose that the opinion of Billy's mother is true, that O'Cormick has kidnapped Billy and is holding him hostage to force her into his bed, as a condition for Billy's release."

Sergeant Corbin said, "What makes you think that's a possibility, Captain Jamison? Have you been shown the threatening letter Billy told me his mother received?"

"No. But several coincidences associated with O'Cormick have been brought to my attention, one of them just hours ago, which suggest the idea that Billy has been kidnapped rather than assaulted and killed. This theory needs to be confirmed on evidence." James paused to take another sip of his coffee and then continued, "One of these coincidences is that the day after Billy vanished, in the late afternoon of June 22nd, Declan O'Cormick left Philadelphia on an extended trip, which, I'm told by employees of his, is to continue until July the 5th. And, on the morning of June 23rd, the day after

Billy's disappearance, O'Cormick halted work that had been going on for months and was near completion to build a brick kiln inside the Commonwealth of Pennsylvania's Old Powder House. The workers were suddenly dismissed without notice, before the job was finished, and were not allowed back into the building. The significance of the Old Powder House is that it's quite suited for holding a man against his will and that the work stoppage corresponds with the date on which Billy Best vanished."

"I know that building," Sergeant Corbin said. "My militia duties used to take me there. It's on the north edge of town, and the only other thing on that square of land besides the powder house, as I remember, is a cemetery belonging to the German Calvinists. What is it you have in mind to do, Captain Jamison?"

"As I see it, Sergeant, we ought to find out if anyone's being held prisoner inside the Old Powder House. If Billy is inside, he would have to be supplied with food. Therefore, to determine whether victuals are being brought every day to a supposedly empty building, a watch will have to be kept on the Old Powder House. Since food delivery would almost certainly be made once a day under cover of darkness, I think the surveillance need only be maintained during hours of darkness."

James looked in turn at each of the two men, then said, "Fortunately, there's only one door into the powder house, and anyone using it after dark would have to carry a lantern, because there aren't any streetlamps that far from the center of town, and the moon these days is still in its early phases and not shedding much light. It'll be easy to keep watch on one door. Two men, each watching the door for four or five hours, would be sufficient to learn if the Old Powder House is in use as a prison."

A pensive silence fell upon Sergeant Corbin and Noah Day as they considered what James had said.

Then James added, "I think the two men needed to keep watch should be drawn from the Convention Guard because it is a military organization created by Dr. Franklin as Commander-in-Chief of the Pennsylvania militia, and Billy is a member of the Guard. Besides, I have been authorized by General Washington, the President of the Constitutional Convention, to enlist the aid of all Philadelphians in investigating Billy's disappearance."

Corbin and Day looked at one another, and Corbin said, "I do not have the authority to establish eight hours of nighttime surveillance at the Old Powder House."

"Not even if the watchmen are volunteers?" James asked. "Suppose I meet with the Convention Guard in the East Room after today's session of the Convention. Once I've explained to them why I think Billy might have been kidnapped and put in the Old Powder House then I'll ask for six volunteers—enough for three days of keeping watch—to find out if food is being delivered there under cover of night. If it is, then someone is being held in the Old Powder House, and that prisoner is almost certainly Billy, judged by other circumstantial evidence."

Noah immediately spoke up. "I would consider it an honor, Captain Jamison, to participate in your plan and stand one of the first two watches tonight. I think you'll have no trouble getting five more volunteers. Billy is a well-liked member of the Guard."

"Sergeant Corbin, would you arrange for me to meet with the members of the Convention Guard in the East Room after today's meeting of the Convention adjourns?"

"In light of your commission from General Washington, I think no objection could be raised if I allowed you to meet with the Convention Guard and ask for volunteers to carry out your plan. When Noah and I return to the State House, I'll inform the three corporals in charge of the posts the Guard maintains to bring their men to the East Room to meet with you as soon as the Convention adjourns today."

"Very well, Sergeant. Meanwhile, I'll talk to the handful of persons who live within sight of the Old Powder House, to see if any of them know anything pertinent to our interest in the building."

Because of the isolation of the Old Powder House, just five households had to be asked whether they had seen someone coming to it at night. One of these persons farmed a large vegetable garden on a tributary of the rivulet called Pegg's Run, some eighty yards north of where Sixth Street ended at Vine Street, a quarter-mile from where Fourth Street became Germantown Road. Another of the households where someone could have seen something was at the corner of Seventh and Vine, in the easternmost part of the Spring Garden district. There was also a pair of identical houses, side by side, on Sixth Street just south of Vine. In addition, as James had discovered that morning in inspecting the vicinity of the Old Powder House, there was only one house, near Spring Garden, that offered a view of the powder house door. From the other houses, anyone coming from Declan O'Cormick's mansion or one of his workers' cottages off the Germantown Road would be visible as they went to the Old Powder House, but it would not be possible to see whether they entered the building.

James started his inquiries at the house in Spring Garden from which the door to the powder house could be kept under surveillance. This, he discovered, was owned and lived in by a widower named Owen Jones, a retired house builder.

Because James had learned the benefit of showing those he wanted to speak with his commission from General Washington, he began his conversation with Mr. Jones that way. Then he asked the man what he knew about Declan O'Cormick's purchase of the powder house.

The answer he received to this question revealed nothing new. But when James asked Mr. Jones for his opinion of why the construction of the brick kiln inside the Old Powder House had been suddenly halted, the answer he got struck him as significant. "Since coming to Philadelphia from Wales, I've spent my life building, Captain Jamison, and since I live practically on top of what Mr. O'Cormick was building inside the Old Powder House, I naturally took an interest in the construction of the kiln and often visited the site to see how the work was coming along. In fact, Mister O'Cormick and I spoke three days before he stopped the construction inside the Old Powder House, and he told me then that he was confident his men would be finishing it and have the kiln ready for operation in another three or four days at the most. It seemed to me he was looking forward to having his new kiln turning out bricks to repay what it had cost him to construct it."

"So why did he put an abrupt stop to the construction?" James asked.

"I don't know. Whatever his reason was, it was something unexpected. It certainly wasn't any sudden lack of funds to complete the work. O'Cormick's proud of the quality of his wares and how well they're selling in Philadelphia. He has bragged to me more than once of how much in demand his bricks are among builders in this city, and his credit is good. If he had to go to the banks for money to finish the work, he could have gotten it. But I think he has an ample amount of capital of his own."

James then explained that for reasons associated with the inquiries he was making for General Washington, which he could not divulge, he needed to keep the Old Powder House under surveillance for the next three nights. He asked if Mr. Jones would assist in that endeavor by allowing the men who would be keeping watch on the building to use his home as a vantage point, since it allowed observation of anyone going in or out of the Old Powder House. The retired builder said he would be pleased to accommodate him and General Washington.

James's next visit was to the small house on the five-acre garden plot near Pegg's Run. This offered a view of anyone coming across the open ground from O'Cormick's property on the Germantown Road to the Old Powder House. These householders, a Mr. and Mrs. Ross, reported having seen workmen coming and going every day for months until the work inside the Old Powder House was abruptly stopped. They did not know if there was any traffic at night because they and their children went to bed early.

The occupant of the house on the corner of Sixth and Vine streets, a widow by the name of Kibble, said she had never seen anyone going into the Old Powder House since the workers had left.

Likewise, Mr. and Mrs. Ralph, the couple who lived on Sixth Street in the house next to the Widow Kibble, which she rented to them, had seen no one coming from or going to the Old Powder House at night.

James had just enough time to ride home, take a bite of well-buttered toast, drink a cup of coffee, brush his coat, shine his shoes and their brass buckles, put on a fresh shirt, and return to the State House in time to keep his appointment to meet with the Convention Guard in the East Room.

All but three of the Guards had been able to come to the meeting, and when James explained his reasons for suspecting that Billy Best was being held in the Old Powder House and asked for volunteers to keep watch on the building during the next three nights, to determine if provisions were being taken there, nine of the ten Guards present raised their hands. And the man who didn't volunteer felt he had to explain to James why he couldn't do it.

James then told his nine volunteers that Sergeant Corbin would set up the schedule for them, and that the surveillance would be conducted from a house belonging to a Mr. Jones, which provided a view of the building's only door.

He described to them where the Old Powder House was, and how to get to Mr. Jones's house.

James hurried from this meeting with the Convention Guard to the nearby mansion-house of Mr. and Mrs. Robert Morris to see the performance of *The Prince of Parthia*, which would be the first play he had ever attended.

The Prince of Parthia
Chapter XVI

JAMES CARRIED WITH HIM to the Morris mansion a brief note which he had written in the East Room of the State House and addressed to "George Washington, President, Constitutional Convention." The note read:

Your Excellency,

Believe the missing messenger William Best is alive and I know where he's being held. A day or two more needed to prove hypothesis.

James Jamison

To the sound of genteel music, General Washington and the company of distinguished ladies and gentlemen who'd been invited to see *The Prince of Parthia* were being ushered by livered footmen into the ballroom of the mansion-house, now converted into a theater. James just managed to slip his note to the General before another footman handed both him and the great man engraved programs giving the subject of each scene in the play and a description of its characters along with the names of the actors and actresses who played them.

The ballroom, with its eighteen-foot ceiling and its orchestra's balcony above its entrance, was well suited to its new role. The spacious room's heavy curtains had been drawn across its windows, shutting out the sun and creating a dusky light. At the other end of the space, opposite the wide entrance leading from the rest of the house, a low stage framed by an ingeniously designed, portable proscenium had been set up. From this proscenium a two-part stage curtain was suspended.

Five rows of identically upholstered armchairs—three eleven-chair rows alternating with two twelve-chair rows—had been arranged in shallow arcs facing the stage, which was illuminated by small, evenly-spaced lanterns whose mirrored backstops, shaped like half of a miniature bishop's curved hat, reflected and focused light on the stage. The divided stage curtain was made of the same blue, damasked silk that covered the fifty-seven upholstered armchairs.

Because he was using the invitation sent to Benjamin Franklin, who had endorsed it over to him, James had one of the best seats in this temporary theater, being in the second chair to the right of Washington who, since the performance of *The Prince of Parthia* was in his honor and principally for his entertainment, was seated in the middle of the front row of seats flanked by his hosts, Mary Morris to his right and her husband Robert to his left. In the minutes before the play began, James saw the General break the seal on the note he had handed him, and read it.

Then, leaning forward, so he could make eye contact with James, the General, holding the note a trifle aloft, acknowledged its contents with a nod of his head and put it in his coat.

Then the soothing medleys of the eight-man orchestra ceased and the stage curtain was drawn apart, revealing the painted scene of a street and a temple in an ancient city. The street was crowded on each side with onlookers, as well as the flat rooftops of the houses. David Douglass, the manager of The American Company, who was also an actor and was to play the role of Artabanus, king of Parthia, stepped from the wings in costume, wearing a crown, and addressed the audience, which was comprised principally of the delegates to the Constitutional Convention.

"General Washington, Mr. and Mrs. Morris, members of the Constitutional Convention, and honorable ladies and gentlemen of Philadelphia, we are now in the capital of the ancient kingdom of Parthia, south of the Caspian Sea. The time is the third century before the birth of Christ. A great victory has just been won by Parthia's renowned cavalry of mounted archers led by Arsaces, the oldest son and heir of Parthia's king, a victory which will establish Parthian independence from the empires surrounding it and allow it to expand and become itself, in a few years, a mighty empire. But not until much selfish intrigue, gross hypocrisy and dissimulation, and passions of revenge, envy, and ambition have been quelled.

"In this play, we see what happens in a monarchical government, where all opportunities to gain wealth and position are at the disposal of the crown, instead of being generally available to the sovereign people and their individual merits.

"Ladies and gentlemen, I give you *The Prince of Parthia!* It was the first play by an American playwright presented by a professional troupe, and it is by Philadelphia's own poet Thomas Godfrey, Junior, who because of his unfortunate death at the age of twenty-seven wrote no more dramas. It was first staged eight years before our war for independence."

The Play

Having made his introductory declamation, Mr. Douglass withdraws, a background murmur of excited voices is heard, and a blare of trumpets sounds, suggesting an approaching triumphal procession.

The play has begun.

Two actors in costume walk onto the stage talking, Gotarzes, the King's youngest son, and Phraates, a stalwart of the Parthian Court. Gotarzes says, "He comes, Arsaces comes, my gallant brother, like shining Mars in all the pomp of conquest." Phraates replies, "As far as sight can stretch, all the ways are lined with crowds awaiting the Hero's return! The mother teaches her infant to lisp the name Arsaces, and aged sires who can scarcely speak toss their caps into the air and add their feeble words of praise to the multitude's outcry of joy." Gotarzes remarks, "What pleasure, Phraates, must swell the heart of brave Arsaces on seeing and hearing the happiness he has brought his countrymen!"

Phraates says, "Arsaces will make a fine king when your father dies and he inherits the throne."

The scene then shifts to a dialogue between Vardanes, the King's second-oldest son, and his arch-henchman, the courtier Lysias, who paint a different portrait of Arsaces. Vardanes bitterly laments the adulation of "the servile crowd" for his brother and curses his brother's name. Lysias declares he would rather lose his power of speech "than hail Arsaces" and that Vardanes deserves the praise of the multitude as much as his brother because there's nothing Arsaces has done that Vardanes could not do as well.

In the next scene, we learn that Thermusa, the widow of a neighboring king previously slain in battle with Parthia, whom the King has taken for his Queen, also hates Arsaces, as she tells her confidante Edessa that the *Prince of Parthia* treacherously killed her son, stabbing him in the back. "Cursed be the morn which dawned upon his birth! I shall have my revenge!" the Queen exclaims.

Thermusa also expresses her contempt for "the changeling King" who, though on bended knee has often said he loved her, is now enamored of Evanthe, a beautiful woman the crown prince of Parthia has taken prisoner on the battlefield. Thermusa has heard the King calling fondly to Evanthe in his sleep "while I have lain neglected by his side, except when sometimes in a mistaken rapture he has clasped me to his bosom."

Scene 4 introduces Evanthe, played by Rebecca Wellborn, whose extraordinary beauty as she comes onstage makes some members of the audience who are beholding her for the first time gasp. After waiting for the audience's applause to quiet, she complains to her maid Cleone that duty requires Arsaces to go to the temple to make sacrifices to the gods for his triumph over Parthia's enemies, and keeps him from "my fond heart." For, Evanthe says, she and Arsaces have fallen in love, and "Love is a tyrant." She advises Cleone to avoid it, likening being in love to "being caught in a fowler's net and losing one's freedom."

When Cleone asks her mistress how she came to know and to love Arsaces, we learn that Vonones, son of the hate-filled Queen Thermusa, was holding Evanthe captive and Arsaces rescued her, killing the Queen's son in face-to-face combat during her rescue.

"Arabia gave me birth," Evanthe reports. "My father held great offices in the Arabian Court and was regarded as brave, wise, and loyal by his Prince, whose troops he often led to triumph. In infancy I was his only treasure. On me he wasted all his fondness, which my infant charms beguiled. From my fatal beauty has sprung every turn of my history."

Cleone agrees. "'Tis often so, for beauty is a flower that tempts every hand to possess it."

Evanthe continues her story by telling her confidante that three years before, while bathing in the Niphrates River, a troop of horsemen led by Vonones took her and her maid captive "to force me into his arms."

Act I ends with the king and his three sons—Arsaces, Vardanes, and Gotarzes—in the Temple celebrating Arsaces' victory, and we hear Prince Gotarzes say, "Brother, my soul dilates with joy to see you thus." Arsaces responds by embracing him fondly. Vardanes says in an aside, "Next will be my turn to praise him. I had rather be entwined in the coils of a venomous snake!" To Arsaces' face, he says, "Though I have not the ability to garb my sentiments in eloquence, doubt not my honest love for you, my brave and princely brother, deserving of all our affectionate praise!"

The opening scene of Act II is a prison at night amidst a thunder and lightning storm. By removing most of the stage's footlights a suggestion of nighttime has been created; and the storm's thunder is staged by a booming bass drum, while flashes of lightning are being simulated by uncovering offstage for an instant the light of the intensely-burning lamp Dr. Franklin brought back from France and has leant to The American Company for this purpose. In this ominous setting, Lysias, alone on stage, declares, "This night, sleep shall be a stranger to me. My mind is full of thoughts of overthrowing established order. My spirit matches in kindred rage the thunder and lightning, and taking revenge on Arsaces for refusing me a command in the Parthian army is my only solace."

Vardanes walks onto the scene, exclaiming, "What a terrible night is this!" Lysias, replies, "Some portent lurks, my Lord, beneath this horrific storm. Perhaps the fall of Arsaces." The dialogue of the plotters reveals that Vardanes wants to posses Evanthe, but she has rejected his advances because of the love she has for Arsaces. The advice he gets from his fellow conspirator Lysias is to think only of becoming king and to leave other ambitions aside until that is accomplished. Lysias advises Vardanes not to "trifle time away" but to concentrate his efforts on gaining the throne. Vardanes assures Lysias, "By the powers of heaven and earth, I swear to you I will not rest until I have achieved every one of my ambitions or have fallen silent in death." His co-conspirator praises his resolve and announces his readiness to kill whoever stands in the way of such a worthy ambition.

Arsaces now comes on the scene at the other side of the stage, and Lysias offers to stab him to death with his dagger. But Vardanes says it would be better "to undermine him and plot his fall as part of my father's doom. How easy it is to cheat this tattling, censuring world, where fame and repute name our actions good or bad; and words dress virtue up as vice, and vice as virtue."

Vardanes and his henchman Lysias depart, and Arsaces comes to center stage, saying that he has come to the prison to offer his sympathy to Bethas, the commander of the enemy army he has just vanquished in battle, whose life he spared when the King wanted him executed. "'Tis here that hapless Bethas is confined who only yesterday had every Parthian trembling at his name," Arsaces proclaims. "Now he sits unfriended and forlorn, wrapped in the horrors of this gloomy dungeon. O! 'tis a heavenly virtue when the heart can sympathize with the sorrows of another soul. I'll enter and give my aid to soothe this honorable foe."

Bethas is seen in chains on the right hand verge of the stage putting down a stool and sitting on it. He says as Arsaces approaches him, "To contemplate death in the solitary depths of a dungeon and in chains wracks the soul, because the prisoner has no beloved companion to console him in his need." When Arsaces offers Bethas his condolences, the prisoner thinks he's being ironic and mocking him. Arsaces protests that his condolences are sincere and that he is not mocking him. "Dissimulation never marks my speech nor false words conceal my true sentiments. To virtue and her fair companion truth I have ever bowed, and kept their holy precepts."

Then Evanthe enters the scene, accompanied by her friend and servant Cleone. Bethas, when he sees Evanthe, exclaims, "Immortal gods, is this reality or some illusion to torment me further by reminding me of what I've lost?" Evanthe on seeing Bethas and hearing his voice faints.

Cleone, Arsaces, and Bethas converge over her prone figure to revive her. When she emerges from her swoon, Bethas shouts her name, and Evanthe exclaims, "Oh, my Father!"

The scene closes with Arsaces vowing, "I'll go to the king before he retires for the night and will not quit him, Bethas, until your freedom I have obtained. Once he learns you are Evanthe's father, his own paternal heart is bound to accede to my pleas."

Act III opens inside the palace, with the King and Queen arguing. She upbraids him for being in love with Evanthe, and the King replies, "Why should I blush if heaven has made me with passions you can satisfy no longer? Blame the gods who formed my nature thus, not me!" In the next scene of this Act, the Queen is with her stepson Vardanes and tells him the King is his rival for Evanthe's favors.

The curtain closes and opens on a soliloquy by Vardanes. "Ha, the King my rival! He is also the rival of Arsaces. This will forward my design if I can fire the King's jealousy of Evanthe's affection for Arsaces. The love rivalry between my father and my brother portends the success of my hope to supersede them both."

The following scene begins with the King, in the presence of his sons Vardanes and Arsaces, asking, "But where is Evanthe, where's the lovely Maid? I ordered Lysias to bring her to me with all dispatch, that I may myself convey to her my willingness to grant her father freedom." Lysias enters accompanying Evanthe, who says, "O, royal Sir, thus lowly to the ground I bend in thanks for your goodness to my father. Thy giving hand has blessed me." The King bids Evanthe rise and says that her lowly posture does not befit her charms, which "every heart should exult to behold. But where is your Sire?"

"He said to tell you, noble King, his gratitude had unmanned him and he is not in fit condition to appear before you."

Arsaces then prostrates himself before Artabanus with the words, "Extend thy bounty to me also, father." When the King tells him to rise because such prostration "ill-becomes so worthy a prince," Arsaces says he won't rise until his father grants what he asks.

"Whatever it be, if it exists within my wide kingdom— wider soon to be because of what you've done in battle—it is yours, even were you to ask that I give my crown to you forthwith, rather than wait for nature to take its course."

Arsaces says, "Long and long may you wear your crown, my father, and the blessings of heaven attend you. It is not the unruly transports of ambition that move me. The prize I ask is greater than kingship. For all the dangers to my life in my campaigns to serve thee, my king and father, and all the suffering I have undergone in them, reward me with Evanthe."

The King, taken aback by what he has heard, asks, "Did thee name Evanthe as the sum of thy wished for favor from me?"

"I did, my Sire, I did."

The King walks aside and says, "My promise to grant his boon has been too absolutely made to retract." Turning, he says, "She's thine."

When the lovers are left alone on stage, Arsaces is overjoyed by the King's betrothal of them, but sees that Evanthe looks gloomy. "What means this look of anguish, this mark of sorrow on thy face, Evanthe?" Evanthe sighs profoundly. "What means such a sigh? Some dreadful knowledge seems laboring in thy sweet bosom. What troubles thee?"

"Ah, too soon you'll know what I would hide."

"Out with it! What e'er the doleful news, it cannot shake my devotion to thee. I charge thee, Evanthe, by our mutual vows of love, disburden your mind and let me share in what is so disturbing to you. Tell me the truth you have not spoken."

"Then know, Arsaces, thy father loves me."

"Loves thee?"

"Yea, even to distraction. Oft at my feet, he has woo'd me with the ardency of youth! Didst thou observe, my beloved and loving Arsaces, the reluctance with which he gave me to thee?"

"Yes, I observed it. In giving you to me, he left the impression he was yielding up his own precious life."

"Now you know the calamity that accompanies our betrothal."

"I see before you and me, my dearest Evanthe, a sky of gathering black clouds and a dark sea of menacing waves."

"It is not enough we can foresee the difficulties that darken what ought to be an horizon of natural happiness. What measures can we apply to avoid the rising storm?" Evanthe says.

"The most pressing question for me, Evanthe," Arsaces rejoins, "is whether he will take back his pledge and force us apart. To which question I say no, he cannot without first slaying me!"

"O, my virtuous and loving prince, I fear you speak somewhat insanely and have not weighed as carefully as you should, as heir to the throne of Parthia, what would follow such a conflict between the rightful king and his rightful heir."

"Oh, my Evanthe, that I had been the firstborn of some

shepherd on the plains of Parthia. My scepter, my crook; my subjects, my flock!"

The lovers exit the stage hand in hand to be replaced by the King, with Vardanes just offstage, unseen by the King but visible to the audience. The King says, "I will not think. To think is torment. Now the hot blood of the Furies beats in my veins, the alarm of my love for Evanthe. O, bright heav'nly beings who pity the prayers of thwarted lovers, come to my aid!"

He sees his son Vardanes, and calls to him, "Vardanes, come here! I know thou lovest me without any rivalry."

Vardanes comes forward, saying, "I do, my Royal Sire. Never doubt that I do love you as my father and my king without qualification. Whate'er you would have me do, I will perform."

"Come a little nigher to help me ease the burden of my soul. I need to speak without restraint to someone of sympathetic ear. I want to disburden myself of things too long unknown to anyone except those who participated in them. Your sympathizing, noble nature makes you fit to hear my tale."

"Instruct your loving son who stands before thee in how he may serve to restore thy spirits."

"For now, attending with sympathy to what I have to say will suffice. Of all my offspring but Arsaces—"

"Arsaces!"

"What means this hollow groan? Vardanes, speak! Dost thou know of something amiss in thy beloved brother's conduct?"

"Only this." And he withdraws from his tunic a paper. "I have concealed my knowledge of the intentions of Arsaces to disturb the peace of thy kingdom, only to try to persuade him to desist from their execution. He views thy sacred life with envious hatred, as a bar to his unnatural ambition. It pleases him to imagine the weight of your crown on his head."

Vardanes hands the paper to his father who reads it. "But this is treason! It is a pledge of collusion from Bethas, assuring Arsaces the support of the Arabians in hurling me from my throne! This explains why Arsaces has been so partial to Bethas, not only to deprive me of my crown but to gain the defeated general's support in the courtship of his beauteous daughter Evanthe! 'Tis my earnest command, Vardanes, that you arrest my treacherous son Arsaces along with the recently-freed Bethas, and put them to a dungeon's confinement. Then seize with some cavalry the lovely maid Evanthe for her protection and bring her to me."

Vardanes says, "Aye, my sovereign Lord, I will do it forthwith."

The king hurries from the stage, and Vardanes, left alone, speaks. "I will seize her, but to keep her for myself. It were a sin to put such beauty in the hands of a man in his dotage."

The setting for Act IV is again the prison. Enter Gotarzes and Phraates.

Phraates urges, "My prince, tarry not here but fly! For since last night's horror, which saw thy royal father stabbed to death in his sleep by Lysias, a close ally of thy brother Vardanes, all authority in Parthia has passed to Vardanes since noble Arsaces lies imprisoned within dungeon walls at the King's angry last command. He is charged with wanting to usurp the throne of state, an act he never plotted, I'm certain."

Gotzares says, "Hither I came seeking my unjustly imprisoned brother to solace him in our mutual sorrows!"

"I know, for am I not the one who told you of the tragedy, having been roused from slumber by evil dreams? And wandering aimlessly in the palace garden, wrapped in shadows, I happened upon Lysias, who did not see me, eagerly telling Vardanes, 'Tis done, 'tis done, the cruel Artabanus is no more! The blow he gave my cheek of yore is fully repaid in blood. All hail Vardanes, Parthia's mightiest Lord!'"

"Surrounded thus by lawlessness, what is to be done, wise Phraates? Help me with thy council, for I am of the dead king's body his youngest son, and this regicide weighs heavily on me."

"My advice to you is to fly to General Barzaphernes, thy imprisoned brother's second in command, whose conquering troops are encamped near the city. He loves Arsaces and loved your father. He will see justice done for this foul deed. Before dawn, I dispatched a letter to Barzaphernes informing him of what I heard in the darkness of the palace garden and saying he should invest the city at once. If you leave now, Gotarzes, you will doubtless meet him and his host on the road coming to take the city, the palace, the temple, and this prison."

The next scene is Bethas and Arsaces in chains. "I am the source, my prince, of all your misfortune. Before you shower'd your pity on me, your splendor as a conqueror shone before the world. Evanthe is my offspring, whose beauteous charms move these fatal mishaps forward."

Arsaces replies, "Speak not thus in anger of her! She is all gentleness and innocence, free of all malice and ill temper."

"The gods know, Arsaces, love is in every fiber of her being! But her beauty brings destruction, it seems."

"Restless fears oppress me, Bethas, not for me alone but for you and the radiant Evanthe. Horrid dreams stalk my slumbers. Yesternight, I dreamt I was alone on the shore of a sea of blood and my father was struggling in it not to drown! Vardanes was preventing his success somehow, as is the way in dreams. Through the red billows, I struggled to save my father, but he was unreachable and sank under the waves. I woke with a feeling of powerlessness to change the fate of anyone I pity or love."

Arsaces sees the Queen approaching, and says to Bethas, "Thermusa bears this way, her look full of violence and rage.

Retire, Bethas, I would meet her anger alone." Bethas hobbles off in his chains.

"What means Thermusa, my proud stepmother, by this visit? I cannot believe you come to express pity or forgiveness, for your whole aspect is otherwise. Forgiveness and pity never dwell in people filled with hate."

"Your words insult the memory of my Vonones! I come to kill you, with this dagger, in vengeance for you taking his life. I want to hurl you from life to death to dwell everlastingly in fiery chains and penal fire!"

"If that be thy purpose, why delay? Do the deed at once. I cannot prevent you, wrapped as I am in these chains."

"Oh, thou vile homicide, damned eternally to the flames of perdition! When you slew Vonones, you robbed me of all reliable happiness!"

She moves within striking distance of Arsaces and raises her hand holding the dagger halfway over her head. The Queen says in an aside, "Why this hesitation?" And to Arsaces, "I think I mistook my purpose, or rather how to execute it. To let you live is to let you suffer. To kill you gives you escape from all that lies in wait for you at the hand of your brother Vardanes. Live then, and suffer."

The frenzied Queen exits, and a loud clashing of swords and shouting is heard. Gotarzes and Barzaphernes burst into the scene and quickly strike the chains from Arsaces, as Barzaphernes says, "O, my Prince, to see thee thus forces tears into my eyes."

Arsaces says, "Welcome, loyal friend, beloved brother!" Freed of his chains, he embraces his two liberators in turn. "But why am I released by force, instead of by the generosity of my father, the King, relenting and freeing me? This way, by force, confirms me a lawless traitor canceling my father the King's commands by violence."

"It is a soldier's manner to be blunt, my Lord. Your father, the King, is dead, murdered by a henchman of Vardanes, whose aim is to usurp the crown of Parthia."

"Murdered in a plan of Vardanes! Give me a sword, Barzaphernes, that I may join the fight to put down the usurper! O, Ruler of Creation who ordered it into being, whatever sins weigh against me, I beseech thee to let them not weigh against me today in this struggle, that I and my companions in arms may be victorious! May thy Hand guide us in opposing those who have desecrated in your sight what is by nature right and just."

The curtain opens slowly on the concluding act in The *Prince of Parthia,* accompanied by soft music and the sight of the Evanthe sleeping on a sofa. The music ceases as Vardanes enters.

"Now the shining goal of my kingship comes near with increasing speed. But Arsaces, bane of my hopes, still lives and blocks my way and must be shown a traitor. Yet now I would spend one hour with the fair Evanthe, easing my cares with her love. Her slumbers heighten every feature of her face and figure.

"Fair maiden of glowing form bespeaking a readiness for the joys of love, torment me no more with coyness. When youth warms the blood is the time for love, and youth flies swift away, too soon replaced by the inevitable mortifications of age."

Evanthe, hearing a voice, awakes slowly. "Am I still in the palace of the tyrant who had me seized? In my dream I was with Arsaces crowned with immortal bliss. He led me through groves of flowers as multitudes of shining souls were greeting us with their sublime welcomings." Then she sees Vardanes and the sight of him disturbs her greatly.

"Why this angry look, Evanthe, at the sight of your devoted slave?"

"Leave my sight, vile man. I sicken in thy presence!"

"Arsaces, I suppose, were he to approach thee would sooth thy anger and melt thy icy bosom?"

"Does it gall thee to know I delight to hear his speech, for it joins truth with beauty?"

"I know this! Such praise gives me joy because I know, too, that my rival can only view thy beauty in his imagination, while I have it before me to touch and clasp. Both you and Arsaces are in my power. You to possess and him to kill. Yield me your love, Evanthe, and his life will be spared. There is no other way."

Vardanes starts to lay hold of Evanthe, who exclaims, "Touch me not! You cannot gain by force what you want to have, no more than the beauty of a flower can be enjoyed by trampling it! Would you stain by so foul a blot the honor of the throne you aspire to ascend? Kings are supposed to protect the innocent from villainy, not impose it on them. May you not find some other maiden who can bend to your flame? In me, you will never have that acquiescence without which the bliss you seek cannot be. The ecstasies of love must be by willing engagement."

At that moment then, Lysias with drawn sword rushes into the room exclaiming, "With haste, my Lord, arm yourself! To arms!"

"Damn your interruption!"

"Our lives depend on it, noble Prince! There's no time to spare for other things! The foe is upon us, here! General Barzaphernes has released Arsaces and with his troops, and armed citizens, is attacking along with Arsaces your palace, swearing revenge for the death of Artabanus! We must make haste, my noble Lord, else all will be lost! Thy faithful Guard has repelled the assault three times. But still the rebels return to the attack with renewed vigor."

"Yea, I will lead the van against my brother and repulse him and his cohorts! Now, for a crown or death!"

Vardanes and Lysias hurry away. Left alone, Evanthe clasps her hands and cries, "Be ye partial, ye heavens, to Arsaces and his cause. Grace with victory those who defend the laws you established when you made the world."

Cleone, Evanthe's confidante, enters.

"My Cleone, thou partner of my sorrows and my joys! You are well come."

"My lady, lifeless heaps of men are piling up in the city, and the footing is made slippery by the blood being spilled. I could watch no more from my vantage on the tower and have sought your company."

"What of Arsaces?"

"I saw him active in the fight where the conflict was bloodiest, valiantly leading his forces."

"Oh, I fear for his life. Dearest Cleone, return to your vantage and mark how Arsaces fares. Report to me what you see of him."

Cleone leaves, and Evanthe, moving to the center of the stage, declares, "What torment suspense brings. Scarce do I delight myself by imaging a blissful life with Arsaces than I behold him in imagination cold and lifeless, fallen in battle. Yet if he should die, so too can I. I have here"—she holds aloft a small vial—"the means to avoid the sorrow of life bereft of his love." The curtain quickly closes and opens on Cleone alone.

"Oh, cruel gods—what horror, what anguish, the work of the accursed Vardanes! Arsaces has fallen—I saw it!—pierc'd by a horrid sword wound. How can I tell my mistress such news? Yet she must know!"

Cleone leaves the tower, and a tumultuous, happy shouting is heard as Barzaphernes, Gotarzes, and Arsaces come on stage attended by officers, two of whom lead Vardanes and Lysias in chains.

Arsaces, pointing with his sword at Lysias, says to the officer holding his chain, "Take this regicide to the top of the tower and cast him down as he deserves, to smash on the pavements." And to Gotarzes, he says, "Fly, my faithful brother, and find Evanthe. Bring her here to me!"

"I will do this, noble brother and lord, with all willing speed." Gotarzes hurries off, leaving on stage Vardanes, the officer holding his chain, Arsaces, General Barzaphernes, and others.

"For you, the name of brother is forgot"

"You need not order my death, Arsaces, for it draws near on its own from the wounds I received in resisting you. My breath and my life grow short. Curs'd be Phraates who took with his own body the blow I meant for you which would have been fatal! He paid for his fidelity with his life."

Vardanes drops to his knees, then falls forward on his face, a corpse, and is carried dead from the scene.

Evanthe supported by a distressed Gotarzes comes in. "Lead me, oh lead me! to my belov'd Arsaces! Where is he?" Arsaces sees her and throwing his sword aside rushes to gather her in his embrace. "Arsaces, oh! Thus circled in your arms, I die without pang." And she expires.

"How's this, the most beautiful, most innocent, most kind, most gracious and virtuous maiden alive is dead!"

Gotarzes says, "If my bereaved faculties have durance to tell the tale, it is this. She sent Cleone to observe the battle from the tower and report to her how it fared with you, Arsaces, and Cleone saw the sword-strike delivered from behind by Vardanes that he intended to be your death-blow, which killed instead Phraates, who intercepted it with his body as it descended. Cleone reported Phraates's death as yours because of a similarity between his garb and yours. When Evanthe got from her trusted servant the report you were killed, she took poison."

As his brother concludes his speech, Arsaces transfers his gaze from him to the lifeless form of Evanthe he holds in his arms. Too stricken with grief to speak, he buries his face in her abundant hair and sobs.

Barzaphernes quietly picks up the sword Arsaces flung aside when he went to the dying Evanthe, gives it to a soldier, and with a gesture of his head orders him to take it away. When Arsaces' sobbing over the corpse of his beloved ceases, he gently lowers her head, rises, and goes to where he threw his sword.

Barzaphernes says, "I had it removed, my royal liege, lest your grief impel some act of self-violence."

Arsaces looks around and seizes a nearby soldier's sword and plunges it into his own vitals. As he does this, both Barzaphernes and Gotarzes rush toward him to prevent him taking his life, as they see he intends to do. But they do not reach him in time.

As he dies, the Prince of Parthia says, "Tis vain to grieve me. I go to Evanthe, wedded in death. She is waiting for me. Wear the crown, Gotarzes. You are worthy of it."

The tragic music that has been softly playing since Evanthe's appearance on the scene rises in volume and reaches crescendo with the Prince of Parthia's dying words, and the curtain closes.

Dr. Franklin & James Speak Again
Chapter XVII

AS THE HALVES of the curtain come together, the sound of more than polite applause fills the ballroom-theater, and liveried servants start pulling aside and tying open the room's drapes covering its eight tall windows, admitting the wan sunlight of a June evening into the ballroom-theater, the first step in preparing it for the dancing that will follow the sumptuous buffet supper Robert and Mary Morris are giving their guests.

The curtain of the still-intact stage parts, revealing the twelve players who performed *The Prince of Parthia*, eight actors and four actresses in a line, holding hands and smiling with pleasure at the vigorous applause. The line steps forward and bows to the audience in unison. George Washington stands and adds to his loud clapping a heartfelt "Bravo!" in his commanding voice, at which the entire audience stands and the applause volume increases. Bravos come from various parts of the audience, mostly in the voices of gentlemen but also in the tones of a few ladies. The players in the costumes of their characters take another step forward together, still holding hands, and again bow ensemble to the audience, only this time more profoundly and longer. The cast of the play then disperses and goes behind the slowly closing curtain. The applause continues unabated.

The actors next come forward from behind the curtain in pairs, their pairings and the sequence of their appearances being arranged in accordance with the importance of the characters they have played in the drama and the sympathy each character has evoked. First, Vardanes and Lysias. Then the King and Queen. Then, the Queen's confidant Edessa, and Cleone, Evanthe's confidant. Next, Phraates and Barzaphernes, followed by Bethas and Gotarzes; and, finally, Arsaces, played by a promising young actor named Adam Miggs, brought down from the St. Johns Theatre in New York to play the role, and Evanthe, played by Mrs. Wellborn. The applause for these last two players is so great they are brought back onstage individually. First, Mr. Miggs; then Mrs. Wellborn. Both receive louder applause than any other players, she more than he. Then the two of them appear for one last bow together.

With the conclusion of these accolades for the players, this performance of *The Prince of Parthia* comes to its definitive, memorable end as the applause dwindles to a stop, and the audience is gently ushered toward the mansion-house's dining hall by the servants who escorted them into the theater-ballroom to see the play. Other servants complete the opening and tying back of the ballroom's curtains, and stage hands of The American Company begin taking down the stage and its proscenium.

As James looked around, wanting to talk with someone after his first experience of attending a professionally acted play, he was approached by a lady he did not know but had noticed at the end of the front row of seats, where she had sat next to a common-looking man. She was notable because of her good looks and grooming, her fine figure, elegant attire, and her lack of the fichu, or modesty cloth, usually worn by Philadelphia ladies in low-cut gowns.

"You must be Captain James Jamison, the confederate of Dr. Franklin, who thinks so highly of you that he assigned his choice ticket to you," she said in a velvety voice. "I'm Eliza Willing Powel. What did you think of the king of Parthia and his sons in this play, Captain Jamison?"

During his association with Dr. Franklin James had learned his method for parrying questions he had no opinion on or wished to avoid answering, which was to turn the question around and invite the questioner to answer it. This allowed the questioner to express his or her views on a matter of obvious interest to them.

"Well, madam, I'm not sure I have an opinion worth hearing on that interesting question. What is your opinion?"

"I think a man with as little self-control as Artabanus exhibits in this drama should not be a king. His heir, the worthy Prince Arsaces, seems to have inherited this weakness from his father, as seen in the lack of self-control he exhibits in committing suicide after his betrothed takes her life. The second son, Vardanes, is merely a criminal deceiver, having no respect or regard for either manmade or natural law. In short, Parthia's royal family, as Mr. Godfrey portrays it in his play, is a nest of monarchists morally unqualified to rule. The play holds out some hope that the third son, Prince Gotarzes, who ends up occupying the throne, may live up to the responsibilities of monarchy. But we know too little of his character to be sure. The play does not put him in any situation requiring that he decide important matters. We only see him carrying out the commands or advice of others... Oh, there's my husband waving to me to go in to supper with him. It's been a pleasure talking with you, Captain Jamison. Until we meet again."

After Mrs. Powel's departure, James looked around the room and saw that General Washington had left, and that none of the other delegates from the Constitutional Convention whom he'd met were present either.

He went to the dining room and got into one of the serving lines for the buffet supper, avoiding the one the Powels stood in.

After partaking of the buffet, he sought his host and hostess to thank them for their wonderful entertainment and the buffet. He apologized to Mrs. Morris for his inability to stay for the dancing, and Mr. and Mrs. Morris asked him to give Dr. Franklin their regards and to tell him they regretted he was unable to attend.

At one o'clock that night, James was again knocking at the back door of Franklin Court and, as soon as Mr. Mahoney admitted him, he asked him to take Jenny, who was tied in front of the Indian Queen Hotel, into Dr. Franklin's stable for safekeeping while he went up to Dr. Franklin's library.

The first thing Dr. Franklin asked James was whether he had found the play to be worthwhile. James thanked Dr. Franklin for giving him the opportunity to see a play professionally performed. He said he had found parts of *The Prince of Parthia* "a bit too melodramatic perhaps," but he added that it had contained much that was of interest, and some of the play's language had been genuinely fine. The staging had been ingenious, especially The American Company's use of Dr. Franklin's intensely brilliant Swiss lamp to imitate lightning flashes. The acting had been engaging, and Mrs. Wellborn's performance had been particularly well received, he said.

"Bravo, James. That's a comprehensive review. I see I did the right thing in presenting my ticket to you. *The Prince of*

Parthia was too familiar to me to want to see it performed, having bought several copies of it when friends of Mister Godfrey first published it by subscription along with his poems, when he died. The playwright would doubtless have written more and better plays and further poetry, even a novel, perhaps, had he lived beyond the age of twenty- seven. I think *The Prince of Parthia* is an ambitious political allegory attacking the inherent flaws of monarchy as an institution.

"I knew Thomas Godfrey, Junior, through his father, Thomas Godfrey, Senior, who invented the quadrant, an instrument mariners use to measure the angles of astral bodies above the earth, a highly useful invention for navigating the world's oceans. I wrote an obituary of the father for my newspaper, and did the same for the son when he died. Did you make any interesting new acquaintance at the play, James?"

"A lady named Eliza Powel."

"Ah, Elizabeth Powel. Her father was one of Philadelphia's famous Willing family and a mayor of the city, as has Eliza's husband Samuel Powel also been. He is every bit as wealthy as the Willings, which I suppose is why such a vivacious, handsome woman as Eliza married so dreary a man as Samuel Powel, whose pastime is making silhouettes of famous people, which he collects."

"Before we speak any further, Dr. Franklin, I almost forgot. Mr. and Mrs. Morris requested that I tell you they were sorry you could not attend their entertainment."

"How was Mrs. Powel dressed?" Franklin asked James. "She's a leader of fashion among ladies of quality in Philadelphia."

"She had a small white egret feather in her hair but no jewelry, and no fichu. She wore an elegant, close-fitting yellow gown with a rich purple sash, which showed off her small waist to great advantage. She didn't much like the royal family in *The Prince of Parthia.* She said they lacked the self-control required of proper monarchs, which fits in well with your view of the play, Dr. Franklin, as an allegory on monarchy as a form of government.

"She mentioned you, and thinks you hold me in high esteem since you gave me your invitation to the play. Your opinion evidently matters a great deal to her, inasmuch as she deigned to introduce herself to me because of her belief that you have a high regard for me."

"Elizabeth Powel favors men of political, financial, or intellectual standing, James. She herself is a thinker and a confidante of General Washington. They take tea together with no one else present and for years have written letters to each other. Should you ever have an idea, James, of which you want to apprize the General, convince Eliza that it has merit and he will surely hear of it.

"But we're straying from our purpose. Tell me of the discoveries you have made since reporting to me the results of your experiment with Billy Best's dog, which suggests his mother's hypothesis of his disappearance is probably right."

"Showing you the note I wrote General Washington, Dr. Franklin, may be the quickest way to report my most recent progress. I made this copy of it for you. I gave the note to the General at the play."

Franklin absorbed the note's concise information at a glance and asked, "Where do you think Billy is being held, and how do you intend to prove it?"

"Colonel Zanzinger has informed me of a property owned by Declan O'Cormick that I did not know of when you and I last spoke, which is well suited to incarcerating someone clandestinely. The Old Powder House. It's stoutly built, has no windows that can be opened and only one door, made of iron. And it's isolated. The fact that there are few houses in its vicinity made it a good site for the storage of gunpowder, in case the magazine should ever accidentally explode. O'Cormick was building his sixth brick kiln inside the building and was within a few days of completing the project when he suddenly ordered work on it stopped and refused his workers further entry to it. And mark this, Dr. Franklin. The last day of work was the day Billy vanished. When the workers showed up the next morning, they were not allowed inside the building and were handed the tools they had left inside the day before, I'm told. More significantly, O'Cormick left Philadelphia that day, and his servants say he wont return from his trip until July 5th.

"So here we have an isolated, stout building having no movable windows and only one door, which is made of iron, and its owner abruptly decides to halt work on a major construction project inside it on the day Billy disappears—and leaves town the following day. Why, when he had invested so much time and money in creating his brick kiln, did he abruptly stop the project on that particular day, when, as a man familiar with O'Cormick's project told me, it was within a few days of producing marketable bricks that would repay his investment?"

"How do you plan to find out if William Best is being held inside the Old Powder House?" Dr. Franklin asked.

"If he's there, he would have to be fed, and in order to avoid being seen bringing him food, his rations would almost surely be delivered at night. Therefore, by watching the only door into the building for several nights, I think it can be ascertained whether someone is imprisoned there. If someone is, I would wager it's Billy.

"I've enlisted the help of the only neighbor whose residence permits a view of the door into the Old Powder House and, with

Sergeant Corbin's permission, I've spoken to the Convention Guards and recruited enough volunteers to keep watch on Old Powder House for the next several nights."

"Excellent, James! You've analyzed the problem precisely and done exactly what needed to be done to prove your hypothesis. A debt of thanks is owed Colonel Zanzinger for the interest he's taken in your investigation.

"Now, if Billy Best is being held captive by Mr. O'Cormick, we must consider what should be done to prepare the proper reception for this brickmaker on his return to Philadelphia. The practical question is, of course—once we establish from observation that someone inside the Old Powder House is being provided food—do we immediately free Billy? I would suppose you favor that approach on the grounds that Billy should not be confined a minute longer than he has to be."

"You suppose correctly, Dr. Franklin."

"Decades ago when the powder magazine was being built, I saw and admired the strength of that iron door. It would be impossible to open it without having a key, unless one used explosives or cannon fire. And using explosives would, of course, involve too great a risk to Billy.

"Moreover, if O'Cormick has kidnapped Billy Best and is holding him captive, he's had accomplices, which we must also consider in our planning. My view is that we must not free Billy before O'Cormick and all of his possible accomplices have been arrested. Unless things are managed that way, some or all of the culprits in this affair will likely escape apprehension and justice. The problem you see, James, is how to nab O'Cormick and his accomplices. That's what we have to make plans for."

"You really think O'Cormick would flee Philadelphia and leave behind his many properties if he knew we were on to him?" James asked.

"He might. Kidnapping is a capital offense. Property, even a good deal of it, can weigh but little when life itself is in the balance," Franklin replied. Then he observed, "If Billy is alive, knowing his character, I'm confident, as I've said before, that he either still has Mr. Gerry's letter on his person, intact, or has managed to destroy it. In other words, that he's done his duty to keep the letter he was to deliver from falling into the hands of anyone who shouldn't have it."

James asked, "So how does that observation, Dr. Franklin, affect the practical matter of how to proceed if we obtain evidence through observation to support our deduction that Billy is a prisoner in the Old Powder House?"

"Only in this wise, James, that if circumstantial evidence proves your hypothesis to be correct, and I think it likely will, then we are probably close to answering the other question of great import to us. Is the disappearance of Mr. Gerry's letter still a threat to the security of the Constitutional Convention? You must inform me, James, the instant you have evidence of Billy's whereabouts. Then you and I will have to meet to decide how to ensure that neither O'Cormick nor any of his abettors escapes justice. How many people work for O'Cormick? I would guess as many as twenty from what you've told me."

"That would be my guess also, Dr. Franklin, judged by the seven cottages he has for his workers to live in," James replied. "If anything, 20 might be a somewhat low estimate."

"Let us say 25, then, counting the cook and the housekeeper. That's roughly the number of McCormick's potential accomplices. How many of these might actually have been accessories to Billy's kidnapping and incarceration, do you suppose?" Benjamin Franklin asked.

James considered the question and said, "Among O'Cormick's employees, the cook would prepare the food to send to Billy, and the housekeeper would probably assist her. The Rankin brothers would certainly have been part of Billy's incarceration because they appear to be the executors of whatever O'Cormick decides to do. And one or both of his friends who go with him to the Southwark Theater to see Mrs. Wellborn on stage would likely be involved. If both friends were accomplices, that would make in sum six persons besides O'Cormick to be arrested."

"Then those seven persons will have to be taken into custody at the same time, James, on suspicion of kidnapping and being an accessory to it, which is to say, the crime of depriving a man of his liberty against his will, if we determine Billy is being held in the Old Powder House. We cannot arrest any of them without arresting all of them at the same time. We must, therefore, wait for O'Cormick's return to Philadelphia before acting. Otherwise, we jeopardize holding O'Cormick and his accomplices to account for what has been done."

The Results of Surveillance
Chapter XVIII

JAMES HAD RETURNED home from his conference with Dr. Franklin in the small hours of the night, and consequently remained abed until after nine that morning. When he came down to eat breakfast, he found Grandmère rocking her namesake Anne-Louise in her cradle, singing a French *berceuse* to the baby, one that her mother had sung to her when she herself had been an infant in Normandy. Livy was preparing a breakfast of salted mackerel and thick- cut, thickly buttered, rye bread for James and humming the chorus of Grandmère's lullaby, which she had learned from hearing Grandmère sing it so often to Anne-Louise. The baby was giving rapt attention to the face of her great-grandmother as she leaned over her cradle, singing,

Fais dodo, Colas, mon p'tit frère,
Fais dodo, t'auras du lolo.

(Sleep now, my little brother Colas,
Sleep now and you will have some milk.)

"This little one is *précoce*, Jamie," Grandmère said as James kissed the top of his grandmother's snowy-white head. "Yesterday she has said her first word besides 'Mama.' It is the word 'more,' a favorite word of Americans, which I have often heard them use since coming to live among them. If I am not mistaken, 'more' is the motto of the Americans. It made us laugh—did it not, Olivia dear?—to hear so petite a person say 'more' with such aptness! When she said it, her mother had been feeding her the applesauce and something caused her to pause. Then Anne, she said 'more'!"

James laughed with pleasure on hearing of this verbal accomplishment of his first child.

Following his breakfast and a vague conversation with Grandmère and Livy in response to Livy's question of what he would be doing that day, James left the house, saddled Jenny, and rode to the State House on Chestnut Street, where the Constitutional Convention was meeting six days a week to frame a new constitution to govern the United States.

Sergeant Corbin was as usual at his small table next to the entrance into the East Room as James entered the building and asked him, "Did we hook a fish on our trapline last night?"

"I believe Corporal Whitehouse saw something significant toward the end of his watch, Captain. Noah, why don't you get Whitehouse and meet Captain Jamison over at The Half Moon to tell him everything that transpired during the first night of surveillance."

When the three of them—James, Noah and Whitehouse— were seated at a table in a private room of the old inn, James asked the two Convention Guards to describe their vigils at the Old Powder House.

"As you know, I took the first watch, Captain Jamison," Noah Day said. "From nightfall to two o'clock in the morning, no one came to the door of the Old Powder House. Mr. Jones, from whose front parlor I was observing, made me a pot of coffee to help keep me awake, and he kept me company until midnight, when he went up to his bed."

James asked, "And what happened during your watch, Corporal Whitehouse?"

"It was uneventful until about four in the morning. Then I noticed a light coming across the fields north of Vine Street."

"What happened?"

"The light kept getting steadily closer and finally I saw the person carrying the lantern cross Vine Street and get on the path from the corner of Vine and Eighth to the powder house door."

"Man or woman?" James asked.

"I couldn't tell at first. But when the lantern carrier reached the iron door to the powder house, which has been painted white, some light from the lantern was reflected off the door, and I saw it was a man."

"Short? Tall? Fat? Lean? What age?" James inquired eagerly.

"I'd say in his thirties, more than average height, strongly built."

"Was he carrying anything besides his lantern?"

"It seemed he had a sack with something in it. He held the lantern in his right hand. The sack, in his left."

"How big was the sack?"

"Middling size."

"How was he dressed?"

"It was impossible to tell in the poor light. He wasn't wearing a hat, of that I'm certain. I had an impression he was dressed in the kind of clothes a working man wears, but I couldn't say for certain."

"What did the man do when he reached the door?"

"It seemed to take him quite a while to get it unlocked, as if he was having trouble with the key. Finally he managed it and swung the door open and went in. It was some minutes before I saw his light moving around inside the building behind the thick glass blocks where normally windows would be. It seemed he locked the door behind him before proceeding to whatever business he had come on.

"He wasn't inside long, and when he came back out, his sack seemed to be empty as near as I could tell by the light of his lantern. He stood outside the door awhile, working to get it fastened to his satisfaction, before moving off across the fields in the direction from which he'd come.

"By then, a steady, small rain had come on, and it continued until daybreak when I bade farewell to Mr. Jones, thanking him for letting me use his house for my vigil, and for the cup of coffee he'd brought me after he got up. Then I walked home in the rain."

"Very good, Corporal. And thank you also, Noah. The two of you have given me exactly what I needed. An indication of whether there's someone in the powder house being brought provisions under cover of darkness. From what Mr. Whitehouse saw happen, I'd say there is."

James wrote a simple message for Noah to take back to Sergeant Corbin in the State House.

> Have the Guard continue Surveillance for the next 2 Nights, in accordance with the Schedule you've made. I'm satisfied from what Whitehouse has reported that Food is being taken there under cover of darkness.

James walked over to the nearby Indian Queen Hotel, wrote a report to Dr. Franklin on what the first night of keeping watch had revealed, and delivered it to the letter drop in the west wall of Franklin Court.

Then he rode over to the City Tavern to see if the Jamison Glassworks had received any orders for glassware. Two orders had come in since the last time he'd checked. Then, because he had no urgent task to perform for General Washington and the Constitutional Convention, he rode up to the Jamison Glassworks, where he hadn't put in an appearance for several days. He wanted to confer with Mr. Bartlett, the glasshouse's senior glassblower, and with his sister Jane's husband Lawrence, who managed the production of glassware for Grandmère, the owner of the manufactory, and give them the new orders for glassware.

He returned home in time to eat a home-cooked dinner with his two ladies and Anne-Louise, and found that Mr. Mahoney, Dr. Franklin's majordomo, who was known to Livy, had brought a note summoning him to Franklin Court that afternoon at four.

When James arrived at the backdoor of Dr. Franklin's mansion-house a little before four o'clock, he was admitted by Mr. Mahoney and told that Dr. Franklin was waiting for him, and he was to go up to the new library. Upon doing so James found the good doctor in his usual state of bonhomie.

"Your surveillance of the Old Powder House has had good results, James, as your efforts in this case generally have had. You're again to be congratulated. But we must make certain William Best is being held in the Old Powder House that this Declan O'Cormick owns. The odds are near certain, as you've said, that it is Billy who's in the powder house."

"I've told Sergeant Corbin to continue for three more nights the watches he's scheduled for the Convention Guard, Dr. Franklin. That should be enough to determine the question, I think."

"I agree. I wanted to be sure you and I were in accord on this point, James. It would not do to make a move before ascertaining beyond any doubt that someone is being held prisoner inside the Old Powder House that O'Cormick owns. I would suggest establishing a nighttime watch on O'Cormick's kitchen, and to instruct the man keeping it to follow at a distance whoever comes out of O'Cormick's kitchen, to see where he goes."

James said he should have thought of that and would arrange with Sgt. Corbin to set such a watch.

Franklin said, "I also want to discuss with you a contingency that has occurred to me, James. What sort of reception should we prepare for Declan O'Cormick's homecoming, and when should we arrest him and his collaborators?"

"The four places O'Cormick and his accomplices are to be apprehended, Dr. Franklin," James replied, ticking them off on his fingers as he spoke, "are the mansion where he lives with his housekeeper and cook, the cottage near his mansion where the Rankin brothers live, and the separate homes of his two friends Conall Shaughnessy and Howard Kincaid. Seven arrests at four locations."

"To coordinate that many arrests at four locations, Sheriff Tuttleton and all of his deputies will be needed," Franklin said, "besides some half dozen members of the Convention Guard, who ought to be sworn in as temporary deputies under the Sheriff's authority. Therefore, James, you must go to Sheriff Tuttleton and tell him everything we've discovered. You must convince him that these seven arrests at these four locations are required."

"Come to think of it, Dr. Franklin, besides the four arresting parties, we also need to organize a smaller group to remove Billy from confinement in the Old Powder House. Since the powder house's iron door is so stout, I suggest the men taking O'Cormick into custody get the key to that door from him and immediately send it over to the party rescuing Billy."

"As the French say, James, *d'accord*," Franklin agreed. "Since we have no way of knowing whether O'Cormick will return to Philadelphia early or late on July 5th, the seven arrests and the rescue of Billy should be scheduled for the early morning of July 6th, provided O'Cormick has returned on the 5th. Only that way can we plan a precise time for the action. I think daybreak on the 6th."

"I agree, Dr. Franklin. Daybreak, the 6th of July."

"When you speak with the Sheriff, James, draw up lists of which deputies of his and which Convention Guards are to go on which arrests, and where and when they are to assemble and what each party is to bring."

The Sheriff

Chapter XIX

IT DID NOT TAKE long for James to ride from Franklin Court to the Sheriff's office on First Street. He knew Elias Tuttleton from having conferred with him in recent years while assisting Dr. Franklin in unraveling the mysteries of two violent deaths in Philadelphia. During the course of those investigations, he'd spoken with the Sheriff on several occasions. And the Sheriff had come to admire James, as everyone in Philadelphia had, for the feats that rightfully should have been attributed to Benjamin Franklin, who did not want it known to the public that he was willing to track down public malefactors.

As soon as James entered the office of Philadelphia's principal law-enforcement officer he was warmly greeted by the Sheriff. "It's been such a long time, Captain Jamison!" the Sheriff said, rising from his chair and shaking his visitor's hand. "My deputies have told me you're once again making inquiries, though I've heard no news of late regarding a mysterious, violent death requiring your particular talents."

Sheriff Elias Tuttleton was a strong-looking man of medium height whose brown, alert eyes always reminded James of the color of Dr. Franklin's eyes, though they lacked the merry expression of Franklin's constant good humor. Tuttleton's hair was brown, too, and thick, but beginning to grey. The general impression the Sheriff made was one of reliability and competence, as though he could single-handedly plow a large field between sunup and sundown.

James responded, "It's good to see you again, Sheriff. My investigations this time do not concern a killing, so far as I know. Nonetheless it's a capital crime I'm investigating, a crime like murder, which deprives a person of liberty—kidnapping. I've reason to believe a nineteen-year-old man has been abducted, a member of the Guard providing security to the Constitutional Convention by protecting it from eavesdroppers and spies. I've come to consult you about the disappearance of this young man."

"I heard Dr. Franklin had created such a Guard, Captain, and put my old friend Sergeant Alexander Corbin in charge of it. Would the young man you believe has been kidnapped happen to be the son of Rebecca Wellborn, the actress? She reported to me a few days back that her son was missing, and I recall she said he was nineteen years old and a member of the Convention Guard."

"Yes, that's the young man," James answered. "Based on circumstantial evidence, it would seem a merchant named Declan O'Cormick, smitten beyond reason by Mrs. Wellborn's extraordinary beauty, has taken her son hostage and is holding him until she submits to his lust."

"O'Cormick? Isn't that the man who's fast becoming Philadelphia's foremost maker of bricks?"

"So I've heard. I know he owns five brick kilns and is building a sixth."

"Well, well, well... I can sympathize with the Irishman's passion, though not with the behavior you attribute to him, of course. Mrs. Wellborn is the most captivating woman I've ever laid eyes on. It was hard not to stare at her while she was here with her maid. How far are you in your inquiries, Captain?"

"Far enough to want to report my findings and discuss them with you. But, first, let me show you under whose authority I'm acting this time," James said, handing Washington's commission to Sheriff Tuttleton.

After reading it, the Sheriff said, "I promised Mrs. Wellborn I'd do everything I could to locate her son, but I still have no clue as to the young man's whereabouts. I'd be glad to hear what you've discovered." Then he added, "You know, Captain, I'm an officer of the Commonwealth of Pennsylvania, and act under its authority for the good of the people of this State. I'm answerable only to those who've elected me to the office of Sheriff. Unlike General Washington, I don't concern myself with matters affecting all the States. And, regardless of the high esteem Washington enjoys among the people, including the people of Pennsylvania, and my esteem for you, Captain Jamison . . ." His voice trailed off into silence. Then he concluded his thought by saying, "I'm not compelled by law to do the General's bidding, or expend the resources of Pennsylvania to assist him."

"But that's just it, Sheriff. What I came to talk over with you are ways in which you would uphold the law of *Pennsylvania* against kidnapping. And you yourself just now told me you promised Mrs. Wellborn you'd do everything in your power to locate her son. In providing your aid to the enterprise I have in hand, you would serve two of your constituents who are in dire need. Although as Sheriff you must, of course, apply the law without prejudice, I thought you might want to know that this young man stands high in Sergeant Corbin's esteem. It was his being in the Convention Guard that brought his disappearance to the attention of General Washington, who, as you know, is the presiding officer of the Constitutional Convention."

James then conveyed to the Sheriff all the circumstantial evidence he had collected which had led him to conclude that Declan O'Cormick was holding Mrs. Wellborn's son captive in the Old Powder House. He particularly emphasized that the nighttime surveillance of the powder house by Billy's fellow Guards suggested food was being delivered there under cover of darkness, just before dawn.

Having reported to the Sheriff the results of the first night of surveillance, James continued, "This conclusion must be corroborated by further observations during the next several nights. But, given what I've told you, Sheriff Tuttleton, I hope you agree that this is an urgent matter. Will you pledge to work with us and take the necessary steps to assure justice and the safety of William Best?"

The Sheriff replied, "I'm pleased to hear you say your inquiries are as yet incomplete, Captain, and that you intend to maintain your watch on the Old Powder House to make *certain* someone is being held inside it. And, may I say, I think your surveillance should be expanded to include the probable point of supply as well as the point of delivery. Things would be a good deal more certain if we knew from observation that whatever is being delivered to the Old Powder House is coming from Declan O'Cormick's kitchen. I think I'll assign my best deputy to keep watch tonight an hour or so before dawn at O'Cormick's kitchen door, to determine if someone is taking food from there to the Old Powder House. And I'll tell my deputy to follow anyone coming from O'Cormick's kitchen to see where he goes."

James did not tell Sheriff Tuttleton that Dr. Franklin had given him the same advice, but only said, in commenting on this idea, "That would be very useful."

James went on to say, "It seems unlikely that O'Cormick could have kidnapped Billy Best without help from others. I surmise that possibly as many as four of his employees and two of his friends—the two who seem to share his attraction to Mrs. Wellborn—have helped him carry out this crime.

"I've been told O'Cormick's out of town at present, and won't be back until July 5th. If, as has been almost conclusively proven, he and his cohorts are holding Billy, then the arrests of all the kidnappers, those who abducted Billy and those holding him captive, ought to be made at the same time, to prevent any of O'Cormick's accomplices from escaping justice. If O'Cormick and those who've aided him are not taken into custody, the life of Mrs. Wellborn's son could well be in jeopardy.

"Given the many details that must be taken into account in seven simultaneous arrests, planning for the actions on the 6th, after O'Cormick's return to Philadelphia on the 5th, should begin now. The rescue of Mrs. Wellborn's son from his confinement must, of course, be part of that plan. The laws of Pennsylvania which you're sworn to uphold, Sheriff, must be enforced, regardless of the wealth or the social importance of any suspected perpetrator."

James and the Sheriff then discussed how many men would be needed to accomplish each arrest at the four different locations and for the rescue of Mrs. Wellborn's son from his confinement in the powder house. They also determined how many deputies the Sheriff could supply for each action, how many men the Convention Guard should furnish for each, and where each group would rendezvous in the early hours of July 6th.

James and the Sheriff then decided that the Sheriff would be responsible for determining on July 5th if Declan O'Cormick was in fact back from his trip, for without certainty on that point, nothing could be undertaken.

James went from the Sheriff's Office to the City Tavern to write a note to Dr. Franklin, informing him that he had obtained the Sheriff's cooperation in the rescue of Billy Best and the apprehension of O'Cormick and his suspected accomplices.

After leaving the note conveying this information at Franklin Court, James went home.

Early the next morning, he left his house in the western suburbs without speaking to Livy or Grandmère and rode into town to take breakfast at The Half Moon Inn across from the State House, to be there when Sergeant Corbin appeared for the last session of the Federal Convention before its scheduled two-and-a-half-day recess for the Fourth of July. And looking out through the Half Moon's dining-room windows just as he finished his breakfast, James saw Corbin arriving at the State House, across the street, and went over to invite the Sergeant to share a pot of coffee with him and have a talk.

By the time they'd finished their conference, James had reported to Sergeant Corbin everything he and Sheriff Tuttleton had said to each other, including the happy news that the Sheriff would cooperate in the rescue of Billy and the arrests of his suspected kidnappers. Corbin was especially pleased by the news that the Sheriff was going to set a watch on the kitchen door of O'Cormick's house to determine whether provisions were coming from that point of supply and taken to the Old Powder House.

Can the Convention Be Saved?

Chapter XX

BEFORE ELBRIDGE GERRY had written his letter to George Mason and James had begun collecting opinions and facts on the disappearance of Billy Best, the Constitutional Convention had been sliding deeper and deeper into a deadlock. As the Convention ground on through the high humidity and furnace-like heat of that June in Philadelphia, the debates on how to achieve a stronger union of the States had heated up. The fabric of gentlemanly politeness and respect among the delegates, on which their success depended, had begun to show signs of fraying. And time was running out for devising a basis for a lasting Union of the States.

The question causing the most friction was, how should the States' representation in the two houses of the new Congress be determined? Should the principle remain that each State had one vote and was therefore absolutely equal to every other State, as it was under the Articles of Confederation? Or should the new government be based on a new principle? And if a new principle was needed, what should it be? The most populous States—Massachusetts, Pennsylvania, and Virginia—advocated that State representation in both houses of Congress be based on population. After all, in a republic wasn't it people who were being represented?

In debating the principles of State population versus State sovereignty, another contentious question was involved. Slavery. Should slaves, who were *not* free men but *were* part of a State's population, be counted? Or should at least some portion of them be included in calculating the number of a State's representatives in Congress? Or perhaps the principle of equal State sovereignty and the principle of representation by population should both be dropped in favor of some other way of apportioning representation in the new bicameral Congress. And what would that be? Could a new principle that was both equitable and practical be devised?

Delegates from small States claimed more and more adamantly that the sovereignty of their States would be destroyed if the principle of each State having one vote in Congress were abandoned. According to their argument, if the big States had their way, and representation in Congress were based on the number of people in each State, the big States would exercise a perpetual tyranny over the small States when enacting laws that every citizen in every State in the Union had to obey.

Some small-State delegates were even saying they would leave the Convention rather than submit to representation in Congress based entirely on population. And of course if the small States abandoned the Convention, all hope of replacing the Union based on the Articles of Confederation with a more equitable Union would be at an end, because the Articles of Confederation were rapidly moving the United States toward dissolution. Before it was too late, could a government be framed that would permit the growth of a republic of many States, rather than just the first thirteen, while at the same time preserving belief in government by consent of the governed?

It appeared that most of the delegates to the Convention had arrived in Philadelphia wanting to frame a constitution that would make it possible for the number of States to grow rapidly while at the same time making the unity of the States stronger. But could those goals be achieved without sacrificing personal freedom, justice, and government by consent of the governed? The latter was an American belief identified in the Declaration of Independence as one of the natural rights God has bestowed on mankind, along with the right to life and the right to liberty.

On June 11th one delegate, George Read of Delaware, even stated that he wanted to completely do away with the concept of thirteen sovereign States. He took the floor of the Convention and proclaimed, "Let us frame a government that shall embody *the sovereignty of the United States*, and subordinate the sovereignty of the individual States to that. Too many Americans are primarily attached to their home State. That sentiment must be eliminated, because the concept of State sovereignty under the Articles of Confederation has given rise to a recurring discord which is tearing our Union apart!

"If these conflicts continue, they shall surely destroy the Union. I therefore propose abolishing the States. *That* is the only sure way to eliminate the incessant conflicts among the States. When Americans are no longer beguiled into acting against their true interests by their attachment to their individual States, then, and only then, can the people of the States truly unite."

And the people in the smaller States such as Delaware, where Read lived, would benefit the most by abolishing the States, he said.

Other delegates spoke of their concern that the States which would be formed from the great wilderness between the Appalachian Mountains and the Mississippi River would become so numerous and populous that they would diminish the political authority of the thirteen States that had seaports on the Atlantic. These apprehensive delegates urged the Convention to frame the new constitution in a way that would prevent that from happening and keep the western States under the control of the Atlantic States.

One delegate proposed that, rather than yield to the demand of the big States to apportion seats in Congress according to the number of people in a State, the small States should seek some powerful and honorable European nation to "take them in hand and do them justice."

Old, craggy-faced Roger Sherman, a godly New Englander of the Puritan type, had been a member of the Continental Congress that declared America's independence from the British empire. Thomas Jefferson had once observed of him, "He has never said a foolish thing in his life." At the Constitutional Convention, Sherman declared, "Government is instituted for those who live under it. It ought therefore to be so constituted as not to be dangerous to their liberties. Frequent elections are necessary to preserve the good behavior of rulers."

Sherman had made his living as a shoemaker, a bookseller, a storekeeper, and an almanac writer before becoming a self-educated lawyer, a judge, and a member of the Connecticut assembly and the Confederation Congress.

He was at the time of the Constitutional Convention mayor of New Haven, Connecticut, and reminded his fellow delegates that in New England government officers were elected annually to keep them from developing tyrannous proclivities.

During those June weeks of insufferable heat and humidity signs of consensus on the issue of State representation continued to diminish. Yet even before the armed insurrection of Massachusetts farmers, which had culminated in their attack on the federal arsenal at Springfield in January 1787, many Americans had seen the principle of absolute State sovereignty as a danger to the Union.

Benjamin Franklin, George Washington and many others recognized that to provide an enduring constitutional basis for the Union, a more practical principle than every State being sovereign had to be formulated. Otherwise, the United States could not become the large and powerful nation its resources foretold it should be. It seemed to many Americans that the Philadelphia Convention had been called to attain that goal.

On June 15th, New Jersey's wartime Attorney General, William Paterson, a native of County Donegal, Ireland, proposed a nine-point plan on behalf of the small States. This plan directly challenged the nineteen-point Virginia Plan that the Convention had adopted as a basis for debate. Paterson's proposal to the Convention—which was still meeting as a Committee of the Whole House—was immediately referred to as "the New Jersey Plan."

It retained the key feature of the Articles of Confederation, a unicameral Congress in which each State had one vote.   But it accepted the Virginia Plan's recommendation to add executive and judicial branches to the Articles of Confederation's legislative branch.

Paterson declared to the Convention, "My plan differs from the Virginia Plan in regard to the executive branch by calling for several people to fill the executive function, not one person. It would also allow members of Congress to remove the executive from office upon application of a majority of the State governors." Paterson then proceeded to read the rest of the nine points in the New Jersey Plan for general government of the United States. After that the Convention adjourned to study Paterson's proposal and get ready to debate the New Jersey Plan in comparison to the Virginia Plan.

When the Convention came back into session on June 16th, Mr. Paterson began the debate, proclaiming, "I concur with what my fellow judge, Robert Yates of New York, has said in reference to the equal sovereignty of the States. That is the basis for government under the Articles of Confederation, which were framed during the war and were unanimously ratified by the legislatures of all the sovereign States, with not one dissenting State vote. And what has been established by unanimous approval of the States can only be undone by the unanimous consent of all the States, including Rhode Island, which has sent no delegation to this Convention!"

Charles Pinckney of South Carolina then took the floor. "In my estimation Mr. Paterson is quite wrong," he said. "The Convention, in wanting to replace rather than amend the Articles of Confederation, is not violating any instruction it has received from the Confederation Congress. Rather, the Convention has been authorized to go to *any length* in recommending whatever it thinks will remedy the evils which led to calling the Convention."

James Wilson of Pennsylvania agreed with Pinckney. "The Convention has been empowered to propose anything it deems necessary to the preservation of the Union but is authorized to conclude nothing," he said. "Only the people of the States can approve and give the force of constitutional law to what the Convention may propose."

Wilson then proceeded to compare the two plans, the one proposed by the Governor of Virginia, Edmund Randolph, at the start of the Convention, and the one presented the previous day by Mr. Paterson. His speech was a lengthy disquisition on the nature and purpose of government.

In making his main point he said, "If the legislative authority be not restrained, there can be neither liberty nor stability; and it can only be restrained by dividing it within itself, into distinct and independent houses. In a single house, there is no shield but the inadequate one of the virtue and good sense of those who compose it. In order to control the legislative authority, you must divide it. To control the executive authority, however, you must unite it. One man will be more responsible than three men. An Executive composed of three men will contend among themselves till one of them becomes the master of his two colleagues."

Wilson paused and looked around the room before saying, "The Virginia Plan recommends itself by proposing to divide Congress into two houses; the New Jersey Plan provides for only one house, and is therefore not as good as the Virginia Plan. Moreover, the Virginia Plan calls for a single Executive, whereas the New Jersey Plan would create a multiple Executive. For these fundamental reasons alone, I much prefer the Virginia Plan to the New Jersey Plan.

"But there are also other reasons for my preference. Under the Virginia Plan the new Constitution would be ratified by conventions elected by the people in each State for that explicit purpose. Therefore the Virginia Plan would have the direct authorization of the people of the United States. It would also make the number of people residing in each State the basis for their representation in Congress, and would allow only the will of a majority of the representatives of the people in Congress to make federal laws binding on the people of all the States.

"The New Jersey Plan, on the other hand, in retaining the One-State-One-Vote Rule in Congress, would allow the will of a minority of people in the States to make laws binding on the whole population of America. And the New Jersey Plan would have the State legislatures ratify the new constitution, rather than specially elected conventions chosen directly by the people in each State for that explicit purpose."

The following day was again devoted to comparing the Virginia and New Jersey plans. The next day being a Sunday, the Convention did not meet.

On Monday the 18th of June, the entirety of the Convention's proceedings was devoted to a speech by Alexander Hamilton, the brilliant young attorney from New

York, who disagreed with Roger Sherman about having frequent elections. Hamilton advocated for stronger central government, declaring, "Elections should be as infrequent as possible. I call for a national government where the President and the members of the Senate shall be elected for life, in imitation of the stability of the British government, with its hereditary monarch and unelected House of Lords whose members, like the king, serve for life. I prefer that sort of government to either the Virginia Plan or the New Jersey Plan. In my judgment, neither of these two plans goes far enough toward instituting the strong government the United States requires."

The other delegates from Hamilton's home State of New York, Robert Yates, a New York Supreme Court Justice, and John Lansing, the mayor of Albany, were also disgruntled with the direction the Convention had taken. But their unhappiness had an altogether different source. Whereas Hamilton was unhappy because the Virginia Plan serving as the template for the Convention's debates did not give the federal government sufficient power, Yates and Lansing saw the Virginia Plan as violating the instructions the Confederation Congress had issued in calling for a Convention in Philadelphia. According to these two delegates' understanding of those instructions, the Philadelphia Convention had no authority to replace the Articles of Confederation. But that very thing had been approved by the Convention when, early on, the Virginia Plan had been adopted as a guide for debating the new constitution.

The next day, the 19th, comparisons of the Virginia and New Jersey plans were once more undertaken, and James Madison made extensive comments. "I note, as other delegates have done, that the New Jersey Plan, in which each State has a single vote in Congress, permits a minority of people to make laws for the majority. That defect in the current government simply cannot and should not be tolerated any longer, and the New Jersey Plan embodies it."

When the question was formally put to the Convention as to whether the Virginia Plan was preferable to the New Jersey Plan, the vote was seven States to three in favor of the Virginia Plan, with Massachusetts, Connecticut, Pennsylvania, Virginia, North Carolina, South Carolina, and Georgia in favor of it, while New York, New Jersey, and Delaware preferred the New Jersey Plan. Maryland's vote was not counted because its delegates were evenly divided on the issue, and New Hampshire's delegation had not yet arrived at the Convention.

After this vote, Rufus King of Massachusetts and James Wilson of Pennsylvania both expressed the opinion that the States as they stood should be retained. However, Mr. King added, "Much of the power the States now exercise under the Articles of Confederation ought to be taken from them." During the remainder of that week, the fifth since the start of the Convention, delegates wrangled over whether the Convention had the authority to replace the Articles of Confederation.

It was during this week that Elbridge Gerry wrote his ill-considered letter to George Mason summarizing the most inflammatory remarks made in the Convention and expressing his views on the crucial matter of how the States were to be represented—the letter which had vanished, along with Gerry's paid messenger, Billy Best.

But the delegates to the Convention knew nothing of either Gerry's letter or its disappearance. Nor did they have any inkling of the self-appointed ad hoc committee of Washington, Franklin, Madison, and Hamilton who sought to prevent the potentially disastrous consequences of the letter's disappearance.

Meanwhile, the delegates from the small States became increasingly agitated over the proposal that seats in *both* houses of the new bicameral Congress should be apportioned according to population.

The previous week one of the delegates had remarked in passing that a simple way out of the Convention's dilemma would be to assign the number of each State's seats in "the lower house"—as the U.S. House of Representatives was often called in debate—according to population, while giving each State the same number of seats in the Senate or "upper house."

But that suggestion was not put in the form of a motion, seconded, debated, and brought to a vote.

However, Oliver Ellsworth of Connecticut did make such a motion on the morning of Monday, the 2nd of July, when the Convention held its final meeting before its two-and-a-half-day Fourth of July break. The motion was seconded, and a vote was taken.

The result was an evenly divided Convention. Connecticut, New York, New Jersey, Delaware, and Maryland voted for this compromise; Massachusetts, Pennsylvania, Virginia, and North and South Carolina were against it; and the Georgia delegation was evenly divided and therefore not counted.

Roger Sherman gave the best description of the situation that existed in the Convention after this vote, saying the Convention was "now at full stop."

Everyone in the Convention felt the awful truth of Sherman's plain statement. But no one knew how the "full stop" could be overcome. None of the delegates to the Convention, except the Attorney General of Maryland, Luther Martin, and two of the three delegates from New York, John Lansing and Robert Yates, believed it was permissible for the Convention to dissolve without proposing a constitution that would "meet the exigencies of government" that the Articles of Confederation had failed to satisfy.

After this five to five deadlock and Sherman's "full stop" remark, a solemn hush pervaded the East Room of the

Pennsylvania State House. Then Major General Charles Coatsworth Pinkney of South Carolina stood and was recognized. "I move that a committee composed of one delegate from each State present at the Convention meet over the Fourth of July recess to come up with a proposal to break the deadlock," he said. "I offer this proposal in the spirit of compromise expressed by Dr. Franklin when he likened the Convention's task to the making of a broad table that requires taking something off each side of the boards for the table's top to achieve the needed tight joints."

As a result of General Pinckney's motion, the members of the Convention elected a Grand Committee, or Committee of Eleven, composed of Elbridge Gerry from Massachusetts, Oliver Ellsworth from Connecticut, Robert Yates from New York, William Paterson from New Jersey, Benjamin Franklin from Pennsylvania, Gunning Bedford from Delaware, Luther Martin from Maryland, George Mason from Virginia, William Davie from North Carolina, John Rutledge from South Carolina, and Abraham Baldwin from Georgia, to meet over the Fourth of July break.

It was fortunate that Pinkney happened to remind the Convention of Benjamin Franklin's spirit of compromise, which got the elderly statesman, with his twenty-seven years of diplomatic experience—from 1757 to 1775 in England, and from 1776 to 1785 in France—elected to the committee. And it was exceedingly wise of Franklin to turn down the offered chairmanship of the Committee in deference to Elbridge Gerry, because that allowed Franklin to contribute what he was most adept at providing—a spirit of good-humored compromise; proposing recommendations that would work; and making his experience available in a nonpartisan way. Such influences were much needed to solve the quandary that had brought the Convention to a stop.

Franklin also provided something else—the mollifying effects of good food and drink served in beautiful surroundings when the Committee of Eleven, or Grand Committee, met for the first time on July 2nd, the day it was created, in Franklin's new dining room and the group partook of a supper catered by the City Tavern. Turtle soup, veal pie, broiled and crisped small trout, fresh bay scallops, green beans with bacon bits, walnut and apple salad and vanilla ice cream—made by using ice from Dr. Franklin's year-round icehouse—drizzled with rhubarb sauce.

After this meal the members of the Committee repaired to Dr. Franklin's splendid new library. In the midst of his thousands of beautiful books—and his certificates of membership in the learned societies of Europe and America, and his framed honorary degrees from colleges and universities on both sides of the Atlantic, including honorary doctorate degrees from the two oldest universities in Britain—the members of the Committee of Eleven were served whatever after-dinner drinks they fancied by Dr. Franklin's confidential servant Mr. Mahoney, who, after this service, left the library, and the Grand Committee got down to its assigned work of trying to find a way out of the Convention's dilemma.

The Glorious Fourth

Chapter XXI

THE COMMITTEE OF ELEVEN convened again at nine on the morning of July 3rd in Dr. Franklin's new library at Franklin Court, to partake in his further hospitality and benefit from his years of arranging practical compromises between persons of opposing views to serve a common good. At two o'clock another dinner catered by the City Tavern was provided; and at four the task of finding a compromise resumed in the library and lasted until suppertime.

Early on the morning of the Fourth, well before the Convention's usual ten o'clock meeting hour, the Committee of Eleven assembled in the East Room of the Pennsylvania State House. Sergeant Corbin had the Convention Guard at full strength manning its three posts as if the entire Convention was in session. The Committee worked through the hurly-burly of Philadelphia's explosive, citywide celebrations of the Fourth of July, the noisiness of which penetrated the six wide, tall windows of their meeting room. On Dr. Franklin's instructions, Corbin dismissed the Guard at one o'clock so its members could participate in the Independence Day celebrations, and the Committee members walked the short distance from the State House to Franklin Court to participate in yet another sumptuous repast. Dr. Franklin preceded them in his sedan chair, borne by his four brawny carriers.

Meanwhile, the other delegates to the Convention and the residents of Philadelphia were enjoying the many events and diversions offered in celebration of the Glorious Fourth of July in the city where America's Declaration of Independence had been written, signed, and promulgated to the world eleven years before.

These included military exercises in the tree-shaded promenade behind the State House, where the City Calvary and a brigade of Pennsylvania militia demonstrated their prowess, and where a battery of cannons slowly fired solemn salvos of thirteen shots, one for each State, on the hour, all day long. Noisy fireworks set off at random by energetic boys in every neighborhood of the city also enlivened the day. And there were parades by the city's worker guilds—the carpenters, the printers, the bricklayers, the joiners, the hatters, and all the other craftsmen— throughout the day, as well as parades by English, French, German, Irish, Dutch, Scandinavian, and other fraternal organizations of immigrants, some accompanied by elaborate, horse-drawn floats.

Peale's Museum was an especially popular resort, with its "moving pictures," celebrated dioramas, panoramic paintings of historic moments in the war for independence, and its splendid collection of portraits of the most notable American leaders in the war. Many of the city's numerous taverns and inns offered recitations by professional orators of the sacred words of the Declaration of Independence. Public orations on topics related to American independence and how it had been achieved were sponsored by various societies. The most popular were commentaries on the importance to the rest of mankind of the ideas set forth in the Declaration of Independence.

The pealing of church bells from morning to night called worshippers to the city's numerous churches to give thanks for Almighty God's Providence. The sermons on the war's outcome were highly popular. Sermons on natural law were also preached and well received. Many of these emphasized the wonderful future which awaited the United States if the Convention meeting in Philadelphia succeeded in creating a more suitable government for a nation of many States, in anticipation of the many States soon to be organized in the immense expanse of unsettled land west of the mountains.

The consumption of food and drink accompanying the festivities was gargantuan. Whole hogs and even entire beeves were roasted on huge spits turned by strong men. Spits skewering three or four turkeys at a time were turned by strong boys. Great quantities of drink were consumed—barrels of rum and whiskey, hogsheads of beer, and puncheons of lemonade.

Every civic organization and many of Philadelphia's important institutions gave elaborate banquets—the volunteer fire companies, the Masonic lodges, the workers' guilds, the hospital, the university, the American Philosophic Society which Franklin had organized for the promotion of science, the library society which he had also organized, and the Junto clubs for self-improvement which Franklin had founded as a young man. And at every such gathering, numerous patriotic toasts were drunk along with the consumption of food.

At two o'clock the militia which had been performing in the yard behind the State House joined forces with the Society of the Cincinnati—the fraternal association of commissioned officers who had served in the war for independence—to escort General Washington, President of the Cincinnati, to the German Lutheran Church on Race Street to hear an oration by James Campbell who was noted for his proficiency in classical oratory. This was followed by the Cincinnati's grand banquet at the City Tavern honoring Washington and memorializing the Americans who'd given their lives that America might be free of foreign domination. There were also concerts of music written by Philadelphia's composers and performed by the city's musical societies.

At the Southwark Theater, a performance of the new play *The Contrast* by Royall Tyler, comparing America's republican virtues to England's effete aristocratic manners, was staged, with the renowned actress Rebecca Wellborn in the leading role of Maria.

After the Committee of Eleven concluded its work on the afternoon of the Fourth Dr. Franklin took to his bed to read and drink the French spring water he had grown so fond of during his nine-year ambassadorship to France, and to give his pain-wracked body some well-earned ease. At eighty-one, he needed to recuperate from his efforts to steer the Committee of Eleven in the right direction without its members knowing he was doing so. Much of the text of the Committee's final recommendation was from his fluent pen or written at his suggestion by other members of the Committee. While he rested in bed, professional scribes were making copies of the Committee's recommendation for distribution.

On the Glorious Fourth Captain James Jamison received a report from the Sheriff saying that his deputies had observed food being sent from the kitchen of Declan O'Cormick to the Old Powder House. He received the news just before leaving Philadelphia to enjoy its countryside with his family.

As they had done before, the Jamison family planned to celebrate the Fourth picnicking on the 150-acre estate called Bush Hill owned by James Hamilton, a wealthy Philadelphia attorney and outstanding trial lawyer, who had inherited it from his father, who had also been a famous attorney and a close friend of William Penn, the founder of Pennsylvania. Penn's country estate, named for his first wife, Gulielma Maria Springett of Sussex, England, lay just to the west of Bush Hill.

The steward of Bush Hill, Edward Latham, had been a friend of James's grandfather Samuel Jamison; and Mr. Latham had obtained from his master permission for Samuel Jamison and his family to picnic at Bush Hill whenever they pleased, a privilege Grandmère, Samuel Jamison's widow, had continued to exercise after her husband's death.

A fortnight earlier Grandmère had contracted with Morton's Livery, the livery she preferred to use, to have her favorite driver, Matthew Crowley, pick her up at her home at ten on the morning of the Fourth, along with James and Livy and their infant daughter. She had specified that the carriage must be large enough to then also collect, in the Northern Liberties, Jane Jamison Sheraton, her husband Lawrence Sheraton, their three small boys, and Jane's maid Abigail.

After Jane and her family had been picked up, the carriage went west on Vine Street to the turnoff, two squares past Broad Street, that led to the imposing three-story Georgian mansion and its outbuildings on what was called Bush Hill, the highest eminence north of Vine in that part of Philadelphia's countryside. The drive there was filled with anticipation for the four women and two men who had been to Bush Hill before, and for the two small boys who were old enough to be informed of what awaited them. For Sammy and Jamie, Jane and Lawrence's five-year-old twin boys, this meant standing in front of their father and their uncle as the carriage rolled along toward its destination and listening to the exciting things Uncle Jamie was recounting.

Captain James Jamison was telling his little nephews that at Bush Hill they would see big birds called peacocks with *enormous* tails, like the fan their Mommy was using to cool herself and their little brother Frankie. This made the twins look over at their mother, who was sitting on the carriage seat, facing forward, next to the right hand rear window of the carriage, fanning herself and Frankie, who was sprawled on her lap, sucking the thumb of his right hand and dreamily twirling his hair with the fingers of his other hand. Their mother's maid, Abigail, sat next to her, and Aunt Livy, holding baby cousin Anne-Louise, was on the other end of the forward-looking carriage seat by the coach's other back window.

Uncle Jamie told them the peacocks could open and close their giant tails whenever they wanted to, only their tails were much, much bigger than their mother's fan, and had giant eyes in them that looked STRAIGHT AT YOU! If they were lucky, they might see the peacocks making their tails quiver all over. They might even hear the peacocks SHRIEK!

Another thing Bush Hill had, Uncle Jamie said, was a big house made of glass for growing beautiful flowers from faraway places, which had been brought to the glass house because the man who owned Bush Hill liked beautiful flowers and paid to have them brought there to grow in the sun-warmed glass house he had had especially built for them.

Besides the big glass house where the flowers from faraway places grew, there was a smaller glass house they could go in that was full of the hummingbirds they loved to watch gathering nectar from the honeysuckle in front of Grandmère's house; and they would be close enough to these hummingbirds to hear them thrumming their wings as they zoomed from flower to flower, hovering on their tiny wings whose movements were so fast they looked like a blur.

Uncle Jamie also told his two little nephews who were making their first trip to Bush Hill that there were horses there that were only as tall as they were! And besides all of *these* wonderful things, there were big roosters that crowed so loudly you had to cover your ears with your hands if you were standing next to them when they crowed.

There was also a paddock with big, woolly sheep you could pet. And a dairy where the cows gave creamy milk. And the biggest stone building you could imagine, with high ceilings and lots of light, which smelled of fresh hay and was divided into stalls where horses of the regular size lived, each in its own stall, where it slept on a clean, sweet-smelling bed of fresh hay, and men and boys called grooms did nothing but take care of them and bring them their food and water, and ride them out into the countryside every day for exercise.

Sammy asked his Daddy if he could ride the little horses that were only as tall as he was; and Lawrence, who was listening to every word Uncle Jamie was saying and smiling as he listened, said maybe he would be allowed to do that. They would have to see.

Sammy's twin brother, Jamie, wanted to know if he could be "a broom" when he grew up, and feed and ride the big horses; and his uncle, for whom he had been named, said, "Absolutely!"

Just then James's twin sister Jane, the boys' mother, called out, "Look at the pretty cows in the field, boys!"

And so the trip to Bush Hill went, with Grandmère in the corner of the backward-facing seat next to Lawrence, being lulled to sleep by the gentle rhythm of the swaying carriage and gently snoring. She woke when the rhythm of the carriage that had put her to sleep changed as the carriage turned onto the road going up to Bush Hill. The coach ascended the road to the great house situated on the eminence that gave Bush Hill its name and drove past the grassy paddock of the miniature horses. When the twins spotted them, they called out to their mother and father, "Oh, look at the little horses!"

The carriage came to a stop behind the kitchen wing of the big house at Bush Hill, where Edward Latham, whom Grandmère had informed of the hour of their arrival, came out of the kitchen to welcome them. As soon as the carriage stopped, Sammy and Jamie pestered their father to take them back down the hill to the pasture with the little horses. Taking hold of their father's hands as soon as they were out of the carriage, one on each side of him, tugging him in that direction, they cried out, "Come on! Hurry up! Come on!"

Nothing would do until they had gone with their Daddy to inspect the paddock of miniature horses.

James stayed behind with the ladies and the two smaller children to help the coachman and Mr. Latham take the picnic things down from the top of the carriage and load them into the pushcart waiting to convey them to the place where the Jamisons customarily picnicked at Bush Hill, a shady grove of tremendously old white oaks. The grove had been cleaned of its underbrush many years before and had grown a carpet of small ferns, fine wild grasses, and tiny purple and pink wildflowers. A breeze seemed always to be pleasantly stirring the dense foliage of these large white oaks.

Grandmère and her deceased husband had discovered the grove with the guidance of Edward Latham on their third picnic visit to Bush Hill, during the time when they liked to picnic with both Edward and his wife Nancy who, like Samuel Jamison, had passed away.

A smooth path led from the kitchen wing of the house to the shady grove, and James had no trouble trundling the pushcart full of picnic things along it with the help of Mr. Latham. Grandmère had brought five old quilts to the picnic, and she had her grandson spread three on the grass under the trees. Two quilts were laid side by side for serving and eating the picnic, and the other three were spread separately in comfortable places nearby for napping after the picnic.

Mr. Latham declined Grandmère's earnest invitation to join them, saying he'd already accepted an invitation to a Fourth of July feast with the other servants at Bush Hill. Just as Mr. Latham was saying his goodbye to Grandmère,

Lawrence and the twins returned from their expedition to the paddock of the miniature horses.

Grandmère had chosen the menu for the picnic, and had seen to the preparation of its dishes, the cooking of which had begun the day before and had not been completed until that morning. She and Livy had prepared the pork in cider, a specialty of Grandmère's native region of Normandy in France, following a recipe she'd brought with her when she'd immigrated to America as a young woman. Livy and she had also fixed the rice pudding cooked in cream. Grandmère had obtained some Norman spiced sausages and a medley of Pennsylvania country cheeses from a fellow native of Normandy, who had a farm on the other side of the Schuylkill River, not far from Grandmère's house in the western suburbs. Livy had baked three loaves of Dutch Bread and prepared a jar of apple butter to go with them.

Grandmère's granddaughter Jane and Jane's maid Abigail had been assigned the chicken with egg and cream sauce, and the oysters rolled in breadcrumbs and fried in butter, which had been prepared fresh that morning. Jane and Abigail also furnished the pressed wild duck, the two rhubarb pies, two gallons of spring water, and two gallons of cider, one hard and one soft.

The two branches of the Jamison family each brought their own cutlery, plates, drinking glasses, and napkins.

The leisurely partaking of the picnic, including one of the rhubarb pies, took several hours, since it was accompanied by much good-natured family banter and tending to the needs of the children.

Afterwards, James and Livy and Lawrence and Jane walked off the meal by taking the twins to find the free-roaming peacocks. They located several and saw them open and close their immense tails, fly up to the limbs of a big tree, and—to the special delight of the twins—heard them SHRIEK.

They also visited the fancy brick chicken coop where the giant roosters lived with their hens, secure from foxes and weasels. After that they took the twins to see the wonders of the Bush Hill greenhouse, the hummingbird aviary, the sheepfold, and the magnificent stable of Bush Hill racehorses, breeding mares, and studs.

Meanwhile, Abigail entertained the two infant children until they fell asleep, and Grandmère napped on her quilt with her special pillow to cushion her head, while a white shawl she had knitted protected her from the grove's cool breeze and satisfied her modesty.

When the family reassembled after their post-picnic doings, it was to take some liquid refreshments together and eat another helping of rhubarb pie if they were so inclined.

Then, in remembrance of the meaning of the holiday, they read the Declaration of Independence from beginning to end to an accompaniment of birdsong, sunbeams, bees, and the rustling of the breeze in the white oaks.

In pairs, they read a part of the magnificent birth certificate of the United States of America before handing the copy of the Declaration of Independence, which James had brought to the picnic, to the next pair of readers.

James and Livy read the two-paragraph beginning of the Declaration, each of them reading a single paragraph. James started.

"When in the course of human events, it becomes necessary for one people to dissolve the political bands which have connected them with another, and to assume among the powers of the earth, the separate and equal station to which the Laws of Nature and of Nature's God entitle them, a decent respect to the opinions of mankind requires that they should declare the causes which impel them to the separation."

Then Livy in her fine voice continued. "We hold these truths to be self-evident, that all men are created equal, that they are endowed by their Creator with certain unalienable rights, that among these are life, liberty and the pursuit of happiness. That to secure these rights, governments are instituted among men, deriving their just powers from the consent of the governed. That whenever any form of government becomes destructive of these ends, it is the right of the people to alter or to abolish it, and to institute new government, laying its foundation on such principles and organizing its powers in such form, as to them shall seem most likely to effect their safety and happiness."

This introduction expressed the beliefs Americans considered "self-evident" because their experience of transforming a Stone Age wilderness into towns and farms, generation after generation, for eight successive generations, had taught them to believe as a people in government by, for, and of the people.

Then came the long middle section of the Declaration detailing the offenses of George the Third—his crimes against the natural law of God—which disqualified him from being a monarch Americans had to obey.

Grandmère and Abigail read this part of the Declaration, alternating the twenty-eight sentences cataloguing the king's offenses and the descriptions of the unsuccessful efforts of Americans to find a peaceable solution to his tyranny, which forced them to fight a war to leave the British empire.

Grandmère insisted on reading this section of the Declaration because, she said, she had experienced the tyranny it described and remembered it well.

That left Jane and Lawrence to complete the reading of the Declaration, which they decided to do by reciting the conclusion in unison. "We, therefore, the representatives of the united States of America [sic], in general congress assembled, appealing to the Supreme Judge of the world for the rectitude of our intentions, do, in the name, and by the authority of, the good people of these colonies, solemnly publish and declare that these united colonies are, and of right ought to be, free and independent States; that they are absolved from all allegiance to the British crown, and that all political connection between them and the State of Great Britain, is and ought to be totally dissolved; and that as free and independent States, they have full power to levy war, conclude peace, contract alliances, establish commerce, and to do all other acts and things which independent States may of right do. And for the support of this declaration, with a firm reliance on the protection of divine Providence, we mutually pledge to each other our lives, our fortunes and our sacred honor."

The resounding words of the Declaration of Independence, which had been addressed to the nations of the world left the picnickers in a somber mood. And the two couples, James and Livy and Jane and Lawrence, decided to take another walk, each couple by themselves, hand in hand, leaving their four children in the loving care of Grandmère and Abigail.

Along toward seven, with the shadows of evening lengthening, the carriage from Morton's Livery returned, as scheduled, to pick up the Jamisons and return them to their respective homes in the Northern Liberties and the western suburbs of Philadelphia.

Once home, as night fell on the American metropolis they enjoyed the cheerful popping sounds of the last fireworks being set off by young Americans in triumphant memory of the war that brought America independence from the dominance of foreign beliefs.

July 5th

Chapter XXII

AT THE CONVENTION'S FIRST session, following the Fourth of July recess, on July 5th, Elbridge Gerry, as chairman of the Committee of Eleven, reported the Committee's three-part recommendation for the new constitution regarding representation of the States in the bicameral Congress. Gerry declared, "We, the members of the Committee of Eleven, agree that the three parts of our recommendation cannot be separately debated but must be considered as inseparable.

"The first part is that the people of each State should elect to the first house of the new bicameral Congress one person for every 40,000 of their State's residents, including persons indentured for a term of years, and three-fifths of all other persons, except Indians not paying taxes. The second part is that bills for appropriating money and fixing the salaries of officials of the United States should originate in that house. And, third, that in the second house of the bicameral Congress, each State shall have the same number of representatives, regardless of a State's population."

The Convention having heard this report, George Washington opened proceedings for comments and recognized Mr. Wilson of Pennsylvania. Wilson stood up and exclaimed, "The Committee has exceeded its powers!"

Mr. Madison of Virginia observed, "It would not be much of a concession from the small States to the big States to grant the privilege of originating money bills to the House of Representatives, in which seats allotted to the big States would outnumber the seats held by the small States, since if a small State wanted to introduce a money bill, it could readily find in the first house representatives from its State willing to do that."

After hearing the Committee's recommendation, Gouverneur Morris of Pennsylvania, who, like Wilson and Madison, was from a big State, made a declaration about the significance of the proceedings of the Convention as a whole. He said, "I have come to this Convention as a representative of America and, to some degree, of the whole human race, because the whole human race will be affected by the proceedings of this Convention. I wish, therefore, that gentlemen would extend their views beyond the present and beyond the narrow thinking of the single State that elected them a member of this Convention. If I were to give credence to some of the things I've heard, I should think we had come here to truck and bargain for our particular States. But I cannot bring myself to believe that any of the gentlemen are motivated by such narrowness. We must look forward, to the effects of what we do for future generations of Americans. Those considerations alone should guide us.

"This country must unite under a stronger government than the one it presently has. If reasoning will not so unite it, then the sword will." Morris poured a glass of water from the pitcher at his delegation table, and took a long draught from it, then continued. "Were the States to have equal representation in the second house of the proposed Congress, our experiences under the Articles of Confederation show that the result will be constant political disputes and turmoil. Giving absolute importance to State attachments has been the bane of this country. I wish us to enlarge our thinking to include the true interests of mankind, rather than be circumscribed within the narrow compass of a particular spot. After all, who can say whether he himself, much less his children, will not become next year an inhabitant of another State? Opportunities for improving one's condition are not to be found in one place only in America."

Gunning Bedford, Delaware's representative on the Committee of Eleven, rose and defended the Committee's three-part, unified recommendation. "As the recommendation makes clear," he said, "the lesser States have thought it necessary to put a provision in the proposed new constitution that will be a safeguard or bulwark for them to preserve their integrity as political units. No man can foresee to what extremities the small States might be driven by the oppressions of the large States. In the judgment of the Committee, the recommended equal representation in the second house of the new Congress provides that needed protection and safety for the lesser States without which, it appears, a more just and enduring Union cannot be formed." Bedford paused and looked down at his notes before proceeding.

"Then there is this to be considered. We have been sent here to confer and devise a more stable and just Union of States than the present general government under the Articles of Confederation affords the country. The people expect us to do that, and the present condition of the Union demands that it be done with dispatch, as an urgent need. Would it not be far better that a plan for an improved general government which might not be perfect in every way come out of this Convention than no plan at all? I think so. I do not know where other gentlemen spent the Glorious Fourth, but everywhere I went I heard expressions of anticipation that this Convention will produce a plan for a stronger Union than the present Articles of Confederation provide. As our esteemed Dr. Franklin has said on more than one occasion, compromises are unavoidable when one is devising a plan of government for a vast extent of territory."

Oliver Ellsworth from Connecticut, another small State, supported Bedford. Ellsworth affirmed, "I am ready to accept the compromise the Committee has recommended because it is evident that some compromise is necessary if the Convention is to achieve its purpose. And I can think of no clearer or more practical compromise than proportional representation in the first house of the new Congress and equal representation in its second house."

Hugh Williamson of North Carolina responded, "Although I do wish to hear the Report discussed, the recommendation of the Committee is the most objectionable of any I have yet heard."

Mr. Paterson of New Jersey, the most ardent spokesman for the smaller States and a member of the Committee of Eleven, said, "I am ready to freely discuss the three-part recommendation of the committee, whose parts cannot be separately discussed. But Mr. Morris's reference to using the sword to achieve unity among the States is not conducive to any useful agreement!"

Mr. Gerry observed, "If some agreement for a better Union, based on a set of rational compromises, is not forthcoming from the Convention, America is certainly laying itself open to foreign interventions of a military kind."

George Mason, Virginia's representative on the Committee of Eleven, stood up and said, "The Report is meant, not as a specific set of propositions to be adopted, but merely as a general basis for accommodation. Because if some ground of accommodation in this conflict over representation in the Congress is not soon found, the Convention will not be able to achieve its required purpose. However liable to objections the Committee's recommendation might be, it is preferable to an appeal to the world to settle the dispute *for* Americans, as I now hear some gentlemen alleging could happen.

"It could not be more inconvenient to any gentleman to remain absent from his private affairs, than it is for me to be here in Philadelphia. But I would rather bury my bones in this city than expose America to the consequences of the dissolution of this Convention without our having done anything to correct the situation we've been sent here to correct."

It was then moved, seconded, and approved that the first part of the Report's recommendation, that each State elect to the first branch of the new Congress one representative for every 40,000 of its inhabitants, and that the definitions that would apply to what constituted "inhabitants," would be discussed.

Gouveneur Morris then said, "This arrangement does not use a State's wealth *and* the number of its inhabitants to decide how many representatives it should have in the first house of Congress. Yet a State's wealth as well as the number of its inhabitants will be what this branch of the new government will in fact be representing. A savage state of society, it has been shown, is generally more favorable to liberty than a civilized state of society. It is only when men acquire a taste for property that the restraint of government is needed to make property safe.

"If I am right and that is so," he continued, "and providing security for property is the main object of government, then wealth ought to be one measure of the influence due those possessing property who are to be affected by the decisions of government. This line of thought may seem new, but it is just.

"I very much look forward to the range of new States which will soon be formed west of the mountains. But I think provision should be made to ensure that the Atlantic States prevail in the general government, as for years to come most of the wealth will be found in these older States.

Hence provisions ought to be put in the new constitution to prevent the not yet formed, or even named, interior States from outvoting the coastal States. This can easily be done by allowing Congress to fix the number of representatives each State is to have."

John Rutledge of South Carolina then stood to speak. "I agree with Gouverneur Morris that property is the principal object of civilized governments, and that if a State's population becomes the sole criterion for its representation in government, the Atlantic States will soon be outvoted by representatives of new States in the fast-growing interior region west of the Appalachians. Therefore, I advise that, in allotting seats in Congress, discussion of the initial recommendation in the Report be deferred until provisions are devised for taking into account the amount of money a State contributes to running the general government."

Mr. Mason of Virginia stated emphatically, "New States should enter the Union without any sort of political discrimination and be considered equal to the States already in the Union."

Then Mr. Randolph responded, saying, "Gentlemen, I want you to know that I concur most assuredly with Mr. Mason's view. New States must be treated as completely equal to previous States."

Mr. Rutledge then made a motion that wealth should be a factor in apportioning seats in Congress. This motion was defeated, nine to one: Massachusetts, Connecticut, New York, New Jersey, Pennsylvania, Delaware, Maryland, Virginia, and North Carolina all voted in the negative; and only South Carolina voted in the affirmative. Georgia's delegation was not present in Convention.

While these contentious discussions were taking place in the Convention, indicating that apportionment of seats in Congress was still a live, unresolved issue, Captain James Jamison, Sheriff Elias Tuttleton, and Sergeant Alexander Corbin were sitting at a small, round worktable in the armory attached to the Sheriff's office. The subject they were discussing was the plan for arresting Declan O'Cormick and his four employees and two friends suspected of participating in either the kidnapping or the imprisonment of William Best, or both.

The Sheriff began. "We have seven persons to arrest tomorrow morning at four thirty in the morning, at four different locations," he said. "And we also have to accomplish the rescue of William Best. I've obtained warrants for these arrests, and have made the arrangements to transport these suspected lawbreakers to the Walnut Street Jail Annex. We must decide how many and which men to assign to each arrest and to the rescue of William Best—and who will be in command of each group. I'll assign four of my five deputies to this effort, leaving just one deputy on duty in the Sheriff's office. I understand, Alex, that a dozen of your Convention Guards have volunteered to participate?"

"That's right," Corbin replied.

"I think it best that I have charge of Declan O'Cormick's arrest at his residence on the Germantown Road, along with those of his housekeeper, Lucinda Belacre, and his cook, Esther Wallsend. From the information you provided, Captain Jamison, O'Cormick's overseer, John Rankin, and his brother Michael are strong men in the prime of life, and Michael Rankin may be disposed to resist arrest. So it seems fitting, Alex, that you should take charge of those arrests. As you probably know, the Rankin brothers live in one of the tenements O'Cormick maintains for his workers next to his brick kilns and mansion on the Germantown Road. My choice for the person to lead the arrest of O'Cormick's associate Conall Shaughnessy, at his residence on Race Street, would be my most experienced deputy, Hector Sheppy, and I'd like my Deputy Charles Fuller to lead the party arresting Howard Kincaid, the other associate of O'Cormick who may have helped him carry out the kidnapping. For releasing William Best from his confinement in the Old Powder House, you are the natural choice, Captain Jamison. Do either of you object to any of my choices or have any corrections or additions to make?"

Sergeant Corbin said, "The names of my men who, in my judgment, would be the best ones to participate in each arrest, Elias, are these. For arrest number one, which you will lead, Corporal Adam Bomberger, Corporal Thomas Whitehall, and Private Samuel Evarts.

"For the second arrest, Corporal Richard Chapman and Private Peter Broadhurst. To go with me to arrest the Rankin brothers, I think Private Noah Day would be best since he's seen both brothers and can identify them on sight. I'd also like Private George Kosh, the stoutest of the Convention Guards to come with me on this action, along with Private Adam Farrier. I'd recommend Privates Samuel Banks and Henry Greenbough for the arrest of Mr. Kincaid.

"And I've told Private Donald Cavendish to go with you to arrest Mr. O'Cormick, so when you get the key to the iron door of the Old Powder House from O'Cormick, Cavendish—who's got a reputation for winning foot races— can take it swiftly to Captain Jamison to unlock the iron door and free Billy Best.

"If you agree with all these assignments, Elias, I'll meet with these volunteers this afternoon at the State House, when today's session ends, to discuss what's expected of each man, and I'll tell them exactly where and when they're supposed to rendezvous tomorrow morning, and what to bring."

The Sheriff said, "I'd like to attend that meeting, too, Alex, with my Deputies Sheppy and Fuller. They'll be the leaders of two of the arresting parties, and that way your men can meet their leaders and ask them questions, if they have any, and we can get to know them."

James said to the other two, "I'll go to Mr. Jones's home tomorrow morning at four. It's near the Old Powder House. That's where I'll wait for the key to the iron door to carry out the rescue. As you know, Mr. Jones has allowed us to use his home for our surveillance of the powder house, and he told me we may do so for as long as we want. I have an extra horse I'll take with me for Billy Best to ride home after we rescue him. At a quarter past four I'll leave Mr. Jones's house and go wait outside the Old Powder House for delivery of the key."

The Sheriff replied, "And I'll have my men assemble at four at the corner of Germantown Road and Callowhill Street to arrest O'Cormick and his household servants. I'll tell Hector's party to assemble at The Turkey Cock—that's a tipling house on Race Street at Second that stays open through the night."

"I think Callowhill and Germantown would also be a good place for me to have my men meet, Elias, since the tenement where the Rankin brothers live is only a short distance away from O'Cormick's mansion," Sergeant Corbin offered. "Should my men come armed with their usual muskets and bayonets, or should I give them pistols?"

Sheriff Tuttleton replied, "I think they should use the weapons they're accustomed to using. Also, having some of our men with muskets and bayonets will give our actions a military look that should make the arrests go more smoothly."

At four o'clock that afternoon, while at home waiting to go into town to inform Dr. Franklin of the plan to apprehend

Declan O'Cormick and his suspected accomplices in the kidnapping of Billy Best, James Jamison received a note by messenger from Sheriff Tuttleton. It read,

> Conall Shaughnessy and Howard Kincaid have both been seen at their homes. The action tomorrow at dawn can go forward as planned. O'Cormick is also at his home.

An hour later, when James spoke to Dr. Franklin in his library to tell him the particulars of the planned arrests and Best's rescue, Franklin responded, "You and Sergeant Corbin and the Sheriff have done well, James. Let us hope everything goes as planned, and that at this time tomorrow young William Best will have been at liberty for most of a day—and that we have Mr. Gerry's letter.

"I would suggest only one improvement. Since the young man you're rescuing does not know you, it might be better to have Mrs. Wellborn's maid Celta with you. That way, Billy will not be taken aback by the sudden appearance of two strange men. The sight of Celta, I think, would allay any fear in him which the sight of you and your companion might arouse. We cannot be certain of the state of Billy's mind after two weeks of solitary confinement, and we ought to take that into account.

"You could pick Celta up on your way to the house of the accommodating Mr. Jones and give her your second horse to ride. She could ride double with Billy in returning him to his home in Southwark after the rescue. I presume you will be returning the young man to his mother in person, and therefore could retrieve your second mount then.

"Perhaps it would be good for you to go after we finish here, to arrange this detail with Mrs. Wellborn and Celta. I'm sure Mrs. Wellborn would appreciate knowing of the effort that is going to be made on behalf of her son tomorrow at dawn."

"What you advise, Dr. Franklin, speaks of your empathy for others, and I accept the advice you're giving me. I was going to go now to Mrs. Wellborn anyway, to inform her that, God willing, her son will be returned to her tomorrow morning. I'm sure she'll be amenable to having her maid accompany me so Billy will be reassured by seeing a familiar face when I rescue him."

James found Mrs. Wellborn having supper with Celta when he arrived at her house in Southwark. James's news delighted both of the women, and Mrs. Wellborn was pleased to learn that, besides James, the Sheriff, Sergeant Corbin, and Dr. Franklin had helped plan her son's rescue.

It was most gratifying to her that James's investigation had proven the correctness of her theory concerning the disappearance of her son. She asked no questions about his planned liberation, but simply said she had confidence in James as the person in charge of freeing him from confinement, and looked forward to having her William home on the morrow.

When James told her that Dr. Franklin had suggested that Celta, as someone known to Billy, ought to be among his rescuers, she immediately assented. Celta herself was eager to be part of the rescue, but wanted to know if Kemper could come with her. When James told her that that wouldn't be possible since they'd be going on horseback, Celta said Billy would recognize Kemper more quickly than any person, and that she could carry the dog in front of her in a saddlebag slung over the withers of the horse she'd be riding. Since James could think of no argument against that arrangement, he agreed to it and told Celta he had a saddlebag large enough to accomode Kemper.

James had to ride home from Southwark through a heavy, wind-driven rain. The storm's fury did not abate or show any sign of slacking during the whole ride.

Triumph

Chapter XXIII

THE STORM WAS completely over by the time James rose from bed the next morning.

The only lingering sign of it was the dense overcast that blotted out the stars. As James went to the stable to saddle Jenny and Cheval, he missed not seeing the familiar luminous arc of the Milky Way in the sky.

The atmosphere was moist, fresh-smelling and serene as he rode Jenny into town, trailing Cheval behind him on a halter, and then went south on Fifth Street to Rebecca Wellborn's residence in Southwark.

Celta and Kemper were waiting for him as arranged. James had put three bricks in one of the attached saddlebags, to act as counterweights to the one in which Kemper was to ride, and Celta put the harness and leash she'd made for the dog in with him. The small white terrier fit neatly into his saddlebag, his paws on the rim of the leather pouch on either side of his black nose and black eyes. He seemed to like being in the saddlebag, and seemed to know something was happening. Their horses jogged along in the dark, James in the lead with a lantern, as they headed to Mr. Jones's house.

When they got there they found that Mr. Jones had some coffee ready. He hadn't heard of Celta or Kemper, because the last time James had been at his house he hadn't known he would be bringing them to participate in the rescue of Billy Best. The retired house builder was offered, and ate, one of the mustard and sliced pork sandwiches of German rye that Celta had brought along to have for breakfast.

A little after four in the morning, James and Celta walked over to the Old Powder House with Kemper to wait for the key to the iron door to be brought from the arrest of Declan O'Cormick. The powder house was silent and dark. Kemper showed no sign of smelling anything significant, and lay quietly on the ground beside the locked door. The eastern sky was taking on a faint tinge of gray, suggesting the coming of dawn. But still the runner who was to deliver the key to open the door did not come.

When the predawn light became sufficient to see nearby objects, James left Celta and Kemper and went around the east side of the building where he could look out across the fields to the north, in the direction of O'Cormick's mansion. He thought he saw, far off in that direction, some movement that might be a man, but he wasn't sure. He returned to Celta to tell her what he thought he'd seen.

Fifteen minutes later, a militiaman in uniform, trailing his musket, hastened around the east side of the building. It was the runner with the key, Donald Cavendish.

"The arrests at the O'Cormick place did not go well," he said, out of breath and leaning forward, with his hands on his knees. "That's why I'm late, Captain Jamison. When we arrested the two women they became hysterical and screamed their heads off! O'Cormick heard them and set the latch on his door and went out the window. The Sheriff was banging on the door but of course O'Cormick didn't answer because he'd gone out the window onto the porch roof, thinking to escape. But the Sheriff had that covered. He had put two men with guns in the yard, and they nabbed O'Cormick after he jumped to the ground in his nightshirt.

"And then Mr. O'Cormick had trouble finding the key, or so he said, until the Sheriff told him in no uncertain terms it would go against him at his trial, if he didn't cooperate with an officer of the law engaged in the execution of his duty, and he ordered O'Cormick to produce the key forthwith. There was also an argument over the wording of the warrant being served.

"There was further delay as we tried to get into the bedchamber where, O'Cormick finally informed us, the key was in a drawer of his tallboy. A ladder had to be fetched from the stables, and we had a man go into the room, which was latched from inside, through the window O'Cormick had jumped out of."

Enough light was now in the sky to permit James to extinguish his lantern, but even though he had sufficient light to get the key into the iron door's lock, he had difficulty turning it and getting the door open. Finally, he managed it, and Kemper dashed into the building, barking—he had evidently smelled Billy. Celta quickly followed the dog, then James and Donald Cavendish went inside.

They found in the dim grey light of the building's interior a young man on a miserable pallet, smiling and rubbing the ears of and petting Kemper as the dog licked his face, wagged his stub of a tail, and jumped around barking. Billy Best looked like the shipwrecked sailor marooned on the desert island in Daniel Defoe's novel *Robinson Crusoe*, or perhaps like a bearded Viking soon to set sail for Ireland in a long ship on a raid to get more gold jewelry like the big gold ring he wore. That comparison was more apt, not only because of the ring but because the handsome young man showed no signs of a shipwrecked sailor's deprivations. The only outward indications of his two weeks of confinement were his thick blond beard in a city of clean-shaven men, the filthiness of his clothes, and the bag of straw that was his bed.

Billy rose from his pallet when he saw Celta hurrying toward him. As they embraced, she cried. But Billy did not cry.

He did not seem any longer the innocent young man he had been when he vanished. He seemed a self-possessed young man, worthy of his mother calling him "William."

Celta introduced Billy to James as "da gen'lman dat found where you be kep'." Cavendish she called "one o' da fellahs what come tah arrest dat pirate dat put yah here."

Billy said, "Thank you, Sir" to James and nodded at Cavendish. He replied to Celta, "I'm afraid I put myself here, Celta."

Kemper all the while was circling Billy, and every now and then jumping up on him and barking to get his attention.

The bearded, unkempt young man said to James, "There's something I have to do right away. I must deliver a letter to a man staying at the Indian Queen Hotel. That I allowed myself to be distracted from delivering it is why I ended up here. Can we go right now to the Indian Queen?"

"So you have the letter?" James asked.

"Right here," the young man said, patting his shirt. "Under my shirt. It's sweaty but still sealed."

"The Indian Queen is on the way. We can stop there on our way to Southwark. Shall we leave? You don't have anything to take with you, I suppose?"

"Nothing except the letter and the clothes on my back. I leave to Mr. O'Cormick the tunnel I started digging with a chisel someone lost in here, which I found."

With that, William Best, his three rescuers, and his dog Kemper left the Old Powder House. On the way to the Indian Queen, Cavendish rode double with James and Celta rode behind Billy on Cheval, with Kemper in the saddlebag in front of Billy.

The hotel's Negro doorman, seeing Billy dismount, said, "Welcome back, Suh. I sees yuh got yah little dog still."

Donald Cavendish said good-bye as James entered the

Indian Queen with William Best and Celta, who stayed in the lobby with Kemper on the leash she had made for him.

George Mason and his son John were in the hotel's dining room, awaiting their breakfast. Mason was surprised to see Captain Jamison in the company of a fair-haired, bearded man in dirty clothes coming toward his table, and was even more surprised when the disheveled young man handed him a soiled letter addressed to him with the words, "This is for you, Sir. From Mr. Gerry. He told me to hand it to you and only you."

Mason took the letter uncomprehendingly as its deliverer took one step back and made a courteous half-bow.

James said, "This is William Best, Mr. Mason, the member of the Convention Guard that Mr. Gerry paid to bring you two letters, the second of which he is just now delivering because he was kidnapped on his way to give it to you. He's only just been released from his confinement."

"I got fresh clothes fah you on yah bed, Billy, an' I'm goin' to fix a bat' fah you. Cook be makin' a propah meal fah you, aftah you clean up."

Mrs. Wellborn said, "That's good, Celta." And, addressing her son she said, "While Celta's fixing your bath, William—which you certainly do need—you and Captain Jamison can tell me of your adventures among the cannibals."

"And I, Mother, want you to tell me of my father. All the things I began asking you as a boy," William Best replied firmly.

"Certainly. You're a man now, William, and I can speak with you of things you could not comprehend as a boy. After Captain Jamison leaves, I'll tell you the history of my family and the lineage of your father, how Celta is related to you, and anything else you want to know. But, for now, let me just say I gave you the name 'Best' at your baptism because your father died fighting to put down an uprising of serfs in Denmark before he and I could marry, and before we even knew I was carrying you. Because of the noble rank of Johan's parents, I did not think they would find my baptizing you with their son's surname agreeable, when I wasn't married to him. I gave you the name 'Best' because as the offspring of Johan, you represented to me the best."

"Please tell us, William," James said, "what happened after you and Kemper left the Indian Queen Hotel on the 22nd of June." Turning to Rebecca Wellborn he continued, "Your son, Mrs. Wellborn, went to the Indian Queen just now, immediately after his rescue, to deliver the letter he was to have delivered that day, a letter given to him in confidence by a member of the Constitutional Convention for delivery to another delegate."

"I became impatient, Captain Jamison, while waiting for Mr. Mason," Billy stated. "And I decided to attend to some business of my own that I felt needed to be taken care of without delay, which I thought I had time to do before Mr. Mason came back from his excursion. The business I wanted to take care of was to confront a man who sent my mother a threatening letter. I was determined to stop his insulting conduct.

"I knew the man's name and looked up his residence in the Directory. So Kemper and I walked there from the Indian Queen and found him at home. I should never have done that. I was not in control of my passions. I'm to blame for what happened then."

Hearing this, Mrs. Wellborn asked, "And what did happen when you confronted Mr. O'Cormick?"

"He laughed at me. Called me a peppercorn, an innocent who didn't know up from down. That made me mad and I went for him, which only proved that what he was saying was true. We wrestled and in our struggle he threw me down, and I must've hit my head on something that knocked me out, because I woke up in pitch darkness and silence in that place where you found me, Captain Jamison. I had no recollection of being carried there. I cried out for help, of course, and the effort to shout made my head hurt."

"Did Mr. O'Cormick visit you while you were captive?" Rebecca Wellborn asked.

"He never came. He only spoke with me that once in his house when I confronted him about his letter to you. Kemper had not been allowed to go inside his house with me."

James asked, "Were you fed well?"

"Food came once a day early in the morning, when it was still dark. But there was always enough of it to last the day. I learned not to eat it all at one time. It was usually a stew with plenty of meat in it. I had water from a hogshead and a tin cup to drink it with, and a tin plate and wooden fork to eat with. The same man always brought the food. Usually, I was asleep when he came and I never saw him, but it was always the same man when I was awake. Whenever I did see him and try to talk to him, he said he wasn't allowed to speak with me. Once he told me, in reply to a question I asked, that his master would deal with me when he came back from a trip he was on.

"I was alone in the silence of that place for fourteen days. I kept track of the days by scratching a mark every day on a brick. There was plenty of time for me to think."

As William Best was saying this, Celta appeared, to announce she had his bath ready and took him away. Before he left, he kissed his mother on both cheeks and shook James's hand in thanking him.

"I, too, wish to thank you, Captain Jamison," Rebecca Wellborn said in extending her hand to James as he took his leave of her. "Your diligence is commendable and has relieved me of a great anxiety."

"You do me too much credit, Mrs. Wellborn. I could not have found William on my own. Many people provided me the information by which I located him. You and he are well thought of by those who know you."

"He's a young man of the best ancestry. I don't know how, Captain, but he seems different to me now from the way he was before his disappearance. His confinement seems to have done him good."

"I didn't know your son before, Madam, so I have no way to compare how he is now with how he was before he was imprisoned. But I will say, from what I've seen of him today, that he seems to be a young man of promising understanding."

"That's it exactly! You've put your finger on it, Captain. William's understanding seems much greater now than it was before his captivity."

"It has been a pleasure to have been of service to you, Madam," James said as he left the actress. "And it has been gratifying to have been part of a happy outcome for your son in a situation that many feared would turn out otherwise for him. I compliment you on perceiving the nature of the situation he was in when Celta and I and others did not."

"My sister is often too emotional in her judgments, Captain Jamison, though her loyalty to me is unshakeable. What'll happen to O'Cormick?"

"There will be a judicial hearing followed by a trial—probably more than one trial since others abetted O'Cormick in the kidnapping of your son. To deprive a person of liberty is in the eyes of the law as serious a crime as murder, and it must be punished severely. I would not be surprised if O'Cormick was hanged."

"Oh, I hope not!!"

There was still time for James to stop at Franklin Court on his way to the City Tavern to have some additional breakfast, before the good Doctor left to attend the July 6th session of the Constitutional Convention. And when James reported that William Best had been freed from captivity and still had Mr. Gerry's letter in his possession, unopened, Dr. Franklin was exceedingly pleased. His pleasure increased when James informed him the young man had insisted on giving the letter to Mr. Mason straightaway, and had done so.

"That boy is a paragon! My assessment of him and Sergeant Corbin's have been vindicated. And what you have accomplished is also wonderful, James, and should be acknowledged in some way. I'm sure General Washington will agree and will think of a way."

"May I say, Dr. Franklin, meaning no disrespect with regard to yourself, that although everyone described this young man as having an aura of childlike innocence, it appears he has noticeably matured, and should no longer be referred to as a 'boy' or be called 'Billy.' And in regard to whatever accomplishments you may attribute to me, permit me to point out that I could not have done whatever it is you think I've done without the help of Celta, Kemper, Mr. Yarden, Colonel Zanzinger and his assistant Mr. Latrobe, yourself, and others. I did not act alone."

"Nothing of importance, James, is ever accomplished alone," Franklin observed. "My long life has taught me that. But it has also taught me that important matters are never accomplished without someone taking charge of them and arranging the efforts required to accomplish them. In this instance you provided that leadership.

"Thank goodness everything has turned out so well for Billy—excuse me, *William*—though it probably will not turn out so well for Mr. O'Cormick and his accomplices after the law has its way with them."

William's Surprise
Chapter XXIV

HAVING HAD A GRATIFYING second breakfast at the City Tavern, James rode over to the Sheriff"s nearby office, to report to him the rescue of William Best and to learn all that had transpired during the arrests of O'Cormick, his cook, his housekeeper, and the other suspected allies of his in kidnapping Rebecca Wellborn's son.

Six of those seven persons, the Sheriff said, were now inside the Walnut Street Jail Annex, awaiting a hearing on Monday morning before Judge Robert Atlee. The seventh, Conall Shaughnessy, had been put in the Annex with the others but released on a bail of 250 pounds sterling, which his arresting officer, Hector Sheppy, the Sheriff's foremost deputy, with permission, had allowed Shaughnessy's wife Dardivia to post with the court presided over by Atlee. Sheppy was reading law with Judge Atlee, the Sheriff said, to take the Pennsylvania bar examination and become a lawyer.

The Sheriff also told James, "As anticipated, Michael Rankin resisted arrest, despite the four men under command of Sergeant Corbin, one of them renowned for his strength, and brawn, who were sent to execute the warrants for his arrest and that of his brother. Finally, with the help of Sergeant Corbin himself, he was handcuffed and put in one of the carriages I hired to deliver the miscreants to the Walnut Street Jail Annex.

"No unusual incidents occurred in the arrest of Howard Kinkaid, which was led by Deputy Fuller."

The Sheriff laughed while recounting to James the antics of Declan O'Cormick in trying to evade arrest. "Besides jumping out an upstairs window, after fastening the door to his bedchamber from inside, O'Cormick when finally arrested tried to talk his way free of the law. The man has the talent for gab the Irish are noted for! He claimed the part of the Germantown Road where he lives has never been officially incorporated into Philadelphia County, which was why, he said, he bought land there and built a house and his first brick kiln there. According to this piece of audacity, the Sheriff of Philadelphia has no authority to serve a warrant on him in that part of Philadelphia."

Then Tuttleton said in a tone entirely devoid of amusement, "He'll find out otherwise when he's brought before Judge Atlee on Monday."

However, when he described to James the arrest of the women who protested by shrieking and crying, the Sheriff seemed genuinely distressed. "I'm not sure there's a case against the cook, Esther Wallsend, who said she never did nothing but cook what O'Cormick wanted cooked and sent it by Michael Rankin where he told me it should go, or the housekeeper, Lucinda Belacre, who said she had only kept the house in order and on occasion helped her friend Esther Wallsend in her cooking. Confining the young man against his will in the Old Powder House was certainly a crime. But was providing him food to sustain his life a crime? Kidnapping is a terrible offense against manmade and natural law, because stealing a man's liberty is like depriving him of life, which is what makes slavery so offensive to God, the Author of all life."

"Well," James said, "on Monday all of that will be up to Judge Atlee to decide, and he is surely able to do so, for in whatever pertains to the spirit and letter of the law, and its applications, he is a master."

"I agree, Captain Jamison," said the Sheriff. "The Judge and I have worked together as officers of the court on many occasions, and I have the utmost regard for his knowledge of the law, as apparently you do, too. How is it you're acquainted with Judge Atlee?"

"The judge and I met when we were both engaged in the same affair involving an application of the law, he as an old friend of Dr. Franklin, and I as a recent associate of the good Doctor. Judge Atlee impressed me then as a master of his profession. He impresses me also as being extraordinarily disinterested."

James left the Sheriff's office and went home to be with Livy, Grandmère and Anne-Louise the rest of that day, all of Saturday, and the Sabbath, his part in the affair of the vanishing messenger being at an end, except for appearing in court the following Monday to give testimony—along with the Sheriff, the Sheriff's deputies, Sergeant Corbin, and members of the Convention Guard—in the arraignment of O'Cormick and his supporters.

On the way home, he stopped in Appletree Alley to tell Colonel Zanzinger and his assistant Mr. Latrobe the happy outcome in the affair and to thank them for their assistance in solving the mystery.

The usual Sunday meal of the Jamison family after church, which this week was at the home of Jane and Lawrence in the Northern Liberties, was especially welcome to Captain Jamison. Apart from being free of the task General Washington, Dr. Franklin, Colonel Hamilton, and Mr. Madison had assigned him, this was the first time since the affair started that he'd been with his entire family to eat a meal except for the picnic at Bush Hill on the Fourth of July. It was the first time in weeks he'd spent two consecutive days entirely with Grandmère, Livy, and Anne-Louise. It was appropriate that the blanket of humidity and heat which had been stifling Philadelphia had been replaced by wholesome summer weather.

James appeared at nine thirty on Monday morning, July 9th, at the State House on Chestnut Street and entered the Court Room on the ground floor, opposite the East Room where the Constitutional Convention was meeting. This half of the ground floor of the State House was identical in its dimensions to the East Room. But because a good portion of the courtroom was occupied by the imposing, high structure at its front from which the judge looked down on the opposing attorneys and their clients, it seemed smaller than the East Room, even though it wasn't.

Just inside the railed-off area for public seating were other benches, for persons giving testimony. On the far end of those benches, where he had thought he might sit, he saw Celta, Rebecca Wellborn, and her son. On the far end of these witness benches, closer to the door into the Court, James saw Sheriff Tuttleton, three of his deputies, Sergeant Corbin, and four Convention Guards.

He nodded and smiled at William Best and his mother and her maidservant; and they returned his greeting with friendly nods and smiles of their own as he strode over to sit with the Sheriff and his Deputies and Corbin and his Guards.

The Clerk of the Court, Charles Sheavers, was arranging papers at his desk to the right of and beneath the judge's massive high perch. Jason Bolt, the Court's Sergeant-at-Arms, was doing the same at his desk in front of the three-tiered jury box, which had a bench for four jurors at each of its three tiers. The benches for the public were empty because today's proceeding was only an arraignment. The proceeding was scheduled to start at ten.

At a quarter to the hour, the three defense lawyers, Mr. Reeves Preen, Mr. Arthur Stackpole, and Mr. Stephen Harrow, and their clients—the five men and two women being arraigned—entered the Court and took their seats at the defendants' tables. An additional table and extra chairs had been needed to accommodate the appearance of so many persons before the Court at the same time. Guards accompanied each defendant, and in the case of Michael Rankin two guards stood behind him. As soon as Declan O'Cormick spied Rebecca Wellborn on the other side of the courtroom, he turned the chair in which he sat so he could look at her without giving too great an impression of not respecting the Judge.

The Prosecutor for the Commonwealth of Pennsylvania, Mr. Jeremy Birk, arrived five minutes before Judge Atlee entered to preside on high at the front of the Court. Once he was in his chair, the doorkeepers locked the Court's double doors and no further entry would be permitted until the Judge pronounced the day's proceeding terminated and left the room by way of his private entrance.

As Robert Atlee took his seat, Mr. Bolt, the Court's Sergeant-at-Arms, in his strong, herald-like voice told everyone to rise, that the Court was in session, Judge Robert Atlee presiding. And after Atlee was seated, Birk told the assembled lawyers, witnesses, and defendants they could be seated.

The Judge then stated that the examination into the facts of the confinement of William Best, a citizen of Philadelphia, against his will would proceed, to determine whether the facts warranted a trial on the charge of kidnapping against the owner of the place where Mr. Best had been discovered, kidnapping being a capital offense in the eyes of the common law and the statutes of the Commonwealth of Pennsylvania; and if the facts appeared to warrant it, to set a date for trial.

"Mr. Birk, proceed as to the fact of confinement, if you would," the Judge said.

"The State asks Mr. William Best to enter the witness box and be sworn to testify under oath as to the fact of his confinement."

William Best rose, entered the witness box, and was sworn in. Birk put the question to the witness, "Do you solemnly swear under oath that you were detained against your will from the afternoon or evening of June 22nd until the morning of July 6th in the building commonly known as the Old Powder House?"

"Yes, I was."

"And was your confinement solitary, that is, during it were you deprived of the society of other persons?"

"I was. I saw no one except occasionally the man who brought me my food, and he never answered the questions I asked, nor engaged in conversation, saying he had been ordered not to; and because he usually delivered the food when I was asleep, I seldom spoke with him. I never had sight of anyone else."

"Did he say who told him not to speak with you?"

"No sir, he did not."

"And was the place of your confinement the building called the Old Powder House on the northern outskirts of the city?"

"It was."

"Thank you. That is all. You may return to your seat."

Judge Atlee asked, "Do any of the lawyers representing the defendants in this hearing want to deny, dispute, or challenge any of the facts the witness has just sworn to under oath?"

One at a time, in turn, Mr. Preen, Mr. Stackpole, and Mr. Harrow rose and said, "No, Sir."

"Ask your next witness to come forward to testify as to the ownership of the Old Powder House, Mr. Birk," Judge Atlee ordered.

"The Commonwealth now calls the Keeper of the Rolls, Mr. Andrew Sparrow." And Mr. Sparrow was duly sworn in as a witness.

"Mr. Sparrow, you are the Keeper of the Rolls regarding persons who hold title to and own property in the city and country of Philadelphia?"

"I am."

"And can you tell the Court who owns the building commonly known as the Old Powder House in the vicinity of the north end of Seventh Street where it comes into Vine Street?"

"I can. I have that information here in Ledger 412, Second Series, page 69, which I have brought with me for my testimony before the Court," Mr. Sparrow said, holding up in both hands a large volume bound in calfskin.

"And who might the owner of that property be?"

"Mr. Declan O'Cormick, Esquire. He is recorded as having bought that property on March 28th, 1786—and I am still quoting from my book—'to build a brick kiln inside it.'"

"And can you describe the character of this building, please?"

"It is a large, substantial building, octagonal in shape, with walls of double brick, having no moveable windows, ventilated by means of a cupola on the roof designed for that purpose. It has but one door, made of iron."

"That is all. You may return to your seat," the judge said. "Mr. Birk, do you have evidence that Mr. O'Cormick ordered the incarceration of Mr. Best?"

"I do, your Honor. I have two witnesses to that fact. I ask Mrs. Esther Wallsend to come forward and take the oath."

After O'Cormick's cook was sworn in, the Prosecutor for the Commonwealth of Pennsylvania asked her, "Are you the cook for Declan O'Cormick's household?"

"Yes, Sir."

"And how long have you worked for him in that way?"

"The better part of ten years, Sir."

"Did he at some time in the past month order you to prepare meals to send outside the house, meals that would be picked up very early each morning, while it was still dark, by his foreman Michael Rankin?"

"He did."

"And do you see Michael Rankin here in Court?"

"I do. That's him over there at that table, sittin' next to his brother John. The burly one in the manacles," Esther Wallsend said, pointing at Michael Rankin.

"Thank you, Mrs. Wallsend. You may return to your seat."

"I ask Michael Rankin to come forward and enter the witness box to be sworn in," Mr. Birk continued. The tall, strong man of good features and blond hair, in manacles, rose from the defendants' table and shuffled forward because his ankles as well as his wrists were in irons. He was the only defendant so restrained. His two guards followed, one on each side of him.

Charles Sheavers, Clerk of the Court, read the oath to him requiring him to tell the truth, only the truth, and the whole truth in the sight of God. But he said nothing in reply, only nodded his head.

The Clerk said, "Mr. Rankin, you must say 'I do,'" whereupon the witness grunted something indistinguishable.

From his Judge's place on high, Robert Atlee asked, "Mr. Rankin, will you tell the truth, the whole truth, and only the truth with God as your witness that what you say is the truth?"

"I guess."

"The Court will take that as an affirmative reply. Proceed, Mr. Birk."

"Mr. Rankin, are you employed by Mr. Declan O'Cormick as one of his most trusted workers in the capacity of general foreman of all the men who work at his several brick kilns? I'll put it more simply. Have you under cover of darkness been taking food every day for the past two weeks from Mr. O'Cormick's kitchen to Mr. Best in the Old Powder House?"

"If you say so."

"Your Honor, I have witnesses who can testify that they saw this man pick up sacks full of something at the kitchen door of O'Cormick's house under cover of darkness, and can further testify that they saw him take those sacks inside the Old Powder House for whose door he had a key."

The Judge told the accused to answer the question, but he remained mute. Atlee then told Birk to dismiss Michael Rankin, and recall William Best, still under oath, to the stand; and when William Best was in the witness box, Birk asked him, "Do you, Mr. Best, see here in Court the man who kept you supplied with food while you were confined in the Old Powder House?"

"I do."

"Would you please point him out?"

"It's that man, Michael Rankin. He brought me my daily ration of food, though I did not know his name until just now."

"Thank you, Mr. Best. You may step down and return to your seat."

But instead of leaving the witness box, William Best asked a question of Judge Atlee. "May I say something, Your Honor? It's important."

"It's irregular to allow a witness to testify to something he has not been asked. But I will allow it since you say it's important and you seem to be a sensible young man of substantial character, and this is a preliminary hearing. Go ahead. What do you want to tell the Court?"

"Your Honor, I have not said that I want Mr. O'Cormick prosecuted for kidnapping me, and I refuse to ask that a charge of kidnapping be brought against him on my account, and I would protest the charge if it were. It was my fault I ended up as I did. I went to his house. He did not seek me out or assault me, or have someone bring me to him by force. I sought him out, I assaulted him. That man over there, the third one from the left,"—and he pointed to Mr. Kincaid at the defendants' table—"he was there. He saw me try to hit Mr. O'Cormick and wrestle with him. He can tell you. The last thing I remember was going for Mr. O'Cormick in the parlor of his house, in front of his fireplace. The next thing I knew I was waking up alone in pitch blackness and absolute silence, with an aching head and a lump on the back of my head that was too tender for me to touch.

"It is all my fault, your Honor, that we are here today, and I regret and apologize for my imprudence. If I had had more self-command, I would never have gone to Mr. O'Cormick's house or assaulted him once I got there."

In the courtroom's silence following this speech, a composed, rich female voice rang out, every syllable of her utterance clearly enunciated and melodious. "Bravo, William. Bravo. You make me proud." What she said was accompanied by her genteel clapping.

After Mrs. Wellborn's applause stopped, the silence continued until Judge Atlee said, "Mr. Preen, Mr. Stackpole, Mr. Harrow, Mr. Birk. Please follow me to my chambers. We need to confer."

William Best continued in the witness box while the conference of the lawyers and judge in the Judge's chambers went on for nearly an hour.

After Birk, Harrow, Stackpole, and Preen returned to their places and the Judge was back in his chair on high, Robert Atlee made a speech.

"Mr. Best, of course, does not get to say what the law is or whether it applies in any given circumstance. Nor can he, on his personal cognizance, declare a person exempt from the operation of the law. The law belongs to society. It is their common possession for their common good. To allow persons who are not judges to decide whether and to whom it applies would be anarchy and the destruction of society.

"There must, of course, be allowance for mercy, because no one can in enacting a statute comprehend all the contingencies of human life. But the law cannot allow or condone applauding anyone's exemption from the law. That is not mercy. That is disorder and disrespect for the law, and the end of human society.

"This hearing on the conduct of Mr. Declan O'Cormick will continue, and all witnesses will attend to give their testimony as required. Otherwise they will be held in contempt of the law and punished accordingly, no matter what their personal and private opinions or judgment may be.

"This hearing will resume tomorrow at ten. Court adjourned."

The Needed Compromise (Barely) Achieved

Chapter XXV

ON JULY 9TH, as William Best—commonly known as Billy before Declan O'Cormick sequestered him—was surprising Judge Atlee, his mother, and everyone else in the courtroom of the State House by taking responsibility for what had befallen him, the debates of the Constitutional Convention in the East Room of the State House, just across from the State House's courtroom, continued to flounder.

The compromise recommended by the Committee of Eleven—led by Benjamin Franklin—had not been accepted. And if the issue of how the States were to be represented in Congress was not resolved, the Convention was certain to fail. Should such a disaster happen, and the Articles of Confederation remain in effect, it was unlikely the United States of America could survive.

The delegates to the Convention could not even agree on what was to be represented in Congress. Was it persons? Was it States? Was it wealth? Or, was it some combination of these? The views of the delegates strongly differed on this question. The day Elbridge Gerry, as chairman of the Committee of Eleven, reported the Committee's recommendation to the Convention, Rufus King of Massachusetts said to his fellow delegates in the East Room, "Property is the primary object of society, and therefore property ought to be the primary qualification for election to Congress."

Pierce Butler of South Carolina agreed. "It seems to me," he told the delegates at the Convention, "that the more the subject of representation is studied, the less it appears to me that the number of a State's inhabitants ought to be the sole criterion for representation in Congress, and that wealth ought also to enter into the matter in a significant way."

Charles C. Pinkney, also from South Carolina stood up and said, "I beg to differ with my fellow South Carolinian. Wealth is too changeable, too difficult to calculate, and too injurious to the non-commercial States, to provide a basis for calculating a State's representation in Congress. The number of inhabitants of a State is the only just and practical rule for apportioning representation in Congress," Pinkney concluded.

But what about the small States? Their delegates contended vociferously that there had to be some provision for equality among the States in the new constitution. Otherwise, the Convention would be creating a tyranny of the majority that would be just as dictatorial as the tyranny the majority was experiencing under the Articles of Confederation.

But even on this subject there was no unanimity. William Davie, a thirty-one-year-old lawyer from North Carolina, a small State, said, "The number of people in a State ought to be the standard for election to the first house of the new Congress, and property should be the standard for obtaining a seat in the second house of Congress."

On July 6th, the day Declan O'Cormick was arrested, the Convention created a five-man committee comprised of Nathaniel Gorham, Rufus King, Gouverneur Morris, and Edmund Randolph who were from the three largest States in the Union—Massachusetts, Pennsylvania, and Virginia— and John Rutledge from South Carolina, to study the Report of the Committee of Eleven and recommend changes to it.

The next day, July 7th, Roger Sherman of Connecticut, a small State, rose in Convention to say, "The small States have more vigor in their governments because in the large

States it is more difficult to know the real sense of the people. Therefore, the more influence the large States are given in the government we are devising, the weaker it will be. To give the small States an equal vote with the large States in the second house of the new Congress will create a stronger government than apportioning seats in both houses according to State population, as the large States want done."

Regarding the need for compromise, James Wilson of Pennsylvania declared, "While I think of myself as having a conciliatory temper, firmness in upholding the principles of justice and right is sometimes a duty of higher obligation."

William Paterson, the presenter of the New Jersey Plan in opposition to the Virginia Plan, said, "The small States will never be able to defend themselves against the more populous States without an equality of votes in the second house of Congress. My view on this matter is fixed."

Gouverneur Morris replied, "My only fixed commitment is to do what should finally appear to me to be right. I oppose giving an equal vote to all the States in the second house of Congress—or anywhere else in the new government—because wherever such equality exists there will be 'another Congress.' If the small States were to be treated as equal to big States, regardless of their having less than a majority of the country's population, that would thwart the will of the majority, as is happening daily under the Articles of Confederation. The small States are demanding not *equal* rights for their citizens, compared to citizens in the more populous States, but *greater rights.*"

The problem for the Convention was to agree on what was right and just in principle. And, so far, neither side in the dispute would budge on what it regarded as being so, nor was either side willing to compromise on its understanding of how its principle could best be served. Each side had, as

Gouverneur Morris said in reference to himself, a fixed idea of what seemed right and just to it, and viewed any other concept as absolutely wrong. Thus a sense of hopelessness and deadlock was building on both sides of the quarrel.

The division among the delegates on the apportionment of seats in Congress was polarized. One delegate noted that this truly "threatened the Convention's existence," even though the Convention generally recognized that the Articles of Confederation had to be replaced. Another delegate stood up and said, "Because of the dispute over State representation in Congress, the Convention is scarcely held together by the strength of a hair."

William Paterson, the foremost advocate of the small States' interests, asked his opponents with sarcasm unbecoming a gentleman, "If voting according to population is so good, why has the Convention made all of its decisions using the principle that every State has one vote, regardless of its population?"

Roger Sherman from Connecticut declared, "I move that final action on the Report of the Committee of Eleven, which has recommended allowing equal votes for the States in the second house of Congress, be postponed until after the Committee of Five's study of the Committee of Eleven's three-part recommendation." His Connecticut colleague Oliver Ellsworth seconded his motion. The motion carried, six to five, with Massachusetts, Connecticut, New Jersey, Pennsylvania, Delaware, and Maryland in the affirmative and New York and the four Southern States in the negative. So it was that the Convention adjourned until Monday the 9th of July, without deciding on whether to accept the report of the Committee of Eleven.

When the Convention came back into session on the 9th, the Committee of Five recommended calculating the specific number of representatives each State would elect to the first house of Congress in the First Congress that would convene under the new U.S. Constitution. The Committee of Five, four members of which were from the three States having the largest populations, estimated those numbers, based on the rule of one representative for every 40,000 inhabitants, including indentured servants, and three-fifths of a State's slaves. The total number of representatives in the first house of Congress thus computed was fifty-six. The Committee of Five also recommended that Congress be authorized to adjust, through legislation, the number of Representatives each State would have in the first house *in future Congresses*, as information on changes in the population of the States became available.

Mr. Sherman of Connecticut rose and asked, "Pray tell me, my learned colleagues, in this calculation of fifty-six representatives in the first house of the new congress was any estimate of a State's wealth employed, or is population its only reference?"

Mr. Gorham of Massachusetts, a member of the Committee of Five, replied, "The calculation has had some regard to supposed wealth. The principle of one representative for every 40,000 inhabitants could not be exclusively used in the calculation, for two reasons. Using only the principle of population, the number of representatives in the first house of Congress would soon become too numerous. And since most of the country's wealth will remain in the Atlantic States for a considerable time, rather than be found in the new States formed west of the mountains, the Committee of Five thinks it necessary to give the new Congress the power to decide on the future number of representatives each State will have in Congress. This is to prevent the Atlantic States from being overwhelmed in Congress, which is what would happen if the rule of one representative per 40,000 inhabitants were to be automatically applied."

Mr. Gouverneur Morris, another member of the Committee of Five, rose and stated, "The recommended number of representatives each State is to have is little more than a guess. The Committee intended little more than to bring before the Convention a matter for consideration."

"Why has Delaware got only one representative in the first house of Congress while Georgia, with a smaller population than Delaware, has two?" inquired a delegate from Delaware.

To this Gouverneur Morris replied, "The second member for Georgia represents the Committee's guess that its rapid growth in population will soon merit that estimate."

New Jersey's Attorney General, William Paterson, said, "The combination of estimated wealth and numbers of inhabitants is too vague a rule for determining a State's seats in Congress. For this reason New Jersey is against the Committee of Five's proposal in this regard. Patently, slaves are inhabitants, but I can regard them only as a kind of live property, like a horse, and a species of wealth. Are they to be simultaneously considered as both wealth and inhabitants? They have no personal liberty, no self-determination. They are owned by someone, and have no faculty themselves of acquiring wealth but are themselves property, and like other forms of property entirely at the disposal of an owner. Why should a man in Virginia have a greater number of representatives in Congress in proportion to the number of his slaves? Is this equitable? Moreover, if slaves are not represented in the government of the States where they reside, then why should they be represented in the government of the United States?

"What is the true principle of representation in a republican government?" Mr. Paterson continued. "Is it not the necessary expedient of the people choosing individuals to represent them because it is inconvenient—that is to say impossible—for the whole people to come together to represent themselves? Surely it is. But if it were expedient for the whole people to assemble and vote directly on making the laws, would the slaves vote? They would not. Not having themselves the faculty of acquiring property, the principal end of civilized society, they would not be counted part of society, would not be one of the people who vote. Why then should they be represented in a constitution devised to govern a free society in which the people have been historically and eminently self-determining? I am also against counting slaves in any system of republican or representative government because calculating representation by counting slaves, even if only a portion of their number is counted, is a powerful incentive for continuing the institution of slavery and its attendant evils."

Mr. Madison attempted to rebut Mr. Paterson's reasoning. "May I remind the Convention that Mr. Paterson's view on representation in a free society, despite its being genuine, would forever silence the pretensions of the small States to have an equality of votes with the large States?" Madison said. "This is because there could never be such equality of representation in any part of the government were all the people, of all the States, to assemble and vote directly to make the laws of the country."

Madison went on, "I suggest that a proper ground for compromise on this issue would be to have the first house of the new Congress chosen according to the number of the free inhabitants in each State, and the second house of Congress, which is to be the guardian of property interests, chosen according to the whole number of each State's residents, including slaves."

Mr. Butler of Georgia agreed, stating, "I warmly concur with Mr. Madison's reasoning regarding the justice and necessity of considering wealth in apportioning seats in congress."

Mr. King, a lawyer from Massachusetts, said, "I have always expected that the Southern States, as the richest in the Union, would never join with the Northern States on any basis which did not recognize and give weight to their superior wealth. Eleven out of the thirteen State governments have agreed to consider slaves in the apportionment of taxation, and in my view that principle ought also to apply to representation in the legislature of the general government for the Union."

By a vote of nine to two, with Massachusetts, Connecticut, New Jersey, Pennsylvania, Delaware, Maryland, Virginia, North Carolina, and Georgia in favor and New York and South Carolina against, the Convention agreed to elect a second Committee of Eleven to deal with the continuing dilemma of how to apportion seats in the new bicameral Congress. This third special committee on the subject of State representation was instructed to submit its recommendation as soon as possible. It consisted of Mr. King of Massachusetts, Mr. Sherman of Connecticut, Mr. Yates of New York, Mr. Brearley of New Jersey, Mr. Gouverneur Morris of Pennsylvania, Mr. Read of Delaware, Mr. Carrol of Maryland, Mr. Madison of Virginia, Mr. Williamson of North Carolina, Mr. Rutledge of South Carolina, and Mr. Houstoun of Georgia.

Nothing further was attempted before this session of the Convention voted to adjourn.

The members of the Convention were desperate to resolve the issue of State representation in Congress. This was amply demonstrated by their appointment of two committees of eleven members each to address the matter, and then designating a *third* committee, having five members, for the same purpose. Every delegate knew that unless this central issue of representation was resolved, and soon—it had already preempted all other business since the Fourth of July recess—a replacement constitution for the Articles of Confederation could not be framed and there would be no new constitution to present to the people of the States. Were that failure to occur, the Convention would have to adjourn *sine die*—without having set a date to reconvene—and without having accomplished anything. Nor would there be any chance before it was too late of organizing another convention to remedy the deterioration in general government that had taken place under the Articles of Confederation.

And, looking forward into the future of the new nation, unless a compromise on State representation in Congress was forthcoming there was no prospect for a Union strong enough to facilitate the rapid growth of the powerful, prosperous republic that Americans wanted the United States of America to become.

The most alarming thing was that, despite all of this, the members of the Convention were not moving in the direction of a compromise. In the middle of July, Alexander Hamilton returned to New York in frustration at being constantly outvoted by his colleagues in the New York delegation, Robert Yates and John Lansing. They themselves went home not long after Hamilton's departure, leaving New York completely unrepresented at the Convention. The reason Lansing and Yates departed was their belief that the Articles of Confederation needed only to be amended—not rewritten and replaced as Hamilton believed—in order to solve the undeniable problems the Union was experiencing under that constitution.

The departure from Philadelphia of all three of the men in the New York delegation to the Constitutional Convention reduced the number of States represented at the Convention from eleven to ten. However, the arrival of the New Hampshire delegation of Nicholas Gilman and John Langdon at the end of July brought that number back up to eleven.

Between July 5th and July 16th, the two different Committees of Eleven and the Committee of Five repeatedly went over the same ground, sifting it ever more finely and casting somewhat different seed upon it, hoping that a different plant would spring forth. But nothing came of these reiterations because the supporters of the two principles—the different sizes of the State populations on the one hand, and the equal sovereignty of each State on the other—were not disposed to compromise.

Several times, in passing, it had been proposed during the "Full Stop" of the Convention that a compromise was available—that State representation in the first house of Congress could be based on the size of the population in each State, while in the other house of Congress the same number of seats could be allocated to every State, regardless of the size of its population. That arrangement gave each side in the controversy what it wanted in *one house* of the new, bicameral Congress, *but not in both houses.* This was the essence of the compromise that had been recommended by the first Committee of Eleven, under Dr. Franklin's influence.

The Convention just as stubbornly refused to adjourn *sine die,* because neither side in the dispute over State representation in Congress wanted to be blamed for the failure of the Convention to frame a new constitution.

Every Sabbath during this impasse which had brought the Convention to a halt, delegates attending the Convention went to the church of their choice and prayed to the Lord God

Almighty, Maker Of the Heavens and the Earth, and All That Exists and the Laws By Which They Exist. And their prayers were exactly the same. That God would move the Convention in the direction of an agreement in line with their idea of what was right and just.

On Saturday afternoon, July 14th, Caleb Strong, a forty-two-year-old country lawyer from central Massachusetts where Captain Daniel Shays had his farm, and the least talkative of the four men in the Massachusetts delegation to the Convention, asked to have the floor in order to make a few remarks before the Convention adjourned to observe the Sabbath.

After being recognized by the President of the Convention, he declared, "The Convention has been much divided in opinion recently. In order to avoid the awful consequences of that division, an accommodation has been proposed. A Committee has been appointed, and though some of the members of it were averse to any equality of votes among the States, the Committee has recommended such an equality.

"It is agreed on all hands that the Confederation Congress is nearly at an end. If no accommodation takes place, the Union itself must soon be dissolved.

"It has been suggested that if we cannot come to a general agreement, the principal States may form and recommend a scheme of government themselves. But will the small States in that case ever accede to it? Under those circumstances, it is probable that only the large States would embrace and ratify it. The small States have already made a considerable concession in agreeing that money bills will originate in the house of Congress elected on the basis of population. Naturally, the small States expect some concession made to them by the large States in return."

Having made these down-to-earth, matter-of-fact observations, Caleb Strong sat back down at the Massachusetts delegation table.

His calm remarks appear to have had an effect, for at the Convention's session on Monday, July 16th, the first after Strong's country-lawyer speech, the crisis was finally resolved. The Convention at long last voted to adopt the three-part proposal Dr. Franklin had steered the first Committee of Eleven into recommending to the Convention. That the first house of Congress be elected from districts having 40,000 inhabitants, which house of Congress would have sole power to originate bills appropriating money from the U.S. Treasury and setting the compensation of federal officers, while in the second house of Congress each State was to have the same number of representatives.

Franklin had not spoken during the long days of contention following the first Committee of Eleven's recommendation. He seemed to think the Convention would eventually embrace the obvious compromise that could overcome the Convention's stalemate.

On July 16th, before the vote on the compromise, delegates from several States spoke in favor of what had been repeatedly alluded to but not voted on. Had the compromise not happened, a majority of the members of the Convention might well have left Philadelphia and gone home without writing the Constitution of the United States of America. The two propositions on State representation in Congress, as two parts of the same compromise, however— the contending principles of State population and State sovereignty—effectively strengthened the Union of States. Had the Convention not agreed to this compromise, the vision of the United States of America as a rapidly growing, self-determining republic of continental proportions would, in all likelihood, not have become part of the world's history. Caleb Strong's simple, down-to-earth speech to the Convention on

July 14th reminded the delegates that time was running out and it was time to stop avoiding what it was necessary to do.

With the New Hampshire delegation not yet having arrived in Philadelphia, New York's delegation having gone home in despair, and the Rhode Islanders not having participated, the vote of the ten States present on July 16th in the East Room of the State House was five to four. Connecticut, New Jersey, Delaware, Maryland, and North Carolina were for the compromise; Georgia, South Carolina, Virginia, and Pennsylvania were against it; and the four-man Massachusetts delegation was divided in its opinion and therefore not counted—Gerry and Strong for the compromise, King and Gorham against it.

The First Committee of Eleven' s proposed compromise, devised by Benjamin Franklin of Pennsylvania, strongly supported by Virginia's George Mason, and presented to the Convention by the Committee's chairman Elbridge Gerry of Massachusetts, would have failed on the 16th of July, 1787, had the New York delegation still been at the Convention, because Yates and Lansing would certainly have voted against it, judging by their previous voting records. That would have brought the vote to five States for and five against, with Massachusetts split and not counted.

Likewise, when the vote was taken on July 16th, had either Gerry or Strong voted no, the compromise would have failed, because the vote of Massachusetts would then have been counted among the States against the compromise.

But the New York delegation was not present, and the positive votes of Strong and Gerry did offset the negative votes of King and Gorham and split the Massachusetts vote.

Franklin's farsighted wisdom of July 2nd, when he let the vainglorious Elbridge Gerry chair the First Committee of Eleven was, of course, crucial. Gerry's chairmanship of the

First Committee of Eleven committed Gerry to supporting the compromise Franklin steered that first Committee of Eleven into recommending.

Naturally, during the remaining two months of the Convention, the delegates dealt with many contentious and momentous constitutional issues, such as how the President of the United States ought to be elected. But once the issue of State representation in Congress was settled, the fear that the Convention could fail, the feeling that had gripped their minds during the twelve days after the Fourth of July, vanished.

With the compromise of July 16th achieved, the way was clear for a successful Convention.

The first complete draft of the Preamble to the U.S. Constitution, which was to replace the Articles of Confederation, was presented to the Convention on August 6th. It read:

> We the people of the States of New Hampshire, Massachusetts, Rhode-Island and Providence Plantations, Connecticut, New-York, New Jersey, Pennsylvania, Delaware, Maryland, Virginia, North- Carolina, South-Carolina, and Georgia, do ordain, declare, and establish the following Constitution for the Government of Ourselves and our Posterity.

That initial Preamble was flawed in two fundamental ways.

First, because it was not at all certain the people of all thirteen of the States named in it would in fact ratify it.

Secondly, even if all thirteen of the States named in the August 6th draft of the Preamble did ratify the new constitution, they would not be the only States which would be consenting to its authority, and establishing the new constitution. As the United States of America grew, every State that joined the Union—which eventually would number fifty, thirty-seven of which did not even exist or have names in 1787—would eventually ratify the Constitution and give it authority by consenting to live under its provisions.

The initial Preamble of August 6th, therefore, had to be revised to correct these fundamental flaws. The Preamble's second and final draft read:

> We the people of the United States [i.e. the people of every State that joins the American Union of States under the U.S. Constitution], in Order to form a more perfect Union [of States], establish Justice [among the States], insure domestic Tranquility [within every State], provide for the common defense [of the States], promote the general Welfare [of the States], and secure the Blessings of Liberty to ourselves and our Posterity, do ordain and establish this Constitution for the United States of America.

The people of every State that has consented to live under the authority of the U.S. Constitution have established its authority for America's general government.

The reading of the final draft of the Constitution of the United States of America in the East Room of the Pennsylvania State House was the first order of Convention business on September 17th, 1787. The signing of the document was the second item of business in that concluding session of the Constitutional Convention in Philadelphia. But before the signing occurred, Dr. Franklin rose from his place, holding in his hand the manuscript of a speech he had written. Franklin announced, "My friend James Wilson will read this speech on my behalf, if you please, because the stones in my kidneys and bladder make standing on my feet for longer than a few minutes at a time extremely painful."

It was the final speech of the Convention. It read:

"Mr. President, I confess there are parts of this constitution I do not at present approve, but I am not sure I shall never approve them. For, having lived long, I have experienced many instances of being obliged by better information, or fuller consideration, to change opinions, even on important subjects, which I once thought right, but found to be otherwise. It is, therefore, that the older I grow, the more apt I am to doubt my own judgment, and to pay more respect to the judgment of others. Most men indeed, as well as most sects in Religion, think themselves in possession of all truth, and that wherever others differ from them it is so far error. Thus the Church of Rome is infallible and the Church of England is never wrong in their forms of worshipping God and their theologies. But though many private persons think almost as highly of their own infallibility as of that of their sect, few expressed it so naturally as a certain French lady, who in a dispute with her sister, said 'I don't know how it happens, sister, but I meet with nobody but myself that's always in the right.' *'Il n'y a que moi qui a toujours raison.'*

"In these sentiments, Sir, I agree to this Constitution with all its faults, if they are such; because I think a general government necessary for us, and there is no form of government but what may be a blessing to the people if well administered, and I believe further that this is likely to be well administered for a course of years, and can only end in Despotism, as other forms have done before it, when the people shall become so corrupted as to need despotic government, being incapable of any other. I doubt, too, whether any other Convention we can obtain may be able to make a better Constitution. For when you assemble a number of men to have the advantage of their joint wisdom you inevitably assemble, with those men, all their prejudices, their passions, their errors of opinion, their local interests, and their selfish views. From such an assembly can a perfect production be expected? It therefore astonishes me, Sir, to find this system approaching so near to perfection as it does; and I think it will astonish our enemies, who are waiting with confidence to hear that our councils are confounded like those of the builders of the Tower of Babel; and that our States are on the point of separation, only to meet hereafter for the purpose of cutting one another's throats.

"Thus I consent, Sir, to this Constitution because I expect no better, and because I am not sure that it is not the best. The opinions I have had of its errors, I sacrifice to the public good. I have never whispered a syllable of them abroad. Within these walls they were born, and here they shall die. If every one of us in returning to our constituents were to report the objections he has had to it, and endeavor to gain partisans in support of them, we might prevent its being generally received, and thereby lose all the salutary effects and great advantages resulting naturally in our favor among foreign nations as well as among ourselves, from our real or apparent unanimity. Much of the strength and efficiency of any government in procuring and securing happiness to the people depends on opinion, on the general opinion of the goodness of the government, as well as of the wisdom and integrity of its governors. I hope, therefore, that for our own sakes as a part of the people and for the sake of posterity, we shall act heartily and unanimously in recommending this Constitution (if approved by Congress and confirmed by the State Conventions) wherever our influence may extend, and turn our future thoughts and endeavors to the means of having it well administered.

"On the whole, Sir, I cannot help expressing a wish that every member of the Convention who may still have objections to it would, with me, on this occasion, doubt a little of his own infallibility, and, to make manifest our unanimity, put his name to this instrument.

"I therefore move that the Constitution be signed by the members of this Convention using the following formula, 'Done in Convention by the unanimous consent of the States present, the 17th day of September in the year of our Lord one thousand seven hundred and eighty-seven, of the Independence of the United States the twelfth. In witness whereof we hereunto subscribe our names.'"

Rufus King of Massachusetts seconded Franklin's motion, and Gouverneur Morris, William Blount, and Alexander Hamilton, who had recently returned to the Convention, spoke in favor of it. The motion carried by a vote of ten of the eleven States present. South Carolina's four-man delegation split; yet when the proposed Constitution was signed, all four members of the South Carolina delegation heeded Franklin's advice and signed. Hamilton signed for the State of New York as its sole representative present.

Only three of the delegates who had participated in the daily work of the Convention during the four months it was in session, and in so doing had been actively engaged in framing the Constitution of the United States, refused to sign the finished document—Edmund Randolph and George Mason of Virginia, and Elbridge Gerry of Massachusetts. These three stalwarts of the Convention did not sign what they had worked so long and hard to produce because, it seems, they deplored the absence in it of a Bill of Rights specifying and protecting the personal rights and liberties of Americans. (The First Session of the First U.S. Congress soon remedied this defect by writing a twelve-part Bill of Rights, ten of which the people of the States ratified.)

After signing the final draft of the Constitution, the delegates to the Convention adjourned, the task that had brought them to Philadelphia having been completed. Then they went to the City Tavern to eat a farewell meal together before returning to their individual, separate lives.

Aftermaths

Chapter XXVI

IMMEDIATELY UPON RECEIVING the records of the Federal Convention for safekeeping, on the morning after the completed Constitution was signed, George Washington departed in his carriage for his beloved plantation Mount Vernon overlooking the Potomac River in Virginia.

As Washington headed south in his coach and four from America's foremost city that Tuesday morning, the four inscribed and signed parchment sheets of the proposed Constitution were on their way to New York in the custody of the Convention's Secretary, Major William Jackson, for delivery to the President of the Confederation Congress, which had authorized the Philadelphia Convention. Also in Jackson's custody were a cover letter and a Resolution from the Convention to the Confederation Congress, both dated September 17th, 1787, and both signed by George Washington as President of the Convention.

The letter said that what the Convention was sending to Congress was "that Constitution which has appeared to us the most advisable." The letter suggested a new constitution had been written to replace the Articles of Confederation, instead of amending the Articles, because the Articles made each State's sovereignty paramount, which was clearly impractical. How could the general government "secure all rights of independent sovereignty to each State, and yet provide for the interest and safety of all of them"? the letter asked. The cover letter also declared that during the Convention's four months of deliberations in Philadelphia, its constant concern had been to serve what ought to be the concern of all Americans, "the preservation of the Union, in which is involved our prosperity, felicity, safety, perhaps our national existence."

The Resolution which Major Jackson conveyed to the Confederation Congress from the Convention, which had been passed unanimously, asked Congress to forward copies of the proposed Constitution to every State legislature, with the instruction that the people of each State be authorized legislatively to elect a State constitutional convention to consider the proposed Constitution for ratification and inform the Confederation Congress whether they ratified or rejected it. When nine States ratified the proposed Constitution of the United States of America, it would take effect for them as their new charter for general government, as specified in Article VII of the document.

Having received these three documents, the members of the Confederation Congress closely examined them and held probing discussions of the proposed Constitution, and voted to follow the Resolution's advice and send the proposed Constitution to the thirteen State legislatures, with the recommendation that each one authorize the people of their State to elect a State ratification convention. That congressional decision was greatly facilitated by the return to the Confederation Congress of James Madison and nine other members of the Confederation Congress who had been delegates to the Philadelphia Convention.

While all of this was going on in the Confederation Congress, the newspapers of the land began to get and publish copies of the signed Constitution and the Convention's Resolution. Thus, the people of the States were getting their first look at the proposed Constitution and the Resolution concerning how its ratification was to be handled. Consequently, a few weeks after the Convention in Philadelphia adjourned, the thirteen State legislatures, including Rhode Island's, began receiving the proposed Constitution from Congress. And only Rhode Island's legislature refused to authorize the election of a State ratification convention.

Of the twelve State ratification conventions elected by the people of the States, Delaware's was the first to ratify the proposed constitution. It did so on December 7th, 1787, by the unanimous consent of its thirty members, eleven weeks after the signing of the Constitution of the United States of America in Philadelphia. The constitutional convention of Pennsylvania gave its approval five days later by an overwhelming two-to-one vote of its 69 members. On December 18th, New Jersey's convention ratified the new Constitution by consent of all 38 of its members. The 26 members of Georgia's convention unanimously ratified on January 2nd, 1788.

A week later, the Connecticut convention ratified by a better than three to one margin (128 to 40). The following month, on February 6th, 1788, the huge Massachusetts convention of 355 delegates—the largest in any State—voted to approve the new Constitution, 187 for; 168 against. Maryland's State convention consented on April 28th, 1788, by a six to one margin, 63 for, 11 against; South Carolina consented on May 23rd, 1788, 149 votes for, 73 against. And on June 21st, 1788, New Hampshire ratified 57 to 47.

The New Hampshire vote fulfilled the requirement of Article VII of the U.S. Constitution, that when nine States had approved the proposed constitution, those nine States had for themselves replaced the authority of the Articles of Confederation and established a new republic under the new authority of the Constitution of the United States of America. Therefore, as of June 21st, 1788, the consent of the peoples of Delaware, Pennsylvania, New Jersey, Georgia,

Connecticut, Massachusetts, Maryland, South Carolina, and New Hampshire had established a new mode of Union, a new general government, a new republic based on the unprecedented political concept of government by consent of the governed.

The people of the State of Virginia ratified the Constitution of the United States on June 26th, 1788, in its State ratification convention; the people of the State of New York did so on July 26th. The vote for ratification in Virginia was 89 to 79; in New York, 30 to 27.

Of the remaining two States, North Carolina and Rhode Island, North Carolina rejected the proposed Constitution on August 4th, 1788, because it had no Bill of Rights. Rhode Island did not elect a State constitutional convention until 1790 and was the last of the thirteen "Atlantic States" to join the new Union. It did so on May 29th, 1790, by a two-vote majority of its State constitutional convention. North Carolina joined the new republic after the First Session of the First U.S. Congress wrote a Bill of Rights to add to the U.S. Constitution and sent it to the States for ratification. The North Carolina vote, on November 21st, 1789, in its second State ratification convention, was 194 for ratification and 77 against.

On March 4th, 1791, Vermont became the first State having no Atlantic port to ratify the U.S. Constitution. In 1792 and 1796 Kentucky and Tennessee became the first two trans-Appalachian States to ratify the Constitution of the United States of America and become part of the new republic.

Thus the chief aftermath of the Philadelphia Convention was that those who said it had no authority to replace the Articles of Confederation were proven wrong.

All of the Atlantic States finally ratified the new Union set forth in the new Constitution, and the vote of the Confederation Congress itself favored its participation in the ratification process. Altogether, 27 elected bodies of representatives of the American people—the Confederation Congress, thirteen State legislatures, and thirteen State ratification conventions—approved the new Constitution.

Of the framers of the new Constitution, Benjamin Franklin died eight months after George Washington was sworn in as the first President of the United States under the Constitution of which Franklin and Washington had been the indispensable supporters. Washington served two terms in the presidency, being elected both times unanimously by the Electoral College created in Article II, Section 1, Clause 2 of the new Constitution. He refused nomination for a third term. Washington's death at age 67 occurred at Mount Vernon, two years and nine months after he ended his service as the first president of the United States under the U.S. Constitution.

James Madison, having been an outstanding cabinet officer in the administrations of Presidents Washington and Jefferson, became the fourth President of the country he had done so much to help found. Alexander Hamilton after brilliantly transforming the finances of the United States of America as Washington's Secretary of the Treasury and making the nation a solvent, credit-worthy republic was killed by a political rival in a duel. James Wilson became an associate justice on the first U.S. Supreme Court, but a few years later, because of imprudent speculations in western lands, died in debt, one jump ahead of the law, as did also Washington's super-wealthy friend Robert Morris for the same reason. Gouverneur Morris, the leading writer on the Committee of Detail that provided the final wording for the U.S. Constitution, became U.S. ambassador to France at the outset of the French Revolution, which coincided with Washington's first inauguration. Elbridge Gerry, whose vote in Philadelphia on July 16th was essential to the Great Compromise that permitted the U.S. Constitution to be written, became, in Madison's second administration, the fifth Vice-President of the United States, despite his not having signed the Constitution. His creativity in winning elections added the pejorative word "gerrymandering" to America's political vocabulary. The decades of friendship between George Mason and George Washington did not survive Mason's opposition to ratifying the proposed Constitution in Virginia.

Roger Sherman became at age seventy a U.S. Senator from Connecticut and an outspoken supporter of Hamilton's highly successful policies on national and State debt, sound currency, and the regulation of commerce and manufacturing. Rufus King, Nathaniel Gorham, and Caleb Strong, delegates to the Philadelphia Convention from Massachusetts, became respectively a U.S. Senator, a debtor who died bankrupt, and governor of Massachusetts. William Paterson of New Jersey was elected to the U.S. Senate from New Jersey and later appointed by Washington to the U.S. Supreme Court. During Washington's administration, John Rutledge of South Carolina, who chaired the committee that reported to the Convention the first complete draft of the U.S. Constitution on August 6th, 1787, became chief justice of the U.S. Supreme Court.

After the Philadelphia Convention, Edmund Randolph, one of the three active participants in writing the Constitution who refused to sign it, changed his mind again and supported the Constitution's ratification in Virginia. He became the first U.S. Attorney General.

Luther Martin, an ardent anti-federalist, retired as Maryland's Attorney General after the Philadelphia

Convention to devote himself full time to his lucrative law practice.

The judicial hearing of Declan O'Cormick before Judge Atlee in July ended in his being sentenced to 14 months in the Walnut Street Jail—not the Annex, but the Jail—one month for every day he had kept the 19-year-old William Best confined against his will, and a fine of 280 pounds. William Best was fined 30 pounds for assaulting Mr. O'Cormick, who did not press charges. O'Cormick's housekeeper and cook were let go with a stern admonition to be more attentive to knowing and obeying the laws of Pennsylvania: that ignorance of the law was no excuse for breaking it. Both women quit the employ of O'Cormick.

The Rankin brothers were sentenced to one year in jail for the older brother, John, and two years for Michael. Conall Shaughnessy, O'Cormick's close friend, had to forfeit half his bail and Howard Kincaid was fined 100 pounds.

Rebecca Wellborn immediately paid the fine levied against her son, and continued her discussion with her friends Carl and Kristen Waldemar on the possibility of accompanying them on their planned trip to their native Denmark, to make their three grown children acquainted with the land of their ancestors. Mrs. Wellborn was interested in meeting her beloved Johan's parents and having her son meet his Danish grandfather and grandmother. Rebecca Wellborn, born Margaret Godolphin, also wanted to place bouquets of white daisies at Johan's tomb, knowing that white daisies were his favorite flower. She wrote a letter in Danish to the Jarl of Jutland, with the help of her friend Kristen Waldemar, asking permission for her and William to accompany his nephew and his nephew's wife on their visit to Denmark.

Permission for them to come was immediately granted, and Andrea Sorina Griffenfeld, Johan's mother, enclosed a note with the Jarl's reply, saying they had to stay with her and her husband during their visit to Denmark.

Rebecca and William sailed for Copenhagen on September 19th, 1787, with Kemper and the Waldemars on the Danish ship *Orenens Hjerte* ("Eagle's Heart"). When Johan's mother saw her grandson William, she wept.

The visit of the Waldemars lasted almost a year, because during the visit their oldest daughter was courted by and wedded to a young Danish nobleman. Mrs. Wellborn received two wedding proposals and turned them both down.

When Carl and Kristen Waldemar returned to Philadelphia in 1788, William Best and his mother stayed on in Denmark, she as a companion to Johan's mother and William as a confidential assistant to his *farfar* (paternal grandfather) who said "Vili" looked exactly like his son at the time of his death.

William Best replaced his dead father Johan as the heir to the titles and estates of the Griffenfeld family after the proper legal proceedings had been attended to.

On instructions from her half sister, Mrs. Wellborn, Celta sold the house in Southwark and sent two thirds of the proceeds to her sister, keeping one third for her and her husband, Noah Day. (Noah had courted Celta almost from the moment of their first encounter, and proposed to her a few days after the signing of the U.S. Constitution.)

It was late in the afternoon of Sunday, September 16th, 1787, the day the Constitution of the United States of America was being professionally inscribed for signature the next day, that James Jamison entered Benjamin Franklin's library for the final time, though neither he nor Dr. Franklin knew it was the final time. James was answering a summons from Dr. Franklin, delivered by Mr. Mahoney the previous evening.

He found Franklin at one end of his immense library table, in the company of Washington, Hamilton, and Madison. Franklin's guests were imbibing choice French vintages, and the master of Franklin Court was drinking a bottle of his usual French spring water.

The smiling, always affable Franklin, using his gold-headed, cherry-wood cane, rose from his place at the head of the huge table as soon as James entered through the library door. The other three men also rose as Franklin said, "We're celebrating, as you see, James, the successful conclusion of our efforts to devise a more perfect Union for the States of the United States. Please take a seat here by me," indicating the empty chair to his left. James sat in the proffered chair, and everyone else also sat down. "We want to express our appreciation for your part in that success, James, by your prompt recovery of Mr. Gerry's wayward and potentially disastrous letter."

Washington rose again and said, "I'm sure you recall, Captain Jamison, the last time the five of us gathered around this table. I know I do. It was with a sense of foreboding regarding the consequences that could befall the Convention if Mr. Gerry's missing letter should fall into the wrong hands. In token of our appreciation of your prompt recovery of the letter, which relieved our anxiety, I have the honor of presenting to you, Captain Jamison, a token of our appreciation."

Whereupon Hamilton brought up from under the table a sword in a gleaming scabbard, adorned with a knot of thick gold braid at its hilt, and handed it to Washington who went around to where James was sitting and handed it to him with a slight nod, then returned to his chair.

Dr. Franklin said, "I bid you draw the sword, James, and read to us what is engraved on its blade."

James did so. The inscription said, "For Captain James Jamison in recognition of his service to the Constitutional Convention. Philadelphia 1787."

Franklin led the gentlemanly applause and murmurs of "Hear! Hear!"

The last time James and Franklin conversed was two years later, on September 12th, 1789, the day after James's grandmother, the widow of Dr. Franklin's longtime friend Samuel Jamison, died. James went to Franklin Court to inform Dr. Franklin of that sad news.

In admitting James to Franklin Court, Mr. Mahoney asked him to please wait while he went to see whether Franklin could receive him. "Nowadays, Captain, it's not always possible for him to have visitors," the faithful Mr. Mahoney explained. In a few minutes, however, he returned and asked James to please accompany him.

The sight of Franklin in his extremely emaciated condition was shocking to James. The advanced state of his kidney and bladder stones had finally subjected America's most eminent scientist and foremost statesman to feel continuous searing pain, which had forced his attending physician to prescribe laudanum or liquid opium as a palliative. But this opiate, although it eased the intolerable pain, caused Franklin to lose his appetite to such a degree that he'd become a merely skeletal figure, barely recognizable as "Dr. Franklin."

There was, however, no lessening of Franklin's mental acuity and remarkably little loss of his interest in life, considering the pain he was suffering.

After James conveyed the news that had brought him to Franklin Court, Benjamin Franklin said in a somewhat slow but distinct voice, "So many of my old friends, James, have died, it seems it is perhaps time for me to follow suit. I trust your dear grandparent did not suffer at the end?"

"She died in great peace, Dr. Franklin. Livy and I, Anne-Louise and the baby, spent a pleasant evening with her on Thursday, and I found her gone the next morning when I went to her room. There was a look of great serenity on her face as she lay in her bed, and her eyes were open. I suppose when she went to sleep the evening before she recited the prayer she taught me as a boy, 'Now I lay me down to sleep. I pray thee, Lord, my soul to keep. If I should die before I wake, I pray thee, Lord, my soul to take.'"

"To die that way is a blessing. She was a good and gentle woman. When Anne-Louise and Samuel found each other in their youth, they each became the chief blessing in the other's life. Your grandmother firmly believed God sent his Son into the world to redeem the sins of everyone who would accept his death as a loving sacrifice for that purpose. And that belief enabled her to have the sanctified self-love that God wants all of us to have, so we can fulfill his great commandment to love our neighbors as ourselves. Tell me, James, will your Grandmother's passing affect your plans for the future?"

"Perhaps next summer, when the winter snows have melted from the mountain passes and our little Benjamin is better able to withstand the rigors of a wagon trip over the mountains on rough roads, we may go west. Livy and I have been talking of doing that. But of course we could not leave Philadelphia as long as Grandmère lived."

"Well, you and your dear wife have my best wishes, James, whatever you decide to do. America is a big country, favored by nature with extraordinary advantages of climate, soil, navigable rivers, big lakes, pure springs of water, vast forests and grasslands, arable soils, abundant minerals, ample fisheries and wildlife. Now that we have a practical constitution, we can fulfill our destiny to be a great nation—prosperous, powerful, and populous—provided America's people maintain the Constitution her elected representatives have written and they have approved."

These were the last words of consequence Franklin spoke to the grandson of Samuel Jamison, his friend from his earliest manhood.

Over the winter, James and Olivia decided to move to Pittsburgh. They were still in Philadelphia, however, on January 17th, 1790, when Benjamin Franklin died at age eighty-four. Two days later, on January 19th, carrying their two small children in their arms, bundled-up against the cold, James and Livy walked in the funeral procession with the tens of thousands of Philadelphians who accompanied the remains of one of the most accomplished Americans who ever lived to their final rest in Christ Church cemetery, where they were laid as he desired beside those of his wife Deborah and his first son, Francis Folger Franklin, who had died of smallpox at the age of four.

When the National Assembly of France received the news of Franklin's passing, it voted to wear mourning in his honor.

Finis

Acknowledgments

Lauren Frances McElroy, my daughter and a skillful professional editor, has enhanced *Benjamin Franklin & The Vanishing Messenger* in many ways, in its details and by her criticism of some of its larger aspects, improvements that I as author failed to notice and am most grateful to have called to my attention. She also relieved me of many administrative burdens. Without Laurie's help, I might not have been able to complete the job.

Curt Pedersen inspired me to imagine "things Danish," and provided details such as "Kemper" for the name of the story's exemplary terrier.

Mike Ebert, Charles Heller, and Dave Hurley provided the sort of friendly encouragement every author needs to see a challenging literary endeavor through. I also thank Charles, a well-read patriotic activist, for his relevant bibliographical tip.

David Damitz of Advantage Computer in Tucson kept things moving by promptly and courteously correcting my electronic missteps and getting me back on track again.

I thank Julie Gard for her artistic prowess in turning the idea I gave her for a cover into such a fetching and intriguing image, and for her work on formatting the text.

Grace Walker helped with the advertising pamphlet launching the Galloping Giraffe Press which the Benjamin Franklin detective trilogy has inaugurated.

And of course without the unfailing devotion of Ony, nothing could have been accomplished, simply because there would have been no point in doing anything.

Finally, it must be said that this historical fiction could never have been contemplated without the many works scholars have written on the Philadelphia Convention that took place in Philadelphia from May 25th through September 17th, 1787, and without the hour-by-hour, day-by-day, speech-by-speech, contemporaneous notes on the proceedings of the Convention that James Madison made, which are the principal source of everyone's knowledge of that four-month gathering in Philadelphia. I am likewise indebted to the scholarly works on the Americans who were delegates to that Convention, particularly Walter Isaacson's biography of Franklin and Ron Chernow's biographies of Washington and Hamilton. It almost goes without saying, that I alone am responsible for the use I have made of this trove of scholarship.

JHM

The author with Milou

IF YOU ENJOYED THIS BOOK

Please write a review on amazon.com.

This is important to the author, and helps get
the word out to others.

Visit:
Galloping Giraffe Press
www.gallopinggiraffepress.com

All Galloping Giraffe books are available
through Amazon.com

The First Book

in the

Benjamin Franklin

Detective Trilogy

Benjamin Franklin & The Quaker Murders

Philadelphia, September, 1785. Benjamin Franklin is certain of Quaker stonecutter Jacob Maul's innocence, despite Maul having been jailed for murder after a second woman's corpse is found on his property with bruises to her throat. Franklin also knows that if he becomes known to be willing to involve himself in the most serious personal problems of others, he will never be left in peace. Everyone in Philadelphia will be seeking his help with their troubles.

So in strictest secrecy Franklin recruits maimed Revolutionary War veteran Captain James Jamison to be his legman. No one must know that he and Jamison are even acquainted. The reader accompanies Jamison as his pursuit of the killer leads him through Philadelphia's markets, taverns and poorer neighborhoods, and as far afield as the college at Princeton and a farming community where everyone speaks German. Questioning informants as varied as a free black laundress, former Hessian mercenaries, and the midwives of Southwark, Captain Jamison discovers pivotal information with the help of his French grandmother's comely maid, Livy, and makes progress in both the investigation and healing from the wounds the war has inflicted on him. Meeting with Jamison in the dead of night, Franklin applies his extraordinary analytical abilities to the facts Jamison gathers. But will Franklin's judgment and genius alone be enough to meet the challenge of confronting the murderer?

The Second Book

in the

Benjamin Franklin

Detective Trilogy

Benjamin Franklin & The Innocent Duelist

May 5th, 1786. Dawn. A misty, isolated field on the banks of the Schuylkill River outside Philadelphia. Two men disembark in silence from a rowboat and meet two other men for a duel. The moment the count for the duel ends, the younger duelist shoots into the ground, but the other duelist falls over—dead. How could the surviving duelist be arrested for murder and locked away when he shot into the ground? His father, a wealthy merchant, begs newly married Revolutionary War veteran Captain James Jamison to exonerate his son, because of Jamison's seeming success in solving the case of The Quaker Murders the year before.

But what no one but Jamison and Benjamin Franklin know is that it was Benjamin Franklin who solved the mystery of those deaths. Can Franklin help the young duelist escape the hangman?